OF FAITH AND FI

Geoffrey Hotspur And The War
For St. Peter's Throne

Evan Ostryzniuk

KNOX ROBINSON
PUBLISHING
LONDON • New York

KNOX ROBINSON
PUBLISHING

1205 London Road
London SW16 4UY
&
244 5th Avenue, Suite 1861
New York, NY 10001

Knox Robinson Publishing is a specialist, independent publisher of historical fiction, historical romance and medieval fantasy.

© Evan Ostryzniuk

The right of Evan Ostryzniuk to be identified as author of this work has been asserted by him in accordance with the
Copyright, Designs and Patents Act 1988.

All rights reserved. No part of this publication may be reproduced, stored in a retrieval system, or transmitted, in any form or by any means, without the prior permission in writing of Knox Robinson Publishing, or as expressly permitted by law, or under terms agreed with the appropriate reprographics rights organization. Enquiries concerning reproduction outside the scope of the above should be sent to the Rights
Department, Knox Robinson Publishing, at the London address above.

You must not circulate this book in any other binding or
cover and you must impose the same condition on any acquirer.

A CIP catalogue record for this book is available from the British Library.

ISBN 978-0-9567901-6-3

Manufactured in the United States of America and the United Kingdom

Visit our website to download free historical fiction, historical romance and fantasy short stories by your favourite authors. While there, purchase our titles direct and earn loyalty points. Sign up for our newsletter and our free titles giveaway. Join our community to discuss history, romance and fantasy with fans of each genre. We also encourage you to submit your stories anonymously and let your peers review your writing.

www.knoxrobinsonpublishing.com

To Wendy,
a fair maiden and clever companion

The Patrimony of Saint Peter

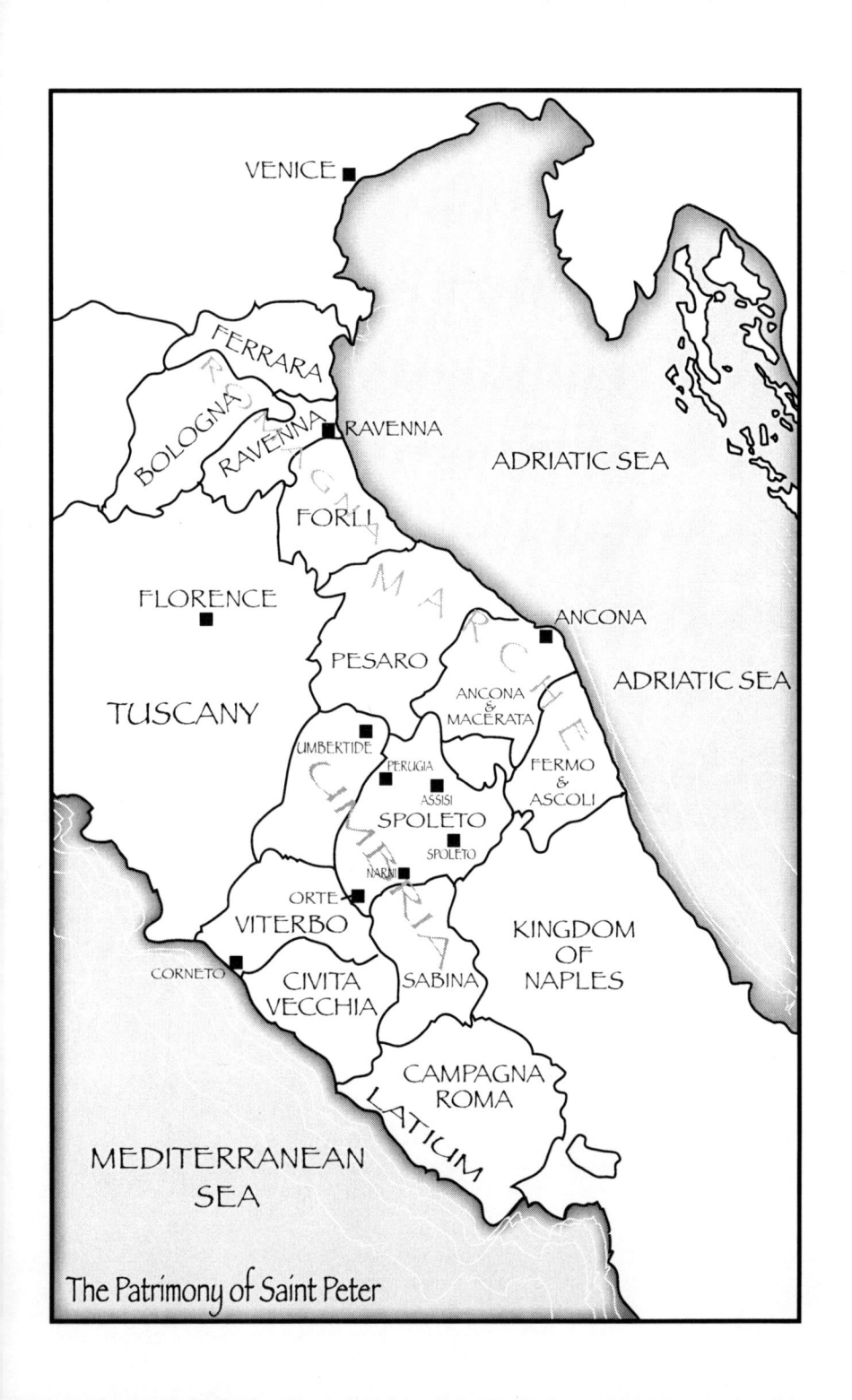

CHAPTER 1

Avignon, France
March 1394

THE gaming hall at the Blue Boar alehouse was a riot of men of manifold ranks placing bets, exchanging silver and hazarding odds, but the moment the squire dressed in a blue-grey doublet rattled a small leather drum, all matters were dropped and silence ensued. It was now the turn of Geoffrey Hotspur to throw the dice.

"How many wagers are gathered for my cast, Roger?" Geoffrey asked his friend and fellow squire.

"Throw and we shall find out," Roger answered, affecting indifference. "The mystery lies in the result, not in the act."

Geoffrey paid his friend no mind for he was already scrutinizing excited faces and listening for fat purses. He was sure Lady Fortuna would grant him a big win on this night, but he felt compelled to stoke the fires of enthusiasm to make himself worthy of such a favor. To frustrate the anxious players, he leisurely adjusted the pleats of his doublet, which was still buttoned to the neck. Its color suggested integrity, and it went well with his grey hose and blue cap.

Geoffrey shook the dice in rhythm with his agitated heart, while raising and lowering the leather drum as a priest would a chalice. He was about to make his cast when he pulled back and again, turned towards his friend and asked, "How much was the butcher up before it all came undone for him?"

The crowd jeered, with the most vulgar making rude gestures and indiscreet references to the caster's mother, while others shouted to him to throw the dice. Those endowed with better sense than to bet on this tricky game simply laughed at the squire's impudence. When no answer came forth, not even from the unfortunate butcher, Geoffrey fixed his gaze on the Gamesmaster, whom he found standing on a raised platform that gave him the full view of his gaming hall.

In addition to assuming the role of setter for all manner of wagers, the Gamesmaster was the owner of the Blue Boar, as well as its brewmaster and credit-giver, which meant that he was the highest appellate court in the house. "Let us not have a casting of accounts now, gentle squire. I am sure the respected butcher desires that no one measure the weight of his meaty losses," the Gamesmaster declared.

"He lost seven sous and a penny," Roger whispered as several bettors began to bandy about exaggerated numbers despite the interdict. This was far more than the poor butcher's monthly earnings, even as a papal victualler.

"Is that all? Seven paltry sous? Mercy of God, I thought it was a bishop's ransom!" But Geoffrey was no longer looking at his fellow player, for his blue eyes were now fixed on the remaining bettors. The crowd laughed, but soon the call went up again for Geoffrey to cast, with cries of "main point!" and "have at us!"

The caster acquiesced. Confident of his success at plucking more silver from the crowd than what might have been without his antics, Geoffrey gave the drum a final shake before throwing the dice onto a small leather mat.

"The main point rolled is 'five'," the Gamesmaster announced and inscribed the result on a slate.

"That's too bad, Geoff," Roger said and clapped a hand on his friend's shoulder. It was quite an effort, since not only was he shorter than his

OF FAITH AND FIDELITY

fellow squire, his own shoulders were sore from that day's sword practice.

"Why is it too bad?" Geoffrey asked. "No, it's not my lucky number, but I will wager on these spots nonetheless."

"The number is five. Should you not pass the drum?"

Geoffrey guffawed and returned Roger's shoulder embrace. "Did I knock that much sense out of you with my buckler today? It was quite a blow, and for that I am sorry. You are like a brother to me. But let me remind you that you are in the Blue Boar: 'Five to nine are fine; less or more abhor', so have faith." Geoffrey twisted his head to face the crowd. "Does my main point stand?"

The crowd gave a roar of approval and the Gamesmaster nodded.

"Still, five is nothing to boast about," Roger said.

"You worry too much. No, it doesn't look good for my chance point, but that should bring the wagers up now, shouldn't it? And that's what we want!"

Geoffrey threw a few sharp glances at those players he knew to be freer with their silver and rubbed his aquiline nose. The longer he cast without definitive result, the higher the pile of coins. The Gamesmaster nodded for one of his retainers to collect the pot.

"Tell us how generous your patrons are, Gamesmaster!" Geoffrey shouted.

The Gamesmaster did the sums on his slate before announcing a sum of four gros, three half-gros and six pennies.

"That's not even three sous, you tight-fisted bastards!" Geoffrey chided. "You'll have to do better than that or I will abandon my next cast and publicly charge you all with meanness and cheating on your tithes!"

"I suggest you pray before you cast again, boy," someone said, "because now I'm betting against you."

Geoffrey's eyes darted around the circle until they found the face that belonged to the voice.

"What makes you think I haven't been praying, old man? Do you not see how I make the sign of the cross as I cast?"

A chuckle rippled around the circle, but most players and watchers were discussing the odds on the squire taking the pot with his next cast.

"Be mindful," Roger whispered. "He is the duke's man. A knight in good standing."

Geoffrey raised his eyebrows and smiled genially. He scrutinized the man and recognized the high quality green doublet, wide belt that sagged well below the belly and wool cap that was popular at court. He might have been one of those knights whose armor he would clean, Geoffrey thought, in the days before he was made a squire.

"I see that you cast the most difficult number to repeat, so now let us have that chance point already, since I know you'll have to make enough crosses to bless us all!"

"Then let it be so!"

Geoffrey snapped his wrist and threw the dice to the far end of the mat. Each die showed three spots – a neutral result, a sentiment confirmed by the low murmur of the crowd. Some were pleased that the tall squire would have to continue, including the squire himself, who with a fiercely challenging glance all but commanded the remaining players to increase their wagers for the next cast.

"Thank the Lord it wasn't a seven," Roger said, "and now we can forget about that awful five." He shifted uncomfortably. Despite the Holy Peace between the kings of England and France, the English were only tolerated in Avignon. This was the home of Pope Clement VII, the French claimant in the war for St. Peter's throne, while King Richard supported Pope Boniface in Rome, who was Italian. So, Roger knew that it would not take much to cause someone in the hall to set upon the two squires.

"Such strange numbers tonight," Geoffrey mumbled. "I was expecting a seven, but this is good. As our green knight just said, I should have a long series of casts ahead of me."

"Unless you throw out, of course."

"I'll throw you out if you don't cease with the dark thoughts. Instead, look how the trickle of silver has become a torrent. Now *that* is a prayer against me."

Geoffrey did not ask the Gamesmaster to recite the tallies. He merely rattled the dice while he silently counted up to his lucky number. He would not risk blowing into the drum for fear of aiding demon luck in dissipating this good charm. Then, with great care and attention, he trickled the ivory cubes onto the mat.

Someone breathed out "twelve." Several players crossed themselves. It was a very dangerous number to throw for future luck in the game, but for now it did not matter. The 'twelve' gave courage to a few more players to lodge bets while two timid players, who had dropped out after the first round, re-entered for the third. Once everyone was satisfied, the Gamesmaster announced that the pot was just over ten sous.

"Half a pound of silver already!" Geoffrey cried. "By Jesus' noble passion, shake those coins for me so that I can hear them. I am in want of inspiration!"

"You are in want of my wrath," the green knight warned and he threw the dice back at Geoffrey. "Again!"

For the next two casts Geoffrey's lucky number – 'nine' – cancelled out the curse of 'twelve'. Wagering peaked and dropped, filling the pot to a full pound, which someone argued was the largest single collection of wagers the Blue Boar had seen in a week. The Gamesmaster was about to duly mark the new amounts when he saw that his slate was full, so he called a short break until one of his retainers brought him another.

"That's quite the pool of silver, Geoff," Roger said. "You know you could pass the drum and call it even. Remember, a little loss is better than a long sorrow."

Geoffrey shook his head. "Would you yield at the first knockdown in a pass of arms? A poor knight you will make. No, we must have a result."

Roger ran his hand through the thick, dark curls on his head. He was keeping his hair long, while Geoffrey had decided to closely crop his, as a few of the knights at court were doing.

"You remember that that we are wanted at court tonight," Roger said. "His lordship the Duke of Lancaster will be present, which means that he will have something very important to say."

"What? Has he finally decided which pope to support? You know as well as I that he is a vassal of both his majesties, Richard and Charles, so it doesn't matter."

"I believe it's something else," Roger tried to explain, but Geoffrey was no longer listening.

Then it happened. Once the awkward dance of the dice was over, the players counted and recounted the spots that mattered. A groan went up. Geoffrey had made his point. He shouted and threw his purse at the feet of the Gamesmaster. "Load it up! And a round of your best ale for those who bet against me!"

It was a good win, so good that between the ritual congratulations and hearty backslaps a desperate few touched Geoffrey's casting hand in the hope of sparking their own luck. Most of the patrons knew Geoffrey well. He frequented gaming halls throughout Avignon and made aggressive wagers, but what distinguished him most was his height. Geoffrey towered over most men, a feature made all the more striking by his narrow frame and youthful look. He was eighteen or nineteen years old and like his fellow squires, he was expecting to be apprenticed to a knight this campaign season.

"What will you do with all that silver, squire?" the green knight shouted. A serving maid brought in a wooden platter laden with pewter tankards.

OF FAITH AND FIDELITY

"I should spend it on drunken harlotry, of course," was Geoffrey's vulgar reply with an eye on the maid. Even the stoic Gamesmaster allowed himself to chuckle along with the crowd.

"Maybe this victory is the Lord's way of telling you to put that money away for your marriage," a player joked.

"Nonsense!" Geoffrey cried. Then, posing as a grave supplicant, he added, "Don't you know that wagering is a sin? Our Lord would never send me such a brutish message."

Roger started to say something to deflate his friend's exuberance, but the Gamesmaster anticipated him.

"Play on, good squire, for the dice grow cold. Lady Fortuna is an impatient mistress."

Roger tried again. He had been friends with the orphan Geoffrey Hotspur for about ten years, ever since the duke had paired them at the onset of squire training, so knew how Geoffrey could let loose his passions.

"The dice will still be here tomorrow," Roger said.

"But I am here tonight! Have some ale, Rog."

The next series of casts ended in a hurry. After making the fortunate 'seven' on the main point, Geoffrey threw, or crabbed, out on the chance point with an unexpected 'three'. However, his losses were small – not more than a sou and a half, as the players had wearied of the squire's good luck and so had shied away from early wagering. Satisfied that he had successfully demonstrated his prowess, Geoffrey grandly passed the drum.

The dice quickly traveled the circle. The mood darkened with two successive throws of 'twelve'. Geoffrey threw out twice in a row, losing him half his first-round winnings. Another small victory for the squire was then eaten up by his generous bets against other casters, as Geoffrey began to make it a point of honor to add two pennies to the highest wager.

"Why don't you encourage Lady Fortuna to turn her radiant face once more to me, Rog?" Geoffrey asked half in jest. "You refuse to partake of the game, yet without pain of conscience you drink the free ale and share in the good cheer. Why, if I didn't know you better I'd swear you were a Franciscan."

Roger laughed and confessed his negligence. However, after Geoffrey lost for a third time in a row, Roger fretfully peered through the slats of a shuttered window in order to gauge the hour.

"Don't forget that we're expected at court before vespers, which should be upon us very soon. If the evensong bells catch us in this hall, it will be too late. Did you hear me, Geoff?"

"What? Oh yes, yes, Roger, right after I win back my money." Geoffrey then drew Roger aside and whispered. "My lucky number is back. I saw the serving maid bring in nine tankards and the dice just showed me another nine at the bottom of the drum. That hasn't happened for more rounds than I care to remember. It's true!"

Roger sighed. "Should I ask the Gamesmaster how much you are up or down? I see that the green knight has left. That does not bode well."

"Does it matter how much I'm up or down? The Gamesmaster is still preaching at his lectern. On my oath, I am not some petty tinsmith who needs to count his grubby black pennies every time the sun shines. I don't finger my purse like a friar. If I win, I shall share; if I lose, I shall return what is owed. Please, do not trouble your conscience for my sake, as it will do your humors no good." Geoffrey held up the leather drum before Roger's face and rattled it.

"I do not wish to be late for court – that is all – but it would serve your interests if you were sure of enough silver to buy those bits of armor you still need. No knight would take you on campaign with what paltry gear you have now."

"Very true, my friend, but there is plenty of time for all that. The campaign season cannot start for another month." Geoffrey cocked his cap to show that he was in earnest about staying.

"Your cast, monsieur!" the Gamesmaster ordered.

Roger grabbed Geoffrey's casting hand. "Check your purse, for all that is holy! Campaign or no campaign, do you really want to lose what little you have, and your dignity to boot?"

Geoffrey wrested his hand away, causing him to spill the dice. "Look what you have done, fool! My luck is sure to turn sour now. If it will keep you from making more mischief, I will do as you say." Geoffrey dumped the contents of his purse in his hand and raked through the coins. "It seems as though I shall shortly be in need of silver," Geoffrey announced, "and I pray that one of the good gentlemen here will honor himself by sharing his so that I might continue." He assumed that he was few pounds down, but only the Gamesmaster knew the true figure and Geoffrey would not lower himself to ask.

"He can wager on tick," the Gamesmaster said. "I will allow it."

"But at what price?" Roger asked. "If he borrows three pounds now, will you be demanding six when time is called?"

The Gamesmaster reviewed his slates. "No," he said at last. "I shall demand no percentage on any amount the good squire shall require of me. I trust that he will honor any debt he might incur, and with speed. Let him play on and have Fate make the result."

"My word is my bond and any statement of wager I might make is as good as gold," Geoffrey said.

Roger took Geoffrey aside and said sternly, "Had you some property to serve as surety, then I would hold my tongue, but you have no family to stand behind you and his lordship pays no one's bills." He regretted having to remind his friend that he was an orphan, but his posturing had left him no choice.

"You cut me to the quick, Rog, but I forgive you." Geoffrey turned back to the Gamesmaster. "Pay him no mind."

The Gamesmaster nodded to acknowledge the pledge then gestured that the casting should continue. The Gamesmaster's credit line unleashed whatever restraint Geoffrey had for wagering, but the results did not improve: for every one gros Geoffrey won, he lost three. At the first peel of the evensong bells the Gamesmaster called time.

"Let us play on, for the love of Christ and his most pure mother!" Geoffrey cried as he watched the crowd melt away. Several serving maids entered and began to collect the gaming gear.

The Gamesmaster stepped off his dais and approached Geoffrey and Roger. "That is all, I'm afraid. My license forbids any and all manner of gaming between evensong and the woman's curfew, and I am not a man to defy the authorities."

Geoffrey felt the frustration of the moment welling up inside his breast. His eyes darkened, but he held himself with the decorum of his station and declared himself quit for the day. He made a slight but not undignified bow to the Gamesmaster and then turned to Roger to say that they were leaving. However, at their first motion towards the hall's only exit, two men in full harness moved to block it.

"And what about your debt, good sir knight?" the Gamesmaster asked with that light touch of sarcasm for which he was known.

"What is owed?" Roger asked.

"Ten pounds of silver."

Roger's mouth dropped, but Geoffrey looked unaffected by the immense ransom.

"You will be repaid," Geoffrey declared and he drew himself up to his full height. "I honor all my debts, however base. You can rest assured that when I have collected the agreed amount, it shall come to you. Have faith in my fidelity."

"My rest comes with the debt's rest, I assure *you*. You have one month to settle with me," was the Gamesmaster's cold reply.

"You shall have it when the good Lord has blest me with it."

OF FAITH AND FIDELITY

"Let me repeat the contract in full so that you are not confused. You have one month to repay the precise amount of money you owe me, in good silver, and if the whole sum does not reach me in time, then the debt will grow by four sous for every week you delay redemption."

Roger nearly burst with indignation. "There was no such contract! You said no percentage. Ten pounds of silver in thirty days? It can't be done!"

The Gamesmaster gave no indication that he was intimidated by either squire. He lifted his slates and pointed at the figures.

"I did indeed say no percentage, but the duration of the offer was never stipulated. Now it is. The offer is good for one month only. In truth, you should be thanking me for granting your friend such generous terms, I could make just cause for putting him in the gaol until someone redeems his debt."

"Very well. Let us make it so. *I* will stand as surety for my friend," Roger declared. "My name is strong enough. What say you to my offer?"

"I do not deny that Swynford is a strong name. If that is your desire, then ..."

Geoffrey put a hand on his friend's arm. "It is agreed, monsieur Gamesmaster," he said. "I accept your conditions."

The Gamesmaster gave a curt not and allowed Geoffrey and Roger to leave the Blue Boar unmolested.

Once the squires were gone, the Gamesmaster turned to his guards and ordered: "Find Jean and tell him that I have work for him, *now*."

San Donato, Tuscany
17 March

The doctor crossed the threshold, closing the heavy oak door behind him.

"So, is he dead?" William Godwin asked. He was keeping himself just beyond the doctor's reach, since he was deathly afraid of bleeders, cuppers, herbalists, and other medical mischief-makers. In truth, he would not have been within arrowshot of the newly made corpse had a sense of duty not called him forth.

The doctor ignored the question and its speaker, since the right of first address did not belong to him, and instead approached a stately figure standing alone by an open window. They exchanged a few words in Latin, nodded grimly and made respectful bows to each other before the doctor departed without another word.

Godwin had taken a couple of tentative steps towards the open window before a rush of servants, now given leave to do their funerary duty, bumped him all the way into the mournful chamber of the deceased.

Chancellor Salutati smiled at the comedy and then after straightening his bent back turned towards the open window. The early spring sun was just beginning to warm the verdant Tuscan hills, its still weak rays slowly advancing across the raw fields, through tumbledown villages and into the manor of San Donato that dumbly watched over them. He noticed a clutch of peasants about to begin their daily drudgery. If only they knew, he thought, that Florence's greatest captain, the soldier who once protected this valley and its leading city, was now gone.

With the help of Fate they appeared in Florence at the same time, nearly twenty years ago – John Hawkwood as invader and he as the young chancellor. But the peculiarity of Italian politics is such that the good citizens of the Republic brought them together to save the city from her enemies, from within and from without. And they were successful. As Captain of the People, John Hawkwood fought the wars that kept Florence paramount while he, as Chancellor of the Republic, Coluccio di Pierio di Salutati, ensured that peace and prosperity ruled over chaos and ruin.

The chancellor watched the villagers waddle down grassy paths towards the fields until his eyes fell upon evidence of one of their few failures: the charred remains of a barn. It was the mark of Clement, the false pope, and served as a vivid reminder that despite all efforts made, the frontiers of the Republic were never wholly secure. His armies had invaded Italy several times to claim the throne of St. Peter, since two pontiffs were elected by two factions of cardinals in 1378, but this year's expectations were different. Clement was using Italian captains this time, instead of relying on French princes, so that the lords and cities of the Patrimony would not view his campaign as a foreign invasion.

Salutati shook his head in disgust. If this schism within the Church was a matter of faith, like with the Eastern Church in Byzantium, then the war would be just, but the divisive element was fidelity: who should submit to whom. The pope in Rome was the true pontiff, of course; Clement had never been properly elected. The French cardinals had been arrogant to place one of their own on the throne of St. Peter. And now, they are back in Avignon. The more's the pity.

"Are you here to dig his grave?" Godwin asked in a voice laced with invective. He had succeeded in swimming against the tide of servants and was now standing where the doctor had been. "You tried to bury him once with ill-conceived plans; are you now prepared to dirty your own soft hands to finish the job?"

"My duty is grave enough without spades full of your spite sergeant. I am here only to ensure that your late, great master is accorded all the dignity he deserves, and that no hands reach out to snatch what is not theirs." He noticed that the English sergeant had a ruddy face as a result of the cold and his beard was greyer than he remembered.

Godwin took the mild insult with equanimity, since now that he was retired from soldiering he could afford not to care a jot for this jump-up clerk's reproaches and innuendos. He cared only that his late master's reputation remain unsullied and that he receive that to which he was entitled.

"It should and will be Sir William when I return to England," Godwin retorted with affected dignity. "There'll be no marrying Italian bastard princesses for me, upon my word. Only the purest English roses for this old stick, and when I buy that piece of land what my father once tilled for his lord, aplenty of pieces'll come knocking, along with their good 'sir fathers so-and-so' ready to share their titles." It was an empty boast and Godwin knew it, since even with the not inconsiderable fortune he had accumulated, his long time away from England would make it difficult to enter the titled ranks with any speed, and he was too old to earn his spurs for the sake of a knight's fee. Not that he wanted one anyway, coming as it did with oaths of fealty and tedious duties, not to mention stubborn peasants and rapacious priests. He would be his own man.

"Or I'll buy an inn. I'd name it the Tabard and blazon it with whatever bloody charge takes my fancy."

Salutati thought about having the sergeant flogged for impudence, with an extra twenty lashes just for being English, such was the nature of the offence to the esteemed servant of the Republic, but he was not in a mood for violence and he begrudgingly needed the old man's counsel. As it was, the slight presented the chancellor with the opportunity to broach a subject that any respectable citizen would denounce as impolitic during this early period of mourning.

"You have been in this country far too long, for you are starting to sound Italian," the chancellor teased. "I hope your purse is heavy enough to balance your ugliness on the scales of a young heart. Perhaps you should give thought to marrying a widow, or an old spinster. Their spousal expectations tend to be, how should I put it, somewhat less rigorous."

"I'm a patient man, *signore*, and very selective. Scales or no scales, weights come in different measures, each no less valued than the next."

"And what if the greatest bastard of them all decides to throw *his* weight across your path? What if Clement decides that the chivalry of France should be the only riders of roads in and out of Italy? French princes are already contesting Genoa and until the Visconti are overthrown, Milan stands behind Clement." Salutati nodded at the open window. "There is war already in Umbria, and Genoa is in turmoil. I have been told that you do not travel well by sea, so unless you possess some charm that allows you to pass through frontiers unmolested, you might have to remain in Florence for another year – at least. But now that you are no longer in our service, well …"

He was exaggerating the danger, since even during times of intense conflict only the most reckless lord or foolish city would dare sever all channels of trade and communication. But that was beside the point; all the chancellor needed to do was bother the sergeant enough for him to throw up some useful words.

"You would never dare imply that I was ever in league with Clement. You of all people should remember the slaughter at Cesena. If Sir John Hawkwood was wholly loyal to your republic, then so was I, for his bond was my bond. Now I am far too old and care far too little to start making friends now." Godwin stuck out his chin and squinted to show his defiance, a gesture that was as good as a badge, but he also clenched his fists to diffuse what anger the wily chancellor had stirred in his soul.

Yes, he remembered Cesena. When Clement was still Robert Genevois, Papal Legate to Italy, bent on conquest of the Patrimony, and he had only been Chancellor of Republic for a couple of years before they had come to blows. He, Salutati, had rallied half of Italy against returning *fidelitas* to the French pope, and he, the papal legate, had retaliated ferociously by ordering his army to murder the defenceless citizens of that eastern city Cesena. He was known as 'Robert the Butcher' from then onwards. They had both learned lessons on the dangers of arrogance that day.

"It is not new friends that worry me, but rather old ones," Salutati said. "We are a lush island amidst a very turbulent sea. Alliances are shifting, allegiances are withering. It would pain me to hear that you had been murdered by someone whom you thought to be true. There is honor among thieves, to be sure, but does the same hold for condottieri? Were I to issue you a letter of safe conduct embossed with the Great Seal of the Republic, it might become your death warrant. Tell me, Sergeant Godwin, once you step beyond the *contado*, who will you trust to let you walk freely? You do know that your late master's companions-in-arms, Brandolino Brandolini and Ceccolo Broglia, have decided not to renew their *condotti* with Boniface's brother, the Duke of Spoleto, and have instead gone over to Clement, don't you? Of course, you all were in the famous Company of St. George together, so I suppose a few threads of that old tie of fellowship might still hold."

"Why did they not sign with Boniface, if it's reconquest of the Patrimony that they are after?"

"Well, it's all the same, really, but I believe that Boniface wants to ensure the men's fidelity to his brother as well as to himself. And besides, it is the duke who is leading the campaign."

Godwin squinted and cocked his head to the right. He was genuinely surprised and for a moment doubted the chancellor's words. It was not that he thought the men in question were incapable of switching sides mid-campaign; they were and had many times before. Rather the old sergeant was troubled by the painful truth that Salutati had received the news before him.

When Captain Hawkwood had been just a petty condottiere with no more than a dozen lances to his name, Godwin was his man responsible for gathering intelligence, a position he held at first with resentment then with pride and covetousness until the day he sheathed his sword for the final time and announced that he would swear no more oaths until his ultimate confession. The work also made people afraid of him, especially Italians, and even more so Italians in high office, hence his pugnacity.

"That must mean they are with young Malatesta Malatesta of Rimini," the old sergeant mused. "Well, they have chosen a reputable captain, upon my word; it has nothing to do with me, mind you, or my late master, anymore. Why don't you just buy these wayward captains back for his holiness in Rome? Your republic has silver beyond measure, especially after you gouge your fiendish tax out of my late lord's fat estate."

"Yes, but think for a moment, my good sergeant. Captains Brandolini and Broglia are very expensive condottieri. They each command a company of five hundred men-at-arms and the horses to bear them. Even having been elected Captain of the People in Bologna, young Malatesta does not have a war chest big enough to be able to afford them, and the false pope's supporters in Umbria do not belong to the wealthiest order. We can be certain that only one man is underwriting this venture." Salutati gave Godwin a meaningful look.

"You mean Clement. You're not afraid of Boniface losing the Patrimony, are you? That will never happen. I have yet to meet a man, woman or child in Italy who wants to see another French pope in Rome. But, of course, it has nothing to do with me."

Salutati explained the situation in the slow voice he reserved for his children. "Nothing is certain other than the lord of Avignon is pouring money into the Patrimony, and he will stop at nothing until it is under his thumb. We are, of course, still loyal to Rome and this will forever remain so, but we cannot afford to enter the fray on the field. However, should the Patrimony fall, we would be surrounded by enemies gorged on the fruits of victory. Then all of Italy will be aflame and you will never reach home, sergeant." Salutati gently placed his hand on Godwin's shoulder.

"I suppose none of the other cities in Tuscany would risk lending men or money either if you don't," Godwin said.

"If we are much longer together the other mourners will begin to suspect a conspiracy brewing, so I shall make my offer brief. I need you to visit an old friend of your late master's. Giovanni Tarlati."

Godwin knew the name – he knew all the names.

"You old devil, you. He's leading the siege of Narni now, isn't he?" Godwin said just to prove that he was still up on events. "Won't chance one of your own men, I see. Well, it has nothing to do with me."

Salutati assumed a grave expression. He had anticipated the sergeant's reluctance to submit to him and was fully prepared to throttle his independence. "You do know that Hawkwood's estate is under probate until his final will and testament is validated by the courts and approved by the chancellery, don't you?"

Godwin gave the chancellor a blank stare.

"Well," the chancellor continued in his slow voice, "that means that all documents left in possession of the late captain of the people cannot be removed from San Donato until they are properly sorted, including those that did not belong to him. By the custom of your old company, my good sergeant, you were obliged to keep all your financial records with your late master. So …"

Godwin leaned into the chancellor. He was breathing heavily. After a pregnant pause, the fatal weakness of his situation struck him.

"By thundering Jesus, do you mean that I must continue to wade in this cesspool of greed until you say otherwise?!" Godwin's voice dripped with loathing. He knew well that lawyers and other parasites had to poke through Hawkwood's property before anything could be done, but he could not believe that it would take long, considering that his late master had been scrupulously organized. He also knew, however, that if he wanted, Salutati could prolong this probate thing for as long as it suited his own ends. The chancellor had him over a barrel.

"Will you accept my offer then? You need only report to me and you should not find cause to draw your sword," Salutati said quickly, hearing approaching footsteps.

OF FAITH AND FIDELITY

"Do I have a choice? I am almost a prisoner here."

"You are free to choose. That is one of the glories of our republic. But you are also free to fall. This should not be an onerous task for you, my good sergeant. All that is required of you is to listen to Tarlati and hand him a bag of coins. Broglia and Brandolini are too far, so that is all. You loyally served Sir John Hawkwood for twenty years by listening. You may consider this as your final service to him. It would be his wish."

Godwin gave the chancellor a sharp look for his presumption, but upon seeing one of Hawkwood's daughters rounding the corner, he merely nodded and walked away.

Spoleto, Patrimony of St. Peter
March

Andrea Tomacelli liked the rush of cold wind against his face as he galloped across the open field, for it not only enlivened his flesh, but also helped him concentrate his thoughts. And there was no shortage of thoughts to concentrate. This was to be his year, the year he would bring the war between the true pontiff in Rome and the pretender in Avignon to a close. For four long years he had struggled to bring back the Patrimony of St. Peter under the control of his brother, His Holiness Boniface IX, who had made it Andrea's duty with his appointment as Papal Legate to the Marche shortly after the election of Boniface, then Pietro, in 1389. His view of the great citadel of Spoleto in the distance reminded Andrea about how the refusal of the pretender to submit had obliged them to turn to the Way of Force to reunite the Church. Everyone knew this. They had started with the lords of central Italy who owed his holiness *fidelitas*. However, some of those very lords were quite content with the decline of papal authority, and aided by the heretic Clement and his confederates, who had been making war in Italy for nearly a generation, it allowed them to create their own patrimonies. It was quite a delicate matter, so the papal legate understood that in addition to a strong hand, respect was needed. One false move and all of his work would be undone; popular communes would seize cities, petty lords would invest castles, and all of them might switch their *fidelitas* to the false pope in Avignon. He had to be bold, but he also had to be careful. As he rode up to the gates of the citadel, Andrea recalled that the failure to engage such a policy was at the heart of his younger brother's, Duke Gianello's, abject failure to secure his part of the plan, and this failure was why his elder brother had sent him here.

At their most recent meeting in Rome, Andrea had to stifle his laughter while Pope Boniface recited the litany of disasters that had befallen poor Gianello in recent months: his poor winter campaign in Umbria; his mistake not to relieve the city of Narni, besieged by the wily Malatesta Malatesta and Giovanni Tarlati; and his inability to retain the services of two very important condottieri – Brandolini and Broglia. As a result, many lords of the Patrimony were now looking at Malatesta as their champion and with him the false pope in Avignon.

"I have only myself to blame, Andrea," Boniface had concluded. "I should have sent someone from Rome to advise him, or kept a closer eye on things myself. But you know the situation here; plots multiply like a pestilence, and I suffer accordingly."

"He should have known better," Andrea answered. He would make no excuses for his brother. "The Patrimony is not Naples. The north has been polluted by agents of the pretender and his French protectors. The natural order has been distorted, and it is up to us to make it right again. Remember when the French pontiffs ruled in Italy? Their moral degeneracy and callous disrespect for our ways caused cities to revolt, and many remember that."

"You too have been intemperate of late," Boniface said after a thoughtful silence. "Your response to your capture at Macerata last year was rather excessive, don't you think? Do not mistake me for being lax in military matters. I am the captain of a free company too, only mine consists of cardinals."

For once during his campaign in the Marche Andrea had overextended himself and, as a result, he and his captains were captured in an unequal pass of arms. He blamed his captain-general, the popular condottiere Boldrino da Panicale, and after their release fatally stabbed him during a heated argument over who had been responsible for the defeat. However, the scandal had unfortunate consequences. Panicale's company reacted badly to their captain's death, and so after recovering his body, its lances voted to abandon the papal legate and for several weeks rampaged in papal-controlled territory. This was only a minor setback for the Church, as the pillaged land was soon reclaimed and no other company left the papal legate's service, but Andrea soon discovered that the incident had made some lords even more wary and, as a result, they were less willing to come to terms with him. Well, so be it, he decided. Panicale's death was regrettable but not unpardonable in his mind, and if nothing else it taught him to keep a close on eye on his captain-generals.

"If my zeal for serving the heir of St. Peter has clouded all judgement of virtue, then I beg you relieve me of my sacred duty to you, the Church and my Saviour so that I may follow the path of a true penitent. Grant me only mercy. But tell me, so that I might retire with a kind word: have I not been successful in executing thy holiness's will?"

"Such excessive sentiment does not become you, my brother, and if you are looking for someone to grade your competence, you would do well to return beneath the soft hand of your tutor. Beware of mistaking vanity and pride for prowess and dignity. The holy work of the Church provides toil enough without adding to it your venial sins. It is the spirit of your execution that I question, not your dedication."

Both brothers knew that many saw the demise of Captain Panicale as a sign that the new pontiff and his family lacked the prudence necessary to enforce papal will in the Patrimony, let alone with the condottieri who administered the conduct of war in Italy. Pietro Tomacelli's elevation to the papacy had gone smoothly, but failure could turn the cardinals against him, just as it had in 1378 with his predecessor, Urban VI. The schism was born out of failure to show proper *fidelitas*.

Andrea wanted to justify himself, call his brother naïve in the ways of warfare, but he knew it would be foolish to turn this debate into a family quarrel. All Rome viewed the Tomacelli as provincial upstarts, irrespective of Boniface's devotion to duty, so any scandal, failure or misstep could signal the onset of a rapid return to obscurity. Several leading Roman families were rumored to be conspiring to reduce the civic authority of the pontiff and to bring the Curia under their collective control – again. If he, Andrea, could bring the war in the Patrimony to a quick and glorious end, then his brother would be grateful and his opponents fearful.

"My arts are wholly devoted to the service of my lord," was Andrea's reply, "and I have many who serve me out of duty and the belief that the Church's cause is just. If any of them have acted in an unjust matter in the execu- … fulfillment of my command, then I accept the blame for any transgressions that may have resulted." Had not a swell of emotion risen in his breast, that would have been all, but he could not resist adding some fiery words to underscore his heated feeling. "However, we are all fallible, and we lesser men are still honing our skills and steeling our dedication to preserve the true heir of St. Peter."

Boniface gently squeezed his brother's arm, just as he did in their youth, when Andrea would allow his passions to rule his reason. "Be careful about shifting blame, Andrea. Unambiguous resolution of troubling matters is often needed, sometimes demanded, naturally, if service is to be properly discharged, but keep the circle of your enemies small, especially within your own camp. You are an excellent *miles Christi*, a soldier of Christ.

Yesterday cannot be changed; however, it is our duty to ensure a fortunate tomorrow."

Andrea took the reproach well, for how could he rail against he who sits upon the throne of St. Peter and thus holds the keys to Heaven? And yet, in temporal affairs, his holiness might not have all the answers. "The will of the Church is universal, your holiness, and must be obeyed by all, high and low," he said.

"True, but there are the laws of men and there are the laws of God. If one is violated, so too is the other. Man is born corrupt and as such must earn the grace of God. Of course, the cause of the Church is just, so it should remain absolute, but keep in mind that any violation of the law on behalf of our cause must also be *just*. I, like any king, am bound by custom. This is the policy that I would have all my flock respect and obey. All that is done in the name of the Church and the supreme pontiff must be done in a *just* manner, including the conduct of war."

Boniface paused. Andrea held his breath in anticipation. Should his brother see it fit to take the title of Papal Legate to the Marche away from him, Andrea was not sure what he would do. The blow to his reputation would be severe, but it would be worse for his brothers, since they were too far apart on how to recover the Patrimony, and that bothered him just as much. Victory was within his grasp, despite one brother's foolishness and the other brother's caution. That was a certainty. If only he would be allowed to assume absolute control of all papal forces in Italy, then his mighty fist could clench and squeeze the remaining resistance out of the Patrimony. He could put all in order – the dignity of the throne of St. Peter demanded it.

"I have endeavored to fulfill the letter and the spirit of your orders to the last detail, and if my performance has been disagreeable in any way to your holiness, then I beg you tell me with all due haste. There is nothing that would sadden me more than to suffer your displeasure."

"We must help our brother in Spoleto," Boniface said in a slow, deliberate manner. "Gianello has done poorly, as I have told you with great heaviness of heart. I cannot be at his side at this moment. Rome needs me. We must win back the condottieri our dear Gianello has lost. We must reinvigorate confidence in the papal host there. Umbria is the keystone in the arch of the Patrimony of St. Peter, and unless we are assured of the fidelity of all the lands of the Patrimony, we will not be able to heal this schism that afflicts the Church. We will not be able to defeat Clement and take the war to the enemies of the one true pontiff. Could I spare men from Rome, I would. Instead, I send you, Andrea, to advise your brother. You are worth a dozen companies."

Andrea felt the wave of calm sweep over him as he rode up the final path to the gatehouse. He had had a few doubts, but now he was certain that his older brother wanted him to assume full command in central Italy. If he planned well, the entire Patrimony of St. Peter, from the Mediterranean to the Adriatic, would be in his hands, meaning in his holiness the supreme pontiff's hands, by the end of the campaign season in November. Then he recalled how he had explained his strategy. "I would be honored if your holiness would hear my proposal on how we can rectify the situation."

Boniface nodded.

"You say Gianello's army is ... how should I put it ... demoralized and ill-equipped to execute the Lord's will," Andrea began. "Then we require more men-at-arms, and that will take some time. However, until this need is satisfied, we must serve up some small victories and secure a frontier. That should demonstrate our resolve. Coordination is imperative, especially with my host still encamped in the Marche. Once this has been done and we have collected great strength, we should issue forth with the full weight of arms. We must build such a wave as will wash away all before us, like the Flood, and my army will be the Ark. I have been preparing for this moment ever since you made me Papal Legate. I shall give you the details in due course. Do you have an inventory of cities still loyal to your holiness? Has our dear brother at least provided you with a list of unengaged condottieri in the area? The winter hiring fair is long past, but this does not wholly remove from us the possibility of finding reputable captains."

Boniface recited the names of fortified towns and cities he was confident were still true, and he even gave voice to the clans that ruled them. He was blessed with such a remarkable memory for detail that some were saying he should have been appointed papal treasurer. As for condottieri, his holiness had to admit that he was only familiar with the most famous, and they were all in pay elsewhere. "No, I must rely on you, my brother. Are you capable of restoring the Patrimony?" Boniface placed his hands on Andrea's shoulders.

"I am your man and your brother. Your will shall be done." Andrea bowed and took a few steps backwards. He then dropped to one knee and kissed the papal signet ring to acknowledge his brother as the Vicar of Christ.

"Beware of placing too much upon your own shoulders, my son. A burdened man has trouble looking up. Do not be so proud as to avoid sharing the load with others, including me."

Andrea could not be sure if these words were a gentle reproach, veiled warning, or polite suggestion. It mattered little. Success would ease any burden. "Of course, your holiness."

Boniface said and he held up his index finger. "Our time is ended. The cardinals await my pleasure. Rise and go, Andrea. Godspeed!"

CHAPTER 2

None of the armorers who plied his trade outside the city walls would give Geoffrey Hotspur credit to buy so much as a used jack, the cheap type of boiled leather coat used by common archers, let alone the pieces of plate and mail he needed to complete his harness to the level demanded by his lord.

"You're a fool to throw away this chance!" Geoffrey yelled after yet another rejection. "I don't see any other men of His Lordship the Duke of Lancaster queuing up to buy your wares!" He waved his arms behind him and nearly hit Roger.

"If you want charity, visit a monastery!" the armorer yelled back. "Do I look so daft that I would give a nameless squire anything but the back of my hand? Out with you!"

"I have a name," Geoffrey said as his drew back his shoulders.

"What is it?" the armorer sneered.

"Geoffrey Hotspur!"

"Never heard of you!"

"Ask anyone at court. They all know me."

"I won't bother to bend my knees for nothing. There are a hundred of you lot up there claiming something or other, and all of it backed by hot air and none of it by silver!"

Roger sighed and stepped forward. "I'll stand surety for whatever my friend might need here. My name is Swynford." He pulled out a signet ring embossed with the Swynford crest and thrust it as the man.

The armorer looked Roger up and down. "Yes, well you certainly don't look like a common squire, so I agree. Your friend can only have refurbished stuff though."

"I cannot let you do this, Rog," Geoffrey said. "This man has no cause to refuse me."

"It is done."

"It's not right. You are too generous."

"Not at all." Roger made a dismissive gesture.

"I should just walk out."

"You will not. Come now, time is fleeting. You know we have to muster soon."

"Very well," Geoffrey concluded, having thrice denied the offer.

After fully trying the patience of the vendor, Geoffrey picked out a full leg harness complete with leather cuisses for his thighs, iron poleyns for his knees and greaves for his shins, plus a bag of laces and rivets for likely repairs. Combined with the coat-of-plates he had recently won off a poor knight and the simple iron helm he had earned from months of sweeping the duke's stables, the result was a serviceable kit.

Once they had packed up the gear and were trudging back along the muddy path of Armorer's Row, Roger asked Geoffrey why he was willing to accept his pledge for debt to the armorer but not to the Gamesmaster in the Blue Boar the other night.

"Not for the life of me would I let you become beholden to such a knave. It would have insulted you. With such essential craftsmen as these, however, my debt is worthy of your trouble. And the cause is good. Campaigning with the duke? God be praised!"

"God be praised, indeed. A *chevauchée* is better than sitting in halls, that's for sure," Roger said, "I just hope that we get to see a true pass of arms, and not just pillage whoever we are pillaging."

"You worry too much, my friend." Geoffrey slowed his stride so that Roger would not fall behind. "You will make for a melancholy knight. Do you know where we are to campaign?"

"Had you not been spending so much time with the ladies, you would have heard that his lordship is issuing forth to punish several of his vassals for not showing the proper *fidelitas*. They have been using the excuse of their devotion to Clement not to attend court and pay homage to his lordship."

"We will bend their knees and doff their caps for them, then!" Geoffrey whipped his arm back and forth as though he was wielding a sword.

"Would you do that?" Roger asked.

"Do what? Cut them in half? Of course!"

"No. Would you withhold *fidelitas* from your lord for the sake of your faith?"

"You want to be ordained a priest, not a knight," Geoffrey teased.

"I'm serious. I know we squires are forbidden to discuss the schism between Rome and Avignon in halls, but I am curious."

"Well then, I would deny your question. I understand fidelity as faith, my friend. Were I to break my bond with my lord, I would also be giving offense to the Lord."

"But it happens all the time," Roger said.

"So? A bond can be mended, forgiveness can be given, restitution can be made."

"Now who sounds like a priest? But I understand you."

Geoffrey nodded at a pair of young maids as they passed. He was tempted to approach them, especially since one of them was exceptionally tall.

"You were saying, Rog?"

"I was just wondering when we will muster for this *chevauchée*."

"The sooner the better. I've been waiting so many years for this," Geoffrey said with such enthusiasm that the maids turned around to look at him.

"Yes, well, we shall see. I just hope my shoulder will be strong enough." Roger massaged his right arm.

They were walking in companionable silence through one of the poorer areas of the Outer City when Geoffrey said, "I should like to ask your advice, Roger."

"Does it concern the heart, the soul or honor? With you, it could be anything."

"I'm afraid I misunderstand you completely. My soul is pure and will be devoted to but one, when the time comes."

"Your soul may be whole, but your heart seems to have fragmented, with pieces left in every quarter. And I dare say the rest of you is fairly corrupted as well."

"Man is born fallen, so his body by nature is corrupt and fated to decay. We cannot pretend otherwise."

"Did you learn that from your days as a novice?"

"Rather from my nights. The days were devoted to hard labor while the nights were labored with strict devotion to the psalms. I hardly got any sleep, as I recall."

"And for what kind of deliverance did you pray?"

"As it was a time before my voice was restrung for manhood, I would say that I prayed precisely how the monks instructed me."

"And in Avignon you continue your education at the feet of the city's most ardent maids. Does that make you a Franciscan or a Dominican, I wonder? Regardless, you stink like both orders."

"Frail of flesh, am I, with respect to the gentler sex, upon my honor." Geoffrey placed his left hand on the right side of his chest, away from his heart.

"No doubt you respect the frail flesh when honoring your commonest desires, but let us not have notions of sin enter into this."

"By faith, my friend, you have hit the nail on the head, for it is indeed the worst of sins that is torturing my soul."

"Then let us have a casting of accounts."

"Ah! There it is? Are you a seer, Roger, or do your thoughts naturally turn to such base things."

"That would make me an alchemist then, now wouldn't it, or rather the opposite of one. What have I said? Your dithering makes me dizzy."

"Casting of accounts. The issue is money and where I can find some." Geoffrey shifted the clutch of new armor to his other shoulder. "I still need a horse."

"Debts are a terrible thing," Roger sympathized. "Had I more than a shilling or a sou, I would gladly give it to you, but I only have my name for support. Do you really want to make use of someone else's silver? There is the wretched Gamesmaster to consider, after all, and his reputation for enforcing the terms of his bonds by less than peaceful means is well known. Of course, while we are considering the matter, there are the Jews …"

"Fie! I would rather with the fiend entrust my soul than borrow anything from those haters of honest men. Some debts cannot be countenanced. I will most readily pay a debt of *fidelitas* to my lord and master. I am bound as a Christian to pay the debt of faith to my Creator. I will be honored to pay the debt of virtue to my order when Fate befits it for me to be made a knight. But a debt done with coin soils the very word. The only time I will worry myself over a bond for the loan of silver is when it is stuck to my backside!"

"Well, now that we've ruled out Jews and the Gamesmaster, I hasten to add that it would be very unwise to ask his lordship for a gift or a loan. He would most certainly strike you off the campaign roll for such an offense."

"Absolutely. I would never ask him for money – only for the opportunity to serve and earn some. What about His Grace King Richard?"

"*Our* King Richard? Richard *Plantagenet*? Are you mad? First of all, I hardly think you'd be permitted an audience, and second, even if you were to succeed in being admitted to the great hall, you would no doubt be led to some forgotten chamber, where you would languish until you got fed up and left of your own accord. Of course, I don't suspect anyone would reject your request outright, out of courtesy, but the *chevauchée* would be over long before you received a proper reply."

"Well, what then? I no more wish to offend than betray you, but truth be told you are well served by your distinguished name, and that cursed armorer is right – I am unknown."

"Our lordship would not keep you in halls if he saw no worth in you," Roger protested.

"Yes, well, this situation cannot last for long. I need to join the *chevauchée* if I am to retain my place. What have we now, Rog, eighteen years behind us? Nineteen?"

"Does it matter? The time for our training is almost at an end, although you need more lectures on shield-bearing. You still leave yourself open, I have seen."

"All the better to lead my opponent to exactly where I want him."

"What? To stab you?"

The squires continued to jangle and jape as they wound their way through the Outer City, but they failed to heed their lengthening shadows and were well past the small side gate by which they had left Avignon proper when they realized their mistake.

"Oh, for the love of all that's holy, now what do we do?" Roger said. "We cannot be late in halls again and risk the wrath of his lordship."

"Well, we might as well just proceed to the Merchant's Gate. It's closer, I believe."

"Do you know the way? None of this looks familiar and it stinks of the devil's bowels."

Geoffrey laughed and shoved his friend on ahead of him.

"Mind my shoulder!"

They walked for another half hour, keeping the tall Merchant's Gate within sight.

"Ugh! What a wretched place," Roger said as he looked around at the disorderly collection of rickety huts that had grown up on the southern slopes of Avignon. "What sort of people live here?

"None of the sort you might be familiar with, Master Swynford. Those who have no place in the city proper, I'll wager. I'd burn the lot down if I knew it would do any good, although good is not what this marvel is known for."

"And what is it known for? Don't tell me you've swum in this sty on your own."

Geoffrey smiled and changed the subject. "Darkness has stolen my vision. Can you still see anything?"

Roger shook his head.

"Hmm, well I know of a square down from the Merchant's Gate, and by my reckoning it should be straight that way." Geoffrey pointed ahead.

"And you wouldn't take me? Fie on you!"

"Would you have come? I think not. Ha! Here it is! Doubt me no longer."

"Had I been here once, I would be quick to forget it." Roger looked around and made a sour face.

"Then there is no time to lose leaving it."

As the squires were crossing the square, one of the nameless alehouses on it erupted with a violence that showered splinters of shattered wood as far as their feet. Angry shouts and terrified shrieks punctured the fetid idyll, all but stifling the moans of a bloodied man lying across a ruined door. A column of men, inflamed by the dangerous combination of drink and wrath, poured out of the alehouse on unsteady feet and set upon the prostrate man. They were quickly followed by women, who shrieked at the men to lay off, warning that their violence will alert the night watch.

"That looks familiar," Geoffrey joked and they stopped to watch.

"That might have been you at the Blue Boar the other night if it wasn't for me," Roger said. "I don't see that man on his lordship's *chevauchée* anytime soon."

Geoffrey used the break to relieve his stiffening shoulders, and so levered his net full of armor onto the ground. After witnessing one bloody pummeling and the start of another, Roger turned to his companion.

"Well, I've seen enough. Should we hasten to the gate, Geoff?"

"Why don't we just duck into one of the better houses here until this mess gets dragged back into the tavern where it belongs?"

"There are no 'better houses' within a stone's throw from here."

"I'd like to make a beeline for the gate, but look how the fighting spreads. We might just have to slice our way through, and soon. Another late night and his lordship will have my hide." Geoffrey clasped the hilt of his sword and smiled.

"You're joking, I hope."

Not wishing to place his new kit at risk, Geoffrey nodded and relaxed his grip, but the squires had not taken more than a couple of steps towards a better house when a loud voice pounded the backs of their heads.

"And where d'you think you're going with that fine sack of goods?!"

Geoffrey and Roger turned to the voice and saw a very large man with no teeth and matted hair pulled over his left eye. Two men lay at his feet, half drowned in a puddle of mud.

"What have we here then?" the giant drawled. "It looks to me like a couple of *routiers*." He cocked his head sideways and yelled behind him: "Hoi! Stop that! We's got other work to do. The *routiers* are back, and what's more they're English bastards. Let's get 'em a-fore they make some nasty business!"

"We are men of the Duke of Lancaster," Roger declared. "It would be wise…"

"Don't talk to this wretch as though he was worthy of such courtesy," Geoffrey cut in and then turned to the ruffian. "Trouble us again and I will run you through. As ugly as you are, I dare say your head would look good on a spike!"

The call of '*routiers*' was the clarion that ended the brawl. Those who were armed, however crudely, abruptly reined in their fury and gathered around their new captain. While bandits were common in France, the word *routiers* rang harshly in Geoffrey and Roger's ears, since they knew that it specifically referred to English brigands, and as such was an effective rallying cry.

Geoffrey and Roger retreated a few steps but halted when they realized that they could not reach their refuge before the mob would be on top of them. Geoffrey's hand trembled with excitement as he again sought a sure grip around the familiar hilt. A fluttering filled his temples and his feet grew as cold as ice.

"It looks as though our lance is made, Rog," Geoffrey announced. "This should be merry practice. Only tell me we face nine fools and I will be glad."

Roger steeled himself as well, since any thought of a negotiated settlement was quickly dispelled by the ring of furious faces.

"I'd like to say there are *none* of them, but Fate is unkind, for she is offering us double your number." Roger flashed his dagger at a group that was now moving to encircle them.

"Then we must be quick about this so that we are back in hall in time for lauds. Let's have at them!"

Roger nodded and set his guard for attack, but Geoffrey was already striking, quickly drawing blood from two of the brutes. Roger parried a couple of awkward passes, sending his assailants reeling backwards, and then used this gap in the action to yell, "We must stand together or we'll be hacked apart!"

Geoffrey heard the warning and shifted his guard to create the standard back-to-back defence they had learned from their swordmaster.

But the mob was not frightened away. Led by the instigating giant, the dozen-odd men remaining broke into two groups; the smaller group fought the squires at close quarters while the larger one maneuvered around the clash of arms, looking for an opening to stab or slice. Both groups cried *"routiers"* at the moment of attack. A deft twisting move by Roger opened the hand of one fighter and Geoffrey forced another to retire with several cuts to his thighs and chest, but even with their superior skills and arms, the squires could not remain unscathed. The giant made good use of his long reach by hacking into Geoffrey's left shoulder with a fish knife, but the clumsy angle of the blade drew little blood.

However, Roger was caught in the calf by a rough weapon and struck in the head by a stone, which skewed his eyesight enough to make him retreat into an even more defensive guard.

Geoffrey, ignoring his damaged shoulder, took down another attacker, whose gaping facial wound scared off yet another, but it was not enough to end the battle. Seeing Roger stagger, the giant shifted his attention and quickly lunged at him, striking home just above the heart. The reckless move gave Geoffrey the opening he needed to pivot and thrust upwards, catching the giant deep beneath the ribcage. Roger and the giant stumbled a few paces before slumping to the ground. Geoffrey now stood alone, with a few close and more distant foes ranked against him. But his instinct was to protect his friend, and so with his free hand he reached down and pulled Roger to the cover of his heap of armor.

The surviving band of angry revelers now took their time surrounding the lone squire. Geoffrey snatched Roger's dagger out of his limp hand to double his chances, even though he had precious little training in such advanced swordsmanship. What was worse, though, was that the stance left him dangerously exposed.

The circle was beginning to close anew when one of the besiegers jerked upwards and fell to the ground. In his place stood a man in a wide-brimmed hat holding a bloodied knife. The mob froze, but that only gave time for the stranger to slash the sword-hands of two more brutes. The confusion was too much for the attackers, and with their leader felled, the company broke up and fled.

The stranger considered melting into the darkness too, but his safety was not assured. He was certain that other men were on their way, leaving him with no doubt that he would fall victim to their blind rage as well. And then there were the squires to consider.

"How was it that you came to aid us and not them?" Geoffrey asked as he attended to his friend, although he held his sword at the ready. Roger was nearly unconscious and losing much blood.

The stranger wiped his knife on the back of one of the fallen and adjusted his hat. He grimaced when he saw the wounded squire. He could not leave them to the night. "I recognized by your badges that you are men of Gaunt. I assumed that he would be discomfited to learn that two of his squires were found murdered in the Outer City. He might even reward someone for saving the two unfortunate men."

"Your judgment is sound. What is your name so that we may repay you this debt of honor?"

"Your friend is bleeding badly. I know the guards at the Merchant's Gate, so we had better get him there as soon as possible." The stranger carefully lifted Roger by the shoulders and nodded for Geoffrey to take his legs. He had revealed himself, but not his name, and the distraction of the wounded squire would give him time to come up with a plausible story and false name. He was glad he wore that hat, since at least the wide brim coupled with the darkness obscured his features.

Spoleto

"Remind me, Corrado: has your lord declared for his holiness the true pontiff in Rome and proper heir to the throne of St. Peter, or is he still defiant, like so many others in Germany?" Andrea asked the condottiere Corrado Prospero. His real name was Conrad Prosperg, but it had long since been Italianized. Andrea was standing several yards away from his brother's captain-general because the German was too tall for his liking. He was also uncomfortable with the man's dour demeanor and pockmarked face.

"And what lord might that be?" Prosperg answered with genuine surprise. "My *condotta* is with His Lordship the Duke of Spoleto, and so my first duty is to him. I cannot recall the last time I was in Bavaria and no one is demanding my return. Why does this concern you?" Prospero put down the enrolment list they had been reviewing and concentrated on the papal legate. He spoke in the clipped Italian of the local condottieri, although his voice still resonated with the accent of his homeland. Swathed in an unmarked, pitch black, riding surcoat, the German captain exuded austerity.

"Because we cannot have distractions. Clement is throwing silver around out of desperation and, if you will forgive me, some lords might be tempted into sin. If His Lordship the Duke of Bavaria, for example, demands you go over to Malatesta Malatesta, would you follow him into sin?"

"Your brother has hired me to captain his army."

"His army is the same as his holiness's army," Andrea interjected.

"Please let me finish. What you say is all true and irrelevant, since my conscience does not enter into this. My faith is strong and will remain unchanged no matter who declares for whom."

"Your faith is a matter of salvation, not conscience, but let's set that aside for now. Are you saying that you are more devoted to a piece of parchment than to the Lord, that your fidelity is stronger to Earthly covenants than to divine ones?"

"Not at all. There is a division between the two, and I would not denigrate the latter by setting it next to the former. That will not do. If you want to take the Patrimony before Clement does, then I suggest we discuss the material composition of our army and leave to others their spiritual needs."

True to his reputation, Andrea thought, the German was of sanguine disposition, like his brother Boniface, to match his dour look. He was a man of few words but great dignity.

"I am of the same opinion," Andrea said. "Now, I think you will agree that I have done well in the past week, if you will return your attention to the list."

"I have read it. Has your brother? Where is he? Is he no longer a part of the war council? If not, I worry more about my *condotta* than my soul."

"I sent word to him," Andrea said quickly and gave a dismissive wave. "Now, as you can see, while my brother lost Broglia and Brandolini, I brought Giovanni Colonna with me from Rome and I signed a young condottiere from the Romagna named Bosio Attendolo. I don't think you know him, since he only has ten lances."

"Having Colonna will help. The coffers are low at the moment and I assume he brought his war chest with him. He's a good captain. The men will be pleased. With the militia I recruited and my company, we should be able to relieve Narni soon."

"I disagree. We haven't enough men to take on both Tarlati and Malatesta, should the latter arrive with his main brigade. Their horsemen still outnumber ours, and I cannot redress the balance without archers, and you still only have *half* a company. Your impetuosity surprises me."

"Yes, well, I'll only have half a company until I get the rest out of

Narni. As good as they are, they cannot hold out indefinitely."

"I understand. However, Giovanni Tarlati is in charge there, and he is a skilled captain. Malatesta has supplemented his company with a brigade of Bretons, a dangerous combination. Whether he does this to frighten people or because he lacks good men, I do not know." Andrea wanted to inform his captain-general that he had already established contact with Tarlati.

"Tarlati is not a skilled captain and I doubt he has the fortitude to maintain a long siege without resorting to terror, which is why I believe we should strike now. We need Narni intact if we are to have a safe rear. No one has forgotten Cesena."

Andrea was very concerned about Captain Prospero's men. Half of his company of 600 veteran heavy men-at-arms was all that was preventing Clement from capturing Narni and thereby controlling the upper reaches of the Tiber River valley as far as Orte. Should those key towns fall, the Patrimony would be sealed from Rome.

"So, what do our numbers look like?" Andrea asked.

"Aside from my company, we have the duke's retinue, a growing company of local militia, and a few free companies under *condotta*." Prospero sighed and stared at the table. "The numbers are here." He pointed to a list next to the map of the Patrimony. "The free companies are small and led by young condottieri. No lords from outside the duchy have ridden to our cause, but many remain in their castles awaiting our arrival. I also put the word out that we will recruit free lances."

"Withdraw that order," Andrea said abruptly.

"I beg your pardon?" Prospero took a few steps towards the papal legate.

"Forgive me, captain. I suggest that we rescind that order. Begging for free lances makes us look desperate. We are not. The larger condottieri will come to us."

OF FAITH AND FIDELITY

A messenger entered the hall and bowed deeply first to Andrea and then to Prospero.

"We have more good news, captain," Andrea said. "My crossbowmen do exist. A company of crossbowmen has been engaged and is on its way. God be praised!"

"How long before we see them?"

"They were to embark for Italy the day after this message was sent. If the date here is correct, that would make it ten days ago."

"Embark? Where are they coming from?"

"Barcelona."

"Barcelona?"

"Yes, Barcelona."

"Are there no other crossbowmen available? Italy is strewn with them."

"Gianello contracted some from Genoa, but the civil disorder there has kept them at home. All other respectable companies are either already engaged or doing essential garrison duty somewhere, like at the castles of lords refusing to submit to his holiness."

"I suppose we should be grateful," Prospero sighed.

"Let us call the war council," Andrea proposed. "The captains should be informed that we are nearly ready to make our mark."

"Jean Lagoustine! What are you doing out here past compline?" the guard said. "Don't tell me that the Ga ..."

An angry look from Jean shut the guard up. His name now revealed, Jean could only finish the guard's story and find a way to leave the gatehouse as soon as possible. He got the guards to tear up bits of cloth to bind Roger's wounds and encouraged Geoffrey to cradle his friend's head and keep him conscious. Carrying the wounded squire had strained his back, so he rolled his uneven shoulders to relieve the muscles. The lower right shoulder was already growing stiff, Jean felt, and he shook his head at the memory of that night four years ago when it was broken by a defiant but hopelessly indebted knight. That was in his early days with the Gamesmaster, and he learned his lesson about watching his back.

"We owe you a debt, Jean Lagoustine," Geoffrey solemnly stated. "Just as the greatest honor is to save a gentleman's life, so is it the worst of dishonors to let it go unacknowledged."

Jean wanted to laugh. The Gamesmaster had instructed him to shadow Hotspur and squeeze whatever money he could out of him, or get the Swynford squire to contribute. The tall squire was penniless, by all accounts, but a favorite of Gaunt, and Jean knew how to bide his time until the opportunity to collect presented itself. He had worked for the Gamesmaster since he ran away from that nasty chandler his father had arranged to take him. He was an apprentice for years and had learned nothing but how to drink.

"What is your rank," Geoffrey continued, "so that I might know how to address you?" He was starting to regain his composure.

This was a good question, and Jean was prepared for it. He had used the silence of their flight to the Merchant's Gate to refashion himself, since he could now expect to meet this squire again, likely in or around the Blue Boar. "I am a chandler."

"You sure you're not a cutler? You handle a knife better than some of my fellow squires."

"If I'd had a candle, we'd been snuffed out by now."

"True. How was it you came upon us? I would pay you and your family a visit," Geoffrey asked. He saw that Jean looked like a typical villein: heavy-set, face dark from the sun, strong but unrefined voice. However, he was impressed by how far to the right his nose pointed, as though it had been broken several times. The man was a fighter.

Jean could not appear ungracious, but he was intent on pushing the squire off this line of questioning. "The bandages are poor. You must get your friend out of here."

"We must get him back to our halls. I cannot do it alone and you can easily go by way of Gaunt's palace as any other, if I know Chandler Street right. Your journey will be not much affected on any account."

Jean was caught, but he still attempted to extricate himself from this easy favor. "My wife is no doubt frantic over my continued absence at this late hour, for beyond the walls evil is free to stalk the honest man. I shouldn't tarry."

"But you have good reason, and now a fair story, with which to redeem your lateness," Geoffrey countered.

"True, but Gaunt's halls are not as close as you might think," Jean reasoned. "Why don't you call for a litter? I'm sure the other squires would come to your aid, if only to hear *your* tale of this night's adventure."

"There is no time. I too see how poorly the bandages dam the blood."

Jean stared at the pale face of the wounded man. Roger was now bleeding through and Jean calculated that he would be dead by morning, and with him a large measure of surety for the English squire's debt.

"We shall take your companion to the Hospital of St. John," Jean declared. "The chandlers support a chapel there, and so the monks should have no trouble accepting a request from me. It is not far from here and the hospital is cloistered."

A nod from Geoffrey settled the issue. With help from the anxious captain of the night watch, Jean saddled a barely conscious Roger on Geoffrey's back, while Jean assumed responsibility for the arms and armor. Payment of a few gros to the captain opened a secret door to the city.

Jean had been right when he said that the monks who administer to the ill and infirmed at the Hospital of St. John would be amenable to taking in the wounded squire. With the efficiency for which they were famous, they bundled Roger into a warm cell with an attendant novice to watch over him and recite prayers. Jean was also honest about the guild of chandlers sponsoring a small chapel, although he neglected to mention the Gamesmaster was the patron of the hospital's other chapel, and so the monks recognized Jean from his frequent checks on its construction. Therefore, a few words were all that was needed to ensure silence on the matter of Roger's injuries and identity.

After seeing that his friend was comfortable and well-tended, Geoffrey left Roger to the care of the novice. He found Jean at the end of the corridor.

"I shall stay the night and pray in the chapel your guild so generously funds. Once again, I thank you. These monks look to be a capable lot."

"Are you not worried about your soul? I should warn you that the chapel was consecrated by priests ordained by bishops loyal to Clement. You are English, unless your king has finally come around to supporting the one true pontiff." Jean was only half joking. Such matters little interested him since he never attended mass and the Gamesmaster told him to ignore it. As for final confession, whenever that might be, he believed that if the priest is true, the Lord will hear him.

"I am not taking the sacrament and have no need to listen to a cleric. I shall be praying alone. I shall find peace no matter who blessed the chapel."

"I take my leave of you then. I have gathered more than enough threads to weave a fine tale … for my wife. We chandlers are more accustomed to the small daily struggles with wax than sword fights with drunken bruisers." Jean adjusted his cloak and turned to go.

"Fare thee well, Master Jean, and may fortune smile upon you. You must let me buy you a quaff of ale or two as a small gesture of my thanks. I know a great many excellent taverns in this holy city."

The only time Jean wanted to see Geoffrey again was when he had the money he owed. "I would be honored, particularly as we are rarely blessed with visits from English squires down on Chandler Street, even at our alehouses. However, I am shortly to embark on a commission that will take me far from Avignon. The guild has decreed it, I'm afraid."

"I wish you well, then. Should you see fit to recommend a welcome host on your street in your absence, then I am sure to come, but as the *chevauchée* takes me away from Avignon too, we shall have to wait for winter to fulfill our pledges."

Jean turned back towards the squire. "*Chevauchée*? Did I hear you correctly in that you are about to embark on a *chevauchée*?"

"Of course. We should muster shortly." Then, seeing the anxiety appearing on the Frenchman's face, Geoffrey added, "On my oath, it is not against France. We are to strike somewhere in the Guyenne, as far as I know."

While Geoffrey was worried the Frenchman might harbor ill will against him on account of his possibly having to slay his countrymen, Jean, was gripped by the fear that the squire would fall out of sight, or worse, that he would have to track him across half of Christendom. The Gamesmaster had taken a risk by accepting the debt of the nameless Geoffrey Hotspur. Of course, that was when the Gamesmaster was sure that the clarion of war would remain silent, leaving the alehouses and gaming rooms of Avignon full. It was easy enough to follow the squire between the halls of the Duke of Lancaster and the Blue Boar, but the thought of having to leave the safe environs of the city filled Jean with dread and loathing. And Jean was certain that his employer would command him to do so.

"Are you sure this is not just rumor?" Jean said. "Men are fickle of speech and I have not heard anything from the guild of chandlers, whose ears, I must say, are not made of wax. The truce between England and France includes the greater and lesser lords of both kings, and the truce is still in force, as far as I know."

"There is no reason I can think of why a chandler should know the minds of great lords, and I don't believe in rumor," Geoffrey declared as a matter of course. "I received my commission only today, from the noble hand of his lordship himself. With His Grace King Richard now bringing order to Ireland, Sir John is the highest ranking English knight in France, and so is above reproach and beyond question. If he commands that a *chevauchée* be undertaken, then so it shall be. But come; let us repair to the chapel, should you wish to question me further. I will share with you whatever I possess, for I am still in your debt." Geoffrey patted Jean's shoulder and went to find the chapel of the guild of chandlers.

Jean tried to suppress a smile. Instead of thieving away, he escorted Geoffrey along an arcade and through a pair of roughly hewn stone posts that were serving as the temporary entrance to the chandlers' chapel, pending additional funds to complete the vestibule. As Jean admired the well-set rafters and comforting solidity of the structure, Geoffrey made straight for the altar, threw himself on his knees and began reciting those fragments of Latin verse he could still remember from the time before he was brought to the halls of Gaunt. Jean was surprised and amused in equal measure by Geoffrey's radical shift in demeanor. He found it difficult to reconcile the image of the lusty, arrogant youth he had seen wildly throwing dice in the Blue Boar and hacking down ruffians on a muddy square with the one that was now hunched in devotion, remorseful and seemingly on the verge of tears.

Distracted by some shuffling, Jean watched Geoffrey rise and go to a row of stubby wooden chairs anchored to the north wall. Jean followed and sat beside him.

"I find it warm in here," Jean said to dilute the stifling solemnity, "but at least it dispels the winter chill. How fare you now, master squire?"

Geoffrey lifted his head out of his hands. Although his lips had ceased to move, his thoughts were still filled with bits of prayer tinted by regret and annoyance: regret for his having included a third party into the night's melee and annoyance at the realization that it might jeopardize his place in the *chevauchée*. Upon hearing the chandler repeat his question, Geoffrey could not refuse to answer.

"I must confess; a heavy sadness weighs upon me. The monks assure me Roger will recover – all signs point to it, they say, but all the same, I am troubled."

Jean was keen to leave the hospital, but that word 'troubled' held him back. Compelled to say something that might draw the squire into his confidence, Jean adapted a speech the Gamesmaster once made when Jean himself had expressed doubts about his work after having laid a solid beating on a delinquent debtor. "The feeling will pass. You are weary from spilling blood. You require distraction. You fulfilled your duty to your friend in deed and in prayer, so the time has come to look forward. Let us depart from this place and speak of other things." Jean took Geoffrey by the sleeve and tried to drag him up, but he would not budge.

"I will remain. Go, if you wish."

Jean sighed as quietly as his frustration would allow. He was indeed anxious to go, but he had to know more about Gaunt's war plans. The Gamesmaster was also in the victualing business and some of Gaunt's knights had debts. So, after a respectful pause, he began to probe. "You don't think that your friend … Roger … will be well enough to join the campaign, do you? After all, the campaign season is swiftly upon us." This was quite true. Occasionally, someone would launch a winter campaign for the sake of surprise or bravado, but only the foolish attempted to march horses and men-at-arms across country during the spring thaw.

"We are to muster in less than a fortnight at one of Sir John's castles. My conscience would allow me to travel without Roger, since my fidelity to Sir John surpasses all, but his injury is a bad sign, the monks' assurances notwithstanding."

"You are a good friend," Jean said. "I wish I could advise you, but I know little about such matters." A lengthy silence grew between them. Another monk entered the chapel.

"Should I decline the invitation, it would not only insult the dignity of my lord, but with every other squire in Sir John's court already enrolled for the *chevauchée*, it would shame me beyond any hope of recovery," Geoffrey said slowly, as though shaping his thoughts with his words. "I am told there is a certain age at which a squire becomes a jester, and as such is treated as a laughing stock." Geoffrey emitted a deep sigh.

Jean found himself on the horns of a dilemma. Should he convince the English squire to remain and watch over his friend, it would take more time than patience for the Gamesmaster to collect his debt, with the corollary that he, Jean, would get the blame. Should he convince Geoffrey to go on the *chevauchée*, however, he would in all likelihood have to follow, risking life and limb in the dangerous French countryside. Then again, should the wellborn squire quickly recover from his wounds, he might be able to procure the money for the Gamesmaster from his own family. Jean grimaced in frustration. With nothing more to resolve that night, he stood up and made ready to depart. "You will sleep here tonight?" Jean asked.

Geoffrey nodded.

Jean clapped him on the shoulder and left the chapel, no less troubled than when he had entered.

CHAPTER 3

GEOFFREY was being punished. His Lordship the Duke of Lancaster had heard about the scuffle in the Outer City and so had decided to make an example of him by sending him on a fool's errand.

"I will not allow any member of my household to add fuel to the fire burning around St. Peter's throne," his lordship had said. "Clement has not raised his sword against His Grace King Richard, or me, and I do not want to give him just cause. Do not interrupt! I will not hear about *your* just cause. Clement has declared his campaign season started and so far it is not against us. Now, this is what you will do."

Geoffrey listened with horror about how he was to sail to Florence the next morning with a band of old knights and collect the remains of the mercenary John Hawkwood. They were calling it a royal commission, since King Richard appointed it himself, but in Geoffrey's eyes it was nothing more than a humiliation. The only concession his lordship would make was that he could visit his wounded friend, as long as he was in halls before nightfall.

As he was passing the Blue Boar, Geoffrey spat as he thought about how he might miss the *chevauchée* and nearly caught Jean's boots as he was rounding the corner.

"Hey! Is that the thanks I get for saving your ass? Well, I've had worse."

"A thousand apologies! Jean, isn't it? I'd go in for a drink with you, but I'm off to see Roger."

"This *is* a happy coincidence. So am I." In truth, Jean had no desire to see either squire, but the Gamesmaster had ordered him to check on his investment.

As they were walking, Geoffrey gave Jean an account of his unfortunate meeting with the duke. The man was a stranger, although he was hardly spilling secrets, but Geoffrey just had the urge to talk. Roger was in hospital and the other squires were not close, even though Geoffrey often shared their company and bought them ale. He knew that they called him Percival behind his back, but he was not bothered by it, although Lancelot was more to his liking.

"The only manner by which I would ever happily concede to travel to Florence would be in the ranks of a crusader, like how Richard Lionheart went to the Holy Land to cow the Saracens," Geoffrey concluded.

"I am told Florence is full of wonders, a place where fountains flow with silver and chapels are made of gold."

"A place ruled by men without rank, you mean. I'd rather not be so fenced in with florins that I cannot see the heavens. But it's the purpose that troubles me most. I mean, I don't see what the fuss is all about. This Hawkwood might have been dubbed a knight and granted arms, but when all is said and done, he really was little more than a glorified *routier* in my mind. What kind of knight was he anyway? He never took up the cross, even though the Saracens threaten the frontiers of Christendom, and from what I hear he was no one's man and changed lords as often as he shaved his beard. He was as common as a cart road. I have half a mind not to go and let my sword earn my forgiveness with his lordship."

"Don't be so hasty," Jean said. "Think of it as a chance to shine in a company of your peers. A *chevauchée* is an opportunity to prove one's worth, you will agree, so why not this? You cannot afford to remain in Avignon with idle hands, by any reckoning. A royal commission can be a lucrative venture. Just as well, you could go to Florence and *then* join a campaign when you return. It is close by fast ship." Jean was hoping the hint of money would remind Geoffrey of his debt.

"I don't see how collecting a corpse, even for the king, will open any doors for me. I was given no task, not even as a cup-bearer, so what kind of service is there to prove my worth?" Geoffrey kicked a stone in despair.

"Well, if you will not find favor with the English, then perhaps you will with the Florentines. Gaunt's man you might be, but you can still call yourself a freeman."

"How can a money-lender make a knight? I would rather earn my living picking fights with drunken louts than humiliate myself by counting pennies for a sinful … whatever." Geoffrey waved his hand to disperse the confusion clouding his thoughts.

Jean heard an echo of his own uncertainties in the squire's vacillations. Jean's service as a modest but effective debt collector for the Gamesmaster's network of alehouses in and around Avignon had been entered into voluntarily between men of equal station, although of unequal means. He was not a bondsman, strictly speaking, but he could not just walk away from one of the most powerful men in Avignon. If the Gamesmaster paid him well, or would allow him an interest in any of his gaming halls, then his doubts would vanish. Jean knew that one day a collection will go against him, and he will find himself either dead or in a dungeon. The Gamesmaster could find another poor but broad-shouldered peasant to take his place, so he was alone. Fear held Jean fast. Should he break with the Gamesmaster, he had enough influence to ensure that Jean would never again find a place in Avignon. He was thinking about a way to secure himself when he bumped into the squire.

"What would your companion, Roger Swynford, say about all this, do you think?" Jean suggested. "Perhaps he would want you to go."

"Roger. I should not leave him alone, but I would rather suffer a thousand deaths than defy my lord. And if he mends well and goes on the *chevauchée* without me while I sit idle in a distant land? I don't know." Geoffrey looked up at the sky and beat his chest. "May the devil take me away from this cursed life!"

Seeing that less subtlety was required, Jean said, "Does not the jangle of silver call you to duty, though?"

"What makes you so sure that I need money?" Geoffrey cocked his head and looked at Jean.

"All squires need money." Jean began to count on his fingers. "You will need to complete your harness; I've seen your kit, since I carried for you last night. Remember? You will need to eat. You are not pledged to a knight, it seems, since you have no true place on this royal bones commission, as you say. The *chevauchée* is out for you, at least at the moment. Am I missing anything?"

Geoffrey shrugged his shoulders. "You reckon well, but this is not a simple as rolling a taper."

"Listen," Jean continued. "If you stay, you have nothing; if you run to Gaunt's *chevauchée* without his knowledge, his lordship will send you back in shackles. If you fulfill this modest task of keeping out of trouble, I am certain that his lordship would reward you when you return. You could go off to fight in some petty feud between German cities or in a punitive expedition against some troublesome peasants in Frisia, I suppose, and no one would be the wiser, but you haven't the men to form a proper lance, and what would be the point of your enlisting as a common soldier? It would be beneath you."

These last few words were like daggers in Geoffrey's heart. He was already so low that he could see only darkness beneath him. And the chandler was right. As much as he would like to find proper service as a squire, he did not have the means to do it.

At the Hospital of St. John the infirmarian led the squire and his chandler friend through the now familiar maze of the hospital to the convalescent cell, where the monk raised a finger to his lips and pointed at the open door. Peering inside, the visitors saw a surgeon wiping a streak of blood from his patient's right arm. Beside him on the floor sat a brass pot filled to its fluted brim with a dark, viscous liquid. Roger looked pale and tranquil, as though he had reached a pleasant end to a long journey, but when his eyes fell upon the hesitating figures crowding the door, his face brightened. With a weak hand gesture he invited them in.

Geoffrey entered first. He ignored the bloodletter, who was still gathering his instruments, and instead sat down on the stool closest to the bed, nearly kicking over the pot in his haste. Abandoning the rules of propriety that dictated he should at least mumble a simple blessing when visiting the sick, Geoffrey launched into a recounting of his audience with the duke. "… and my final destination is to be England, Roger, to present the remains of this Hawkwood to King Richard in person," he concluded.

Roger said not a word during his friend's exposition, but his eyes and ears were attentive, so once silence returned to the cell, he raised himself up and delivered his piece. "I am not a seer, but I have been expecting to speak to you on a delicate matter." His voice was weak and its ethereal quality made Geoffrey very solemn. "I saw something last night that will almost certainly affect our enrolment in the *chevauchée*." Before continuing, Roger raised his unblemished arm, since he could not raise the other, and grasped Geoffrey's shoulder.

Jean, meanwhile, had taken just a few steps into the musty cell when he blanched at the sight of the heavy vessel of blood the infirmarian was taking away. To Jean, the wounded squire looked worse than when they had left him the night before, despite his tidy appearance. The infirmarian brushed passed him, followed by the bloodletter with the instruments of his trade wrapped in a leather case tucked beneath his arm. Jean noticed that the bloodletter had said nothing about Roger's parlous state to Geoffrey, so after excusing himself on the grounds that he had to inspect the chapel of the chandlers, he followed the pair out.

When they were beyond earshot of Gaunt's squires, Jean seized the bloodletter by the arm and showed him to a niche that was once occupied by a Roman fountain. "Will you be dining on pork tonight, old man? For I dare say you let your mind wander and mistook that poor squire for a slaughtered pig, such was the lake of Christ's wine I saw drawn onto this hallowed floor!"

The bloodletter shook off Jean's hand and shifted his package of tools forward in defence, but he did not lose composure.

"Your words make no mince of my work," the bloodletter said calmly. "Remove yourself immediately or your snout will feel my wrath."

Jean barely suppressed an admiring smile. In truth, he had never accosted a bloodletter or any man of healing before. In his native village, all curative powers were entrusted to the wise-women, with their herbs and roots and noxious poultices, while in Avignon his circle of learned acquaintances included at best low-rent alchemists. He gave some ground.

"Forgive my impertinence, master bloodletter," Jean said with an ingratiating tone, "but concern for my friend the squire gave voice to my baser passions. I do beg your pardon." Jean proffered a small bow, but seeing that the bloodletter was making leaving motions, he hurried his speech. "I would be most grateful if you would tell me the full state of the squire so that I might be able to aid in his recovery. I would ask this of the brothers here, but if the truth be told, I doubt their practical ability in these matters. They might have libraries swamped with books and heads flooded with prayers, but I would rather let a miller's wife put a calloused hand on me, should an ailment strike me down, than give one of these novices free reign over my person."

The speech had its intended effect, as the bloodletter guffawed so loud that it echoed along the gallery. Dropping his shoulders and re-tucking the leather roll under his arm, he suggested to Jean that in exchange for a good word about him to his friends, for the monks paid poorly, he would give a free consultation.

"Agreed."

"Well then, it is my duty to declare quite plainly that your friend is not at all fit for fighting. Nor is he in a good state for traveling." The bloodletter then whispered, "I say this because he mentioned a *chevauchée*. Now, that does not concern me, nor do I want it to. For me, I see enough natural corruption of the body to dull any interest in the hacking of men. I will heal bishops and kings, but I refuse to counsel them on anything save diet and convalescence. As to our brave squire here, I say again that his condition is most dire indeed, although his humors are now stable thanks to my ministrations."

Jean wanted to say something to the effect that having seen the amount of blood ministered out of the patient, Roger must be left with only one humor, but he bit his tongue. Now that he had ingratiated himself with the bloodletter, it would be a supreme act of folly to permit his unruly wit to dam up this trickle of knowledge. "This, I am relieved to hear," said Jean. "However, I must broach the question of when we might expect to see the young squire back on his feet."

The bloodletter looked away, as though to review his thoughts, and scratched his cheek. "Yes, well, stable does not mean healed, of course. The squire's blood was strong with choler as a result of his fighting and, most assuredly, thoughts of this *chevauchée*, of which I know nothing, as you now know. As a squire, the boy's choler should be strong anyway, and this hot, dry weather does not ease my labors. That is why I had to puncture several veins in order to return his system to its natural state. He leaked much blood from those wounds, which was doubly unfortunate because they were made near veins where melancholy is concentrated. More encouragingly, I can see that his sanguine humor is a steadier than his phlegmatic humor, so he should remain in good spirits, which should hasten the mending. In all, I give the lad two weeks to recover. Of course, the healing process is in its early stages and I have yet to consult the stars. I should expect to make another visit in a few days or so to bleed him again."

These were not the words Jean wanted to hear and he would not let the tall squire hear them either, having already seen how unruly his humors were. However, the news must be reported to the Gamesmaster at once, since the end of Swynford would mean the end of surety for the debt. So, with the appropriate courtesy Jean thanked the bloodletter for his consultation and let him go on his way. Then, after bidding a curt farewell to the squires, the false chandler made a swift exit.

His brother was late. Corrado Prospero had called the meeting of the war council for noon, which was a generous time already, and now Andrea Tomacelli stood next to his captain-general embarrassed.

"Let us start without him," Andrea said. Had the other captains been present, he would not have undermined Gianello's position in so flagrant a fashion, but Prospero had been with his brother long enough to know his shortcomings. And besides, the fewer people involved in the planning the better.

"Very well," Prospero said. "His lordship's absence allows me the opportunity to bring up a sensitive subject. How will the Patrimony be governed once this is all over? It will affect our campaign, because if it is believed that all fealty will revert to your younger brother, then I fear fewer cities will open their gates to us. That is sad, but true."

Andrea frowned. The German was being impertinent, but if it was a matter of strategy, then he should make the post-war order known to his captain-general. "The lords and cities will be obliged to follow the Egidian Constitutions again. My brother will have his place, but I will be vicar-general and enforce compliance."

"So you are to be the new Gil de Albornoz." It was a powerful name and any condottiere worth his salt knew it. The Spanish cardinal had been vicar-general of the Patrimony of St. Peter in the 1350s and had done what no one had been able to do since the emperors enforced their will in Italy: unite the Patrimony and impose a settlement favorable to his holiness the supreme pontiff. The cardinal had seized the prefecture of Rome, waged war against the rebellious lords and cities of central Italy, and written the Egidian Constitutions that defined the administration of papal territory. Clement and the schism had caused the ruin of the cardinal's victory.

"You flatter me, Corrado. It is the will of his holiness. Are you not in agreement?"

"It is not for me to pass judgment. Lords must be offered precise terms of settlement."

"Submission. His holiness has extended a generous hand, and the lords of the Patrimony would do well to bow their heads to it."

"Yes, submission, as you say. As I was saying, lords must be offered precise terms. Negotiation of as few articles as possible is preferable. We do not have the forces for many long sieges, and Malatesta Malatesta will not remain idle for long, what with all that Clementine money behind him."

Andrea nodded, but he was busy recalling his assessment of the great cardinal. How had Albornoz done it? As a Spaniard in the service of a French pontiff adrift in the turbulent sea of Italian politics, he had succeeded in systematically reducing the opposition to his holiness and in building a structure that might have endured. Andrea had studied the campaigns of Albornoz and the emperors and concluded that a clever strategy and a powerful host would lead to victory over a cabal of enemies, but they were insufficient to create a lasting solution. So, where was the key to the riddle of once and for all pacifying the Patrimony? Andrea found it lying with the Visconti family of Milan. Despite their having more enemies than anyone in Italy, the lands of the Visconti were still intact and under control, and the reason for that, Andrea believed, was that in addition to maintaining a powerful host and controlling the inns of court, the Visconti were ever present on their *dominium*. The Patrimony had remained under papal control as long as Albornoz had been alive, as long as he had remained in the saddle, while the emperors could only ever be a fleeting presence in Italy. The right of conquest meant nothing if the land could not be held. Therefore, Andrea concluded, he had to concentrate command, and to do that he needed to have control of all the condottieri who had been hired to defend the interests of the Church. If unifying command meant usurping control from his younger brother or imposing his will on the war council, then so be it. The throne of St. Peter was at stake.

The city walls sliced away the last glimmer of orange sun. Shadows slipped into oblivion, torches crackled to life and church bells everywhere peeled evensong. At any other time Geoffrey would have hurried to the chapel to make his devotions, then run to throw dice at the Blue Boar, but on this night he was sitting on the edge of his cot and twisting his *couteau* to reflect the candlelight against the walls that surrounded him. He was troubled. He had wanted to organize a sumptuous meal at the hospital to raise Roger's spirits and honor Jean the chandler, but his purse was empty and the words that his friend had spoken only an hour earlier were weighing heavily on him. He was still ambivalent about going to Florence. When was the ship to depart? Tomorrow some time. The signs were bad, once again, with Roger's dream the worst of the lot.

Roger had struggled to relate the details of his vision before falling unconscious. Even so, the message was so clear that the words long remained with Geoffrey, constantly striking at his heart. The dream was led by king of blessed memory Richard Lionheart, with all points armed, resplendent in gold and radiating majesty from the golden lion blazoned on his chest. He was at the altar of a magnificent rose chapel, perhaps in France, perhaps in England, perhaps even in Jerusalem, and his face was full of wrath. Geoffrey stood a few steps below him, head bowed and uncovered, his sword lying on the altar. The event had all the trappings of a knighting ceremony, but it could not be that, since Geoffrey was in full battle harness and no spurs were visible. The witnesses to this encounter were many and seemingly ill disposed towards the squire. Geoffrey's torment was compounded by his inability to speak, and each time he would open his mouth, part of his armor would rust until finally the entire harness dissolved into a pool of orange dust, leaving him clad in a penitent's tunic. Then his grace raised his sword and the rose window shattered, allowing a crusader host to float in, each surcoat blazoned with massive crimson crosses. King Richard reached out to Geoffrey and anointed his forehead with the sign of the cross. After Geoffrey bowed, his grace led the crusaders out of the chapel, leaving Geoffrey alone. The scene faded away but for the *couteau*, brilliant and untouched, on the altar. It was when Geoffrey tried to grasp it that Roger awoke.

No amount of prayer could help Geoffrey work out the meaning of this sign, leaving his mind afire with conflicting ideas. Was King Richard truly his grace or was it the Lord, the Savior, the Holy Ghost, or the trinity incarnate as the greatest English king? Should he take up the sword against the infidel? Should he get tonsured and serve the Lord otherwise? He was being given a quest, Geoffrey was certain, but what was it and where would he find the way to it? Did the desiccation of his armor mean that he was too poor, too sinful, too common, or too muddled to be allowed on crusade, or wherever the good king was headed? A sign had been proffered and no more would be forthcoming until he had chosen.

One of the Duke of Lancaster's priests, whom he had immediately consulted, suggested that he ignore the dream, as it might be the fiend tempting him into sin, but that rote assumption did nothing to soothe Geoffrey's soul. In any dream, as everybody knew, the Devil always reveals himself and Roger had not mentioned the presence of the Fallen One in his. Another way to resolve this dilemma could be to visit a wise-woman, but while many such creatures plied their trade in and around Avignon, they were usually expensive, as they had taken to bedecking themselves in silk robes and gold jewelry and calling themselves 'seers' or 'astrologers' as means of pretending to elevated station. Of course, paler versions could be found in the Outer City, but another visit to that hellish pit was unappealing and unlikely. Regardless, he was utterly poor. Even the penny-a-word advice-givers were beyond his means, as he had emptied his shallow purse in the chandlers' chapel to buy a prayer for his stricken friend. Shaking his head in disgust, Geoffrey reconfirmed his belief that the decision had to be his and his alone: should he obey the will of his master and patron and make for Italy, and thereby regain favor at court, or should he risk the wrath of his lordship and find service elsewhere, perhaps fighting on another *chevauchée*?

Ah…the *chevauchée*. If he were not to be permitted to join his fellow squires on campaign, then Geoffrey would be left with no alternative *but* to wander Christendom as nothing more than a sword for hire, since idling in halls was not an option. He laughed bitterly at the realization the he might end up a *routier* after all. The Royal Commission to retrieve the remains of the knight and captain Sir John Hawkwood, however, was definitely on. Then there was the Gamesmaster and that pathetic debt. If he were to follow through on his threat to seize his sword and harness in lieu of payment, the humiliation would be great, and considering his most recent disgrace no amount of patronage could protect him from collection if the Gamesmaster so desired.

Geoffrey shook his head and slammed his fist against the wall in frustration, causing the *couteau* to slip from his grasp and fall to the floor with a loud clang. Geoffrey sighed. He checked his hand for cuts; all was whole. His sword possessed one of the finest edges of any he had seen, and others even had remarked on its perfection, yet never once had it caused him injury. The marvelous weapon had been with him since infancy, and in his heart he considered it his only true possession. Geoffrey recalled that the arms master classified his *couteau* as a broad sword, likely of northern forging. However, he said that the blade was unusually thick, as though someone had taken a two-handed long sword and planed it down for one-handed use. This made Geoffrey's *couteau* heavier than most, but it was so well balanced that anyone with the requisite strength could wield it like a dagger. Neither blade nor hilt bore a stamp that might identify the original smith. There was nothing particularly notable about either the grip or the quillons, and the fuller, straight and true, was without decoration or inscription. The only exceptional part of Geoffrey's *couteau* was found in the heart of the pommel: a mottled crimson orb encased in a thick iron shell.

Geoffrey gripped the leather-wound tang and, making sure that the sharp *derrito* side of the blade did not drag along the stone floor, raised it reverentially until the pommel was poised before his eyes and the full image of the Cross was crisply outlined against the wall. He stared into the orb; its color was so dense that it seemed to absorb all light around it. By now Geoffrey knew every detail of this mysterious pommel, down to the pits and scratches in the iron. The young squire smiled. The odd deflections of light reminded him of the ridiculous childhood fantasies he had once held about his one and only piece of property. For years he had thought that the orb was a massive ruby, the great wealth of his lost family, which he believed had perished during the Black Death, or perhaps been ruined by an evil lord, or some such tragedy, leaving him alone in the world. Then, when he was older and a page in the court of Gaunt, Geoffrey had once secreted the *couteau* out of the armory in order to show off his treasure to his fellow pages, whereupon one of the senior boys told him that the fantastic orb could not be a ruby, pointing out that its mottling could not make it so. Rather, its hue more resembled blood. Instead of causing him to despair, however, this revelation led Geoffrey to a new belief (although it did not prevent him from beating the boy senseless for his presumption). The orb in the pommel might not be a jewel in the literal sense, but it was something far more valuable - a reliquary containing the blood of a saint. The humility instilled in him by the monks prevented Geoffrey from thinking that it could be the blood of Christ, but he knew in his heart that the blood must have coursed through the veins of someone of great sanctity and virtue. After considerable research, Geoffrey drew up a list of candidate saints. He prayed, consulted local scholars and even examined several blood-related relics to compare, but it was only when his lordship let slip a fateful name during one of their interviews that the epiphany struck and Geoffrey divined the name of his patron saint. In 1375, during one of the darkest hours of England in France, the royal army under the Duke of Lancaster was about to be driven out of Calais when the cries of the infant Geoffrey alerted them to the impending French attack. His lordship was able to regroup and preserve what was left of English France – on St. John's day. That was when Geoffrey started to believe that deep inside the pommel of his *couteau* was preserved a few drops of the blood of John the Baptist.

 The ringing of a hand bell pulled Geoffrey back from his thoughts. A page was walking down the corridor, calling for lauds. Could it be so? Could he have been contemplating the dream, the *couteau*, his Fate for so many hours? With great care Geoffrey wrapped his *couteau* in its oiled cloth and placed it in his chest. He had decided. Duty to his lordship came before all. He would join the commission.

"What say you, good squire?" Jean greeted with forced conviviality. "I knew you would come. Avignon has become old for both of us." He stared up at the sun. It was almost noon.

 "So, you've come to see me off, have you?" Geoffrey said with gratitude. "I am glad."

"In truth, I am crossing the sea with you. Remember how I told you that my business might require me to leave Avignon? Well, the signs are right for travel, if my fellow guild members do not deceive me. I am told there is a place for me with this commission of yours, and it makes better sense to journey with friends than with none." Jean was wearing a yellow jupon and a dark brown cloak.

Geoffrey's voice distracted some important-looking men in rich robes and feathered hats, who were sorting a collection of vellum scrolls further along the dock. After some scrutiny, one of them broke from the group, roughly pushed passed the false chandler and, without introducing himself, addressed Geoffrey.

"Your name wouldn't be Hotshit by chance, would it?" He was a large, imposing figure of a knight, with a long moustache and round belly that stretched his green surcoat.

"My name is Geoffrey Hotspur, sir, the Duke of Lancaster's man."

"It matters not what you are called," said the knight with casual disregard. "If his lordship wants you on this commission, then you are. It matters little to me. Wait, I know you." He scratched his cheek as he took full measure of Geoffrey's height. "Yes, you're that squire who makes wild wagers. You were in the Blue Boar the other night."

"Indeed, I was, your lordship."

The green knight coughed out a laugh. "I'm surprised the Gamesmaster let you leave in one piece, or are you missing something there beneath your doublet? Well, no matter. Tell me, boy, who is your father?"

"I do not have a father, sir," Geoffrey said plainly.

"Well then, who *was* your father? Would I have heard of him?"

The interrogation made Geoffrey uncomfortable, but he would neither lie nor stretch the truth. "I do not know who my father was, sir, or my mother. I am an orphan, sir."

The knight made a disapproving noise through his moustache. "A charity case," he mumbled. "I might have known. Well, get yourself together, orphan squire, and stow your gear. The tide goes out anon." He returned to the party of English dignitaries.

Geoffrey was annoyed that the green knight had not introduced him to the commission, but he calmed himself with the belief that time must be pressing and proper introductions would be made on board.

"You should stay close to him," Jean whispered. "Make yourself known to as many lords close to court as possible. A lengthy journey on a cramped vessel should allow it."

Before Geoffrey could answer, he felt a tug on his doublet. He turned and saw the loaders gesturing at a couple of moored ships.

"Oh, I see. Well, the barque flying the English royal standard must belong to our commission, so find a place for my things on board," Geoffrey ordered.

The loaders were about to go when something stopped them in their tracks.

"No, no, no!" the green knight yelled. "Not that one, you fools! Throw his gear on the supply ship, over there."

Geoffrey followed the loaders to a small round-hulled vessel with three thin poles poking out of its deck. He was aghast.

"That isn't some kind of Saracen horror, is it? I've never seen a boat like that before," Geoffrey cried. He was astounded by the ship's fragile appearance and sharply curved hull. "They're not allowed in port! God's bones, not even the bloody Venetians can sail up the Rhone without leave!"

"You like wagering," the green knight yelled, "so climb aboard, squire! I know I'm not game for it!"

Geoffrey turned around, but the knight was already gone.

Jean, fearing yet another threat to the squire's departure, put his hand on Geoffrey's shoulder. "Not to worry. I've been on these things before. Safe as anything, I tell you." Jean had never been on such a strange vessel, but there was no turning back now. "Come; let us talk to the crew."

Jean approached a group of sailors working with the loaders. After exchanging a few words, he returned to Geoffrey, who had not moved.

"The crew is Portuguese, not Moorish." Jean smiled. "They're taking your commission's supplies and assorted goods to Pisa. They don't speak French and I don't speak Portuguese, but they do well in Catalan. I can get by in Catalan. We chandlers do a great business in Catalonia, you know. And to answer your other question, this horror, as you put it, is a *caravel*, a Christian Portuguese device they use for fishing and trading. It's one of the fastest and sturdiest vessels plying the Mediterranean."

Geoffrey stared up at the curious craft that was to ferry him far across the sea. It was certainly larger than the many flat-bottomed kogges that pass through Avignon during the trading seasons, but certainly smaller than the wide galleys that formed the backbone of the navies of great kingdoms. His overall impression was that the caravel could not possibly handle anything but the calmest waters.

"How can we be sure this thing won't capsize?" Geoffrey asked. "I see no oars and with all those sails dangling the winds will most certainly blow us into the next world, if they don't throw us upon some rocks first."

"Both possibilities are highly unlikely," said Jean. "The Portuguese are the best sailors. They know how to play the wind and turn it to their advantage. After all, they managed to reach Avignon all right, didn't they? They were hardly conjured. And besides, we won't be seeing much shore to risk being smashed by it."

Geoffrey looked at Jean in alarm and astonishment. "That is outrageous! Now tell me in all truth that these sailors have common sense and we will travel as a group, as is proper custom."

"Look who knows so much about sailing! There is no need. The caravel is faster, so we will be arriving at Pisa about a day ahead of the others. If I, a lowly chandler, have confidence in these men, then I should imagine a brave squire in the service of a great English lord should have as well."

"This is madness!" Geoffrey exclaimed. "We'll get lost, or swallowed up by a sea monster!"

Jean was becoming exasperated. He would be damned if the squire's fear of sailing vessels prevented him from leaving Avignon and the Gamesmaster behind. "Trust me, or rather trust them. Why do you think they hang so many sails? Different winds require different sails, if they are to be of any use, or so I am told. Come now. I see that the commission has already boarded and the moorings are cast. We must be away!"

Jean took Geoffrey's arm and led him up the gangway. Once aboard, Geoffrey stamped the deck timbers a few times to ensure that the vessel was worthily built and then, to distract himself from his fears, he went to the central deck to see that his gear had been properly stowed. Meanwhile, Jean went to the starboard railing to have one last look at the great city.

Just as the last barrels of pitch were being laded onto the caravel, a page came running hard along the dock. He caught Jean's eye and he watched the boy reach the foot of the gangway, where Jean heard him ask if a squire named Geoffrey Hotspur or a chandler called Jean Lagoustine was on one of the departing vessels. Jean moved to the head of the gangway and demanded that the page declare his interest in the men he had just named.

The page was breathing hard and had difficulty speaking. "I belong to the Hospital of St. John," he heaved. "The monks sent me on account of a squire named Roger Swynford."

"Well, what of him?"

"Are you either one of the men whom I seek?"

"Why, of course. I can't be both, can I?"

"What, sir?"

"I am Jean Lagoustine."

"Oh, I see. Well then, sir, the squire is dead."

CHAPTER 4

T HE smaller the distant shore appeared, the more nervous Geoffrey felt about sea travel. While the Portuguese sailors were showing a great deal of skill furling, unfurling and shifting the numerous sails, the thought of losing sight of land reinforced his sense of isolation, for it was after they had cast off when Jean informed him that he was the only member of the Hawkwood commission on board. The chandler had learned that the captain was approached at the last minute to take the poor squire, since the royal barque was full. That was yesterday, and since then Geoffrey had been distracting himself by sorting, cleaning and polishing his gear, interspersed with the occasional talk with Jean Lagoustine. As he stood at the gunwale, he now thought about Roger, the duke, the Blue Boar, his fellow squires, and how well the preparations for the *chevaucheé* were going. He was the odd man out again, as when the duke had removed him from the monastery at the age of eight or nine, or when the other pages would talk about their families and he would have nothing to contribute, or those times with his fellow squires, when they would visit a clothier and he would have to watch as they spent silver to their hearts' content. Geoffrey looked down at his blue-grey doublet and fingered one of its worn edges and sighed.

"You'll worry a hole in that thing if you don't stop," Jean said.

Geoffrey looked around and saw the chandler approaching with a pair of flagons. He took one and raised it to salute the chandler. For someone in the trades, this Jean Lagoustine was quite an affable fellow, he thought. He was already on good terms with the captain of this diabolical caravel, he could talk to the crew and he had succeeded in learning where the best wine was stowed. Perhaps when he was knighted, he would ask the chandler to be one of his sergeants.

"If I could put my hands to better use, it wouldn't be a problem. Perhaps a tournament will be held in Florence when we arrive. I brought my full harness, such as it is. Didn't you say you were in Italy once, master chandler?"

"I must admit that what little I know of that fair land comes from my fellow guildsmen," Jean said, carefully spinning a credible yarn. "They tell me that Pisa is a wealthy town with warehouses full of oriental spices, and that its women dazzle in fine raiment such as compliments their unrivalled beauty. If we are fortunate, we might be able to spend some pleasant nights there before moving on to Florence."

"We? Your business is in Florence?"

"There, as well as in other cities," Jean quickly said. "Now, come away from there, or you'll get seasick. I've been up and down the Rhone more times than I care to count, so I'm used to this pitching, but I see you are still nervous. Listen, we'll be on open water only for a day or so before we near Corsica, if that makes you feel better. Until we do, why don't you regale me with stories about the court of the great Duke of Lancaster? You must have a thousand of them."

"Well, Roger is a much better troubadour than me, but I suppose you must be interested in what goes on in the great hall. Damn! I should have sent him a message when we docked in Arles." Geoffrey stamped the deck.

"Well, you could have, but how would you receive a response? By cloud?" Jean took the squire by the arm and pulled him forward. "He has the prayers of both of us, so he should be all right."

Geoffrey nodded and Jean led him to the stable middle of the deck, where their gear was stowed.

"That's the lot then, is it?" he said, pointing at Geoffrey's poor harness.

"I assume *you* have nothing other than your wit to protect you," Geoffrey accused and took a long draught. He found the wine sweet, but on the whole to his liking. It did not have the astringency of the French varieties, but it had the body.

"Well, what would I know about such things? I'm just a chandler. Even when I served in the town militia, we would only wear leather jacks or gambesons. None could afford a noble hauberk, even if it were allowed."

"The Avignon militia must be better equipped than *that*," Geoffrey argued. "The garrison looks almost as dignified as knights."

"I was referring to my village. The lord forbids his villeins from carrying arms or wearing iron. Of course, that was many years ago."

"That must mean your lord protects your village with sufficient vigor. You should have been content and proud." Geoffrey took another swig of wine.

"I just hope you feel as safe in your rather original harness there."

Geoffrey placed his hands on his hips and looked down at the chandler. "Do you want to hear about the duke or not? I could just as well reassemble my harness."

Jean pulled together some crates to create a bench and table. As the squire spoke on one of his favorite topics, the ladies at the court of the Duke of Lancaster, Jean considered the power he now had over the squire, not only in communicating with the crew, but also by his knowledge about the death of Roger Swynford, not to mention Geoffrey's finances, his position in court, and his martial skills. The question Jean put to himself, then, was how he could turn that power to his advantage. The Florentines might make him a gift of some florins and maybe the commission had some money for him, but he should not expect that. The other squire was dead and Gaunt had banished this Geoffrey Hotspur from court, so those sources of silver were dried up. He should expect the royal commission to remain in Florence for about a week, so he might find opportunity there. The Gamesmaster had given him the names of some of his partners in Italy, whom Jean could contact if he had any silver to send to Avignon: a cloth merchant in Pisa, a couple of minor bankers in Florence, some low-ranking papal functionaries in Rome, Viterbo and Amalfi, and other discreet, reliable men scattered in Umbria, Genoa and Bologna. This gave Jean an idea; the squire liked wagering and Florence had no shortage of gaming halls. He even might be able to reap some reward for himself, enough to build up the courage he needed to leave the Gamesmaster.

"… and you know, I think it was the green knight who fell flat on his face in front of the bishop," Geoffrey was saying. He had changed the subject. "He never introduced himself, then, in the Blue Boar or at quayside. Wait." Geoffrey raised his head and sniffed. "Is that onions? What time is it?"

Jean had only been half listening, but the scent of cooking renewed his attention. He looked at the sun. "Must be noon. Great stories, master squire!"

Geoffrey stood up. "I had better stretch my legs. Go and see what's on the brazier for us."

Jean grimaced and was about to go when he felt a hand on his sleeve.

"I see a vessel on the horizon," Geoffrey announced. "Might that not be his grace's barque? And look! There is another ship trailing close behind."

Jean squinted into the distance. "You know the other ships are following a different route. Come; let's eat."

But Geoffrey was already running to the forecastle. Jean followed. From the new vantage they recognized tiny fishing boats, identified a few lumbering kogges and even spotted the occasional broad-beamed bireme, its twin banks of oars propelling the craft swiftly over the waves. No royal standard sailed into view.

Geoffrey was crestfallen, but then he saw one of the biremes veering

OF FAITH AND FIDELITY

towards them. "By all that is holy, what is that vessel doing, Jean? Maybe *that's* the barque and it has recognized us. It's still far, though."

Jean squinted into the eastern horizon and confirmed that the bireme was aggressively maneuvering. "It could be corsairs," he speculated. "I'll tell the captain."

"Corsairs? We'd better put on arms then."

"Don't excite yourself. This vessel can outrun just about any other. Stay here and keep watch." Jean was about to go when he stopped short and turned around. "If you please, master squire."

Left alone, Geoffrey could not keep his eyes off the approaching vessel. He searched the masts for a red banner blazoned with the gold lions of the king, but he saw nothing, not even a simple pennon. He was about to step off the forecastle when Jean intercepted him.

"The captain says that it cannot be corsairs," Jean said. "Look closely at the deck. The crew has formed a wall of shields, or more precisely, a wall of well-marked shields. Corsairs have neither the discipline to form close ranks nor charges to mark their shields. She is a war vessel, but the captain assures me that they are not uncommon in these waters."

After another sweep of oars, the strange bireme discharged a series of thin black streaks from behind its palisade of shields. Within moments, the dark swarm was overhead, bringing with it a breath of wind and a piercing wail.

"Quarrels!" someone shouted. The word was unmistakable in any language. It was quickly followed by a trumpet blast to signal the caravel's neutrality.

Jean dropped to the floor of the forecastle and pulled Geoffrey down beside him. They waited in silence for the bolts to strike. When no blows arrived, they raised their heads and peered over the railing. Nothing. Even the crew looked astonished.

"They missed," Jean said. "Let's hope that gives us time to fly out of range."

"Oh, I don't think they missed," Geoffrey said. He was standing now.

"What do you mean?"

"We weren't the target. Look over there!"

Jean stood up and turned to see where the squire was pointing. Another vessel was coming at them out of the west, and on it they could see clusters of armed men crowding the gunwales and shouting.

"*Those* are corsairs!" Jean cried.

"God's hellions! We're caught in the middle!" Geoffrey declared. The memory of his and Roger's dusting off of the ruffians in the Outer City rushed back to him and his hand instinctively reached for where his *couteau* should be. "We must prepare to defend ourselves. Is this vessel armed?"

The captain barked an order and they looked down to see the sailors scrambling across the deck. He then turned towards the forecastle and waved for Geoffrey and Jean to climb down. After exchanging a few excited words with Jean, the captain rushed to the other end of his ship.

"Well?" Geoffrey asked.

"The captain says that he still cannot identify the first vessel," Jean answered in a quiet voice, "but it appears to be the lesser evil of the two." He stared at the bireme that launched the volley of quarrels.

"So? What are we to do?" He grabbed Jean's arm.

Jean turned to Geoffrey. "*We* are to join the ranks of crossbowmen and engage the corsair vessel."

"What do you mean crossbowmen? I don't fight alongside crossbowmen. I'm getting my *couteau*!"

"It shouldn't come to that. Our two-to-one advantage should be enough to scare those wretched corsairs away, so hold steady."

A bolt slammed into the forecastle next to them.

"Let's go down to the hold and collect those crossbows, shall we?" Jean suggested.

Jean and Geoffrey picked their way through the frantic sailors as they brought down sails and put up their own palisade with whatever was handy. When they reached the center deck they met a dozen men newly clad in thickly quilted hoquetons and brandishing an assortment of arms. One of the men turned to Geoffrey and shoved a crossbow and a dozen quarrels into his hands.

"You're recruited," Jean said, who quickly received one too.

"I said I was getting my sword. Good Lord, this is heavy," Geoffrey said as he weighed the device in his hand.

"What's the matter? You do know how to use one of those things, don't you?"

"Of course, but the crossbows I trained with were much smaller. They were French."

Jean examined his own crossbow. "I think these are Italian, or maybe Spanish. It's all they have. Very nice workmanship though …"

They were given no more time to debate the merits of crossbow design, for someone was already shoving them into ranks. As they stumbled across the deck with their new company, Geoffrey and Jean saw that most of the other sailors had sturdy polearms and falchions, but only rudimentary armor, while the remaining few were busy filling gaps in their defence with crates and barrels. Soon Geoffrey and Jean were back on the forecastle with a dozen others.

"We had better at least try to span these things," Jean said after watching the sailors work their weapons.

"We haven't a choice." After tucking the quarrels into his belt, Geoffrey pulled the flaccid drawstring along the tiller of the crossbow and hooked it onto the nut, but he soon found that he had considerable trouble winding it back with the rack. The span of the crossbow was greater than he was used to, which made the draw considerably long, but with some extra effort he managed to pull the string taut. However, the lock was complicated, and after several attempts at securing the nut the tension of the string put too much stress on Geoffrey's injured shoulder and his grip slackened. The drawstring sprang back, nearly taking his thumb with it.

"Ahh! Damn this contraption! Now I know why the Church banned these things. They're dangerous for the shooter as well as the target. How are you doing, Jean?"

"I'm close, but nothing yet. Maybe together we can span them." Not waiting for a reply, Jean dropped his crossbow and went to help Geoffrey. The Portuguese sailors, meanwhile, had shot a few random bolts at the oncoming corsair vessel.

"We need a better ratchet or some sort of pin," Geoffrey said as he wound back the drawstring. Together they got it securely hooked onto the nut and Jean had nearly slipped the trigger lever into place when the tension trapped in the crossbow began to waver. This time the stirrup loosed itself from Geoffrey's foot and the device went careening into the front wall of the forecastle.

"You're right. We need a better ratchet," Jean admitted. The crossbow was not damaged, but it did leave a deep gouge in the timber.

Geoffrey then tried to help Jean with his crossbow, but the end result was the same. As they stood and stared at the infernal devices, pondering another attempt at arming them, another volley of quarrels screamed overhead, though lower this time, from the war vessel. Geoffrey looked up. He saw that the crossbows had done some damage to the corsairs, judging by the limp bodies being thrown overboard, but they seemed no less determined for their losses and were now forming into small heavily armed groups. The sight reminded him of his *couteau*. He should have just muscled through and retrieved it in the first place instead of following that bloody chandler. He could almost feel the hot hilt of the powerful broad sword in his hand and he clenched his fist. In the hateful eyes of the corsairs Geoffrey saw the ruffians he had cut down in the Outer City, the ones who had wounded his friend and got him banished from court and on this horrid caravel.

"Let's get off this tower!" Geoffrey commanded as he kicked the uncooperative crossbow out of Jean's hands. "We're not doing any good up here. Help me with my harness so that I can join the others when the real fighting starts."

Jean was too slow to restrain the furious squire, so he followed him off the forecastle and through the mess of sailors finding places for the final clash. When they reached the center deck, however, they found Geoffrey's armor scattered in every direction.

"By Jesus' noble passion, I am lost!" Geoffrey cried, and he fell to his knees to collect whatever pieces he could.

"That's only about half your harness," Jean said as Geoffrey counted what he had.

"It'll have to do. Go find the rest."

Geoffrey went to his chest, which now formed a part of the middle section of a long palisade, and threw it open. He found his *couteau* near the bottom, and after throwing off its protective cloth, he set it aside to search for his pourpoint, helm and arming hose.

"Do you have another sword?" Jean asked. "I don't know how to wield a polearm and you saw me with the crossbow."

"Where is the rest of my harness? I told you to search for the lost bits."

"It's all gone." Jean slashed the air with his hand.

"What?" Geoffrey had nearly emptied the contents of his chest.

"I said 'it's all gone'. You must have another sword in there somewhere."

"What happened to that dagger you had the other night?" Geoffrey mumbled. He found his pourpoint at the very bottom.

"That won't do against this lot."

Time was running short. The taunts and threats of the corsairs were growing louder. The efforts of the war vessel were not deterring them, especially now that they were almost fully shielded by their target vessel – the caravel. For a moment, Jean thought about hiding in the hold, but he was certain that either the sailors would find him or a sea serpent would, when the ship was finally pierced and sunk. The squire had proved an excellent swordsman, and so he decided to try his luck with him.

Geoffrey flung his short training sword onto the deck and then scrambled to throw off his doublet and throw on his pourpoint.

"How much time do I have?" Geoffrey asked.

"Time for what?"

Geoffrey grunted as he tugged at a brass buckle. "Time for this!" He jabbed his uninjured thumb at his tangled coat-of-plates, which he had pulled out from beneath a crate of olive oil.

A desperate cry from the first mate drowned out Jean's response. Two sailors immediately dropped their arms and scrambled into the hold, only to quickly reappear with a large pot and a sack of powder. Geoffrey followed the curious spectacle with his eyes as he fumbled with the coat-of-plates' clasps and watched as the Portuguese arranged the pot over a fire near the stern then poured the entire contents of the sack into it. Geoffrey looked at Jean in surprise.

"He was yelling for soap," Jean explained. He picked up the training sword and crouched in the shadow of the palisade.

"Now's not the time to be washing, for the love of Saint Mary! Is our plan now to act peculiar in the hope that the corsairs will be too confused to kill us?" Geoffrey threw the difficult coat-of-plates to the deck and instead resumed fastening the twenty-four buttons of his pourpoint.

"It's a weapon. I heard about it from a Venetian trader who had fought the Turks. When the corsairs ram us – and they will – our sailors will wash their deck with the soap and make it too slippery for them to attack. It works well against fully armored knights. I say, let them try, if it gives another breath before dying."

Geoffrey grunted. After the pourpoint's last button was secured, he dropped to the deck to have another go at his stubborn coat-of-plates. He had sorted out the clasps and was adjusting some twisted links when he felt a hand pulling him to his feet.

"Get off! I don't need to see them throw the soap, Jean!"

Geoffrey shook his shoulder, but the hand remained fast. He was about to throw a punch when he looked up and saw a falchion-armed sailor. They exchanged a few mutually unintelligible words, but the sailor got his message across when he pointed out to sea. The bowsprit of the corsair vessel was pointed directly at the hull of the caravel. Within moments the ram would strike. A tremor of hatred went through Geoffrey as he finally saw the ugly faces of the sea raiders. Geoffrey looked around and saw that each sailor was preparing himself for the violence of brusque contact. His head began to swim and his hand trembled in anticipation. He looked down at his coat-of-plates and then back at the corsairs. He shook his head in anger. "Time, time, no time," he whispered

Geoffrey grabbed his *couteau* and staggered to the center mast. The stench of boiling soap filled his nostrils and he could hear the gurgling slurry. All thoughts of his harness melted away as he watched a group of sailors roll the soap pot over a series of rods towards the expected point of impact.

The other bireme, meanwhile, was moving away, now that the caravel had finally given the corsairs full cover.

"What on Earth?" Geoffrey said. "Leaving us to our fate, the bastards! Cowards!" Geoffrey stood up and shook his fist.

"Get down!" Jean shouted. "They wouldn't spend all those bolts for nothing. I think they're trying to get around us to make the corsairs the piggy in the middle."

"They won't make it," Geoffrey said without inflection.

The first mate yelled something and all who understood grabbed hold of a mast, a crate, or something solid. Geoffrey looked around and found a loop of thick rope. In the tense silence that suddenly fell upon the caravel's crew and passengers, everyone fixed his eye on the angry ram accelerating towards them. Geoffrey shivered just before it struck. A terrifying crack split the air. The deck trembled and Geoffrey was thrown onto a pile of rigging. The next sounds were sickening thuds and scraping of grappling hooks seeking purchase in dense timber.

Geoffrey raised himself in time to see the soap being poured onto the enemy vessel. The Portuguese were lucky. Some of the boiling sludge blinded the more dangerous looking corsairs and they dropped their weapons into the sea below. Others, however, were already pulling the grappling chains or bringing boarding planks and ladders up to the gunwales. Furious attempts to dislodge the steel hooks were met with a shower of arrows, forcing the sailors to seek cover or be cut down.

The corsairs charged in waves at three fast points and set upon the sailors in less time than it took to load a crossbow, easily forcing them back. Once they had cleared the palisade and were stumbling over other obstacles, the first mate yelled to counter-attack. The sailors needed no encouragement. This was their caravel and the ferocity of their cries was enough to convince Geoffrey and Jean that they would defend it to the last breath. The makeshift armies collided. Falchions swooped, driving deep into the heads and shoulders of the corsairs, while swords thrust to skewer bellies.

The sailors made a good showing for a while, but the steady stream of support arriving unchecked soon threatened to turn the tide against them. The remaining sailor-crossbowmen fore and aft realized that they were too few to affect the outcome of the battle, so they abandoned their platforms and joined the fray, picking weapons off the dead and dying on their way.

OF FAITH AND FIDELITY

Geoffrey felt most confident fighting around the center mast. He had tried to thrust himself into the heart of the melee, but he discovered that he could not wield his *couteau* with effect in the ranks of polearms, so instead he fell back a few paces to take on anyone who might come through. He quickly downed one surprised corsair, who had climbed over the backs of his own men in order to get behind the sailors, with a slash across the belly, and he nearly decapitated another, who had crawled through a gap in the palisade, with a spin move.

An older sea raider saw the talented warrior kill two and then three of his companions. He shouted an order to a fresh band of corsairs and aimed his dagger at Geoffrey. Immediately a trio of men with barbed spears pushed through a narrow gap near the forecastle and advanced on the squire.

"Geoffrey!" Jean yelled from behind the center mast. "On your left!"

Geoffrey faced this new threat and furrowed his brow. He could see the giant with the one good eye, his wounded friend and the chandler who had aided them.

"Have at you!" he cried and brought down his sword with all the force he could muster. In an instant two spears became four sticks. The third spear got stuck in the deck when Geoffrey dodged a long thrust and knock it down with his pommel. As the corsairs stumbled from the sudden loss of arms, Geoffrey took advantage and dispatched them in quick fashion.

The old sea raider then decided to take matters into his own hands. Ensuring his grip on a dagger and a long Saracen scimitar, he advanced on Geoffrey through the same gap as his companions. Geoffrey decided not to wait and went to the attack, but all his movements were skillfully parried. He staggered a little when the caravel rolled, exposing his injured shoulder long enough for the corsair to strike it obliquely with his scimitar.

"God's mercy!" Geoffrey cried out. "You'll pay for that, you dog!"

The blow did not open the wound, but the searing pain that resulted forced Geoffrey to step back and use the empty soap cauldron as a shield while he steadied himself. He glanced at the main battle and saw that the sailors had lost over half the deck. Then a whoop went up as the corsairs conquered the forecastle.

Geoffrey looked around for Jean and prayed that he was nowhere near. He would not suffer the shame of being in debt twice to that chandler, not when the odds were even. Geoffrey tried to flex his left shoulder, but the pain was too great. The corsair was approaching with great care now, but he would soon be upon him. Geoffrey tried to remember all the moves Gaunt's swordmaster had taught him and for which situations, but all the stances required balance, and with his useless left arm and the pitching of the deck, he was not confident he could parry even a single blow now. Balance was the key. Balance. Like his *couteau* was balanced. Geoffrey weighed his sword in his hand. He would only have one chance. Without a word he kicked over the cauldron and brought back his arm as far as he could.

The corsair flinched when he realized what the squire was doing, but the residue of soap trickling out of the cauldron slowed his movements. Geoffrey flung his arm forward and launched his sword like a spear at the heart of his opponent. The *derrito* edge of the blade struck the corsair across the neck and stuck into a mast as he tried to spin away. Clutching his spurting wound, the old sea raider staggered sideways and went over into the sea.

"Nice work," Jean said. "Now we just need to take care of the rest of them."

"Who have you taken care of today?" Geoffrey yanked out his sword and looked around for another opponent. The deck was awash with blood, bodies and all manner of broken wares. He saw his leg harness, bent and twisted, beneath the stairs that led to the aftcastle, but he could discern no ranks of either sailors or corsairs – just small groups of tired men trying to overthrow one another.

One group suddenly went down like ninepins. The mysterious war vessel had completed enough of its maneuver to give range to its crossbowmen. However, the second flight of quarrels struck corsair and sailor in equal measure. Then the shooting became indiscriminate, as though the crossbowmen decided it was better just to destroy the crews of both ships in order to ensure total victory.

"Christ!" Jean yelled. "We're done for now! I said they were corsairs. Can you swim?" He looked at the cauldron and wondered if it could float.

"Of course I can't swim! I'm not a fish!"

A series of flashes from across the water distracted them. Like that original volley of quarrels, they rose high in the sky, but unlike them, they rained down on the caravel.

"They want to burn us!" Jean cried as he watched flaming bolts set fire to some crates.

"So much for neutrality!" Geoffrey huffed. "We must rally the men to make a final stand before we go under. The corsairs are done for, but if those 'bowmen are too cowardly to board us, then maybe …"

"Oh, maybe what? Show them your badge of the Duke of Lancaster and pray they do homage? Besides, I doubt there is anyone left to rally. Surrender is the best option now."

"What! Surrender to whom? I will not submit to a band of Saracens or whatever ungodly souls inhabit that vessel. It is better to die, sword in hand." Geoffrey reaffirmed the grip on his *couteau*, but for all his brave words about a rally, he was at a loss on how to do it.

The caravel lurched as the newest attackers rammed the join between the locked vessels, throwing the cauldron overboard. Another volley of fiery quarrels set the corsair bireme fully alight and she began to list. Someone grabbed the tiller of the caravel in the desperate hope of steering her away, but he was immediately felled by a dozen bolts. The crossbowmen tightened ranks and took careful aim at the deck of the caravel. Sailor and corsair alike raised their hands or dived into the water.

Jean saw a crossbow pointed at him and heard a call to surrender. He punched the sword out of the squire's hand and yelled. "We submit!"

CHAPTER 5

Florence

As much as Chancellor Salutati enjoyed deploying the grand gesture to demonstrate his power and magnanimity, he preferred its clever cousin the discreet interview for his own amusement, not to mention protection, particularly when it concerned affairs of state. He had arranged for Sergeant Godwin to meet him in the cellar of a copper-beater, whose shop was connected by a tunnel to the Balia, the chancellor's place of work. Salutati met his spies in clandestine places all over the city, but he had selected this one for his audience with the Englishman because it sat next to a Medici bank, where the old sergeant kept some of his money.

Heavy stamping on the cellar stairs announced Sergeant Godwin's arrival.

"Did you bring an elephant with you, Hannibal, or are you trying to wake the whole city? Not all of us are deaf, you know," Salutati said.

"This damp will be the end of me," Godwin muttered. "Could we not meet in a garden? Put on a light, for all that is holy! You'll get nothing out of me if I fall and break my neck." He tripped on a chamber pot and stumbled the final steps into the cellar.

Salutati removed the shield from his lamp. "Your face is red. Did you run here all the way from Arezzo?"

Godwin straightened his surcoat and rubbed his eyes. "I ran all the way from Narni." Godwin looked around. "Can't even be bothered to offer your best man a thimble of wine, I see. Well, so be it. So, if Arezzo is on your mind, then I will start with that. You will be pleased to hear that the commune of Arezzo remains a friend and ally of Florence, although only because they fear the return of the Tarlati. Giovanni Tarlati has a large company under him and he controls the cities of Cortona and Chuisi. Oh, and Clement's captain-general, Malatesta Malatesta, recently gave him command of his company of Bretons." Godwin spat at the overturned chamber pot. "I had a bloody difficult time getting through those heathens, let me tell you. They are prowling between Viterbo and Orte doing their worst. My guess is that Malatesta is covering his siege of Narni from the west. Everything east of the city is controlled by the Tomacelli."

"That is all very useful, sergeant, but should I assume that you genuinely met *Signore* Tarlati? You made him the offer? Did he remember you?"

"Such questions and they all have the same answer. Of course. I never failed Hawkwood and I didn't fail you. Yes, Tarlati took the money. I expect he will parley with Andrea Tomacelli any day now."

The chancellor nodded, but inside he was resentful. The Tarlati was and had always been an enemy of Florence because of Arezzo, since the chancellor considered that city essential to the eastern defence of the Republic, and so to give him any part of the wealth of the Republic was distasteful. But, the Tomacelli needed Florence's support, if not with men, then with money. The Visconti, the French and half of the Patrimony were pressing on the throne of St. Peter. Had the Duke of Spoleto not made such a mess earlier in the year, then he could have ignored Tarlati and let him meet his fate in the field against the Tomacelli.

"What was his mood?"

"Who? Tarlati? The same as always – dour, angry, thumbs his nose at just about everybody. He likes me though. I ate well while I was in his camp. He rambled on about taking the western Patrimony by himself."

"Cut from the same cloth, I suspect," Salutati said in Latin so the sergeant would not understand. "But what about his company? I don't want to see it marching on Arezzo anytime soon."

"It is a good company, well provisioned, though they complain of late payment, like everyone else. Oh, and I don't suppose *my* silver has been freed from that probate thing, has it?" Godwin was skeptical that the lawyers would have completed their poking around the Hawkwood estate in a week, but he had to ask.

"Sadly, that probate thing has yet to be settled. Even I cannot rush such matters. However, should you be short of silver, I might be generous enough to give you an interest-free loan until all is done."

"And how long will this settling take?"

"Several more weeks, at the most. Of course, I could encourage them to accelerate the process, but I have been informed that your late master's affairs were quite complicated. I already have my hands full fending off his widow and her anxious claims. It seems as though she too wants to leave Florence at the earliest possible convenience."

Godwin emitted a deep sigh that was noisier than the clanking of the chamber pot. "I'm not surprised. Well, maybe I'll try my chances in Lombardy and trust you to send me my share to England. I know a few notaries who can help me with that."

"Very well. You are welcome to stay, of course. I should expect that the Republic will need to parley with Tarlati again, so if you would like to remain in my service, I would not be opposed."

"No more service for me, chancellor."

"Well then, at least stay and visit with your compatriots. Your King Richard has sent some knights to collect your late master. They should arrive soon. You could regale them with tales of great adventure from days long past. They might even take you with them back to England."

"By sea? Never! I will tell them a few stories, though."

The sunlight nearly blinded the prisoners as they were dragged out of the hold and herded off the mysterious war vessel. They had been bound by their captors, who remained anonymous, and given no instructions other than to keep their mouths shut and to follow a deeply tanned, heavy set man into a pen set up on the dock.

"Any of you recognize the port?" Jean whispered. He and Geoffrey were with half a dozen Portuguese sailors. "Is it Pisa?" The Gamesmaster had a partner in Pisa, and if he could somehow get a message to him, then all should be well.

The sailors looked around and shook their heads, but then one of them whispered 'Corneto', but he dared not say more.

Jean was not sure where Corneto was, but considering that they had been locked away in the ship's bowels for about a day and a half, he reckoned that it was in either Italy or Sardinia, maybe France, but he was sure he knew all the names of the southern French ports, and Corneto was not among them.

"Have you heard of the place, Geoff?" Jean looked at the squire. He stood even taller in this group than amongst his fellow squires in Avignon. His hair and pourpoint were sooty and his left shoulder sloped a little as a result of the wound. "Geoff! Can you hear me?" He looked closer and became worried by what he saw. Geoffrey's blue eyes were covered in a glassy sheen and he was staring into the distance. He must be in a stupor, Jean thought. The squire had said very little in the hold. The boy takes things too much to heart, Jean determined, recalling their meeting in the chapel in the Hospital of St. John.

Jean moved to jolt his companion, but the heavy set man cuffed him in the head with his hand and yelled, "Quiet, or you'll follow the corsairs into the drink!" He then ordered a cohort of two dozen crossbowmen clad in crimson and yellow surcoats surround the pen.

Catalan! Jean thought. Then he had an idea, if he could get anyone to listen to him.

A delegation of richly clad men, jangling with each soft step they took, appeared at the head of the dock. One of them called out "Sergeant" and pointed at the dock. The heavy set man waved back and ordered some dock workers to make a table out of a pair of empty barrels and a wide plank. He then rolled up a barrel himself for him to use as a stool. After rapping his fist on the plank a few times, the sergeant pulled a book out of a satchel and ordered the crossbowmen to form the prisoners into a queue.

"They're going to sell us!" Jean whispered in astonishment. He recognized the sergeant's book as a ledger, like the Gamesmaster used to record the movement of silver through his hands and what was owed him. He had no time to lose. Jean bullied his way to the front of the queue, which the sailors were happy to allow, and he soon found himself face to face with the man in charge.

"Good master sergeant, let me say to you that we are very valuable," Jean declared in the finest Catalan he could muster.

The sergeant looked up. "You are to speak only when spoken to, but if you want to be the first to join a bank of oarsmen on a galley, then so be it. Age!"

"I am a man of the Gamesmaster of Avignon," Jean said and raised his chin.

"Of course you are," the sergeant replied disdainfully. He was a lean forty years of age, bald but for a narrow grey fringe encircling the crown of his head. "What is your age?"

"You don't understand. You see ..."

"Answer the questions and spare yourself some pain. The longer you try my patience, the more you succeed in prompting me to have you flogged. Now, what is your age and trade, and don't say corsair or anything funny, or I'll have you beheaded on the spot." The sergeant repeatedly tapped the ledger with his finger to indicate that he was ready and waiting.

Jean understood. "Well, I really don't know how old I am; however, I have been in the service of my lord, *the Gamesmaster of Avignon*, for five long and trusted years." Jean gave a knowing look, but the sergeant still ignored him.

"And I suppose your lord is also *gamesmaster* to our holy father the pope himself, or perhaps he serves both pontiffs. Well, all that means is that you no doubt have many wondrous tales with which to entertain your new master. Now, tell me something that will be of use or I will have this guard shove his spear up your ass, unless that is one of your games." The guard in question stepped forward and tamped the dock with the butt of his weapon.

"Nothing like that, but he is worth a king's ransom and has friends throughout Christendom," Jean said as the sergeant rose from his barrel. Jean quickened his speech. "If you let me go to Pisa, he has a partner there; I could get whatever money you ask."

The sergeant grabbed a fist full of Jean's surcoat and threw him down. "It's always the most enjoyable with the first one," the sergeant threatened, "and the time goes by so quickly."

Jean continued to talk as the sergeant placed a boot on his back. "Why would I tell you falsehoods when I know they might mean my life?"

"Why do they all tell falsehoods?" the sergeant echoed. "I care not. Now, one last time. Where did that spear go? Oh, it's beneath your tunic. Quickly: age and trade!"

"There is a squire with me," Jean croaked as he felt the cold, sharp tip of iron start to wedge between his cheeks. "He's worth a lot of money. A man of Gaunt, the Duke of Lancaster."

"Oh, for the love of all that is holy!" the sergeant cried. "I'm tempted now to cut out your tongue. I doubt if we could get much for you with it."

"Look, look! Behind you with the others! The tall one with blue eyes."

The sergeant faced the prisoners and saw Geoffrey. He motioned for the guard to step back and lifted his boot off Jean's back. "He is tall – I'll grant you that – and he has the build of a good squire. That pourpoint he's wearing tells me something though. Well, I see no one stirring at the head of the dock, so I will be indulgent for the time being. *You*, down there, speak Catalan with a Provencal accent, so you could be from Avignon."

Jean crawled to his knees and told about the squire's debt, the Gamesmaster's interest in him and the royal commission to retrieve Sir John Hawkwood's body.

"Bring him to me," the sergeant ordered a guard.

Geoffrey did not resist, but he walked with such quiet dignity that the other prisoners were astounded. The sergeant held up a hand and Geoffrey stopped. After looking the squire up and down, the sergeant turned to the guard and said quietly, "Get Captain Vilardell."

The guard ran to the delegation of richly clad men and within moments one of its members was striding purposefully along the dock, a crimson and yellow striped mantle flowing behind him.

What is it, Alfonso? I'm a busy man and why is this ledger not open?"

In a low voice the sergeant re-related the part of Jean's story about Geoffrey being a valuable squire.

"A man of Gaunt, you say? I don't believe it. And the other is his valet?" The captain looked at Jean. "Well, why doesn't your master make the plea himself? Never mind. I'm a busy man, so *I* will ask the essential question." He turned to Geoffrey, who was regarding him no differently from the sergeant or his fellow prisoners. "Do you swear upon your honor that you are a man of Gaunt, the Duke of Lancaster?" the captain asked in court French.

Geoffrey heard the refined nature of the captain's words and brought himself up to full stature. "I am indeed, sir. And who might *I* have the honor of addressing?"

"I will ask the questions and you will answer them truthfully. What were you doing aboard that vessel we sank? We found no other squires, English or otherwise."

"Truthfully, your lordship, I was on way to Florence at the behest of my king," Geoffrey said slowly. He was still disoriented and his eyes would not focus. "I will say nothing else until you tell me your rank and station."

Captain Vilardell raised his eyebrows and smiled. "I would have you beaten for discourtesy, but I see someone already has." He slapped Geoffrey's injured shoulder.

Geoffrey winced, but he did not cry out or curse. He quickly recovered his composure and again stood silent.

Vilardell interrogated the Portuguese sailors about these out-of-place men and found that they corroborated Jean's claims. The captain and Sergeant Alfonso exchanged a few quiet words.

"Hawkwood? I find it difficult to believe that someone would make up such a tale. I am intrigued. And what is worse, I'm in no position to pass judgment," the captain said, "and time does not favor a detailed inquiry." Turning to his sergeant, he commanded, "Lock them up somewhere on quayside. They will not be sold today."

They were rounding a corner of the customs house out of sight of Captain Vilardell when Sergeant Alfonso Sanchez stopped. "Put the Portuguese in the customs house," he ordered his guards and he handed one of them a small pouch. "Here is some silver. That should take care of it. Now, you two come with me."

Geoffrey and Jean looked at each other, but said nothing. They followed the Catalonian for a few hundred paces before Jean finally broke the silence.

"So, are we to get private cells? That would be worthy of our stations."

"The captain said that the squire here might be worth something, not you." Sergeant Alfonso stopped and asked a woman about some vendors.

"You brought me along to carry your victuals then? I am not as strong as I look."

"No, but you are as stupid as you look. Squire! You have the advantage of height. Look down this street and see if there is a money-changer, like the woman said." While Geoffrey was distracted, he pulled Jean to the side and whispered, "Do not think for a moment that I have forgotten about this debt the squire has with your Gamesmaster. In exchange for saving your life, you will give me a third of his debt. You have until we part company to do so."

Jean felt his chest contract. He had been hoping that the golden words about the royal commission outshone those of the silvery debt. However, considering that the Catalonian appeared willing to defy his captain, he might have some room for negotiation. In the meantime, Jean thought it wise to remain in the sergeant's good graces and learn a little more about him, his captain and his company.

"At least tell me how long I have to collect the bounty, my good sergeant," Jean said. "Our destination is Florence but no further. What is your company, aside from an excellent collection of crossbowmen, and where is it headed?"

The party passed a row of money-changers, four strumpets, two blind beggars, and a cargo vessel undergoing repairs before Sergeant Alfonso answered that the company's next destination was Viterbo, about a two-day march from Corneto.

"We are called the St. George's Company of Crossbowmen of the Vintners Guild of Barcelona, and do not forget it. Viterbo is a papal city, so someone there should be able to verify your story about King Richard wanting to collect Hawkwood's body, unless of course you revise your tale in the meantime."

"Why can you not send a messenger now?" Geoffrey asked. "My company will be missing me by now. And I would like my sword back. Your captain has recognized my rank, so you have no just cause to hold it."

"The captain recognized no such thing," the sergeant said. "And *my* company is in a hurry. A messenger can be sent from Viterbo, by the bishop, if he cares enough."

"But my *couteau*, master sergeant. I cannot be presented to his grace the bishop without it." Geoffrey's hand went instinctively to his side.

"Your what?"

"The broad sword your men took from him on the caravel," Jean explained.

"Oh, that. Nice piece of steel. Look, you should be thankful of what generosity the captain has offered."

"At least tell me that it is safe …"

"Enough! That sword belongs to the company now as a prize from our victory over the corsairs. Maybe the captain will let you redeem it, but until then, I do not want to hear another word about it. I can still put you in the customs house with the others, so be warned, boy!"

Alfonso entered the hall of the master victuallers. Captain Vilardell had entrusted him to find a man who could arrange the essential support for the crossbow company for the duration of their time in Italy, from negotiating provisions to procuring women of a certain trade. He had approached several victuallers and was discussing terms with another when he heard Jean's voice behind him.

"You know, there are ways of making even the smallest rations go further without adding to their cost."

The sergeant turned around and said angrily, "If you are trying to cajole me into cheating my companions, the captain and the sacred hair of St. George, then you will come to regret it."

"You misunderstand me, my good sergeant. What I was about to explain is that I know well how victuallers of all sorts and stations operate, and not always to the good of their patrons. I have had dealings with them on many occasions, both Roman and Avignonese, so I am well versed in their intrigues and in spotting their falsehoods." Jean was about to add to a list of his skills when in some confusion he asked, "The sacred what?"

"Hair. The relic sewn into our gonfalon is a few strands of hair from St. George," Alfonso explained. "You don't think we have St. George himself enrolled in our company, do you? Anyway, intrigues and falsehoods are corruptions of all men, including victuallers, so don't be troubled on that account. But time is fleeting, so I am willing to listen to what you have to say if only you will be quicker about it!"

Jean held up his hands as a conciliatory gesture. "My only suggestion is that it would do no harm if you were to consult me when negotiating with these men. Accountability is their weakness, since they stand close to the war chest, so we would do well to make that our shield. I once served in the papal household in Avignon, so I know their methods of reckoning, true and otherwise," Jean lied.

The sergeant did not respond, but if he was half as good a judge of character as the Gamesmaster, then at least Jean had planted the seed of his own usefulness in the Catalonian's mind. The interviews continued.

Geoffrey was unimpressed by the hall, and so he sulked behind Alfonso and Jean, but the false chandler continued to proffer unsolicited advice. He was not rebuffed, and even succeeded in saving the company a few florins. In the end, Sergeant Alfonso hired an aging victualler named Antonio, who had worked for crossbow companies before and agreed to supply the complement of 175 lances of crossbowmen and nine sergeants with smiths, leather-workers, wrights and joiners for repairing crossbows and building shielding devices, a cohort of sappers to dig ditches, some cobblers, numerous carters, and cooks. Antonio wanted to include a priest, but Alfonso declared that the sacred hair of St. George was all the divine blessing the company needed.

"You do not resent me?" Andrea Tomacelli asked his younger brother as they hunted in the papal forest near Spoleto. The sky was clear and the trees were starting to leaf.

"What is that you say?" Gianello asked. He took off his cap and shook out his long hair.

Andrea repeated the question.

"No, not at all. Anything that Pietro says is right. Wine?" Gianello reached into his fur coat and pulled out a wineskin. He took a long draught before offering it to his brother.

"No. It is too early for me, and you should refer to him as 'his holiness', even if we are alone." Andrea saw a hare scamper in the distance, but he decline to draw his bow. He was not keen on hunting at the best of times, and he had brought his brother into the forest for a private discussion. "It is important for us to show that the family does not suffer from internal discord. Despite the recent defections by several condottieri, I am confident that we can drive the cursed Clement out of the Patrimony once and for all."

Gianello threw down the wineskin and unslung his bow. He had made the full draw before the hare slipped behind a fallen log, out of sight. "He'll be back," Gianello said and carefully unset the arrow. "I agree with you – can I call you 'Andrea', or should it be 'His Lordship Papal Legate to the Marche'. I jest, but I am as confident as you that together we should create a formidable host."

Andrea maneuvered his horse so that Gianello's view was blocked. "I should tell you that I have been in contact with Giovanni Tarlati," he said seriously. "This does not trouble you, I pray."

"Not at all." Gianello shrugged. "Tarlati is a good man. Excellent hunter and decisive."

"How can you say that, when he abandoned you in January?" Andrea frowned. This was not what he was expecting to hear. "You might have taken Perugia and Broglia and Brandolini would have renewed their

OF FAITH AND FIDELITY

condotti with you. What did Prospero do? He was your captain-general, after all."

"Prospero? Oh, he and Tarlati had a good many discussions about how to pursue the campaign. When Tarlati began to regain the fidelity of the smaller cities on my behalf, Prospero complained that he was taking too much booty, or some such detail. There was so much talking that I cannot remember what everyone said."

"And then what?"

"Then the weather turned cold and we agreed to suspend the campaign. That is all."

Andrea was surprised by this casual recounting of last winter's failure. "And your captains received their pay and whatever else they could extort out of those small cities, no doubt."

"They received some pay, yes, but only for a month. I was sorry to see them go, Captain Broglia in particular – the man knows how to run a company – but I saw no purpose in keeping the host together and have it feed off my *dominium*."

Andrea was now doubly glad that he had come to take command of the papal venture in the Patrimony – all of it. Gianello needed his strong hand to lead the campaign.

"Out of the way, Andrea! I will not leave this forest empty-handed." Gianello reset his bow and scanned the distant trees.

Andrea smiled thinly and moved aside.

To keep Geoffrey and Jean out of trouble, or from bolting, Sergeant Alfonso entrusted them to the care of Antonio, the master victualler, who immediately set them to work shifting supplies and minding carts. This did not bother Jean, since it allowed him to keep a close eye on the squire. However, when it was clear that Geoffrey was content to simply load and unload sacks of flour and barrels of ale and that his wounds were healing cleanly even without the aid of a bloodletter, Jean turned his attention towards the inner workings of the company, so that by the time they reached Viterbo, he had worked out that he could replace Antonio at a moment's notice. In truth, he was already working so closely with the master victualler that he was present when Captain Vilardell rushed into the main pavilion and declared that he had finally received his promised *condotta*.

"I have been blessed," the captain declared, slapping the contract on a table laden with books and other accounting tools. "We are now part of the host of his holiness the supreme pontiff under the name of Gianello Tomacelli, the Duke of Spoleto. I was able to finagle a larger bonus, but by and large I accepted the generous terms proposed to me in Barcelona, plus a little extra for destroying those corsairs." He wiped a drop of wine from his mouth with the sleeve of his mantle.

"The duke is here?" Antonio asked.

"No, of course not. The bishop signed on his behalf," Vilardell said.

Alfonso and the other sergeants, who had been waiting impatiently for their captain to return from the negotiations with the bishop, slapped him on the back and offered hearty congratulations.

"It is time to celebrate," Vilardell declared. "Come! Let us retire to my lodgings."

Everyone followed the captain out of the pavilion, except Jean.

Left alone, he furtively looked around and quickly made himself aware of the contents of Captain Vilardell's *condotta*. Thus, he learned that Captain Vilardell and his St. George's Company of Crossbowmen of Barcelona were obliged to remain in the service of the Duke of Spoleto for three months with an option for a further two months of service, should the duke demand it. These two stipulations made up the main body of the *condotta*, Jean reckoned, since the Latin terms *'ferma'* and *'ad bene placitum'* were written with the largest and fanciest script. Focusing on the *ferma,* Jean learned that each crossbow lance, which had to consist of two men in good health and of necessary strength, would receive twenty silver florins per month in white money. This rate was a bit above the archer standard, Jean calculated, since the average was given in the marginalia. At 175 lances, that came to 3,500 florins per month. In addition, each of the company's nine sergeants would be paid 20 florins per month while Captain Vilardell himself was to receive a full 200 florins per month. For the *benvenuta,* or the speedy and successful march to the mustering point at Spoleto, Captain Vilardell, as head of the company, would get another 500 florins. Thus, the total value of the *condotta* was 16,640 florins. Jean skimmed over articles on division of booty, immunity from taxes, sworn promises not to ravage allied territories, and others. One item that caught Jean's eye, however, stipulated that Captain Vilardell had wide discretion on deploying his men in battle. To balance this privilege, though, the *condotta* required that the company travel to the mustering point by the route determined by the duke, that the company not partake in other military activity along the way or at the final destination, unless for purely defensive purposes or for the preservation of the company, that the company be fully complimented in men and arms so that if upon arrival the company was found to be deficient in any way, whether in arms, armor, men, or health, some or all of the terms of the *condotta* could be declared null and void. Captain Vilardell also was to immediately receive a *prestanza,* or cash advance, of 30% of the first month's pay (ex-*benvenuta*), which Jean reckoned came out to 3,492 silver florins.

"God's bones, that's a lot of silver!" Jean exclaimed. He returned the *condotta* to its original place.

"The captain wants to see you two," Alfonso said, as he poked his head in the tent.

The voice startled Jean and he leapt back from the table. "You mean the squire?"

"No, the King of Jerusalem. Of course, the squire! What's his name? Geoffrey Hotswill?"

"Hotspur, a man of the Duke of Lancaster. That should be remembered."

"Just go!"

Jean found Geoffrey near the edge of camp exchanging pleasantries with a group of young women, who had come down from the city proper to visit the Catalonians. When Jean told him that Captain Vilardell had important news for them, he clapped his hands and bid the ladies a good night.

"I am known, at last," Geoffrey said as they accelerated their pace.

"With those women? I dare say you are, although once they learn you haven't a groat, they'll forget your name."

"With his grace the bishop of this fair city," Geoffrey said brusquely. "I expect he will send me to Florence with a suitable escort. Have you any idea how far it is? I pray I don't arrive before the commission leaves. How many nights were they to spend there?"

"I don't know, although I would be wary about making assumptions."

"As a chandler, I would expect no less from you."

Jean shook his head and bit his tongue.

Captain Vilardell lowered his gaze and waited for his eyes to focus on the trio of his master sergeant, the English squire and the French chandler. "Well, I shall get right to it then, since I'm a busy man and I cannot afford to idle my time away. Which one is the English squire, sergeant? Oh, yes, the taller one." Vilardell pointed at Geoffrey and smiled. "I spoke with His Grace the Bishop of Viterbo regarding the story you spun in Corneto, and he said that a peculiar English embassy did indeed reach Pisa for the stated purpose of collecting the remains of a former Florentine captain of the people for re-interment in England. So, that is all well and good, but the bishop could not say whether this embassy had reported an unexpected loss to its party. Do you understand me, boy"

"Mostly, your lordship," Geoffrey answered.

"Mostly. That means you understand nothing." Vilardell shook his head, and then continued in Provencal French. After summarizing his earlier words, he said, "However, do not despair, for his grace has agreed to send a messenger to Florence to confirm your story. In the meantime, you are to remain with the company until I receive word about what to do with you, whether from Florence, Avignon or England, or Rome for that matter." Vilardell slurred the final few words.

"How long will that take, your lordship?" Geoffrey asked. His heart was already sinking.

Vilardell shrugged. "A few days, a week. There's a lot of fighting to the north of here."

Geoffrey moaned and dropped his head to his chest.

"Then we should stay in Viterbo," Jean suggested.

"*We*? Oh yes, we have to decide what to do with you as well. The slave traders are gone and the bishop won't have you. I suppose I can release you."

"He belongs to a wealthy guild, Berenguar," Alfonso interjected. "In Avignon. It has already cost the company dear to keep him, so let's have them make it up to us."

"Oh, very well," Vilardell said. "A chandler might be useful and Antonio rates you highly. Write to your guild and ask what they'll give for you."

Jean nodded and looked askance at Sergeant Alfonso.

"Ah, but let us not look so glum. As you can see, I am in very good humor this evening, so I offer you some of my company's wine. If there is one thing we have plenty of, it's wine." Vilardell reached for his goblet, and needed three tries to take a firm hold of it. "I suggest you take advantage of my hospitality while I still respect your stations, for bad news could overthrow things tomorrow." He turned to Alfonso.

Geoffrey was not sure what to do now. He looked first at Jean, who seemed to be straining to hear the conversation between the captain and his sergeant, and then around the pavilion. The furnishings were luxurious, even by Avignonese standards, their intricate designs bearing the hallmarks of Iberian craftsmen. An impressive array of crossbows was neatly arranged at the foot of a pile of shields that bore the crimson and yellow crest of the Barcelona vintners guild. Bottles of wine and bowls of fruit covered several tables.

"Please, don't be shy on my account, Squire Hotspur," Vilardell said. He was becoming unnerved by the squire's passivity. "If you are unfamiliar with our wine, rest assured, it is the best. We have only red, I'm afraid, but as an Englishman you should well appreciate it."

Geoffrey nodded and gingerly selected a mid-sized bronze chalice from the closest table and filled it. As he was lifting the chalice to drink, Geoffrey noticed a Greek inscription engraved around its base and several silver crucifixes inlaid around the brim.

"It's good," Geoffrey said after consuming the entire contents of the chalice. The wine had the effect of dulling his nerves and revitalizing his mood. "Strong nose, but a light body. It's not Spanish, I'll wager, is it?"

Berenguar smiled and waved a hand to dismiss his generosity. Then, bolting upright, he announced, "The first to guess the wine's home can keep the cup the young squire is holding. You can play too, Alfonso."

Jean assented to the challenge first. He took the Byzantine chalice from Geoffrey, refilled it, crossed himself thrice out of respect, and took a few delicate sips.

"Sicily," Jean declared with some conviction. "I wouldn't put money on it, but I'd have to say that this wine was poured in Sicily." He passed the chalice to his right.

Sergeant Alfonso took some time before settling on Valencia as the origin.

"Well, I for one *would* put money down – on myself," Geoffrey declared.

OF FAITH AND FIDELITY

"Without question this wine hails from Bordeaux, near the coast I would say. His lordship would supply some to the squire hall on occasion."

"Bravo! The Englishman has won," Berenguar announced. "The wine *is* from Bordeaux, although whether it was made on the coast or inland, our guildsmen did not say."

"You certainly can be trusted to come through on a wager, Geoffrey," Jean said. He then gave voice to an idea inspired by the Catalonian captain. "I wonder. Would you have been so accurate had the chalice not been at stake?"

To Geoffrey, these words were almost blasphemous, but because he was a guest, his strong sense of courtesy held a well-seasoned oath fast on his tongue.

"So, the young squire enjoys gaming, does he?" Vilardell mused. "How…natural. Tell me, Hotspur, what games are favored in your circle of friends? Dice, nine-pins, quek, maybe? What other games are played in the north, sergeant?"

Geoffrey chose to be circumspect about his personal indulgences, merely citing a list of common places in Avignon where wagering was legally attended. He thought it prudent to be modest.

"Oh, Geoffrey here has quite some talent when it comes to Hazard, sir," Jean declared to keep the conversation on topic. "I've not seen him play myself, but his reputation as a skilled and honorable diceman is second to none."

Vilardell nodded, then he opened a large chest and pulled out a small box. "Have either of you seen these before?" he said as he spilled its contents on the table.

A look of recognition slowly transformed Jean's face as he examined the collection of coins, chalices, swords, clubs, numbers, and noble faces. "These are playing cards, aren't they?" He did not want to appear presumptuous, but he was familiar with the novelty. He even recognized this particular deck as being Spanish, since the French and Germans instead employed diamonds, hearts, spades, and clubs as symbols. The Gamesmaster had yet to introduce playing cards to any his gaming halls because he was still working out how to ensure his advantage with them.

"We call them *naipes*," Berenguar explained. "They are made of thick paper and are painted by heretics." He laughed at his petty irreverence and picked up a card that showed a knave wearing a snide expression.

Geoffrey was fascinated. He looked down at the pile and with great care and respect lifted one of the cards.

"It's so light," Geoffrey said, "and colorful." The card crossed the span of his hand. He stared at the patterns and pictures until his eyes lost focus and the images began to dance. Frightened, Geoffrey dropped the card and stepped back.

"They won't bite, squire," Vilardell said as he laughed. "Well, the might bite your purse." He scooped up the cards and repacked them in their box. "The company has an ongoing game with these things. It was started during the last struggle for the throne of Castile, when your master tried to impose his English ways on the Spanish, incidentally." He was referring to the Duke of Lancaster's failed attempt to conquer that kingdom.

"Seven years!" Jean exclaimed. "Doesn't anybody win?"

"The rule, as far as I understand it, is that the last company man alive will be declared the winner, or declare himself the winner, I suppose. You are welcome to join the game at any time, now that you have been accepted as guests of the company. I myself rarely play, since I am constantly inundated with important tasks." Berenguar smiled and refilled his goblet.

"You are fortunate, then, that my poverty prevents it," Geoffrey said. "Otherwise, I would win your company from you."

"Mind your tongue!" Alfonso bellowed. "This isn't the squire hall."

Vilardell waved at the sergeant to calm down. "You would what? Ha, you are a fine guest! Well, then it's good for me that you won't be with us for very long."

The pavilion began to fill with the other sergeants, their companions for the evening and a group of townsmen who were curious about the Catalonians. Geoffrey and Jean were about to go, when the squire recognized several ladies.

"It would be rude of me to leave now, I should think," Geoffrey said as he eyed the younger maids. "Roger would have something to say about this, or at least remember their names for me. Do you think he would have sent a message to Florence by now? Maybe Gaunt?"

A chill went up Jean's spine. He had never thought of that, but of course the Duke of Lancaster maintained regular correspondence with Florence. He sighed that here was yet another thing he had to be mindful of.

"Well, I don't know their names, so you had better just reintroduce yourself." Jean pushed Geoffrey away.

However, Geoffrey had not taken more than a few steps when he saw his reflection in a polished plate and was taken aback.

"I cannot talk to them looking like this." He turned to Jean and tugged at his dirty pourpoint.

Jean looked around until he spotted a company tabard draped over a shield.

"Take this," Jean said as he handed Geoffrey the crimson and yellow surcoat.

"You are clever," Geoffrey said and he pulled it over his shoulders. It was short, but covered most of his pourpoint. "Perfect fit!"

While Geoffrey consorted with the maids, Jean mingled with the sergeants and townsmen. He was hoping to chance upon the Gamesmaster's local partner or at least have someone send him a message, although considering his own attire, he doubted that he could convince anyone that he was much more than a swineherd. He looked down at his jupon; it was in better condition than the squire's pourpoint, since he had used the grooming tools of the master victualler to give it a good brushing, but several buttons were missing and, in contrast to the other guests, had neither blazon nor brocade. The garment was plain grey, which was fine for slipping in and out of the shadows in Avignon, but it made him for all intents and purposes invisible here. He wanted his purple cloak back.

"Sergeant," Jean said, leaving Geoffrey to entertain himself. "It's time you returned our gear. The nights are still cold, so if you do not want to hand over a frozen corpse to the Florentines, do yourself a favor."

Alfonso turned from speaking with a woman, whose own dress impressed Jean for the richness of its fabric and modesty of its style. Her deep blue gown was cut with strict vertical lines and had a row of buttons that ran from the waist to the very top of her neck. Jean was tempted to pluck a few for himself.

"I suppose we can let you have it back," Alfonso said. "None of it is worth anything, except for the sword taken from the squire. Nice instrument. Nearly cut my finger off, it did."

"You have a curious accent," the woman said, whose own voice betrayed exotic origins with its offbeat cadence. "Are you from Provence, east of Avignon, perhaps?"

"I am," Jean said. He could not think of anything else to say, so he just stared at the woman. She had what the troubadours described at almond-shaped eyes of lustrous brown and gently curving eyebrows. He admired the sharpness of her features, although her face was quite pale, which told Jean that she hailed from nowhere near Provence.

"Well, *I* am Catherine, most recently of Rome. These Catalonians have kindly agreed to escort me to Spoleto." She made a small bow in Jean's direction.

"Not for nothing, we haven't," Alfonso mumbled, and an awkward silence fell on the trio.

"Ah, there she is!" Vilardell said and he opened his arms as though to embrace Catherine, but he stopped just short of her. His face was flushed. "My reader. Better than a priest, I say, and much safer. They're all spies now, since the war has heated up again." His took a long draught from his goblet and smiled.

"A reader?" Jean asked.

"Astrologer," Alfonso confirmed. "The captain has decided that he needs an astrologer to read the stars and signs for him."

Jean looked at Catherine again and noticed the badge of astrologers on her headdress: a gold pendant holding twelve tiny rubies.

"And that's *all* she is?" Jean smirked.

"You are with the tall squire over there, I am told," Catherine said. "To earn your keep as his valet, you should take proper care of his wardrobe. Even in Provence, I should think they know better." She smiled and looked at Sergeant Alfonso.

"I should introduce you to him," Vilardell said, louder than was needed. "He won't be with us for long, since he's a man of old Gaunt. We Catalonians are a charitable lot, you will see."

Vilardell took Catherine by the arm, handed his empty goblet to Jean and escorted the astrologer to the opposite side of the pavilion, where by now all the other women had congregated.

Sergeant Alfonso smirked. "She *is* better than a priest."

"Are you sure she's not a spy?" Jean asked. "She has a dubious station." He recalled how the Gamesmaster used such people to keep watch over debtors and high-placed men.

"She carries the papal seal and is known to read for Boniface, but more importantly the captain likes her, and he has good taste."

Both men turned to look at Catherine, who was already speaking with Geoffrey.

"Don't steal the cup," Alfonso warned and he walked away.

Jean frowned at the goblet. He pried off an amber stone from its rim with his fingernail and shoved it inside his jupon.

Geoffrey and Jean stayed until Captain Vilardell could hardly stand, which was when Sergeant Alfonso concluded the evening's festivities. They walked together in silence, each lost in his own thoughts, following the line of steaming braziers that illuminated the main path. As they approached their tent, Jean asked, "Are you in better spirits now? You certainly look much better than you did in Corneto. I believe a miracle was performed when that wine cleared the wool from your head instead of making it. You'd hardly spoken until then."

"I do feel better," Geoffrey answered. "My belly is full and my wound heals. Our captors do make a luxurious camp for themselves. I pray such indulgence doesn't undermine their strength, though they seem to bear it well. Did you watch them shoot this afternoon? It was a marvelous sight. They could unseat a knight at 200 yards, no doubt."

"I saw well enough from the caravel the horror they inflict, so I can do without another show for the time being," Jean said.

"They will do well in the papal host. Part of me wishes I could go with them and fight for the true pontiff, but my duty lies elsewhere. Once His Grace King Richard is done pacifying the Irish, then maybe he will send his own host in aid of Boniface."

Jean shook his head, but Geoffrey did not see.

As they were passing a group of crossbowmen huddled near a brazier, someone called out in Catalan, "Have you come to pay your ransoms finally?" Laughter rippled through the party.

Geoffrey and Jean recognized them as the guards at Corneto.

"You should ask your captain about that, if you could gain an audience with him," Geoffrey retorted. He awaited a return jeer with arms akimbo, but the crossbowmen immediately lost interest and remade their huddle.

Surprised by this reaction, Geoffrey's curiosity got the better of him and he peered into their midst. It was the pile of silver that first caught his eye, followed by the naipes scattered around the coins. A game was on, and Geoffrey could not have felt more at home. Instinctively, Geoffrey leaned in and began to concentrate on the play.

A crossbowman flicked a trio of cards face up onto the mess of coins. "Cacho!" he yelled, and followed the strange word with some babble in his native tongue. Then, just like in the gaming hall at the Blue Boar, some men cursed, others laughed while others called to play on.

Jean frowned. He did not understand. "What?" Jean asked a neighbour, pretending that he had not heard.

"He made a cacho, friend. Look!"

Jean assumed that the Catalonian was indicating the three cards the ecstatic player had used to win the pot. The victorious cards bore the likenesses of three very different men of high rank. They were similar to the cards Captain Vilardell had showed them, but Jean was certain they were not the same. Glancing at some of the other cards before one of the players collected them, Jean noticed that the reverse, or hidden sides, were covered with such an elaborate weave of design that he assumed these *naipes* had been acquired in Moorish lands.

Once the center was cleared and the watchers had quieted down, the dealer patted what looked to be forty cards before proceeding to throw a single card to each of the four players who signaled his decision to remain in the game. Each man furtively glanced at his card, though one was bold enough to show his spectator friends. The player to the right of the dealer alternated a dozen looks between his small pile of silver coins in white and black money, the man opposite him and his lone card before with a confident flick of the wrist tossing three good pennies into the center. Satisfied that the stake was respectable, he nodded to the player to his right, who quickly accepted the wager by adding three more coins.

The other two players, who Geoffrey distinguished as the 'one with the facial tic' and the 'one with the face of stone', were only slightly more hesitant about calling, though neither appeared interested in escalating matters. From this Geoffrey reasoned that the first card was more about assessing the other players than about the card itself.

The dealer issued another round, but judging by the players' sharp reactions Geoffrey surmised that this card carried a weight of consequence far greater than its elder brother: the player with the stony face quickly arranged his pair and slapped them down behind his silver; the player with the tic ground his teeth to reign in the suddenly flaring muscle after a fleeting glance at his cards; the other two made equally cursory reviews of their cards before hiding them against their chests. The crowd began to discuss strategy, although no one dared address the players.

The second round of betting took longer than the first. Stakes were raised and re-raised until the last player buckled under the weight of chance, ending his participation by mumbling an oath and throwing his cards onto the large pile of silver. The three 'survivors' studied one another while pretending to count their coins, examine their cards or stare at the stars overhead. The dealer, anxious to lay another round, motioned that he was about to throw out another card. The 'survivors' made eye contact and gave consenting signals.

The final cards were sent. Each player was hesitant to lift his third card until one of the others did. The audience was hushed in anticipation. The players searched watchers' faces for any hint of passing signals, which was strictly forbidden and punishable by any one of a number of penalties.

Satisfied that the crowd was honest, the players renewed their wagering. This time, though, the bets were made with groats, or *grossi* in Italy. Another man folded. The 'survivors' then undertook a verbal joust, making passes with vicious barbs and obscure taunts to test the other's resolve. Geoffrey took this to be a part of the game also, not unlike his famous wager-raising delays when he was the caster in Hazard.

The pot was up to half a pound when the dealer held his hand over the pile of silver and called for the players to show cards. With confidence and great care the man to the dealer's right laid out two coin cards, which totaled fifteen coins, including one faced with a valet, and the third card, which hosted two swords. The watchers pursed their lips and nodded in approval. The man with the facial tic made a crooked smile as he revealed one club card of very low value and a pair of chalice cards that added up to sixteen, with a mounted knight as the highest. The audience burst into cheers and jeers while the loser merely shook his head and counted his *resto*, or remaining funds.

"It all looks simple enough," Jean noted. He had been as quiet as and no less attentive than Geoffrey. "The wagering is just sequential. The trick is to know the winning combinations and to count the number of cards that the fellow who gives them out has remaining in his hand. I think even you can work this game, Geoffrey." He nudged the Englishman with his shoulder, sending him a few steps closer to the players ring.

Geoffrey mumbled a few calculations that were working in his head. He barely heard Jean's comments, so focused was he on deciphering the subtleties of the game. *Naipes*, or rather this way of playing them, for Geoffrey was sure that innumerable versions existed, looked more complicated than dice but less involved than the pitch-and-toss board games that were popular in English France, like quek. His fingers began to tingle at his sides and his feet felt as though they were about to shuffle of their own will towards the players ring. The stars above sparkled with renewed intensity. Geoffrey turned sharply and pulled Jean away from the crowd.

"What is it? I don't think they've finished playing," Jean said.

Geoffrey spoke in a low but commanding voice. "Ask someone about the number and symbol combinations. Just the winning ones. There is no time for anything else. I think I've figured this game out!"

Jean was about to address the nearest watcher when Geoffrey again pulled him back. "No, not him. He won't know. He's just a watcher. Look at how he stands, all ragged and loose. There is no interest there. Let me see …" Geoffrey scanned the crowd. "Him!" Geoffrey nodded towards a fellow standing on his own. "He is showing himself to be indifferent yet he does not take his eyes off the players. Nor do I see him discussing the game with his neighbors. That's the man to ask, if he will speak, though doubtless he will be more than gracious for our purposes. Go on!"

Jean played the naïve foreigner with the man, introducing himself as a simple chandler and mixing questions about the game with observations about Catalonian customs. He was helped in his disguise by the company rumor of his being the English squire's valet. Meanwhile, another three rounds went by, at the end of which one of the players decided to call it a night, leaving a gap in the players ring. Jean returned the moment he saw it.

"I shall quickly tell you what I've learned," Jean announced. "The best combination is a cacho, or three kings, as they say, that is having three of the four cards in the pack that are blazoned with royal portraits. Don't ask me which kings they are; we can find out tomorrow, if you like. The next best combination is a sequence of numbered cards all in one suit, which is what those symbols spattered over the cards are called. Then comes three number cards, two number cards and finally one number card. He who possesses the highest ranking combination wins. It's as simple as that."

"I'm more worried about the talking, but I'm sure I can impress them with some English rudeness," Geoffrey stated.

Jean looked at him askance. "So, you're jumping in? You should do well, but who will stake you? Unless you're willing to pledge your *couteau*, and I know you are not, then how will you wager?"

Geoffrey already knew from Jean that all his possessions but for the *couteau* had been lost. Geoffrey clenched his sword hand and felt the bronze chalice almost burn his flesh. He did not fancy being parted from it, as it was a sacred vessel, but the lure of the cards was too great. Was it temptation or Fate guiding his will? Perhaps the chalice was meant to serve as a sacrifice, Geoffrey reasoned.

"Ask someone to stake me for this." Geoffrey handed Jean the chalice.

"Who? I'm not a moneychanger. I have no bond of trust with these men."

"You are a chandler, so you should be able to gain a little trust amongst these men. They're not knights or lords, after all."

After making a show of wavering, for he did not want to seem too glad that the squire was again set on gaming, Jean went around the circle with Geoffrey's chalice, trying to convince anyone who would listen to stake the English squire, who had been appointed to a royal commission. He resented being treated as a servant, but he was more troubled by the fear that his failure to elicit an offer would undermine Geoffrey's belief in his false self.

"I shall stake the squire," someone declared.

Jean turned and saw Sergeant Alfonso. Seeing no other takers, Jean reluctantly agreed without discussing terms and passed the chalice to the dealer to give to the sergeant.

"I found someone, although I am not sure whether …" Jean began when he returned, but Geoffrey cut him off with a wave of his hand. He was anxious to enter the game. He was not interested in the details of Jean's transaction.

The dealer gave Geoffrey a square of light-colored cloth and a stick of charcoal. These were his credit tokens, he was informed, with a short tick of charcoal representing half a penny, medium tick representing a full penny and a long tick meaning a groat. A cross against a tick indicated that the wager was being made in white money. A few objected to the squire on the grounds that it was custom that only members of the company and perhaps the odd Catalonian were entitled to play. However, after Sergeant Alfonso made a speech in favor of admitting Geoffrey to the privileged circle because he had fought like a Catalonian against the corsairs, the doubters were silenced. So in the spirit of good will and avarice, Geoffrey was given a place.

Things went bad from the outset. To show he was fearless, Geoffrey wagered aggressively and lost the first three hands without folding once. He wanted the other players to know his name, but not one associated with timidity. The money was flowing freely, as each lance had received its *prestanza* and the provisions were still high. Geoffrey could not keep such a pace for long, but so concerned was he to establish his reputation as an earnest *naipes* player that not once did he count the ticks he was making on the cloth. Then his luck turned and he caught a cacho. Some of the Catalonians hailed him as a hearty fellow and praised his skill. He won small pots in three of the next six rounds and soon found himself with enough money to render the cloth and charcoal unnecessary. Then he felt a tap on his shoulder.

"Perhaps it would be wise to set aside a few coins to redeem your chalice," he heard Jean say. "It would be a bad sign were you to lose it, and should Captain Vilardell hear of it, well, we hardly know these Catalonians, do we?"

Geoffrey looked at his *resto* and saw that it was no larger than anyone else's. To set aside any amount now would considerably impair his ability to wager as boldly as he had been. However, these crossbowmen were lowborn types, and the kind of grand wagering to which he was accustomed was almost certainly beyond their experience; they might take offence and not allow him to join their circle again. It was a difficult decision. So, he wagered for it.

"Tell you what, my good chandler," Geoffrey began. "If the next card dealt to me shows a chalice, I shall take your advice and start saving like a miser. If it does not, I shall see it as a sign that I should carry on without change. What say you?"

Jean gave Geoffrey a doubtful look, but he decided he had best agree, even though the odds were grossly against him. If he argued the point, he might start to sound more like a debt collector than a simple chandler. He wanted to encourage the squire to wager anyway, and this was as good an opportunity as any for him to gain proficiency at a means by which he could eventually profit from the young Englishman. He nodded his assent and stepped back.

The next card cast before the squire bore the likeness of a sword.

By the time the moon was at its brightest, Geoffrey had earned just enough to redeem his chalice, leaving a sou's worth of silver as his winnings. Then the game, by order of Captain Vilardell, broke up for the night.

CHAPTER 6

"Murdered!" Sergeant Alfonso and Jean cried together after Captain Vilardell announced the death of the bishop's messenger.

"I'm afraid so. Some peasants brought in a body from a village near Montefiascone last night. Bretons, apparently," Vilardell explained. "And what is worse is that his grace blames me for the loss. He won't send another and I'll be damned if I'll risk losing anyone." He turned to Jean. "Have you eaten, master chandler?"

Jean shook his head.

"No? Fine, then. I see you won't cost me much. Now, tell me: what has become of that English squire of yours?" the captain asked. "He should be here. No wonder he got separated from his party."

"He is on his way," Jean answered. "He wanted to ask your company treasurer about his sword."

"He's still worried about that thing, is he? Oh well, we must press on regardless. If we delay, my *condotta* risks being forfeit, and it is already April." Vilardell began to pace the floor of his pavilion. The death of the messenger meant that his way might be blocked and he would have to risk his company in battle, with Bretons or whoever else was out there, and he had only eight days to reach Spoleto.

"Alfonso, what else do we need to do?"

"The reader. Shall I still engage her?" Alfonso asked.

"Yes, of course. She has the terms. Just get her to accept them. I am a busy man and we must soon be on our way."

"Naturally, captain. And the prisoners?" Alfonso was acutely concerned about the English squire and the French chandler. They owed him money. He had found the Gamesmaster's partner in Viterbo, a petty moneylender from a family of middling station, and while the man recognized the name Jean Lagoustine and described him as a sturdy fellow of average height with Provencal looks and uneven shoulders, he refused to have anything to do with Geoffrey's debt without a written pledge or instruction from Avignon. Alfonso decided not to tell Jean any of this.

"Yes, the prisoners. I would prefer to leave them here, but the bishop has made me responsible for the squire, since I found him. Besides, he might be Gaunt's man after all, and it wouldn't look good if I lost him." Vilardell shook his head in annoyance.

"We have to take them with us, then," Sergeant Alfonso proposed. "The chandler does good work with the master victualler and the squire has already proven himself as a carter."

"That's just what I was thinking. We need to keep that squire close, though. The baggage train offers too much room for movement. Somewhere in the ranks, I should think …"

"For how long?" Jean asked with a desperate voice.

"For as long as it takes," Vilardell answered. "Now don't interrupt."

"That is all good and well for you," Jean said, "but that will take us further away from Florence. How do we get him to Florence then?"

"Oh, there will be opportunity, I should think. If I send him alone, he will be dead in a day. Ah, Master Hotspur! You've decided to join us."

"Your lordship." Geoffrey strode in and stood next to Jean.

Captain Vilardell nodded and reviewed the company enlistment rolls.

"He can be a *pavesaro* for one of the lances," Vilardell declared to Alfonso.

"Excellent idea, captain," Alfonso said. "He might be a little tall for that, but I don't think the men will object to having a large target in front of them." The sergeant chuckled.

OF FAITH AND FIDELITY

"He is not to be put on the field, you understand."

"Yes, but *I* don't understand, your lordship," Geoffrey said. He turned to Jean for an explanation. Jean told him and for how long.

"A shield-bearer!" Geoffrey cried. He was appalled. A well-trained squire in the service of Sir John of Gaunt was worthy of something more exalted than a rank-and-file *pedite*, a miserable foot soldier, and not even a proper one at that. "That simply won't do. Could I not pledge myself to a knight or be given a place that befits my station?"

Alfonso guffawed. "What sort of knight would take a man who has no harness, no horse, no attendants, and no arms, much less a name? Not even the poor knights of Christ are that desperate!"

Jean threw the sergeant and angry look and then an imploring one at Vilardell, but the captain was not sympathetic either. He did not care for knights of any rank, since they usually held crossbowmen in low regard, except on those occasions when they needed crossbowmen to cover their retreat.

"No. We have no knights here," Vilardell said at last.

A messenger entered the hall and announced that Captain Prospero was requesting an audience with his lordship. Andrea bade the messenger send the captain in without undue haste.

"Why the formality, Corrado?" Andrea asked in a flat voice. He was genuinely glad to see the captain-general, although he would have preferred to meet him at a scheduled gathering of the war council.

Captain Prospero entered unescorted. "I was not sure if you were gathering with his lordship, the Duke of Spoleto," Prospero said, then added: "Why is it so cold in here? Look, your fire is out, or hadn't you noticed?"

"I like the cold. It keeps my humors balanced." Andrea kicked the andiron into the ashes of the hearth, where it produced a grey cloud. "Do you believe that I would discuss this campaign with him in league against you? He is late again, that's all."

"No, of course not, but I thought that perhaps if family matters were on the table, well, you know how famous your family is." Prospero sat down on a stool opposite Andrea.

"There is no pressing family matter on my account," Andrea said quickly. "I am glad you came. Wine? It is a gift from Salutati, the Florentine chancellor, from the last war with Clement." Andrea got up and filled two bronze chalices with red wine from the Chianti valley. He handed one chalice to Prospero before returning to his seat. "I need your opinion on *condotti*. It has become glaringly obvious that the terms my brother offered in January were not commensurate with the value many condottieri place on themselves. Of the famous captains he employed then, you are the only one who took up his *ad bene placitum*. I want to know why. The minor captains were no problem to retain. Altoviti, Montone, Attendolo … they all signed or re-signed with little fuss, but Brandolini and Broglia bolted and others refuse to negotiate. Now, I would like to know: did you stay out of loyalty to my brother or did the offer from Malatesta not satisfy your dignity?"

Captain Prospero had assumed that this question would arise eventually, since the constantly shifting allegiances in this part of Christendom heartily fed the cloud of suspicion that was darkening the land, and so he was prepared – with an honest answer.

"We differed on strategy. It was foolish. Winter campaigns have to be done quickly, or they suffer the result ours did. Your younger brother had trouble deciding whose advice to follow, and the time flew. Brandolini and Broglia refused to risk their reputations further. Captain Broglia was particularly incensed because he wanted to campaign around Assisi."

"And that is the only reason? Surely they argued about such things when in the service of other lords without suffering the need to change sides, money notwithstanding. And besides, the summer campaign is a different matter altogether." Andrea had yet to meet Ceccolo Broglia, even though the distinguished captain had already moved into the Marche for this year's campaign.

"While I cannot speak for my fellow condottieri, having ridden with them on several occasions in the past I believe that they objected also to other aspects of their *condotti*, namely the conditions of occupying towns and castles. The duke, your brother, was not generous in this respect. He wanted to impose papal garrisons on the towns, as opposed to giving them over in provisional jurisdiction to the occupying condottiere. I did argue that he had precious few men for such a broad task, but he insisted. The noble duke even suggested that Broglia give up his claim to Assisi, as your brother believes that this holiest of towns should be governed by the Holy See and not shared with either a *signore* or some communal administration."

"I see why Captain Broglia did not like that aspect of my brother's scheme."

"No indeed. Where do you think much of the silver comes from to fund his company and his school for aspiring condottieri?"

"From the tolls and duties he imposes on priests and pilgrims," Andrea answered.

"Exactly. The duke had the will but not the – how shall I put it – the *virtue* to enforce his prerogative, and so we might conclude that he lost the debate."

"You have yet to mention Giovanni Tarlati," Andrea said slowly. "He had a large company with you."

Prospero's face betrayed no expression. He looked down and tapped the map with his index finger. "We had our differences," Prospero said plainly.

"I heard." Andrea inhaled deeply. "What I don't understand is why you could not decide everything in the war council. I do not wish to insult you, but how was it that each captain was not made to follow the letter of his *condotta*? Amendments can be made, strategies altered, but such things must be done quickly and decisively. Clement must be defeated at all costs, and with speed."

"I do not wish to insult *you*, but your brother allowed it. The *condotti* were signed with him. I could not go against his wishes under such circumstances." Prospero carefully drew his hand over his scalp.

Andrea stopped for a moment to think. He stared into the blackness of the fireplace that he refused to have lit. The cloud of ash had settled, coloring the andiron in a light grey. While clarity of command was all good and well, what he believed would really impress those professional men of war was a solid victory in the field, a strategic victory at a key location for radiating papal authority. He knew well from experience that sometimes condottieri simply cannot be bought, despite the nature of their service.

"But none of this tells me why *you* stayed," he said. "Giovanni Tarlati has your men under siege. Had you gone over to the Malatesta, they would be safe now."

"I am not convinced that Malatesta can take Umbria – he is very young and none of his more powerful uncles accompany him – and I believe that the cities of the Patrimony can be brought back with care and consideration. I do not want to be on the losing side either. And besides, I cannot even contemplate campaigning alongside Tarlati. His way of war is crude and his company unruly. Should I have command, and I now do, I would not tolerate such ruinous and purposeless raids as he conducts in the English style."

"Perhaps, but he did return the fidelity of some cities to my brother."

"Well, yes and no." Prospero scratched his cheek and looked down. "He invested several cities in western Umbria in your brother's name, but we cannot count on them. Neither Tarlati nor your brother left men to govern them, or garrisons."

Andrea eyed the captain carefully, trying to measure his honesty. Corrado Prospero had yet to make a bid to establish himself in a city or carve a lordship out of a piece of captured land, as so many leading Italian condottieri were doing. He was one of the last captains to fight just for money and personal glory. That much was certain, and he was glad that he had pressured Gianello into supporting his candidacy for captain-general. Until such time as he could complete his own campaign in the Marche and unite his and his brother's armies and sweep the antipapal host out of central Italy, he could rely on the solid German captain to keep Malatesta at bay. Then, once carried aloft on the wings of victory, Andrea could have himself appointed Vicar-General of the Patrimony.

"So, you are happy with your *condotta*?" Andrea asked. "You only signed for two months. That does not show much confidence in our cause, I would argue."

"I signed it before I knew you were advising your brother. I am sure to consider signing a three- or four- month contract at the end of May."

"You will want to relieve your men at Narni before then, though." Andrea was still concerned that should they fail to successfully prosecute the war very soon, the fear of losing his company could finally send Prospero to the other side.

"When we are ready to do so. My men are well supplied and can withstand anything the enemy throws at them. Narni can wait," Corrado said confidently, and he took a long draught of wine. He was comforted by the papal legate's open words with him and he was happy to return the compliment of trust.

"I agree, but our task is beset by many uncertainties, so we must apply the greatest force in retaking Narni. We can no longer afford to indulge in half-hearted measures. Tarlati had help from within the city, you know;

it was how his men were so easily able to enter. The walls are intact, according to my sources and yours, which might make our siege difficult. Only the citadel, where your men are standing firm, has yet to fall."

Corrado smiled. "The German emperors tried once to hammer the cities into submission and only succeeded in breaking themselves."

"You are right. I have advised my dear brother that when he takes cities, he should enter in person and set terms. Compromises must be made, but from a position of strength. What he needs are strong vicar-captains, like Tarlati and Malatesta."

"But they are working against us."

"They are working against my brother, the duke, because he both erred and was weak. You are right, though. What we must to do in order to secure our gains is to bring the cities and the condottieri back to our side. We need to be at once righteous and strong." Andrea brought the tips of his fingers together and placed his elbows on the table.

"Do you not mean *right*, meaning holding to a correct and consistent strategy?"

Andrea stared into his wine. He had not intended to use the word 'righteous' with his captain-general, although that was what he believed. "Of course, that is what I mean. Now, you take care of the strength part of our duty and I shall take care of the right part, meaning holding to a correct and consistent strategy. When shall we be ready to march against Narni, captain?"

"We have enough men-at-arms on foot and mounted to issue forth as soon as you raise the papal standard. My company and your brother's retinue will provide the equestrian backbone while the small condottieri companies will comprise the *pedites*. I have also asked your brother to levy a militia, which could form a garrison or do foraging. I should say rather that we are *almost* prepared. We are only short of supporting companies, which I would argue are essential for this campaign. We need crossbowmen, or at least archers. If we weren't relieving a siege, then I wouldn't worry so much, but I will not risk getting bogged down and dodging arrows for the sake of relieving just one castle, however important. Do you know when those Catalonians your brother recruited will arrive? The moment they appear at our gates, we can be on our way."

"I will be honest with you; I cannot say for certain when they will be here. They are a good lot, those Catalonians, but they are awfully cautious. However, I have heard that they've landed."

"Then let us pray they arrive soon."

"Let us pray."

Via Cassia-Amerina

Although relegated to a common *pavesaro*, Geoffrey got some of his dignity back when Captain Vilardell ordered his treasurer to return 'that strange broad sword with the bloody pommel' to him. At the very least, Geoffrey could *feel* like a man of his station while the captain could say, if need be, that he had treated a man of Gaunt with respect. He also was impressed by the compact marching order the crossbowmen kept, forming two dense ranks on either side of a line of wagons that carried their arms and accessories. The ranks were so tight, actually, that Geoffrey could see Jean leading a bullock near the head of the baggage train. Geoffrey's mood improved all the more when he saw the first milestone, as he realized that for the first time in his life he was genuinely on campaign. He was going to war. True, he was without lord or station, while the incessant chatter in Catalan and Italian constantly reminded him that he was not supposed to be on the road to Spoleto with a company of crossbowmen. Nevertheless, he was serving the one true pontiff, if distantly and for a short time, so at least that was something. There must be some meaning in all the trials and travail he had endured, Geoffrey thought.

Geoffrey patted his *couteau*, which was now firmly strapped to his hip, thinking that no matter where he stood in this company, as long as he had his sword with him, he would be the true squire he knew himself to be.

"You know," Jean called out from behind Geoffrey, "the lads here tell me that Spoleto is one of the pope's favorite cities."

"So?" Geoffrey shouted back.

"So, that means the city offers the finest food and most luxurious lodgings, *and* is home to the fairest women in the Patrimony."

"If you have such bountiful wealth at your disposal that you can afford all that, why don't you redeem us out of here?" Geoffrey yelled.

"You never know what Lady Fortuna has waiting in store, squire. And what's more, Spoleto boasts more gaming halls offering higher returns than even Avignon!"

"And even greater penalties," rose a woman's voice from behind them, "for those who wrongly anticipate Fortuna's fancies." The astrologer Catherine rapidly approached on a small palfrey.

"Fie! Wagering is a skill, like archery, or even an art, like war," Jean replied. "I need advice from a woman like I need a nose above my ass."

"You insult me, you insult Captain Vilardell, since he readily takes my advice. Is *that* not a foolish wager?" Catherine answered.

"My wagers might appear foolish to your kind, but rest assured that they are always well considered and masterfully played."

"Let not your conceit be your undoing," Catherine warned.

"Truly spoken, but is it not conceit to pretend to know how the heavens affect the actions of men? As to wagering, I will argue that all possible combinations are known, whether for dice or *naipes*, and so a man can calculate and stake accordingly, if he is as learned as he should be. As to your business, I will ask: to what knowledge or surety can a man cling as an anchor should you portend that he will grow feathers and become a duck on the next full moon? For this he must have faith, and only our

Lord and the supreme pontiff are worthy of this, not some well-plumed strumpet."

Catherine reined in her palfrey and drew alongside Geoffrey. "I agree that faith serves the divine, but – and I ask the good English squire here – is not service to one's lord an act of faith? Is not a pledge a knightly form of prayer that binds the loyal and devoted warrior to his liege?"

Geoffrey looked up at the woman and worked to piece together a clever answer, but Jean re-entered the debate with one of his own. "Worthily said, m'lady, but that is no more than an earthly contract, as the young squire will attest, though one of the highest order. It is an exchange of debts, or rather duties, and an expression of gratitude above all."

"The principles are the same, though the devotion be different. But this is not a matter of faith in principle, no matter how you would aim to fashion it. Not surprisingly, owing to your low station, you mistake the art of reading the signs shown by Nature with conjuring, which I assure you is something completely different. I can only illuminate darkened paths as reason readies me to, but I cannot cut them." Catherine tugged her bodice to give herself more air. She inhaled deeply before finishing her speech. "All combinations are known, as you say, but I hasten to add that a man would do better to employ the well-cut words I offer to improve his odds of choosing the most worthy path than to stumble blindly onwards and be certain of losing all."

Geoffrey laughed. Jean was nonplussed, but he would say no more. Catherine announced that she was wanted by the captain.

"Enjoy your walk, soldiers," she said in English. With a whip of the reins she galloped ahead.

The scouts continued to report good news until several miles west of Orte, when several groups of villagers stated that the army of Clement had recently passed through. They learned nothing else until the company passed empty fields and the air turned with the sweet and awful scent of rotting flesh. The company was ordered to put on arms and the column slowed to a crawl.

After a few, tense miles the vanguard spotted a cloud of dust billowing in the distance. Captain Vilardell motioned for the column to stop and called for Sergeant Alfonso. After exchanging a few words the captain consulted with some of his scouts and then sent an order down the column. The Catalonians spanned their crossbows and began to form ranks, while the *pavesari* scrambled to collect their shields.

"As silly as this will sound," Geoffrey began, "we have stopped."

"Maybe a cart lost a wheel, or someone with a good eye spotted berries in the woods. We haven't done much foraging since we left the coast, I've noticed," Jean said.

"Foraging! What do you know about campaigning?" Geoffrey said with unbridled condescension.

"In my village we called it 'starving', but what would *you* know about that?" Jean retorted.

They saw Sergeant Alfonso hurrying towards them from inside the column. "You!" he said, pointing at Geoffrey. "Find your shield! And you, Frenchman, help me get these people behind the 'bowmen."

"What is it, sergeant?" Geoffrey asked.

"I hope it's the advance scouts, but they're kicking up a lot of dust for two riders," Alfonso said.

"Could it be Bretons?" Jean asked.

"Could be a lot of things, but looking around here, I'm expecting the worst. Now, move!"

The *pavesi* were thick and heavy and painted bright crimson and yellow. Geoffrey was not sure how to hold the monster, and twice he nearly knocked the crossbow out of his companion's hands, but a fellow *pavesaro* helped him ground the shield and it was soon steady. He looked down at his harness and grimaced. Having neither money nor a benefactor, Geoffrey had been obliged to take what the Catalonians cast off, so in addition to his pourpoint, he could now boast of an old hoqueton that was stripped from a dead corsair, a basinet helmet, some leather leg protection, and a pair of vambraces to give his forearms the additional strength needed to hold the loathsome crossbow shield.

The crossbowmen kept one eye on the mysterious cloud and trained the other on invisible targets in the woods. A tense silence enveloped the company. Even Captain Vilardell was unusually still and quiet, Geoffrey noticed, and he wondered if the Duke of Lancaster was showing the same vigilance on his *chevauchée*. Geoffrey turned to his neighbors and saw that they had their fingers resting on the trigger of their crossbows, which were being held steady just above his ears. Geoffrey tightened his grip on the shield and returned his attention to the road ahead.

At two hundred yards a brace of riders formed out of the dust. Some of the men raised their heads to get a better look. Geoffrey let his left hand slip from the shield-grip to the pommel of his sword. He heard coughing and praying in the ranks, but he was content to remain silent, with mouth taught and jaw set. Several more men appeared, on foot this time, staggering closely behind the riders. The tension seeped out of the company when the crossbowmen recognized the scouts. They were dragging three prisoners with hands tied behind their backs.

Geoffrey watched Captain Vilardell gallop ahead to meet the cohort. An exchange of serious words with the scouts was followed by a brief interrogation of the prisoners, who appeared cooperative. The scouts rode to the baggage train and Sergeant Alfonso took charge of the prisoners. The captain shouted a few orders to the other sergeants and returned to his place at the head of the column.

A sea of murmuring flowed through the company, but Geoffrey was able to understand one word: "Bretons".

The company resumed its advance, albeit in full harness and with crossbows at the ready, but it was slow going. Geoffrey had to carry his *pavese* with him now, as did all his fellow *pavesari*, while the baggage train clung closer to the main column. All life seemed to vanish the further they marched. Even birds seemed too afraid to chirp. The road started to rise, retarding their pace more, and a few men pointed to the smoke rising from the crest of the hill in front of them. When they finally reached the village of San Bernardino, just a few miles west of Orte, the company encountered burnt cottages, overthrown walls and ransacked yards, but a bleaker site awaited them on the village square, where they came face to face with a group of wailing of women standing around a heap of corpses.

"Keep moving!" Sergeant Alfonso shouted. Some of the younger crossbowmen had stopped and were staring at the terrible scene. The column began to bunch and gaps opened in the ranks.

"By Jesus' noble passion! What lord could allow this to happen to his *dominium*?" Geoffrey whispered to himself. He stepped away from his lance and surveyed the devastation. Between the tattered skirts of the grief-stricken women he could see the open mouths and ashen faces of murdered men. Some were missing noses and eyes, but the tunics of all the bodies were stained with great dark blotches. Geoffrey thought about those ruffians in Avignon he had cut down, but he recalled that they looked nothing like this. Then the sweet stench of decaying flesh overwhelmed Geoffrey, and he staggered back, dropping his *pavese*.

"Geoff!" Jean called out. "Get back in ranks before Sanchez sees you!"

Geoffrey seemed to hear, but his feet were slow to respond. Jean left his bullock and grabbed him by his injured shoulder.

"Ow!" Geoffrey turned to face Jean.

"Don't go any further. This has nothing to do with us." Jean looked around for Sergeant Alfonso and saw him rounding a corner with the vanguard.

Geoffrey threw Jean's hand off his shoulder, but he remained rooted to the ground. He looked around the remains of the square with sadness and wonder until his eyes fell on a ruined chapel. He squinted through its empty doorway and saw a scorched altar.

"By all that is sacred I have never been witness to such a vile sight as this!" Geoffrey cried out. "Who would dare despoil consecrated ground in such a fiendish manner yet still call himself a Christian?" He grabbed the pommel of his sword and squeezed with all his might.

"This was a *chevauchée*," Jean declared solemnly. "The fiendish acts visited on this town were planned."

"What makes you say that? This looks like simple banditry to me." Geoffrey felt his heart beat like it never had, and his stomach wanted to overthrow its contents.

"Because bandits would have sacked and run, yet this assault was prolonged. Those poor men over there were killed over several days, judging by the rates of corruption. And the plundering is too ... thorough. Bandits don't burn cottages or pull down chapels, nor would they spend such a long time in one place."

Geoffrey continued to stare at the chapel. "No, a *chevauchée* goes against a lord, to make him submit. This ..." Geoffrey raised his arms to the sky, "does nothing. Pillaging property and knocking down walls is a *chevauchée*; murdering peasants and burning down chapels only serves the Devil!"

"Geoffrey, calm down," Jean began, but Geoffrey was not listening.

"Who would commit such an un-Christian act? Listen! Those women need their chapel. Where will they pray? How will they bury their sons and husbands?" Geoffrey thought about the comfort he received on the cold stone floors of the many chapels he had visited. "Something must be done. We should find the lord of this village. I should expect that he will not tolerate such barbarity, and then ..."

"And then we must return to the column," Jean said as he pulled harder on the squire's pourpoint. "These people have more to worry about than a little old chapel."

"It is not a barn! That chapel was the heart of this village. How long can you live without a heart, Jean? There must be a reckoning! We must go after these Bretons!"

"We cannot tarry. Captain Vilardell must reach Spoleto in less than a week."

"I will go to Captain Vilardell then. He is an honorable man and will know how to give these villagers the satisfaction they deserve."

"Fine, Fine," Jean said and he got Geoffrey back into ranks near the end of the column. The vanguard had already passed through the village and was following the scouts towards an enclosed field.

"You left your bullock behind, master chandler," Catherine said as she trotted along the column. "Antonio is already looking for you."

"I have more pressing matters in need of attention," Jean answered through his teeth. He nodded at Geoffrey, who was ahead of him and staring into the distance with a furrowed brow.

"Is he that affected by this slaughter?" Catherine leaned forward to get a look at the squire.

"And you are not?" Jean asked. "The stench alone would send the Devil himself back to Hell."

"Breton devilry, to be sure, though they cannot be made to take the blame alone."

Jean raised his head and fixed his eyes on the astrologer. "You know who committed this foul deed?"

"I do. The widows here entrusted me with the knowledge. They have no one else."

"Pray tell us, and then maybe the squire won't have to look for them." Jean took Geoffrey by the arm. "Geoff! Listen to this."

They stopped and listened as Catherine told them a harrowing tale about how a band of two dozen Bretons abused the village for days, mutilating and murdering men folk, as they pillaged and pulled down the best houses. No amount of ransom could convince them to leave, but they took everything anyway. What was worse, though, was that the Bretons had refused the dead burial, reckoning that the unholy sight and stench of husbands, brothers and sons would ensure that they were remembered.

"I still see no purpose in this," Geoffrey declared.

"That is because I haven't told you that this is the work of the antipope, the cursed Clement," Catherine said. "He has the murder of these souls on his conscience."

"You must be mistaken," Jean said. "Clement was still in Avignon when we departed. He could not have reached the Patrimony already."

"You are right. It was one of his condottieri who committed this crime, so it is much the same."

"Condottieri?" Geoffrey asked. "Is that an Italian word for knight or count or some exalted rank? I have heard the title several times in this land and I have yet to understand it."

Catherine drew closer to Geoffrey until she could read his anger in the taught muscles in his face. "A condottiere is a kind of mercenary."

"So, they are mercenaries then. I understand."

"In truth, they are much more than mercenaries, and maybe more than knights and counts."

Geoffrey sighed and balled his fist in frustration. "Do tell me the difference, m'lady. Things are far more simple and honest in France. We call a hired sword a mercenary and nothing else. If a condottiere is a captain of a band of mercenaries, then he is the same."

Catherine started to dismount, but abruptly changed her mind and repositioned herself on the saddle. "A condottiere is more than just a captain of hired swords or lances. He is their leader, their arms master, their judge, and the keeper of their reputation. He pays them and makes his company their home. It could be said that a condottiere is the father of his men."

"So he is akin to a prince or a constable with his host convened under his banner for war, then. 'Condottiere' must just be the Italian name for a great lord," Geoffrey reasoned.

"I would not compare a condottiere to a captain-lord or even a king, if you will forgive me for saying so," Catherine said gently, fearing the young squire's wrath, "because in a host of knights these elevated men muster with the great man as a matter of duty and allegiance, bound by personal oaths, and when the campaign ends that same convention of nobility returns to their lands and the common soldiery to their homes, as though the host never existed. The companies of the condottieri, however, do not go home when the days become shorter and the snow threatens to fall. The men-at-arms remain with their captain, for silver, naturally, but also out of respect, and to bask in the glow of his reputation rather than cringe in the shadow of obeisance."

"You sound as though you've spent much time with condottieri," Geoffrey said.

"Rather I've spent much time in Italy. My profession has led me to many fine halls, where amongst the attending courtiers I have met the most famous condottieri."

Geoffrey grabbed the hilt of his *couteau* and stood as though he was about the draw it. "So, do you know the name of the condottiere who ruined this village and its chapel? I need to know." Geoffrey's voice dropped an octave and his eyes shone icy blue with intensity.

Jean silently shook his head behind the squire, but Catherine ignored him. She would not let some French chandler tell her what to do. "Giovanni Tarlati," she said loudly, "of Arezzo."

"I will remember."

The company was setting up camp in the fortified field when Geoffrey, with Jean hard on his heels, met Sergeant Alfonso at the entrance to the command pavilion.

"You should be dining with your lance, Englishman," Sanchez said. "Remember, until you're told otherwise, you remain a soldier in this company."

"I must speak with the captain."

"On what account?" Sergeant Alfonso folded his arms and looked into Geoffrey's eyes.

For his life Geoffrey wanted to say something that would shake the earth beneath them, explain about the despoiled chapel and how restitution must be made, or at least how justice should be done, but he could not find the words. Asked to state his purpose in a straightforward manner, Geoffrey was now not sure precisely what he wanted. He was convinced only that somebody had to pay for the desecration and destruction of that house of God. He began to throw out words like 'heathens', 'damnation', 'church', and 'heart', but his speech was as meaningful as a dribble of rain in the desert.

"Eh? What's that Englishman? You, Frenchman, what's he trying to say, as if I could give a toss. Look here, shield-bearer: get your ass to your lance and don't even think about bothering the captain. We march at first light tomorrow." The sergeant drilled his index finger into Geoffrey's injured shoulder.

Geoffrey ignored the pain. "But they looted and pulled down the church, man!" he cried. "They must be made to pay for this sacrilege!"

Sergeant Alfonso looked at Jean.

"He's troubled by that chapel the Bretons burned. He is seeking to punish the guilty," Jean explained soberly.

"What chapel? I don't know about any chapel. It's none of our concern anyway. And besides, it won't be the last time such a thing happens. *Our war is across the Tiber.*"

"We should stay and clear those bastards off this land," Geoffrey said in a resolute manner. "This Tarlati must be brought to account, if he indeed has these bandits in his pay."

"That sort of act might be ... expensive," Jean answered very carefully. "It is none of our business and I don't think the captain wants to risk losing men for the sake of someone else's vengeance. And besides, the company only has crossbows. If arms came to pass, *we* would be murdered."

"I have a sword and, if I recall correctly, you can handle one as well. And no doubt some of the Catalonians are as familiar. *I* am prepared." Geoffrey recalled the battle on the caravel.

"But, like I and Sergeant Alfonso have said, it's none of our business."

"Not our *business*, maybe, but it is certainly our *duty*. We are Christians, are we not? The strong must protect the weak. If the Bretons were Saracens, then I'm sure the captain would order arming points to be readied. We are not such cowards as to sit by and watch the ravaging of a harmless village, are we? This is not war. This is fiendish cruelty!"

"Listen, Geoffrey. This is not your company and this is not your land. Nor are they mine. Of course, I agree with you in principle, but it is not our decision to make, and if the company were to risk doing 'its Christian duty', as you so rightly put it, I would venture to argue that these villagers might well end up worse off when we leave. And leave we must. His holiness the supreme pontiff's brother awaits us in Umbria. Everything will be done in proper order." He then turned to Sergeant Alfonso. "You will inform the captain about all this, will you not? Oh, wait. He must know already."

"Yes, yes, Captain Vilardell knows everything," Alfonso said. "He also knows that dusk is fast approaching and the camp must be put in order."

Jean's reasoning made a deep impression on Geoffrey and he finally released his grip from his sword. "I will leave it up to the captain's conscience," he declared, "though it pains me greatly. And I will not forget."

CHAPTER 7

Florence

Behind the locked door of his private chamber in the Balia, Coluccio Salutati was reviewing the most recent correspondence from Florence's spies and ambassadors. Having laid out all the essential bits of parchment and paper on the table before him, the chancellor took a deep breath and selected an urgent dispatch from his man in Genoa. As of one day ago, the doge of that key port city still had not reclaimed the confidence of the nobility and some of the more important merchant guilds, which meant that the French were still on their way. Appended to the dispatch was a note from his man in Turin dated two days ago, which recounted popular rumors that the French army had entered Savoy and was marching southwards. If the good weather held, his man reported, the French and their Genoese confederates should close in on the city within a month, two at the most.

The chancellor accepted this report with his usual aplomb and he wrote to his man in Genoa that he should discreetly encourage the doge into believing in Florence's enduring support for his rule short of offering him money or any other material assistance. While Salutati would never underestimate the strength of a French host, he did expect their invasion to get bogged down trying to take the well-prepared castles nestled in the mountains around Liguria, or that a quarrel would erupt in its leadership, disrupting their strategy. The French nobility was the most querulous in all of Christendom and was as likely as not to snatch defeat from the jaws of victory by turning upon itself at the critical moment. The chancellor could not abide by anyone who refused to learn from the lessons offered by history. Two hundred years of failure had taught the German emperors not to meddle in the affairs of Italy, so what made the French think they were so much wiser was one riddle Salutati was not keen to solve.

The chancellor's man in Rome had happier news. The papal host was growing in size and was expected to launch its campaign in the Patrimony any day now. Salutati smiled when he read that Giovanni Tarlati had not taken Narni, despite his numerical advantage, and appeared to be waiting for the main body of Clement's host under Malatesta Malatesta, who had men-at-arms in Perugia, Assisi and Todi. Would he go over to Boniface or would he stay with Clement? He wondered if the money he had given the Arrentine through the English sergeant would be enough to sway his conscience.

Salutati sighed at the futility and destruction of the war between the two popes. If only both men would accept the Way of Cession, then these wars could end, the French could be kept out of Italy, the Visconti could be stopped from expanding their *dominium*, and Florence could save silver. Perhaps even a crusade against the Turks could be called, which would help secure the trade routes to the Levant and save the eastern emperor. He recalled that some students he was sponsoring had recently informed him that the University of Paris was now openly advising Cession to end the schism, and Salutati was in full agreement. The Way of Force had never been an effective tool to reunite Christendom. Yes, he knew about Albornoz, but he also knew about emperors. If Boniface should succeed in restoring the fidelity of the Patrimony, he will still have to confront the Visconti, which would be no small fight, as well as Naples, let alone mighty France. If the cursed Clement should win, he too would be sure to unleash the dogs of war across Italy and Christendom, and then everyone would lose.

The chancellor poured himself a goblet of wine from his own estate in the Chianti valley and sipped it slowly. This state of affairs could not go on indefinitely. Even if Boniface finally won the Patrimony this year, Clement was a man of vengeance, and he would spend every last penny the Church under his control had to pursue the throne of St. Peter in Rome. Resolution of the conflict had to be taken out of their hands. The learned men in Paris were considering it, so why shouldn't he? Salutati quickly emptied his goblet and then sat down to write.

San Bernardino

The camp was unusually quiet, as most of the men had obeyed Captain Vilardell's order to retire early, but Geoffrey could not sleep. The desecration and ruin of the chapel of – what was the name of the village again? – San Bernardino would not leave him. He saw it in the brazier glowing before him, surrounded by wailing women and filled with murdered men. He had never been witness to such horror and he felt insulted by it. Jean had given the impression that such devastation was a common occurrence, but that could not be true. Yet, maybe he was meant to see it, an event made for him as a sign that he needed to get back on the road to knighthood. He thought back to Roger's dream and the appearance of King Richard and his own penitent's tunic. His hellish passage on the caravel was surely a sign as well. He had to find this condottiere Tarlati and force him to submit to repentance and restitution for his un-Christian offence. What kind of man was he, anyway? He must be filled with bad blood, common blood, perhaps even blood tainted by the Black Arts. However, the more Geoffrey dwelled on the chapel, Tarlati and his own quest for knighthood, the more tired he became, so that by compline hour, he was too exhausted to think.

"Have you eaten?" Jean asked. He had been speaking with Geoffrey's lance head and trying to get more information about the company, their destination, the road ahead, and most importantly where the *Cacho* game was being held that night. "You will be pleased to know that Captain Vilardell has given some victuals to the surviving peasants. I was just at the distribution point. Good man."

Geoffrey nodded and leaned back on his unrolled pallet. "Yes, an excellent and most Christian gesture. Perhaps the captain will do another tomorrow and rid this …" Geoffrey stopped himself short when he felt the bile rise in his throat.

"Well, now that we are all sated and comfortable, what say we distract ourselves from the day's horrors with a heady game of *Cacho*? I can almost hear the gentle purr of the *naipes* from here."

"How can the Catalonians indulge in gaming now, knowing what grief and sadness spreads yonder like the plague?" Geoffrey pointed towards the village. He could see a few fires burning amidst the ruins, but most of the hill was smothered in darkness.

"It is precisely because they have been touched by the grief and sadness yonder that they play. They cannot sleep otherwise, and they must be alert to face the dangers of the road tomorrow."

Geoffrey crossed his long legs and rubbed his buskins. The leather needed polishing and the soles were wearing badly. He felt around his pourpoint and found that holes were already forming, even though it had been whole when he packed it in Avignon. Everything was coming apart. Geoffrey sighed as he dropped his head onto his chest.

"Did you hear me, Geoff? I dare say you will be tossing and turning too if you don't balance your humors somehow. You showed a load of choler up there."

"You are probably right," Geoffrey said languidly. "Just let me get rid of this pourpoint."

Several tent rows over, Geoffrey and Jean saw Sergeant Alfonso entering a faintly illuminated pavilion. They followed him in and soon Geoffrey was seated at the players circle, having been faux-reluctantly staked by Jean with the few grossi he had succeeded in prying from the master victualler as a small commission for the profitable sale of some of the company's supplies to the villagers and the promise of a good word to the victualling guilds in Avignon, plus the little money Geoffrey had won the last time out.

The English squire's arrival was not unwelcome, although the Catalonians' demeanors grew hostile after Geoffrey took the first three tricks without even making a cacho. The wins perked his mood, and when he collected his sixth pot after only nine hands, he was feeling as though he could anticipate the cards. He was reminded of the mystery of communion, of that moment when grace filled his heart, while the hideous sights of the ruined village dissolved into crowns and chalices. Without so much as a glance at his *resto*, Geoffrey threw in a handful of coins.

Jean, meanwhile, did not like what he was seeing in the shimmering faces of the other players. The yellow glow cast by Sergeant Alfonso's small lamp revealed faces sick with anger and frustration. These were the same men who only two days ago had indulged and shared a gamer's fellowship with the young squire. Nor was he comforted by Geoffrey's aggressive disposition. He would have to do better than Roger Swynford at keeping the squire from ruining himself. After another wave of dispirited murmuring, Jean slipped out of the shadows and in the low, conspiratorial voice of a confidante told Geoffrey that he should ease up on the wagering, since they had several days yet before they made Spoleto.

"Why should I leave the path that has led me to such green pastures," Geoffrey hissed in English so that none of the Catalans could understand. "What you are suggesting is akin to heresy. You are not a Cathar, are you?"

Jean had to restrain himself from cuffing the young squire on the ear.

This 'Cathar' insult might have meant something in Avignon, since this widespread heresy native to southern France had to be twice rooted out by crusade, but in an Italian village laid waste by a band of Bretons, Jean could let it go. Instead, he tried to think of another approach to keep Geoffrey in the game yet prevent him from stoking the wrath of the Catalonians.

"You are a proper member of this company now, so perhaps you might show a little charity as thanks for their hospitality and faith in you," Jean suggested, taking a page from the book of chivalry. "We could just as well be dragged in chains to Spoleto as to be allowed to march unfettered alongside these good men."

Before Geoffrey answered, Sergeant Alfonso, who was closely watching the interaction between the two foreigners, stepped in and decided to introduce an expensive variation of *Cacho*. Since Spoleto was now only a few days away and the chandler had yet to turn over a single penny to him, he decided to wager on the squire's improving card skills himself.

"We'll play for points now," Alfonso declared. "I am certain the players will agree that the game has become boring."

While some players grumbled, most of them and the watchers made noises of approval. The few players who started to collect their *resto* received a stern look from the sergeant, and they stayed in.

Jean was quick to ask his neighbor what that meant, but Sergeant Alfonso cut him off with "You will see."

Geoffrey started the new *Cacho* with nearly two and a half solidi worth of silver grossi, which Jean mumbled was roughly equal to three sous at the standard Avignon rate – the least of any player in the tent. The crowd grew quiet and the dealer began to shuffle the *naipes*. Caution was now the byword, as each player passed on the first card, and then again, making the first two rounds a bust. Someone suggested switching dealers, but Sergeant Alfonso overruled it.

"Cacho!" Geoffrey cried and he threw his cards in the middle of the ring. The others groaned and revealed their own hands.

"Well done, squire," Alfonso commended. "Now, take the pot and what the 'low man' gives you." He looked at the most dispirited player. "You, over there, pay up!"

The man with the lowest-value hand sullenly counted coins and handed each of the other players the value in silver of Geoffrey's winning hand, plus ten pennies.

"Oh boy, this could be a long night," Jean muttered.

After making another cacho in the fifth round, then following it with a couple of easy wins, Geoffrey was able to put two players out of the game and push up his *resto* to a full four solidi. He was in a wagering frenzy now, dumping silver into the ring the moment he received his next hand. Twice he had a two-card flush in fives, but his high early stakes frightened away the other players, thrice instead of withdrawing from play on low cards he played on and twice he was thumped as the 'low man'. Then Geoffrey handed over 24 pennies in white money to a veteran crossbowman and *naipes* player who had made a two-card flush in crowns with a five and a six plus a card with three clubs, followed by respective 15-penny and 25-penny payouts, which left Geoffrey with a *resto* of half a solidus. It was barely enough to continue. A rough hand fell on Geoffrey's shoulder.

"Blast you!" Jean said in French through his teeth. "That was a fool's call! Now pay attention before you lose your precious *couteau*!"

Geoffrey was about to brush Jean off with his best English oath when they heard a sweeping sound outside the tent. The hour was very late and the group had not invited more players, not even Captain Vilardell. Everyone held his breath; someone shielded the lamp. Someone else whispered 'Bretons', but he was shushed. The sound drew closer then stopped in front of the tent. Sergeant Alfonso, impatient at the dithering and worried looks, pulled aside the curtain and dragged inside a woman carrying a small box. When she threw back her hood, the crossbowmen laughed and exchanged rude comments. The shield from the lamp came down and the dealer collected the *naipes*.

"What is the astrologer doing here?" Jean sneered.

"I have every right to be here," Catherine answered. "You are playing with my cards, after all." Catherine assumed a place behind the dealer.

Geoffrey shot her a surprised glance, then took dumb counsel with his fellow players. To his amazement, it seemed that only he was shocked by this pronouncement. How could they wager with a woman's property? He found something unseemly in it.

"By all means, play on, gentlemen," Catherine said. There were no objections.

The next few hands were weak, giving no one an advantage, but then the dealer announced, "We have matching hands here. We must tally the cards."

With one, five and six plus a premium of twenty for making a flush, Geoffrey's hand added up to thirty-two points. His opponent, a veteran and long-standing member of the company, had also made thirty-two points by holding two, four, six and enjoying the twenty-point premium. The veteran smiled and began to collect the pot. However, Geoffrey took umbrage at the presumption and shooting his arm out with the speed of a crossbow bolt locked down the veteran's arm.

"Just wait one moment, by Saint Mary's holy countenance!" Geoffrey cried. "I can reckon as well as anyone else here and there is no question but we have a shared result. A just resolution would be to divide the pot between us or add it to the next round." Geoffrey appealed to Jean to translate for him, as it was clear that by restraining the veteran Geoffrey had caused more than a few angry faces to appear.

As Jean concluded his speech, the frowns softened into looks of incredulity. Someone laughed and even the veteran managed a thin smile. When the dealer, with an economy of words, explained why the old veteran had the right to claim the pot, Jean leaned over Geoffrey's shoulder and translated. "He says that because he is the elder between you two, you lose the round."

"Well, God's bones!" Geoffrey exclaimed. "What the hell kind of rule is that? His station is no higher than mine and we both owe allegiance to the same lord, and I do mean Captain Vilardell, so what does age have to do with anything?"

The crossbowmen sniggered and called for the squire to show a bit of chivalry.

"What would you have me say, Geoff?" Jean asked, frustrated and annoyed. "That is the custom. Bad piece of luck to lose like that, but there it is."

Geoffrey would not be deterred from pressing his claim. However, in order to preserve the good humor of those gathered around him, he released the veteran, then again turned to Jean. "Tell them that while I might have just, what … nineteen years behind me, the good Lord has seen fit to grant me twelve chalices, which they must agree is sacrally superior to the other suits. If they do not, then ask these good men this: what did our Lord Jesus Christ give to his disciples at the blessed meal on the eve of his most holy sacrifice? It was not a club, for He did not preach that they bring violence to their enemies; nor was it a sword, for that was the symbol of Roman rule; and it was not a sack a coins, for money is forever cursed by the betrayal of Judas Iscariot when he accepted for himself those thirty pieces of silver. He put forth a chalice, and into it poured His blood, so that forever the chalice will be the symbol of the holiest of sacraments. Does that not make my hand superior to the other? Tell the truth!"

Jean had difficultly conveying the precise meaning of Geoffrey's words, but it seemed that the gist of his companion's weighty words was taken in. After a heavy silence, the dealer exploded with laughter. The veteran, who was still the acknowledged winner of the round, slapped Geoffrey on the back and pronounced him the Sir John of the company.

"I must inform you, my dear squire," Sergeant Alfonso said, "that company traditions trump theological arguments when it comes to this simple game, although perhaps your understanding of the card suit hierarchy would be a useful addition. Nevertheless, I am certain you misunderstand. That man is your 'elder' not because he has more years behind him, but because he was wagering ahead of you."

Geoffrey dropped his head onto his chest and said no more.

After Geoffrey lost the next two rounds, even though both times he was sure he had unbeatable hands, he slammed his fist on the ground and declared, "I will not touch another card unless the tent is cleared of women, regardless of any claim on property!"

Geoffrey did not look at Catherine, but others did, and when she realized that no one intended to stand behind her, she left. Sergeant Alfonso followed her into the cool, quiet air.

"Why did you not refuse to go?" Alfonso asked. "Your cause was just and the English squire needs a good kick in the ass, if you'll pardon my rough words."

Catherine gave a forgiving smile. "Prudence, not obedience, dictated my course," she explained. "I did not wish to be the end of things. However, I shall put a similar question to you. You are the ranking soldier here, so why did you defer so easily to a mere *pavesaro*? Have you an interest in keeping the Englishman in good humor?"

"That is two questions, which allows me to refuse to answer both." The sergeant smiled. His aim was to be diplomatic, but not out of respect for her sex. Rather, he feared her power. Alfonso's inquiries in Viterbo had revealed that Catherine was indeed a respected astrologer and not a clever whore, which was his first suspicion. Worse than that was the thought that she might dabble in the Black Arts as well, since it was well known that one easily led to the other, especially with women, whose strength in moral judgments was naturally suspect. The last thing he needed was for this strange woman to put a hex on him.

"It matters not," Catherine said, "for I have no interest other than keeping my *naipes* in good order. I value them highly."

"I shall take care of your *naipes*," Alfonso whispered. "Now go back to your tent. I will be ending the game soon anyway." He thought about the heavy losses the squire had incurred. "Why are you not reading for the captain now? We have a dangerous road ahead, so the watch for signs and omens must be vigilant."

"The captain is asleep and it is difficult to read signs in the dark. I shall wait. I can keep watch while you collect them *and* my fee for their use."

Jean emerged from the pavilion. "You're still here then, are you?" he said to Catherine and then added, turning towards Alfonso, "And you too. I smell collusion out here, and I thought the air was getting rank in *there*." Jean jerked his thumb behind him.

"How's the squire doing?" Alfonso asked.

"I see you do not deny it, and so it must be true."

"So, he is *not* doing well." Alfonso concluded and he shook his head.

"The truth is that he's about to lose the rest of my silver, and I have no more with which to stake him. I cannot understand it. It seems as though the winds of fortune shift with the snap of the fingers. He seems distracted; I don't see the concentration in his eyes as I once did." Jean was at a loss about what to do, since he could neither bodily remove Geoffrey from the players circle nor get him to wager with more sense. He would not ask Sergeant Alfonso for a loan – certainly not in front of the astrologer.

"As you were quick to teach me the other day," Catherine said, "all results are known. To succeed just requires that they be mastered. If your squire will not accept advice on wagering strategy, then perhaps he will be amenable to hearing the names of a few useful combinations that Fortuna favors above all others."

Jean could not help but smile. He did not mind having his words thrown back at him if they could be made to line his pockets. "So, your magic extends to something genuinely useful. I am delighted. Tell me quick before my trickle of silver runs dry."

"You are not worried that I will peck your ear or curse your soul?"

"I am, but my conscience will hound me anyway if I do nothing to help the reckless squire."

Sergeant Alfonso laughed as Catherine approached and began to explain how to count cards at *Cacho*. When she was finished, Jean dashed into the pavilion just in time to watch Geoffrey throw his last pennies into the ring.

Spoleto

The final leg of the Catalonians' journey was uneventful. After hanging the captured Bretons, Captain Vilardell hired one of the few men left in San Bernardino to guide his company away from besieged Narni north to Amelia, where they met one of Gianello Tomacelli's men, who took them the rest of the way through Acquasparta and finally Spoleto. As they approached the main gate, Captain Vilardell saw a black-clad figure riding towards them.

"Identify yourself or be shot down!" Berenguar declared and he nudged Sergeant Alfonso.

"I am he who will prevent you from making an ass out of yourself," Prospero yelled back in Catalan. He reined in his charger only a few feet away from Captain Vilardell and dismounted. "Berenguar, you old fool. Your arrival is as welcome as your friendship. You don't know how much you are needed here."

Vilardell slapped his fellow condottiere on the back, nearly knocking his cap off. "A fool maybe, for accepting a *condotta* with a papal seal, but I am not so old that I cannot knock you from your mount with a single blow."

"With a blow of your horrid breath is what you mean. Have you been cavorting with the fiend again? And what's this about demeaning a holy commission that has been blessed by none other than his holiness the pope himself? I should have you tried as a heretic and take over your company, if only so that it would be properly run."

"You are wrong on two accounts. It is the manner of your dress that is heretical, for one, and there hasn't been a German born yet who could command a company of 'bowmen better than a full-blooded Catalonian."

"You have missed your calling. Your lowborn mother should have sent you to be a jester, not a vintner's mercenary; however, my immediate concern is not your peasant manners but your condition, or rather conditions. Are you provisioned as befits a full company of the best crossbowmen in all of Christendom?"

"Truth be told, my company is well and anxious for battle. What discomfits me though is how our enemy passes with ease and impunity by ducal towns and papal cities. I pray this is not the norm on the lands subject to your rule."

Prospero's face lost its exuberance. Taking the Catalonian by the arm, he began to speak with gravity. "You have always been a watchful soldier, so I shall not insult you with excuses and half-truths. You have indeed arrived at the very moment we need you. But this is no place for such discussions. Come, let us repair to the warm bosom of this old town now dirtied by both ducal and papal feet, where I will tell you all."

The moment he dumped his gear off in his new lodgings, Geoffrey bolted to the citadel to seek an audience with the Duke of Spoleto or the Papal Legate to the Marche about sending a messenger to Florence.

However, at the gate he was redirected to a hall on the cathedral square, where the best he could do without a formal introduction or letter vouchsafing his character was to briefly meet with the court scriveners, who politely listened to his plea and promised to inform their lordships about it at the earliest possible convenience. In answer to Geoffrey's query as to when that might be, the scriveners explained, considering that the current campaign was draining the courts of men and money, that formal inquiries on the squire's behalf needed to be made through other chambers as well, and that recent correspondence with Florence had to be reviewed for references to this matter, it was impossible to say with any degree of certainty. In the meantime, unless the appeal were to be withdrawn, or there were to be an unforeseen change in circumstance, or if Captain Vilardell were to say, otherwise, the *pavesaro* Geoffrey Hotspur must remain with the company in which he is traveling. Before being dismissed with a wave of the hand, the head scrivener handed Geoffrey a scrap of paper embossed with the seal of the Papal Legate to the Marche to validate the meeting.

"You look like how I feel," Jean said the moment Geoffrey entered the room, "and that means I should assume that you did not get what you wanted."

Geoffrey collapsed on a small folding stool and buried his head in his hands. Then, after a moment's pause, looked up at the chandler and asked, "What are you doing here?"

"The master victualler discharged me from my duties this morning. They no longer need me, but that doesn't mean I'm a free man, of course. I am still a ward of the company, just like you, but now I have to beg for my food." Jean smiled grimly at his own luckless fate, but inside he was as angry as Geoffrey at losing his place. He had already looked for the Gamesmaster's partner in Spoleto, but it turned out that the fool had wagered on Malatesta Malatesta taking the city before the spring, and so had fled when it did not come to pass. "So, I'm staying with you. I brought some linen that I liberated from old Antonio, so your crossbowman was appeased."

"Were I a knight, I would be free to ride this instant and *you* could take my place next to the crossbowman," Geoffrey said bitterly.

"Had you some means, you could do the same. Without silver, though, the papal legate's seal is but a key without a lock," Jean retorted. "Now, calm yourself. At least *you* still have a rank in this company."

Geoffrey closed his eyes, took a deep breath and slowly exhaled. "It shows great camaraderie of you to want to accompany me, but haven't you business of your own? There must be a guild of chandlers in this city that would give charity to one of their own. Please, for the love of all that is sacred, don't let my pathetic condition be an obstacle to you making your way."

Jean had to think quickly, or the squire might finally be onto his scheming. "Yes, well, chandlers throughout Christendom are a prickly bunch," he stalled. "Candle-making is an arcane craft. I cannot simply walk into the guildhall and expect them to welcome me with open arms. I have nothing to prove my profession."

Geoffrey rolled his chin on the pommel of his *couteau* and stared at the wall. Then he stopped and jumped up. "We should see Captain Vilardell!"

"What? Why?"

"I have to show him the papal legate's seal. He will be embarrassed when, after asking his holiness to send a messenger to Florence, he learns that his grace already knows that I approached him earlier with the same request."

Jean raised his eyebrows, but he could find nothing to say.

"*And*, I could ask the captain to vouchsafe you to the guild of chandlers."

Geoffrey was out the door before Jean could answer. He followed at a quick pace, and they soon found themselves standing before Captain

Vilardell, the company treasurer and the company scrivener. The company's leading men were seated at a large table strewn with paper, parchment, seals, weights and measures, small bags sagging with coins, notched sticks, and a chequered cloth.

"Geoffrey, Jean, thank you for coming," Berenguar began. He motioned for them to approach the table.

Geoffrey and Jean looked at each other.

"Your lordship," Geoffrey began, "I have just returned from the hall of His Grace the Papal Legate to the Marche, where ..."

"Yes, yes, I am sure it is beautiful and I will visit when time allows, but I am a busy man, so I shall get straight to it. I need you two to form a lance. Not a crossbow lance, for heaven knows I wouldn't let you near such a fine instrument, but a regular men-at-arms lance."

"No, you don't understand, Captain," Jean said.

"Tut, tut, I don't want to hear it. My company needs a guard and Captain-General Prospero says that he cannot spare any men, so I am obliged to recruit any old rubbish I can find."

"You are sending a messenger to Florence to verify my claim that I am a man of Gaunt, are you not?" Geoffrey asked.

"Of course, of course, all in good time. But now I ..."

"And you will take action to ensure the restitution for the spoliation of the chapel in San Berdnardino. It must be made know that this Tarlati conducts war poorly."

"Yes, now keep quiet!" Vilardell slapped his hand on the table, causing his goblet to tremble. "As I was saying, I am commissioning you, Master Squire, to form a lance and enroll it in my company, which means that I formally discharge you from the one you are in now."

"What? You mean a pike?" Geoffrey's heart began to sink.

"Yes, of course that's what I mean. You're English, after all, are you not? The English are quite good with the pike, from what I hear. Or have you developed a fondness for the *pavese*?"

Geoffrey went silent. The rank of pikeman was certainly higher than that of *pavesaro*, but it was still well below that of squire. At least he was still someone's man, so he had a place, but now he had no idea when he might be returned to Florence. Geoffrey caught himself nodding slowly.

"Then we are settled. It was Sergeant Alfonso's idea, I must admit, and a fine one. We are an excellent company, so you should be safe."

Jean and Alfonso exchanged looks.

"So, what will I do?" Jean asked.

"Why, you will help Master Hotspur hold that damned pike!"

CHAPTER 8

Spoleto

"Is his lordship the duke hunting again?" Corrado Prospero asked. He was clad in black again and had his lean frame bent so far over the table of the war council that he looked like an angle iron.

Andrea Tomacelli smiled thinly and chuckled. He was in an exceptionally good mood. "He will be here shortly. He is inspecting the horses."

"Thank the Lord that Vilardell has arrived. Good man. I invited him to share counsel, but he decided to ensure that his men are well fed and in good cheer. He promised to attend this afternoon, though, and give an account of the Breton company he encountered."

"We march at first light regardless. Narni must be relieved and we can sweep aside any Bretons we might encounter along the way. We have the strength." Andrea pointed to the most recent enrolment list of the papal host: 400 mounted knights and men-at-arms of the heavy sort, most belonging to Captain Prospero's company and the remainder to the Duke of Spoleto, 175 Catalonian crossbow lances, 300 men-at-arms on foot, also heavy, under the command of several petty condottieri, and two dozen lances of local militia.

"It is a shame none of your men could be sent," Prospero said, "yet we are about as strong as need be at this moment."

"Once my men have finished with the Malatesta clan in the Marche, then I should be able to spare some. That the young Malatesta felt obliged to send Captain Broglia to Pesaro in support bodes well for this campaign."

Prospero looked at the map of the Patrimony laid out on the table. "I only wish I knew where Brandolini was. Those captains usually campaign together, so if he is not in the Marche, then I don't know where. That troubles me."

"You are not thinking about delaying our advance, are you? Your men are still trapped in Narni. You said yourself they can only hold out for so long." The question was rhetorical; under no circumstance was he about to let even the captain-general prevent the start of this season's glory.

"No," Prospero drawled. "Vilardell met no one between the Tiber and here, and since the young Malatesta has his base at Todi, we can assume that he is still mustering. Brandolini should be with him, or at Perugia. Our scouts have given conflicting reports. He might strike south at Acquasparta; he might strike east at Spoleto, or even further north at Assisi."

"Brandolini is too far away for us to worry about now," Gianello Tomacelli declared as he swept into the room. He removed his gloves and slapped them on the table. Positioning himself between his brother and his captain-general, he began staring at the map.

"You might be right, your lordship," Prospero said as he shuffled to the side. "Nevertheless, we must be mindful of such things. His horses are just as fast as ours."

Gianello did not seem to hear. He placed his index finger on Spoleto on the map and drew a line from there to Terni. "If we can make Terni by nightfall, then we can surprise Narni with a quick advance, and then, since we have the men now, we can move on to Orte, up to Todi, Fratta Todina, Deruta …"

Prospero placed his hand on that of the duke. "If your finger were a battering ram, we would conquer the Patrimony in a day, your lordship. The map lays everything plain, but the war must be played out on the ground."

"Yes, of course, captain, but once we have Malatesta on the run, we should remain hard on his heels," Gianello explained. "I was too slow in January. Am I not right, Andrea?"

"So that he might concentrate his forces in the north?" Prospero said. He was becoming annoyed.

"We will crush him in a single pass of arms then!"

Andrea put his hand on his brother's shoulder. "Let us first secure the south of the Patrimony. Perhaps Malatesta will come to us. How are the horses?" Andrea asked. "They will be the key to everything." The truth was that Andrea had already decided on the strategy for all papal forces: finish pacifying the Marche and secure southern Umbria; encourage condottieri to defect from Clement; reintroduce the Egidian Constitutions; slowly push north towards Perugia. What the papal legate was keeping from Captain Prospero and his brother was that Giovanni Tarlati had already been neutralized by Florence with the help of 50,000 silver florins. Andrea knew of Prospero's dislike for the Arrentine, so he thought that it would serve everybody's interests to keep his negotiations a secret. Of course, he could not take Tarlati's honesty for granted, hence the reason to send an impressive force. Speed and stealth were of the essence.

"For the moment, let us concern ourselves with the march on Narni first," Prospero said plainly.

Gianello was mollified. He went to the sideboard and poured himself a goblet of wine.

"We need to keep things tight if we're to make Narni quickly and in good order," Prospero stated. "Because we are well blessed in horses, I propose a single column with mounted squadrons placed at regular intervals throughout. That should keep the *pedites* moving and temper the strength of the column. Also, I suggest that we not risk weakening ourselves by approaching the city divided. The road is good and the distance is short enough that our pace should not slow."

"Should we not use our mounted knights to screen the column, at least on our right flank, should an ambush await us? You said yourself that we are more or less in the dark about the movements of Malatesta," Gianello suggested.

"With respect," Prospero began, "I would not recommend such a course. Our horsemen, in my opinion, are too heavily armored to serve as a proper screen and I would hesitate to risk the horses on such uneven ground. Had we some quicker mounts, like Illyrian stradiots, then your suggestion would be well spoken; however, as we do not, we should weigh our risks accordingly. Also, I want the horses as fresh as possible when we arrive at Narni, should we have to tilt with Captain Tarlati immediately. Are you in agreement?" He looked at the papal legate.

Andrea nodded. He was encouraged by the captain-general's enthusiasm for the advance. He was worried that the careful Prospero would deploy an array of excuses to avoid campaigning, advising maneuver to engagement, negotiations to demands.

"Where shall we put the militia?" Andrea asked. "They can't be left alone, or they might bolt at the first skirmish."

Prospero nodded respectfully. "You bring up a good point. I'll hold them in front of my men, somewhere in the middle of the column. That should keep them quiet and out of trouble."

The final discussion concerned the order of departure. The papal legate proposed, and his brother agreed, that they needed to show the lords, citizens and commoners, who would be watching the army trail through Spoleto's main gate, an unmistakable chain of command to demonstrate who ruled the Patrimony.

"This host will be bearing the crossed keys of St. Peter, of course," Andrea explained, "so we are led by our Lord, ruler of all that is seen and unseen. However, since all of the *condotti* were signed with my brother, and we are going forth from the seat of his *dominium*, it would be most suitable in all respects if Gianello were to ride at the head of the column, with his ranking knights flanking him."

"And who will follow him?" Captain Prospero asked abruptly.

"You did not let me finish my proposal, captain," Andrea answered. "It would do well for the dignity of this host that the duke be followed closely by its captain-general and the leading agent of the crossed keys. The lesser captains should ride out in order of the value of their *condotti*. Above all, though, we must show that we are true to our purpose."

Prospero gave his assent with a curt nod.

It was called *hastiludia*. Jean has seen it and Geoffrey had even done a bit of it, but neither was well adept at coordinated maneuvering with a pike. On a long strip of flat land that bordered the city they had spent much of the day taking turns tripping each other, and when they finally did get their footwork sorted, they had such trouble holding the pike steady that the moment they began to advance in good order they found themselves drifting to one side and unable to correct. All that prevented total failure or impalement was Captain Vilardell having seen fit to arm them with the shorter English pike, arguing that because there was only the two of them, Geoffrey and Jean formed a *barbuta* rather than a full French or Italian lance, which were complimented with as many as five men and a much longer weapon.

"How many times must I tell you? Your main duty is to keep the hilt steady," Geoffrey explained in an exasperated tone. "That will support me in my effort to hold the point up at the proper angle. If you fail in your simple task, the shaft will waver and the point will get grounded. Do you want to be hacked down like a dog? We cannot join formation practice if you keep making a mess of this, and I do not wish to embarrass myself in front of a group of Italian peasants."

The peasants in question were the locally recruited militia Vilardell wanted to make his guard. With spring planting over, it was common for unengaged villeins of military age to take up such work, if their lords did not disapprove, and on this spring enough such men had arrived in Spoleto to be able to form nearly two dozen complete lances to serve under the Catalonian's banner. Geoffrey's lance was the twenty-fourth.

"Do I really have to remind you that I am a chandler and not a man-at-arms of any rank?" Jean retorted. He was tired and bathed in sweat from the morning's toil of marching up and down the narrow field in notional unison with an English squire who was clearly not interested in working with him. Had the squire been an ox, he would have had no trouble directing him along a straight furrow and back again. Jean had spent enough time tilling the land of his uncles and cousins to know how to make beast and plough agree.

"The pike is not too heavy for you, is it?" Geoffrey chided. "How will I run Giovanni Tarlati through if my pike misses him by a mile?"

"No, of course it isn't. You're advancing too fast and throwing me off balance. Remember that our little company has been detailed to defend men, not attack them. And besides, my grip keeps slipping. I have to get that sorted or my flesh will be flayed off." The truth was that Jean's uneven shoulders were making it difficult to find the necessary leverage, not to mention the squire's great height.

Jean released the hilt, letting the pike drag Geoffrey to the ground. Although a good deal shorter than the French pike and heavier than its Italian brother, the English pike still possessed enough concentrated weight to make it a formidable, if inelegant, weapon.

"Are you sure that this stick of wood is not too heavy for *you*, Master Hotspur?" Jean laughed as he watched Geoffrey untangle himself from the pike. "Although, truth be told, I have seen as many as four men handle this horror, so with just the two of us I don't think we're performing all

OF FAITH AND FIDELITY

that badly."

Geoffrey winced as he raised himself to sitting position and grabbed his left side. "This bloody hoqueton the Catalonians gave me must be some fiendish Saracen device. I think it has bored through my pourpoint and bit my flesh. It's pinching something fierce for sure. Here, master chandler, make yourself useful and help me get it off."

Jean held fast to the collar of the hoqueton while Geoffrey hastily worked apart the clasps, laces and other arming points. When he had finally freed himself from the hard, leather coat, Geoffrey examined his pourpoint and the tunic he wore underneath.

"I don't see a hole," Jean said, turning the piece of armor around in his hands. "Are you certain that's the place?"

"Well, this is where it hurts, and I don't think it requires the deductive skills of a Parisian theologian to find the damage. And look. This area is worn the worst. Pass me that damned hoqueton." Geoffrey closely inspected the inside of his armor, fingering the sections of boiled leather, pulling the brass links that held them together and scratching the few iron plates that still protected the leather. "Ah ha!" he cried. "Look here! One of the hooks has broken and is sticking out, or rather in, like a bloody nail."

"Then it's off to the armorers for us, I suppose," Jean said, hoping to end the day's training.

"I think it might be off to Captain Vilardell or the duke's quartermaster to procure a proper harness," Geoffrey said. "I'm done with this peasant's dress. They might mock me with this pike and refuse me passage to fulfill my duty to my king, but I shall no longer look the part of a common tiller of the soil. Here, you take it." Geoffrey threw the armored jacket at Jean's feet.

"And that brings me to another problem with our lance," Jean said, picking up Geoffrey's hoqueton. "It pains me to say it, but the other pikemen might mock you for *not* wearing something more common. They look to be about a half dozen years older than you, and, well, you do look a bit green for this. Those fancy boots of yours are far too long in the toe for close-quarters work. You wonder why we were tripping all over the place? Well, there's your answer!"

Geoffrey looked down at his buskins and then back at Jean. "You don't expect me to wear clogs, do you?" he retorted. "That would not do."

Jean picked up the pike and began to wrap its steel tip in a protective oiled cloth. "It might unclog your footwork if you did. However, in all truth what you need is something with a squared toe, like what *my* sad old boots have, or a set of sabetons." Jean kicked out his right foot to show Geoffrey his small black leather boot, even twisting it around a bit for show.

Geoffrey wrinkled his nose and turned away. "I certainly will not have my buskins altered," he announced.

"Well, we should deal with essentials first. Let us start with an armorer. I will need some thick leather gloves and patches for my surcoat if I am to continue to anchor our *barbuta*. I still have a sliver of silver on me and I'm sure the name of the St. George's Company of Crossbowmen will do well to secure you a small loan for at least a short hauberk."

Luck was not on their side. As in Avignon, no one, not even the poorest blacksmith, would consider loaning or lending Geoffrey so much as a studded belt. A poor lance in the company of foreign crossbowmen merited little respect, and each time they argued, they were told to either bring more silver or the captain himself to stand surety.

While Jean went to see Captain Vilardell, Geoffrey stormed back to their lodgings. He built himself up to such a white-hot fury along the way that he could hardly see straight, and the moment he was inside he kicked aside a stool and threw himself on his pallet. Why did he ever leave Avignon? No doubt his fellow squires were wreaking havoc in halls and giving hell to the duke's enemies on the *chevauchée*. And then there was Roger, his friend. He would have recovered by now and would be on campaign, or even pledged to a knight. Good for Master Swynford! They would soon be together bullying players at the Blue Boar once again, he reckoned. And concerning his own fate, Geoffrey was sure that the Hawkwood Commission would be asked about him. Ah, those wretched, rusty old knights! What would they be saying? That he failed to attend the departure from Avignon? That he drowned at sea? That he remained in Florence in the service of some money-grubbing banker? No, that was going too far. They were fair and honest men; otherwise the king would not have selected them. Regardless, he would not come out in a good light. The duke would see his failure as proof that he was unworthy to serve him. And now, according to Jean, he was far closer to the holy city Assisi than he was to Florence.

For several hours Geoffrey ruminated over these dismal thoughts, but just as his head was beginning to swim he was struck by an epiphany. He bolted upright. Spoleto, the Catalonian captain's *condotta*, the battle at sea, it all came together. After a month of failure, the Lord was not abandoning his poor squire. Rather, He was giving him a choice: to continue on the path to corruption by fighting as a mercenary in a foreign band or to purify himself by striking his name from the company list and traveling as a pilgrim to the greatest shrine in the land, whither he had been now so clearly led, and there to humbly beg for forgiveness and guidance. It was no accident that Assisi was within easy reach while obstacles had been constantly thrown up on the road to Florence. This was an opportunity to start over on the path to knighthood.

Jean entered at the time the evening fires were being lit and announced, "It's ours!" He was about to reveal the details of some happy news when he was taken aback by the strange attitude of the squire. It was a look Jean had never seen before, even on that day at quayside in Corneto. "Are you well?" he asked, but his question provoked no reaction. He saw that, while

Geoffrey appeared to be relaxed, his hand was maintaining an iron grip on the *couteau* that lay at his side.

Assuming that no response was forthcoming, Jean went up to the squire with small, quiet steps and touched his injured shoulder. "How is it with you, my friend? Has the day exhausted you? I am not ashamed to admit that *hastiludia* took a lot out of me. I don't remember it ever being such hard work. Mind you, I was younger back then and practice day for the village militia was as much a holiday, if the truth be told."

On hearing the word 'friend', Geoffrey turned his head, but he was not prepared to speak, although he could hear Jean babble on about something or other. He merely patted Jean's hand. He felt calm. Even his wounds did not trouble him.

"Bloody hell, Geoffrey?! Haven't you heard a word I've said? Sleep must be overtaking you; you look so peaked. We've got it, I said. It's ours." Jean bobbed in front of Geoffrey's face to get his attention.

"You were saying something about arms? Whose arms?" Geoffrey voice croaked. His eyes slowly focused on the Frenchman.

"No, *armor*. We have, or rather we shall have, some proper armor finally. Captain Vilardell has fixed it. Or maybe I should say that *I* have fixed it through him. I had the good sense to inquire about our *condotta*, and according to one of the clauses, each lance is entitled to an advance on its full contractual pay – a small amount with a small percentage, or a larger amount with a greater percentage, set at the discretion of the condottiere. In truth, Berenguar was quite amenable to the idea of advancing us some cash. The last thing he wants is for his company to campaign in decaying harnesses. However, I should admit that because we are with a local militia and its commission was added to the *condotta* late in an appended subcontract, our pay rate is quite low. Regardless, we need to go together for the silver, since you are the head of the lance."

What Jean was holding back from the squire was that the proposed advance was only half of what they needed to secure their harnesses. The other half, Jean refused to say, he had acquired through a secondary loan from Sergeant Alfonso against the proceeds from the next *Cacho* game and a larger share of Geoffrey's debt to the Gamesmaster.

"You can keep the lot. Where *I* am going, I shall have no need of armor, not the metal kind anyway, just … spiritual armor."

Jean drew his head back and stared at Geoffrey as though he was touched in the head "If you truly feel the need to display your faith then you can sew a cross on your surcoat, as big as you like."

"I am more inclined to follow the Cross than to lead with it. I have had a change of heart, or rather my heart has altered my intentions. What you said about this advance merely confirms it. Oh, cursed coin! All these debts are nothing but a millstone around my neck." Geoffrey looked hard at Jean. "They are a warning, these debts, don't you see? Each coin is a serpent stalking me. Every pile of silver I touch is poisoned with evil. Ignoring my debts of silver has led me to commit the sin of pride, I now realize. Instead, I should have simply avoided them, avoided them completely and run the other way. This *advance* of yours is yet another temptation that will ruin me. I will not touch it!"

Jean was much troubled by these words. It was clear that the Englishman was fast slipping beneath the waters of despair and would soon drown if Jean did not drag him up. But where was he planning to go if he refused to join the papal host? "You're not going on crusade, are you?" Jean asked warily. "I don't recall the pope having called one, either pope. There is Spain though … Have you been talking to the Catalans? No, of course not, since you still do not share their tongue. You're a bit old to be tonsured, although anyone can be, the monasteries being so desperate these days."

Geoffrey held up his hand for Jean to stop. "Let me tell you before you wear yourself out from guessing. I shall follow the Lord to Assisi, the home of St. Francis. You said that it's not far from here."

Jean raised one eyebrow and then the other. Assisi? That was a holy city to be sure, but he could not see Geoffrey achieving anything there. "What makes you think the Lord is leading you to Assisi, Geoff?" Jean asked, genuinely incredulous but being careful not to laugh. "He has not descended to speak with you, has He? Or did this all stem from a dream, like the one Swynford told you about?"

Geoffrey listed the signs that were pointing the way to Assisi. He was clear and calm and not once did he remove his hand from the pommel of his *couteau*.

"But what about that parish chapel Tarlati's Bretons destroyed near that town … Orte?" Jean said loudly so that Geoffrey would hear without mistake. "Did you not pledge to have restitution made for its ruin? As a poor and defenceless monk I hardly think you could make that happen in a hundred years."

Geoffrey looked at Jean without scrutiny. The seed of doubt has been planted, Jean thought. Now, he had to water that seed with a little guidance; earthly guidance, to be precise.

"But what if that crime no longer has anything to do with me?" Geoffrey said. "Perhaps my pledge was born of the sin of wrath, and so is deemed invalid in the eyes of the Lord? I am greatly troubled, Jean. You would not understand." He turned his attention to his *couteau*.

"Maybe you should get a good night's sleep and we'll discuss this in the morning," Jean suggested. "Have you eaten? That could be the trouble. For once there's no shortage of excellent victuals in camp, which is another thing to be thankful for. Come, let us walk a while."

Geoffrey finally agreed after Jean insisted, although he was not hungry. Rather Geoffrey saw the walk as an opportunity to find someone who knew the pilgrim's way to Assisi.

"You know, Geoffrey, no one will grant you spurs should you go to

Assisi, or to any such place. Eventually, you will lose your place in Avignon, and that will leave you with absolutely nothing: no name, no rank, no station. How will you become a knight then?" They were following the city wall near the main gate when Jean had spoken.

"I must not ignore the signs, Jean. I might suffer in this world for my pilgrimage, but it will help pave the way to a greater glory."

"Are you certain about that?" Jean snapped. He was already tiring of the squire's piety. "Say you go to Assisi. Say you pray and chant and beg forgiveness for whatever sins you might have committed. Say you forsake your commission, or rather commissions, with Captain Vilardell, Gaunt and England, breaking your vows, not to mention the ruined chapel. Then what? The only remaining path for you would be the thorny road to the monastery, for no one would take you as a squire again, let alone a knight. And you would have to do it barefoot, which is a certainty considering how threadbare things are with you. I know you haven't the money to become a priest or the connections to become a merchant, so what purpose would it all serve? *Who* would that serve? The Lord? Well, yes, there is some glory in that, but *He* appointed you to your station for a reason and *He* gave you a swordsman's hand. Should you throw that over? I would not. Perhaps *I* could wander off to a monastery and no one would be the wiser, but I don't believe that such a fateful step is for you."

Geoffrey listened to these words while watching a small company of pikemen march together in good order. From a distance the work looked easy, for if a villein no more than a few days off the manor can manage it, so should he – and ten times better – as a trained squire. He was certain of his excellent proficiency in all the essentials of knighthood, whether it be swordplay, riding, falconry, or knowing the virtues of that illustrious station. Geoffrey closed his eyes and tried to imagine his life as a monk. He recalled his childhood in the chapter house of the Cistercians, although all he could find of that memory was the eternal echo of prayer and the bland food. He thought about the hospital, where Roger was being attended with vigilance, and the chapel funded by the chandlers, or was that his lord Gaunt's private chapel? Geoffrey could not be sure. He opened his eyes and suddenly felt very cold.

"I think I should seek some advice," Geoffrey declared.

"I think so too, and I know who you should consult."

"A priest?"

Jean made a sour face. Considering the squire's love of chapels, a priest was the last advice-giver he wanted Geoffrey to see. "No, a reader."

"You don't mean Catherine, do you?"

"You remember her name. That bodes well."

It was Geoffrey's turn to wince. "She is still with us then?"

"She is indeed, and not far from here." Jean smiled.

Catherine was not quartered with the rest of the camp followers. She was reading for Captain Vilardell, and so she had seen fit and received permission to find modest though decent lodgings near his own, just off the main market square. The favor she found in the papal host's newly minted captaincy improved her standing in the town, but she was well aware that should the captains fall from grace or the tide of war turn against the supreme pontiff and his family, she would most assuredly tumble with them. Therefore, she was prudent to hold as many keys to quick exits from her situation as possible. It was for this reason that upon hearing the name Geoffrey Hotspur, with the station of squire and position of the newest lance in Captain Vilardell's company of foreign crossbowmen, that Catherine consented to see him.

"You are very fortunate to find me at home this evening ..." Catherine was about to call Geoffrey and Jean 'gentlemen' but held back. She met them in a dark blue taffeta gown lined with narrow strips of silver brocade. Her headdress was the same as at Viterbo. "How shall I address you? I have learned that your stations have improved."

Geoffrey bristled at Catherine's suggestion that his current and very provisional station of pikeman was commensurate with his dignity. "You may still call me squire," he declared, his pride suddenly aroused. "I yet retain the honors granted before I was so ruthlessly cast upon this land."

"Are you enrolled in Berenguar Vilardell's company as a squire? Is the word 'squire' next to your name on the list of notable soldiers appended to the good captain's *condotta*? You and the Frenchman here, from what I understand, have joined a small company of lances. Is that not true?" Catherine said.

Geoffrey found offense in the insolent tone of the astrologer, but what kept him from issuing a rebuttal was that it would be indecorous and what she spoke was sadly true.

Seeing that the Englishman's bellicosity and the astrologer's haughtiness could easily lead to an abrupt termination of their audience, Jean decided to join the verbal sparring as umpire. "You could call him 'master'. The Duke of Lancaster would not accept just anybody at his court."

"If it is only you who is vouching for his character, master chandler," Catherine said, turning to Jean, "then I have no option at all. I, therefore, must call you 'pikeman Hotspur', although if your character merits such rapid advancement as you think it does, then no doubt I shall soon be calling you 'sergeant'."

Jean winced. He had learned a long time ago that brooding resentment led to anger, anger to violence, and violence to a quick death or expulsion, especially in his business. Therefore, as he saw that both Geoffrey and Catherine had strong currents of the choleric humor running through their veins, he decided to correct this imbalance by showing resignation and humility. Of course, he had to be careful not to make mince of his mummery, since this woman had a wary eye and some advantage over them by virtue of her being so close to the captain.

"'Tis true, of course, that we are a humble lance in the company of Captain Vilardell and that young Master Hotspur is a squire only in France and England by official reckoning, however …" Jean took a deep breath before continuing. "However, we come to you more as supplicants than as soldiers, for we have a request that is well suited to making use of your profession, so I suggest that in the commodious spirit of that which I have just stated, and indeed continue to state, we agree to leave aside the courtesy of rank and station and instead simply address one another by our Christian names, or even not at all, which I think would be better in all regards. What say you?" Jean looked at both Catherine and Geoffrey, who had returned to looking sulky.

Catherine reacted to Jean's rhetorical shift to southern court French with a thin smile that in the dimness of the hall neither man could see. She returned the compliment. "You do not think that the informality implicit in your proposal will not sour our relations? Well, perhaps that is of no matter, for in view of the state in which you approach me," Catherine waved a hand at Geoffrey's dirty pourpoint and Jean's torn surcoat, "I can believe your tale of humility and distress. Therefore, in the spirit of Christian charity and on account of the late evening, which shades you from the prying eyes of my neighbors, I will condescend to hear the jangle of your tale and the jingle of your cash." Catherine folded her arms and retired to a large chair in the far corner of the hall. Her maid, who was standing as witness to this exchange, could not prevent a smile from bending her lips, which she quickly covered with the tail of her shawl. Although she could not understand the French they were speaking, there was no mistaking her mistress's sarcastic tone.

Jean nudged Geoffrey.

"My fellow pikeman is right," Geoffrey began with quiet modesty. During the exchange between Jean and Catherine his anger had melted into sadness, and this sadness tempered his anger, which was more in keeping with the feeling of piety that had recently settled upon him. The astrologer possessed a sharp wit and it had pierced him, and he was glad. "We come to beg a service of you, and it is a service to the soul. Will you consider our request?"

"I agree," Catherine said. "And because you too are enrolled in our respected company of crossbowmen, I shall take but a penny in white money from each of you, so to make this an honest exchange. Hang on to your *grossi*, good soldiers, for prices are high in Spoleto. This is his holiness the pope's patrimony, after all." The small joke relieved some of the tension. Jean sighed and nodded. Geoffrey bowed his head. "Now, come."

Jean figured that the best way to solicit the astrologer's assistance in keeping Geoffrey away from Assisi was to be perfectly candid, since a stark presentation of the foolishness of his convictions might shake Geoffrey into abandoning them. "Hotspur here wants to break his bond with Captain Vilardell and go on pilgrimage," he said. "He wants to retire our lance because he has seen *signs* that it is God's will, may it please the Lord. I have suggested that he be not so hasty in drawing extreme conclusions from such shifts in nature, since he is hardly qualified to understand let alone read them properly, if any signs were indeed revealed to him. We would like you to judge."

Catherine listened in respectful silence. This was a common enough request and normally required little effort on her part to satisfy. For her, the trouble was never in reading the signs once they were laid before her, but in getting her client to dislodge them from his or her memory as truly as possible in the first place. People could be so hopelessly vague. Catherine turned to Geoffrey. "I will not formally read for you, as I am certain that it is not warranted and it might risk you having to pay an additional fee. I see in this the need only for skilful observation. Now, describe to me in the plainest manner possible these 'signs' you say, or rather your friend says, were revealed to you."

Geoffrey was now nervous and unsure. He was about to reach for the comfort of his *couteau* when he remembered that he had left it in his lodgings. For comfort, then, he directed his thoughts towards Assisi, where he would need neither sword nor pike, or any device other than a simple wooden cross to represent his new station. Geoffrey wanted to be resolute in his exposition if only to prove Jean wrong in his doubting him, but recalling the sin of pride, with bowed head he instead concentrated on giving a simple recitation of events.

"Money is tainted," he began. "Coins are cursed. This is what I have seen." The moment the words seeped through his mouth Geoffrey realized how childish he sounded. His words were trite and he hated himself for it. He looked up and saw that Jean and Catherine were in rapt attention. This was more difficult than he had thought, and he suddenly wished Roger was here to help him. But he wasn't, so a different path had to be found. The woman wants a 'plain' report, Geoffrey recalled. Very well then. He knew in his heart that he had been shown signs, so they were 'plain' to him, but the woman had to be made to see them as well. Jean was usually with him when they appeared. Perhaps he could ask the Frenchman to relate what he had seen, even as a doubter, but Geoffrey quickly realized that the Frenchman could not possibly attest to their veracity because the signs were not meant for him. And besides, how could Jean explain that the Lord was revealing to him, an English squire brought up in the halls of Gaunt, a path that would lead him to salvation, or redemption, or grace, or perhaps even to knighthood, when the Frenchman was just a chandler? He took another deep breath and started again. "Every time I touch money, evil strikes. The more money involved, the greater the evil." Geoffrey did not like these words. He did not want to say 'evil' because the Lord does no evil. He wanted to describe the complications, the losses, the troubles that had beset him in relation to the acquisition and need for money. He sighed. "You do not follow me, and I don't blame you."

Catherine leaned forward. "Don't try to relate the nature or attempt to explain the possible meanings of these signs," she advised. "Think of a single incident and lay it out to me as you beheld it then. Recite for me names, colors, sums, anything that might help me see it for myself. Look at that silver plate on the table in front of you. Describe for me a sign as you would describe that plate."

Geoffrey listened intently and his mind began to clear. What first came to him was the ruined chapel near Orte. He described the spoliation and how important it was for him to get restitution. He then mentioned *naipes*, how colorful the cards were, how much silver had flowed through his hands. There was the battle with the corsairs, the uncertainty about his position, and his debt to the Gamesmaster. At the end of his confession Geoffrey slumped in his seat and closed his eyes.

Catherine stared hard at Geoffrey and after a lengthy silence asked, "Do you wager very much, master squire?"

Jean shot her a glance, although he could not be sure if she saw it. This was the one place he dreaded she would go. She might convince Geoffrey to swear off gambling, reconcile or forfeit his debts, or cause him to suspect Jean and Sergeant Alfonso. He readied himself to interrupt her.

"I wager from time to time," Geoffrey answered in a surprisingly indignant tone. Jean was expecting contrition. "I make honest wagers and no one has cause to doubt me."

"You have lost money wagering," Catherine stated.

"And I have won some. It is not thievery or knavery as far as I can see."

"I am not disputing your honor," Catherine patiently explained. "Rather the wagers you win and those you lose are wholly unrelated to your station. Your gaming might be *honest*, but that is irrelevant. These 'money signs', if I may call them that, suggest to me that all the silver you need to fund your ambition in the court of Gaunt must be earned by the sword, or the pike, as it is now for you. That can sanctify your likely knighthood. The same goes for the ruined chapel. A roll of the dice might not be the most appropriate way to collect the money needed for this most noble rite."

Geoffrey pondered Catherine's 'observations' before answering, then with gravity said, "Wagering is not a sin, nor is it against the law, at least in Avignon and most assuredly not here in Italy."

"I did not say it was a sin. I merely said that none of the gains and losses you incur while wagering are the result of Christian labor. Our Lord and savior Jesus Christ might not be telling you that money is evil; he might just be hinting for you to find a better way to earn it. Unless you have seen the sign of the Cross somewhere between Avignon and Spoleto, or a saint has appeared before you, I do not think that these signs are adding up to a particularly divine message." Catherine leaned back in her chair. She was satisfied with her 'speech'. It was the truth, if only a simple truth, unless she wanted to probe deeper, undertake a reading or perform some other divining rite, but she was content for none of these methods to be necessary.

"*I* am thoroughly convinced," Jean said. The astrologer had done her duty by him, and so he wanted to get the squire away from her as soon as possible. "I would never have been able to read those signs so well alone."

Geoffrey ignored Jean. He was listening again to Catherine's words in his head, ensuring that they all followed as they should. "So, should I go to Assisi?" he said timidly after a short silence.

"You may go where you wish," Catherine answered. "What would you do in Assisi, aside from paying respect to the most reverend of saints, of course?"

"I might find the solution to this riddle. I thought I was being led there."

"I cannot tell you that. You heard my explanation, and I do not give it lightly. The only other useful words I can offer are if you want to be a knight, duty is as important as piety, prowess is as important as humility. You must obey the Lord's will, certainly, but that I do not see at issue. However, your duty here in Spoleto, to your captain, is absolutely clear."

Jean sensed that Geoffrey was wavering and that the astrologer's penny's worth of advice would not stay with him. What could he add to finally convince the confused squire that his march to salvation demanded that he remain with those who fought rather than with those who prayed? What other signs might they have seen or other duties they might have pledged that would keep Geoffrey away from Assisi? He had already spoken a great deal about money and wagering, about debts and even about their disaster as sea. Then it struck him when he looked at the glass goblet Geoffrey had clasped in both hands.

"That reminds me, Catherine," Jean began almost offhandedly. "What news have you about Narni? Does Captain Tarlati still hold fast to the siege, or has he raised it, knowing that the hounds of the true pontiff in Rome are about to be let loose upon him? I find that in my idleness I am curious about such things. I must find a way home, after all."

As Catherine related the latest rumors, all of which Jean had already heard, Geoffrey slowly raised his head. Jean looked for a sign of resolution on the squire's face and found it in the tightening of his lips.

"Yes, yes, yes," Geoffrey said quietly to himself. "I have my commissions." He shook his head a few times and stood up.

Catherine also rose from her seat and called for her maid.

Jean remained seated. He was not sure if he had returned the bug of enthusiasm for righting the wrong of the ruined chapel to Geoffrey's ear, but at least he seemed to be thinking about it. Well, he would just have to wait and see where the *naipes* fall regarding Assisi, although he was not through dispelling the squire's flush of sanctimony. Feeling the sharp elbow of the maid in his shoulder as she passed, Jean took the hint and stood up.

"I am grateful to you, Mistress Astrologer," Geoffrey finally said. He finished his wine in a single draught and made for the door.

Catherine nodded. Reading signs of the sort the squire had described was a dicey proposition and open to wide-ranging interpretations, and so she thought it would be best for all concerned that the soldiers leave and allow themselves time to decide whether she had read truly or falsely. There would not be another consultation. After glancing up and down the street, she closed the door behind them.

"We had better get to the company treasurer to collect our advance, or *prestanza*, as it is called here," Jean said to keep the squire distracted. "Captain Vilardell has installed his factors near the citadel, which is only a few streets over. I imagine we'll pass some taverns along the way that might be worth inspecting, if only to make ourselves indispensable to the Catalonians for our knowledge of Spoleto's best ale and most hospitable hosts."

Geoffrey nodded his approval. After the strange and exotic week that had just passed, he welcomed the prospect of doing something that reminded him of his life in Avignon. A passing carter brushed his pourpoint with a trio of wine casks. It was a good sign.

"Captain Vilardell is out," the company treasurer stated bluntly. He was seated at a massive table shared by the treasurers, factors and functionaries of other condottiere companies.

"That much is evident," Jean said, "but the captain – *our* captain – authorized the distribution of a *prestanza* to one of his pike lances and we have come to collect it."

The treasurer made an ugly noise akin to a wheeze, but worse, and flipped through some ledgers. "Nothing here from Captain Vilardell," he said in a monotone voice. "Are you carrying his seal?"

"No," Jean said slowly. "But our names should be in one of your books, and he told us that the money would be given out by the company treasurer. We are Geoffrey Hotspur, squire of the Duke of Lancaster, and Jean Lagoustine ... um ... of Avignon; you are the company treasurer. *Ergo*, you must give us the money."

"Is the captain's mark in the books? Can you show me his seal, or a note written in his hand to the effect of what you claim?" The treasurer held opened one of the company's account books in a provocative manner.

Jean wiped his face with his hand. He was feeling a little flushed. "I'll wager that your precious books say you never gave us a *prestanza* on our pay, and that Captain Vilardell's *condotta* contains our names and ranks. That should satisfy you."

"It will not satisfy me," the treasurer calmly explained. "I do not deny that what you say might be true. In fact, it is true because your names, ranks and complete pay schedule are right here, without error. However, I am also aware that nowhere in of these books or in my head is there a word about handing out a *prestanza*. Now, good day, soldier. There is a war on, in case you haven't noticed, for which I have to prepare. These accounts don't do themselves, you know."

Geoffrey stepped forward and clamped his hands to the edge of the table. He was tired from the day's events and all the more impatient because of it. "Where is Captain Vilardell?" he resolutely but politely asked in such a loud voice that it drew the attention of everyone in the hall. "I know that he is not here, so you need not repeat it. Now, hand over the silver, or I will bring the captain back here so he might shake it out of you. Why should this be so difficult? It's only money, for the love of Christ!"

The treasurer held fast to his phlegmatic disposition. His guiding principle in such eventualities was to recite what he considered to be the infallible logic of company procedure, come what may.

"Master pikeman, should I hear the captain's word on this matter, then I will consider it my duty to oblige your request. Until then, the accounts are closed to you." The treasurer pointed his quill at the door. "Now, I believe our business is at an end. Please escort yourselves back to your lodgings before I have some men, larger and better armed than you …" The treasurer stopped short when he saw a tall, black clad figure enter the hall.

"Give the squire and his friend here their silver," Captain Prospero ordered, and to underscore his authority, he made his address in Catalan. "It is a pittance and you know it. I will make my mark on their behalf, if need be. Best keep the men's spirits up, after all that's happened."

Without another word the treasurer complied, but he also collected witnesses to verify that another condottiere had usurped Captain Vilardell's authority in the disbursement of funds, should the captain question the entry he was now making in a ledger. After dumping a small pile of blackened silver coins on the table, he invited the lancers make their mark where he indicated.

Jean signed with flourish and in script, which brought a scowl to the treasurer's face. Geoffrey printed his name and rank in stubby block letters.

"Your accent is strange," Captain Prospero said to Geoffrey in a brusque Italian as Jean counted and recounted their money before sliding the lot into his belt-purse. "Good heavens, you're tall! Where are you from, soldier?" Side by side, Geoffrey was half a head taller than the German.

Geoffrey recognized Prospero as the rider who had met and embraced Captain Vilardell on the approach to Spoleto. As in Catherine the astrologer's house, Geoffrey repeated his name, station and rank in the court of Sir John of Gaunt.

The captain raised his eyebrows in surprise. "So, you're the English squire Captain Vilardell was telling me about." Prospero switched to French to accommodate Geoffrey's linguistic restrictions. "He informs me that you have a commission with King Richard and that you must urgently make for Florence. Is this true, or is the old captain spinning me another one of his Catalonian yarns?"

"This is true, my lord. Corsairs waylaid our vessel, diverting my fate from its natural course. I am now far from where I ought to be, though now in the service of a noble and most respected knight, I mean captain." Geoffrey bowed.

"There is no need to address me as 'my lord', as much as I would like you to. I am not your lord, for one thing, and for another I am not a knight, count or duke."

"Then how shall I address you, as I am not familiar with either your name or rank?"

Prospero laughed. "Why, I am the captain-general of this fair host," he said. "And what part are you scripted to play in it, pray? I can see that you're not one of my junior captains, for otherwise you would not be here, begging for money from one of these loathsome bean-counters."

Geoffrey felt a twinge of shame upon hearing the captain's request, but he would not deny him. After briefly explaining the nature of his latest commission, he introduced Jean as the other half of his lance, ensuring that the phrase 'my lance' rang clearly in the captain-general's ears. He would take pride of place even in that lowly rank.

"And what plans have you to reach Florence?" Captain Prospero asked. "Or are your English friends planning to spend the winter there? I confess that your captain told me nothing about it."

"I am relying on the grace of our Lord to speed me to that place," Geoffrey answered, though quickly adding, "though not before I fulfill my duty to Captain Vilardell, the Duke of Spoleto and his holiness the supreme pontiff."

"Then you might be waiting a long time, master squire, as the Lord and his mighty choirs of angels avoid that irreverent city like the plague. You would do far better to rely on the size of your purse than the strength of your heart to get you to Florence."

The words 'purse', 'plague' and 'heart' blazed as signs, nearly blinding Geoffrey, but he could not let himself worry about them now. Catherine had warned him off placing too much weight on such uncertain things.

As at the astrologer's house, Jean tried to steer the conversation towards clearer waters. "Our purse is quite small for the moment. However, we are expecting great riches, here and in Florence. Pray tell me, captain, when are we to leave this fine city and enter the field? Is it true that soldiers in Italy receive their wages at the conclusion of a campaign, or are they obliged to await the expiry of their captain's *condotta*? Perhaps the successful conclusion of a siege is enough of an incentive to release promised sums. I would not be so bold as to ask you if these heathen money-changers were not like blocks of stone when it comes to answering simple and honest questions."

"I cannot get you more than your *prestanza*," the captain explained. "Soldiers are paid at the end of the month or upon the expiry of a *condotta*, but I shouldn't worry about that just yet, since I promise that you will have other concerns quite soon. Beg Captain Vilardell, if you wish to see a wider stream of silver, but I dare say his response will be as mine, although you can expect him to use more words."

Jean nodded. He had been expecting such an answer, which meant that the campaign would start any day now. He was not looking forward to getting trapped in it. However, he could not avoid considering the possibility that the swift conclusion of a campaign, whether favorable or not, might loosen their bond to the Catalonian captain and give them enough money to leave Umbria, if all else failed.

"I only pray that Tarlati gets nothing when Clement learns of his crimes," Geoffrey said to Jean with a sneer.

"Tarlati?" Prospero asked. "And what crimes might these be, young squire?"

Geoffrey gave an animated account of the Breton ruin of San Bernardino and that a certain Giovanni Tarlati, a condottiere in the pay of Clement, had ordered it. "He must atone for this," Geoffrey concluded. "It was consecrated ground, for the love of Saint Mary!"

Prospero took off his cap and ran a hand through his hair. "Did you see him?" he said gravely.

"No, but he was known. I expect you will see him, your lordship, kneeling before you in submission after you defeat the host of Clement." Geoffrey smiled and held up a fist.

"He *is* known. You must excuse me now," Prospero said. "I have my own business to conduct here. Master squire, I want to hear about the court of your lord. It interests me greatly. I shall call you when time permits, but for now I suggest you get your kit together and muster with your company. We are to make for Narni in the morning!"

CHAPTER 9

"What do you think would be a proper ransom for capturing Tarlati?" Geoffrey asked Jean as they mustered with the other pikemen on a field outside the main gate. He was thinking about the ruined church and what might be in store for the people of Narni should their city be taken. "You have better knowledge about Italy than me, so perhaps you can suggest a figure?"

Jean gave his fellow pikeman a look of impatience mixed with incredulity. The last thing on Jean's mind was anything having to do with what might happen *after* a battle, including the disposal of prisoners. "How would I know even a drop about such things? You mistake me for that miserable scrivener who tried to deny us our rightly silver."

"I know you are close to Catalonian's head victualler. You must have talked."

Jean sighed. He did not want to say more than he knew, and he knew more than the squire suspected, so he equivocated. "It depends on who is willing to pay his ransom, I suppose" he answered curtly.

"Yes, yes, of course rank is important, but you must have some idea about a scale of compensation. I know a little about the ransoming of English and French prisoners from the stories the old knights would spin, but we are not dealing with proper lords, it seems. Maybe these condottieri are not worth ransoming?"

"I wasn't speaking of rank, Geoffrey. From what I understand, a prisoner's station is less important than the status of he who wishes to pay to free the prisoner. Say you capture this Tarlati fellow. Who will you approach? It might be Clement in Avignon, it might be his captain-general Malatesta Malatesta, or it might be his family. It might even be the men of his company, for all I know. Perhaps no one would offer a groat for him. He is a free soldier, after all, like most of these condottieri. It's all very unsettled, and I'm just a chandler. However, should someone capture our Captain Vilardell, I am certain that the guild of vintners in Barcelona would pay handsomely for his safe return, even if he's not a proper knight."

Leaving the squire to ruminate on his words, Jean inspected his armor. Their advance had bought them just enough to avoid ridicule. Of course, Geoffrey received the best bits, including an old hauberk, but his arming harness was not complimented with protection for his neck, arms or thighs. He was able to finagle a pair of greaves from a fellow pikeman in their militia and he still had the old iron hat the master victualler had given him, so that was in order, but as far as Jean was concerned it all still left him dangerously exposed. His only comfort was that, as a support company, the militia should remain with the crossbowmen, meaning near the rear and out of harm's way.

"I understand," Geoffrey said quietly. "Still, I would like to capture him. He must be made to pay for that poor church. Even if he wasn't present at its pillage and ruin, as the head of that band he has to be responsible for the conduct of his men. Any decent knight would agree. Also, he must be already condemned for opposing his holiness the pope in Rome and the Church."

Jean thought this sort of talk dangerous to their well-being, so tried to put an end to it. "So, you would break ranks then? You would let me wield that ugly stick alone just so that you can play games of chivalry with a powerful condottiere?"

Geoffrey frowned. "Perhaps you're right. To abandon my companions would not do. However, I do not plan to play pikeman for long. An excellent man-at-arms is worth his weight in ..." Geoffrey checked himself. He did not want to arouse bad luck by giving voice to any words for money. "Well, he would be *invaluable* and I could be released from my bond to Captain Vilardell. The papal legate might even find time to read mine and Captain Vilardell's petition to get me to Florence."

Jean again cringed at the thought of being cast into a genuine battle. "Well, let us plan for the here and now. If Tarlati and his company have invested Narni, they must have the men to do so."

Geoffrey nodded and pulled off his new hauberk. It was snug around the shoulders, which might impair swordplay should he have to draw his *couteau*, and the length was not what it should be, as current fashion dictated a longer skirt. Nevertheless, he was content. "How much for me, do you think?" Geoffrey asked while examining his *couteau*.

"What?" Jean asked. "Why tempt Lady Fortuna with such questions?"

"How much would I be worth, you know, in ransom? I fancy a good five pounds."

"A good five pounds of pork maybe. Tell me, though, how do you want to be ransomed: as an English squire or a Catalonian pikeman, or perhaps as something else?" Jean quipped.

"Well, what do you think!? I don't have to explain to you the indignity of having to serve as a common soldier in a common lance. Or do I? As a chandler, *you* must consider this an elevation in station."

Jean was about to issue his rebuttal when Captain Vilardell's quartermaster arrived to issue each pikeman a red and yellow tabard of the St. George's Catalonian crossbowmen – a fustian field *or*, although it seemed more yellow than gold, *per paly gules*, or red vertical stripes, *a cinquefoil sable* in the center to signify grapes. This was certainly a step up from *pavesaro*, Geoffrey thought.

"I suppose you expect *me* to carry this thing," Jean said after he dragged their pike and himself away from the crowd of Spoletan peasants.

"We shall take turns. I know how heavy a wooden stick is for you," Geoffrey replied.

"May the devil take you and your kind, master pikeman. It does not bode well for the journey if you insult me before we've taken a single step forward, and to our deaths, no doubt." Jean ground their pike into the turf and gave it a good shake.

Geoffrey clapped the pike with the crest of his helmet to test its timbre, and was satisfied with the low hum it made. "God's bones, man, do you never stop griping! You should be glad that you're no longer with the mob of camp followers, shining armor and shoveling shit."

Jean shrugged his shoulders and silenced the pike with both hands. He would have liked to say that he preferred his place with the master victualler, since it exposed him to the inner workings of the company, including the flow of silver, but he held his tongue lest Geoffrey suspect his ruse as an artisan. He then peered into the distance to learn what was now attracting the squire's attention.

"My, my, they are colorfully arrayed," Jean said as he watched a cavalcade thread its way down from the citadel. "They might be going to a wedding, or a papal funeral."

"Do those look like war captains?" Geoffrey asked, pointing at the parade. "I don't even see a hint of harness on any of them. It could be an oriental caravan, for all that is holy. At least they're displaying their colors, though. I see the papal keys of St. Peter, the checkered banner of the Tomacelli family, and our standard."

"*Our* standard?" Jean exclaimed. "Are you planning to settle in Barcelona when this is all over? I dare say, your lord might have something to say about that, or is your intention to take over where your master failed those many years ago? I know you English like to court danger, but I never realized just how deranged your kind really is."

"I have pledged to serve Berenguar Vilardell of Barcelona," Geoffrey patiently explained. "He shall be my lord for the duration of this *condotta*, come what may, and so have you."

"Geoff. You are enrolled in his company – that is all. Be careful to whom you offer fealty. You are a paid retainer."

Geoffrey nodded, but he was not in accord with the Frenchman on this matter. His word was his bond, and his bond demanded he serve the Catalonian, even if the captain of crossbowmen was not a knight in good standing. But this was not all. He would not tell the chandler, but it was with this service that Geoffrey hoped to win advantage, for holding to his loyalty and performing his duty, others might notice, and perhaps he could return to being a squire in practice, or even be made a knight.

While the captains and their companies were excited to finally be marching against the antipope, some were wary of their fellow condottieri, especially in light of Gianello Tomacelli's disastrous winter campaign. Captain Prospero recognized this weakness in his army, and so to foster better cohesion in the papal host, he arranged for a banquet to be held in the walled city of Terni, which was the last stop before Narni. He invited a representative from each constituent unit to dine in the citadel with him and the rest of the war council and town fathers.

On the advice of both Tomacelli, who were keen to show their generosity in spirit as well as in victuals, Prospero told his company musicians to skip the introductory fanfare and simply ordered the doors to be opened to all irrespective of rank. One of the first guests he greeted was the English pikeman Geoffrey Hotspur.

"You must be accommodating yourself well to the Spoletans for them to have elected to give you this honor, master squire," Prospero said.

Geoffrey had managed to borrow a blue tunic from the son of a peasant freeholder, as he could hardly expect to attend such a banquet in his well-worn pourpoint, but he girded his waist with his own belt. He was forced to go bare-headed because all he had to cover his scalp was a bascinet helm, but Geoffrey need not have worried on that account, since all the other delegates arrived in the same predicament, leading him to suppose that the fashion currently in vogue in these parts dictated against headwear indoors. He bowed to the German captain.

"Good evening, captain-general," Geoffrey greeted in formal court French. "Yes, I do count myself fortunate. Although, if truth be told, I think that I was the compromise candidate, since I surmised that there was much debate concerning who to put forward for the honor."

"You surmised this?"

"Well, I don't understand much of their language, my lord, and before I had a chance to argue their decision with what words I do know, they pushed me out the barn and directed me towards the citadel. Therefore, I had to surmise or be left out on the street."

Prospero laughed at the unabashed nature of the squire. The English were a talkative race, but they rarely minced words. Prospero then decided that since the local notables were busy talking with the Tomacelli brothers and none of the captains were clamoring for his attention, he was free to spend more little time with Gaunt's man.

"You must be weary of us and anxious to be on your way to Florence to complete your journey, especially since our peasant militia holds but poor prospects for one such as yourself," he said. "I am sorry that you are unable to leave your company and cross into Tuscany, especially since you are attached to a royal commission. I understand better than anyone here the brilliance of majesty. It has been sorely lost in this land."

"Should I understand from your sympathy that you once served a king?" Geoffrey was hopeful that, even though the captain-general was not a proper knight, he at least moved in their circles.

Prospero saw that he had hooked the young squire on the station of nobility, which was precisely how he wanted to gain his confidence so that he might talk freely about the wealthy Duke of Lancaster. "I was once in the presence of his lordship Emperor Wenceslas," Prospero continued, "but I have never served under his banner. Nevertheless, I am still his man. Indeed, I might have been your age when I attended his court in Nuremberg. Tell me: did your king personally bestow upon you this commission to repatriate a great corpse, or did you receive the honor at Gaunt's court?"

Geoffrey latched a thumb onto his belt and worked to come up with a suitably respectable answer. He was naturally embarrassed to admit that Gaunt had attached him to the royal commission as punishment, as exile from Avignon. A pique of vanity prompted him to think that his lordship was grooming him for knighthood, but in the absence of a decent war or family connections, he had to prove to them that he was capable of fulfilling his duty, maintaining the dignity of his lord and remaining humble in the presence of his betters. Geoffrey was more than ever convinced that this, the commission, the corsairs, Umbria, were tests of his mettle. Nevertheless, he gave the captain-general a simple answer. "I have never been in the regal presence of my lord and king. It was His Lordship the Duke of Lancaster who entrusted me with this duty, although the royal commission was created by King Richard, who is now in Ireland making peace and order." Geoffrey could not help but add this news about the Irish war.

"You are close to Gaunt?" Prospero asked.

"I live in his hall," Geoffrey answered.

Prospero was not sure if the young squire was being disingenuous or just naïve. About Geoffrey Hotspur he knew only what Berenguar had told him. Englishmen were scarce in Italy these days, and so reliable knowledge of the lesser courts of France and England was getting harder to come by. Should England be actively drawn into the war for St. Peter's throne, and he was certain of that eventuality, considering the apparent piety and single-mindedness of King Richard, he would like to have some link to that distant kingdom. Commanding a papal host had its benefits, of course, but that did not mean he should not cultivate his options.

"He will be glad to hear of your service with his holiness the supreme pontiff, no doubt. Should all go well tomorrow, I will make your name known."

"Should it be the Lord's will that we prevail, I will be grateful," Geoffrey answered.

"I admit that I don't envy your task tomorrow," Prospero said, trying to sound as reassuring as possible. "Your company isn't very large for this sort of work, but I don't expect too many threats to come your way. The worst might be that you will become bored, for once word spreads that we have an entire company of Catalonian crossbowmen with us, only the most foolhardy would dare to risk assailing our support ranks. Should Lady Fortuna smile in your direction, you might be given chance to chase down a fleeing man-at-arms to take for ransom."

Geoffrey's face registered disappointment. "I would much rather force our enemy to yield eye to eye rather than eye to ass, captain. The pikemen are quite a formidable lot, I should say; otherwise Captain Vilardell would not have brought them under his command. If the truth be told, you should have us form your bottom rank on the field, and then your men will have nothing to do but water their horses and pick their noses." His false praise of the Spoletan villeins rang hollow in his ears, but Geoffrey felt that an expression of loyalty to his company would show him in a good light to the captain-general.

"Don't be so anxious to fight. The campaign season promises to be long this year. The pope's brothers are ambitious, and it is well that they are. You will no doubt have more and better opportunities to prove yourself. Narni will be like … like … when Our Lord was interrogated by that Roman governor. There are many more stations of the campaign to visit before our

Lord and Savior grants us a cool winter."

"Does that mean you believe Tarlati will abandon the city the moment he sees the gleam of our pikes rising over the horizon? If so, then why did he bother taking Narni in the first place? Unless he is trying to draw us into the bosom of Malatesta, it seems like a wasted exercise."

"Now look who is captain-general! Maybe I should have you dine next to his lordship the Papal Legate to the Marche so that you can reveal to him the weaknesses in our foe's strategy? No? Well, tomorrow we shall be made to know what *Signore* Tarlati wants with us here. He moves in and out of sieges as the wind blows. His reputation as a condottiere is one of the lowest, I'm not afraid to say, almost as low as that of an English *routier*, if you'll forgive me. Malatesta can have him. It is to our advantage that he fights and flees for Clement."

"It sounds as though you know him well. Have you crossed swords with the blackguard?" Geoffrey was elated at the prospect of hearing the German captain's war stories. He had been taken aback by the reticence the Catalonians showed when weaving their tales of adventure, as though their company was little more than a guild of petty craftsmen. Rather it seemed as though the crossbowmen were perfectly willing to let the company's magnificent standards and sumptuous baggage train speak of their success. Of course, the Catalonian crossbowmen's reputation was already made.

"The condottiere's world is a small one. I have crossed swords with many. I have fought for one side in the morning and then had to cross the field to fight for the other side in the afternoon. The key to survival, let me tell you, is to treat each day in service as a formal partnership, not a personal oath, and that your enemy considers it as well. To bear a grudge or to refuse reasonable service is tantamount to stabbing yourself in the thigh – debilitating and to no purpose. It would hurt and it might even be fatal, but it would most certainly keep you off the rolls for a long while. No action – no money; no money – no company; no company – no service, except maybe as a free knight or lance, if you'll forgive me. But there are some condottieri who I simply cannot stomach. Giovanni Tarlati is one of them, and he is giving my men hell just a few leagues down the road, and mine his."

Geoffrey wanted to ask about the attitude of the lords and knights of the land around Narni and about whether or not Tarlati could be declared an outlaw by the pope and hunted down, but the dinner bell rang.

"Enjoy the banquet," Prospero said, leaving Geoffrey to find his place unescorted.

"Over here, Englishman," Sergeant Alfonso yelled from across the hall.

Geoffrey hesitated for a moment, but since no one else called his name, he followed the Catalonian sergeant's voice to a table of petty condottieri.

"Sit over there," Alfonso said, pointing to the lone empty place on the bench.

Seeing that the sergeant was content to say no more, Geoffrey introduced himself as a 'squire and man of the Duke of Lancaster and Guyenne', and the others reciprocated. Bartolomeo Altoviti, who commanded the smallest company in the great papal host, belonged to a family of minor nobility near Florence that had fallen on hard times, and as such had sent its youngest son to learn the art of war as a condottiere. He was soft-spoken for a soldier and had the face of courtier, Geoffrey thought. Bosio Attendolo, captain of a company of heavy men-at-arms, was also a young scion of nobility from his home town of Cotignola in the Romagna. In contrast to the soft Florentine, Geoffrey recognized a sharp contemptuous look about him, which was confirmed when he growled at the servants to keep the wine flowing at their table. Similar in attitude if not in appearance was Braccio di Montone, who was polite and betrayed no emotion. Geoffrey found it difficult to size him up, but they would talk later. Montone was as green as the other two captains, but he led a company of veteran Umbrian pikemen that he had inherited from a recently retired condottiere who had served his family. Rounding out the table was an old, morose cloth merchant sent by the city militia.

After the priests had given their blessing and the lords and ladies of the head table sat down, Geoffrey looked for Captain Prospero, but to his surprise both he and the papal legate were gone. Geoffrey watched the Duke of Spoleto rise from his seat.

"Lords, ladies and honored guests," the duke began in a booming voice. "Feel the ground shake from the trembling of our enemy! It grows stronger by the day as we gather strength to defeat the unholy enemy of the Church. We set out from the great seat of this land with the belief in righteous victory, but we have come too late!" He left a pregnant pause before resuming. "I wanted to inform you about the approaching pass of arms to liberate one of our sister cities, to buttress your knowledge of our just cause, but alas our fame has preceded us, for at this very moment those who we had planned to smite are instead joining us as allies, to follow us in our quest to return this troubled land to the warm, secure bosom of Mother Church under the reverend guidance of Christ's Vicar, our Father, the Supreme Pontiff Boniface. Narni is free! Now, when others hear of this bloodless victory, they too will come to us as supplicants, on bended knee with swords sheathed and bows unstrung, to beg forgiveness for raising their sullied hands against the One True Church. Without having shot a single arrow or shed a drop of precious Christian blood, we have prevailed. Now, let us cheer, one and all!" The duke raised a silver goblet.

The hall filled with murmurs of wonder and cries of incredulity. The citizens of Terni looked relieved, as war in their *contado* looked to have been averted. Only the captains showed any hint of skepticism about the sudden change in fortune, but none would openly doubt the duke. All raised their mugs, goblets and Venetian fluted glasses and took lengthy draughts. The governor of Terni called for more wine and ale.

At Geoffrey's table, disappointment and fear made their rounds. Although Bosio Attendolo joked about the wordiness of the duke's speech, it was clear to each man that his reputation was in jeopardy, for without a proper pass of arms none would earn fame or attract new lances. A nervous silence descended on the table.

When the cheer was over and the guests renewed their table chatter, Sergeant Alfonso decided to revitalize the mood by asking, "Has anyone been to the kitchens to see what the good citizens of Terni have deigned to procure for the fine soldiers of his holiness the pope in Rome? I, for one, am tired of pork, which our victuallers seem to favor above all other meats. A nice rack of lamb would do me well just about now, although I don't expect it to compete well with our Barcelona recipes."

"So it is the crossbowmen who have been plucking our country," Captain Montone jibed. "I thought I smelled the rank odor of a foul deed coming off you."

Sergeant Alfonso would have returned the jest had not the hall been suddenly flooded with pages and serving lasses laden with the first course. It was pottage, but the governor had used this special occasion to express his aesthetic sensibilities, insisting that his cooks produce the fancy stew in a rainbow of colors. There was bright green pottage made from peas mixed with spinach, vibrant yellow pottage of turnips with a touch of saffron, orange carrot pottage, creamy brown pottage made from mushrooms donated by the city's best citizens, and others, including one so thick and black that Geoffrey thought that it must have been squeezed from a blood sausage. But no one commented aloud, as hunger kept tongues silent, so it was only after the second course of minced rabbit pasties was served that the table was sated enough for conversation to be rekindled.

Attendolo was the first to broach the subject about which all but the merchant were thinking. "Well, do you think the Malatesta was betrayed or is he simply selling the city? Let us hear opinions on this matter, since we need to replace all fine talk about plans and prisoners."

"What makes you think we won't have prisoners?" Montone asked. "If Tarlati is turning over the keys to the city to the duke, he might just turn over whatever contingent of Malatesta's men might be with him. I, for one, cannot believe that Tarlati took the city by himself in the first place."

"Remember," Sergeant Alfonso began gravely, "the citadel is still held by Prospero's men, so Tarlati has not taken the whole city. But I agree that he must have had help to invest such a well-defended city, and a papal one at that. Tarlati's company is not large, say our sources, although those tongues wagged over a month ago."

"His company is weak," Geoffrey declared.

All eyes turned towards the English squire, excepting those of the old merchant, who was noisily slurping a large helping of turnip pottage.

Geoffrey did not shrink from the attention. Recalling how certain gestures could be used to push up wagers at the dice table, he paused and straightened his posture. He did not mind taking control of the conversation away from Sergeant Alfonso.

"And how would you know?" Bosio Attendolo challenged in such a heavily accented voice that Geoffrey scarcely understood him. "You've only just stepped onto the sacred soil of Italy and are as green as the new grass that rises in the spring. Or are you in league with that bandit Tarlati?" He took a long draught of wine to sharpen his barb.

Everyone laughed, even the old merchant, but Geoffrey ignored this and launched into a passionate account about the destruction of the village of San Bernardino, leaving nothing to the imagination and pounding his fist on the table to accentuate the vilest crimes. When he finished, he looked from face to face.

"That's near Orte, is it not?" Altoviti asked.

Alfonso said that it was.

Geoffrey waited for outbursts and condemnation. He sat still, with hands balled into fists and his knuckles white.

"Typical Bretons," Attendolo sneered as he bit into a hunk of bread. "Once they get their claws into a village, they cannot stand as one. I'm surprised you didn't capture more of the blackguards."

Geoffrey continued to sit agape. Why no outrage about the chapel?

"You know who is a good disciplinarian," Altoviti said, "Malatesta Malatesta. He is very young, but he has a firm hand, *and* he is generous with booty. It's brought him some of the best lances in central Italy."

"I'll wager that Malatesta withheld pay, and that set Tarlati off against him," Montone speculated. "Clement is short on silver, from what I hear."

"Pay or no pay," Sergeant Alfonso said, "that does not answer the question about prisoners. Should there be any, do you think the duke would release them, ransom them or execute them? Keep in mind that we have drawn our swords against Clement."

"Well, it all depends on your *condotta*, doesn't it?" Attendolo suggested. "That is unless, of course, the papal legate decides to declare them anathema and imprison them himself in some Roman dungeon. The urgency of this campaign tells me that our lords might not give such quarter as they have in yesteryear."

"And with any luck my men will have to escort them all the way down to the cold depths of the Castel Sant'Angelo," Altoviti murmured, referring to the immense papal fortress in Rome.

Alfonso sniffed loudly and took a quaff of ale, as though he needed a moment to decide how to respond. He was not obliged by either custom or good humor to say anything. A *condotta* was a private affair between employer and captain that had to be respected. Naturally, some captains struck better deals than others, and should knowledge about a poor *condotta* find its way to the condottiere grapevine, it would reflect badly on the captain, the employer or the soldier who broke the convention of

OF FAITH AND FIDELITY

silence regarding such matters. Good reputations were difficult enough to maintain.

Meanwhile, with the confidence born out of timely consideration and strong ale, Attendolo made his response sharp and brief. "Anyone in my company who captures a Malatesta receives double pay and first choice of trophies."

"I wouldn't mind having that *condotta*," Montone said gruffly. "May I join your company? I believe that I speak for my men when I say that it is certainly possible. However, the Malatesta are notoriously difficult to capture."

The soldiers laughed. Even Geoffrey chuckled, although he scarcely knew who Malatesta Malatesta was or what the Malatesta family meant in the world of Italian politics. In order to keep a toe in the conversation, however, he asked how many of these Malatesta might be found in the army of the antipope.

"There are four – two cousins, a nephew and an uncle," Attendolo answered. "They are neighbors of mine, so I should know. They are holding out against the papal legate in the Romagna at Rimini and Pesaro. One cousin, Malatesta Malatesta is the captain-general. He is a very fine captain, although I am a little surprised to find him fighting for the cursed Clement. After all, Clement is better known in Italy as 'Robert, the Butcher of Cesena', and Cesena is a part of the Malatesta *dominium*."

"Perhaps he's serving not the antipope of Christendom but rather the Prince of Virtue," Montone quipped.

"You mean Giangaleazzo Visconti?" Attendolo asked. "Well, there's no doubt that Malatesta Malatesta is serving that lord, but I put it to you: why can he not serve several masters at once? The Malatesta are as fond of money as the Florentines." He nudged Altoviti, whose voluminous intake of ale had all but made him numb to the ongoing table talk. After readjusting himself on the bench, he squinted at Attendolo, Sergeant

Alfonso and Geoffrey in succession and then, unsure whether or not he had been insulted, decided not to risk causing offence and merely nodded and mumbled something incoherent.

Sergeant Alfonso, meanwhile, thought himself the wisest of the lot. While the others were talking, he and the old merchant had taken and consumed the best portions of the roast duck two pages had brought. He only began to listen in again when Geoffrey spoke up.

"What I don't understand is why Boniface has not just declared the Malatesta anathema for entering service with the antipope," Geoffrey argued. "Excommunication might have divided his clan, or encouraged rebellion against their lordship, thus taking the Malatesta out of the war against the Church."

Montone and Altoviti stared at the Englishman in horror. Sergeant Alfonso remained equivocal about Geoffrey's proposal, but it was Attendolo who was the first to respond. "As the English tend to see things in shades of black and white, I will endeavor to explain to you the subtleties and ambiguities of the situation. The Malatesta hold the vicariates of many key towns in the Romagna and have enjoyed the confidence of the Church in the past. Boniface does not want to destroy the Malatesta – he wants to bring them back into the fold. Should they be stripped of their honors and denied redemption, the Church would then have to deal with a whole new group of families who would claw at each other to replace them. It's much better to deal with known evils rather than unknown ones, I should think. And besides, the Malatesta are a pretty tough lot."

Geoffrey was embarrassed. He needed time to consider this strange arrangement. Could the pope not put his own people in, he thought? In France, the king appoints seneschals and constables to enforce the royal will. Then he remembered that many of these Italian cities and lords were fighting the *French* pope and had fought the *German* emperors, and so they had long ceased to look kindly upon foreign occupiers.

OF FAITH AND FIDELITY

"Let us not forget that excommunication from the Church is the ultimate penalty and as such should not be taken lightly," Attendolo explained. "Boniface has at his disposal the wisdom of his predecessors and is blessed with a strong dose of good sense. I am certain he understands the implications of such a terrible act, and I don't just mean the difficulties of getting absolution. Think of the French. They're marching on Genoa as we speak and they have the support of the cursed Visconti. If Boniface issues a blanket excommunication, then the French will simply ask Clement to do the same, and no one wants a crusade in the heart of Italy. Why, we only just got rid of those German and English companies that were torturing our land. Who wants them back? Considering what happened to Cesena when Clement was here, there's no question but that the antipope could unleash the horrors of the English War upon us. Malatesta is just a soldier, in Umbria to conquer towns; he's not some heretic spreading a false faith. No, such an escalation would be far too dangerous."

"Well," Sergeant Alfonso began, "Holy War or not, I for one am glad that at least we haven't been contracted for a *chevauchée*. Such campaigns undermine discipline, making the men hard to control. Putting words to parchment can only go so far towards keeping order. I could give as many examples as I have fingers of archer and even crossbow companies shattered by the lust for booty." He shook his head and sipped his ale.

"Do not speak too soon," Attendolo argued. "With Andrea Tomacelli at the head of this venture, we might be asked to do just about anything, if the campaign begins to sour. Just remember last year."

Everyone shook his head, even the old merchant, who was finally moved enough by the heat of the table talk to react, and Geoffrey, who did not understand the reference to the murder of the condottiere Boldrino di Panicale.

Satisfied that the first eight courses had been successfully served and well received, the governor gestured for his musicians to play, but all was not well with the governor, as he was visibly discomfited by the continued absence of the papal legate and the captain-general. He feared that his fellow townsmen might start to think that his esteemed guests were snubbing him, or that he had somehow offended the representative of Christ's Vicar. Either rumor would undermine his position, even though it was the papal legate himself who had appointed him rather than the Terni commune. He prayed that the two most powerful men in the city would return before the serving maids, specially dressed in colorful gauze and fruit-shaped hats, brought in the pudding. His prayer was soon answered.

Andrea Tomacelli strode into the hall, closely followed by a large coterie of papal guards. His comportment betrayed a confidence built from success. Trailing at a respectful distance and also escorted by his own band of protectors was a sullen Captain Prospero. With his right hand on the hilt of his sword and the other dangling at his side, he looked troubled but alert. At the tail end of the procession was a man Geoffrey did not recognize.

The hall fell silent. The pudding servers held their places near the kitchens. All eyes scrutinized the returnees, even those of the old merchant, whose natural curiosity could not be contained by his order's dissimulating art of deference.

"That is Tarlati," Alfonso said.

"What? Which one?" Geoffrey asked. He felt a cold shiver run down his spine.

"The one at the end, with the small eyes and broad stride."

As he followed Tarlati with angry eyes, Geoffrey wondered at how such a man, who only a few days ago was terrorizing helpless villeins, could now be an honored guest of a papal legate. His heart began to pound and his right hand instinctively reached for the phantom hilt of his *couteau*. He was responsible for the spoliation of consecrated ground, and so must make restitution. But maybe he already had, Geoffrey thought;

how else could the papal legate accept him?

"Musicians!" Andrea Tomacelli cried out. "Why have you ceased to make pleasant noises? No, you are right. You must change your tune, for this banquet has become grander than was intended. Play a lively melody to help us celebrate the great victory we have won here tonight!" Dismissing his escort, Tomacelli went to his place at the head table, where he exchanged whispers with his brother, the governor and the other great captains. Captain Prospero followed, but he spoke to no one. The musicians, meanwhile, conferred with one another on their next choice of music.

The head-table conference broke up. The governor appeared relieved. The captains remained impassive. The duke and Captain Prospero scarcely hid their troubled looks. Only the papal legate showed signs of elation, and so it was appropriate that he formally address the hall. Taking a gilt chalice in his right hand, he removed himself to the center of the hall.

"Lords, ladies, soldiers of his holiness the one true pontiff, and honored guests." Andrea Tomacelli's voice was loud and dripping with authority. "The first blow against the cursed Robert of Geneva, who calls himself Clement, has been struck. The siege of Narni is over and at midnight tonight that fine city will be back in the sacred hands of its true lord." The papal legate thrust his left hand into his robe, from where he produced a set of large keys and flourished them over his head. "Instead of blood, I give you iron. Instead of a barred gate, I give you a raised portcullis. Yes, these are the keys to Narni! The man who once held them for the black hand of the antipope came to us on this night to beg forgiveness for betraying his holiness. The scales fell from his eyes when he was struck hard by the word that Christ's army was about to descend upon him. Then, like the most humble supplicant, he begged us how he could atone for this grave sin. I answered that for him to pass through the gates of St. Peter he would need a key. He asked where he could find this key. I told him that at the source of his sin there will be the key. After searching with pious intent, he procured these keys from the gatehouse of Narni and brought them to me and asked if they could be refashioned to allow him to gain entry into Heaven. I took the keys to Narni from him and answered that they could be transformed through confession and repentance. Feeling the warmth of grace envelop him, he threw himself at my feet, declared himself wretched and pledged to serve the one true head of the Church however he demanded. I bade him to rise, made the sign of the cross on his forehead and instructed him to remove his company from the city which he had taken forcefully and without right. He now stands before us as our ally and servant of the Church, Captain Giovanni Tarlati di Pietramala." Andrea Tomacelli returned the keys to the folds of his garment and presented the newest captain in the papal host.

Tarlati took several tentative steps forward. For a moment it looked as though he wanted to add to the fine words of the papal legate, but as he opened his mouth he changed his mind and returned to his place.

Led by a broad, sweeping gesture, Andrea Tomacelli gave the floor to his brother, who as the Duke of Spoleto also received the fealty of Narni alongside the Church.

Gianello recognized the part he was supposed to play, but he found that for once he had few lines to recite, especially considering that he had had nothing to do with the victory his brother was proclaiming. He began his oration by distributing even-handed compliments to the captains, lords and ladies of the city, the esteemed servants of the Church, and even the honored soldiers seated at the far table, following this generosity with a statement on how this season's campaign was to be a just war against the enemies of the Church within Christendom. He then began to wax dully on the unexpected glory of the occasion and growing strength of his army until felt his brother tugging on his sleeve. He stopped and the music returned to life.

OF FAITH AND FIDELITY

While the pope's brothers were putting on their show, Captain Prospero was consulting with the officers of his company and Captain Berenguar Vilardell. He was not asked to speak.

"I'm surprised that our captain-general looks so sad," said Montone. "I should think he'd be elated to have his men liberated by such easy means, unless, of course, he was hoping to squeeze Tarlati between the hammer of this host and the anvil of his company trapped in the citadel, but I don't believe Captain Prospero to be so foolish as to have wished for that uncertainty."

Geoffrey found this observation curious. "Do you not think that it would have been more glorious to defeat Tarlati in an honest pass of arms than to win victory by such … passive means?"

"Ahhh, but you do not know Giovanni Tarlati," Montone answered. "It nearly takes the power of angels to bring him to battle. In all likelihood, should our engines have knocked down Narni's walls, Tarlati would have retreated deep into the city, and then we would have had to hunt his men down house by house. Street fighting is for brutes and cutpurses, not proper men-at-arms, let alone aspiring knights, young squire. There would have been blood, ours, theirs and that of the townsfolk."

"I'm sure we could have brought Tarlati to battle outside the walls," Attendolo put in. "His men would not have wanted to starve; it's too early in the season for such risks. Win or lose, his company would have been ruined for the rest of the campaign season. Perhaps he was hoping for relief from Malatesta and received word that he is not coming? Regardless, I do not believe that our captain-general is troubled by the conditions of victory."

"No?" asked Geoffrey.

"No," Montone answered. "The situation is that Prospero and Tarlati bear a not inconsiderable amount of animosity towards one another, long before the duke's disastrous campaign in January." Seeing the curious faces around him, he exploited the opportunity to give a detailed account of the history of the relations between Corrado Prospero and Giovanni Tarlati. The crux of their mutual antagonism, Montone explained, lay in the way they conduct war. Tarlati's great ambition, as anyone in Italy knew, was to become the *signore* of Arezzo, and so his company was made to serve that end. Prospero, however, had more respect for *condotti*, captains and the art of war. A couple of years ago, Montone related, Tarlati and Prospero found themselves on opposite sides of a conflict between two towns, during which some of Prospero's men, who were on a foraging mission, found themselves surrounded by Tarlati's company. They surrendered without drawing blood, but as they were also men of Arezzo belonging to families in opposition to the Tarlati clan, Giovanni Tarlati simply executed them, even though the custom was to hold them for ransom. When Prospero heard about these murders he was outraged, since it besmirched his reputation, which he holds more dearly than his own salvation.

Geoffrey looked for Prospero at the head table and saw him talking to a page, who then approached Captain Vilardell and finally Geoffrey's table, where he addressed Sergeant Alfonso.

"Well?" Attendolo inquired, "What did he want, or was he just complimenting your fair looks?"

"We are to muster with our companies immediately after the banquet," the sergeant explained. "It seems that our captain-general requires more than the brothers of the supreme pontiff and a set of keys to open the gates of Narni."

CHAPTER 10

The city fathers of Terni spilled out of the hall drunk and cheering the bloodless victory of the papal army over the antipapal army, but Geoffrey was in a state of perturbation, sifting through his doubts about the anticipated maneuver. He was wondering why they had to occupy Narni now rather than waiting for dawn. Uncertainties multiplied in the darkness. He recalled the astrologer's words about reading signs without appropriate advice, so held back from drawing any conclusions about Tarlati, the papal legate and Captain Prospero. Nevertheless, he could not suppress the rage smouldering in his breast or the sadness filling his heart when images of the ruined chapel, wailing women and trampled fields entered his head.

"Ahhh! The gracious English squire returns to grace the lesser folk with his exalted presence," Jean slurred. "Shall I summon a choir to sing hymns in your honor, milord, or pay a priest to chant prayers to protect you from temptation? Or maybe it would serve me well to hire a *jongleur* to make a special dance illustrating your charmed life, to perform for the common folk at a penny a head? I could do with a song just about now. The gruel they serve in these papal cities is second only to English fare in the great chain of foul taste!" He was alone, sitting amid the litter of their gear.

"How about showing me a chandler who can fashion a big wax baton with which I can clobber some sense into you. What's the meaning of this devilish pattern that smothers our floor? Have you not heard that we are to muster within the hour?" Geoffrey's initial reaction to the

Frenchman's ridiculous situation was amusement, followed by relief that his foolish companion was distracting him from his doubts about the night's uncertain venture, and ending in annoyance that they would have to hurry if they were to reach the mustering point on time.

Jean drew up his face in a knowing grin. "We can't move if the Catalonians don't move, and the Catalonians won't move if they haven't had their fill of *Cacho*, and they won't've had their fill of *Cacho* until the stack of *naipes* has made three score rounds. When I left them, oh, perhaps an hour ago, they were only on the second score. And that tunic looks ridiculous, by the way." Jean then promptly ignored Geoffrey and began to closely inspect his hoqueton.

After a short silence Geoffrey responded. "I don't think Captain Vilardell will care how far the game has progressed. If the crossbowmen need to rally, then they will rally." Although he felt a pang of regret from having missed the company's perpetual *Cacho* game, Geoffrey comforted himself with the memory of his having dined as a guest of the Duke of Spoleto, the Papal Legate to the Marche and the great captains of the papal host.

Jean looked up. "It was Captain Vilardell himself who established the rule. But I shouldn't worry; time stretches at night. I'm more concerned about us getting lost on the unfamiliar road. I spoke with our militia and none of them has been on the Narni road."

Geoffrey had not taken that possibility into account. He had contemplated more dramatic eventualities, such as ambushes and betrayals, but not the more prosaic threat of getting lost. He was on the point of admiring the earthy, practical nature of his lowborn companion when his thoughts turned to Roger Swynford. What a team they would have made! And make. No file of men-at-arms will be able to stand against a pike pushed by two such hardy English squires.

"You are fortunate that Roger isn't here to keep good order," Geoffrey said. "If I had any cursed silver I would send it to the hospital for prayers and healing. I assume that the *Cacho* game will continue in Narni, so I see some hope yet. I don't want to have to wait until Captain Vilardell's *condotta* expires before I have the means to get out of here. Maybe the duke or the papal legate will put me on the road to Florence. I mean, they must consider my wretched situation at some time." Geoffrey made a dismissive wave of his hand. "Well, those decisions can only be made tomorrow."

Jean froze at the mention of the dead squire. It had been some time since that particular secret had pricked his conscience, but he had little to fear from Geoffrey discovering it. He was still dependent on the Catalonians and himself for protection and guidance in this strange land, which was a big enough lever to tip him away from anything that might compromise their partnership.

"Well, let us hope that by the cock's first crow tomorrow *we* aren't in need of prayer and healing," Jean said, finding his wits once again. He began to fuss with their kit in an effort to distract Geoffrey. "Our pike, I know, is in the wagon with the others. Your harness should be over by your pallet, but don't assume it's all there. The quartermaster's men were quick to dump our stuff and leave."

Geoffrey nodded and set to work. Following Jean's example he examined every piece of his arming harness, but complete or incomplete it was thin gruel. A few good hands at *Cacho*, he calculated, would be enough to purchase the additional bits that would make it worthy of him. Geoffrey unbuckled his belt, removed his borrowed tunic and donned his pourpoint, which seemed to have been cleaned and repaired during his absence. After examining the laces, he attached his leather leg harness and pulled on his hauberk. He then picked up his helm and sighed. The bascinet did not need an aventail, but one would have elevated his dignity. A spit polish ended that review and he set the helm down next to the brazier.

From his kit-bag he pulled out a small pouch and poured its contents onto his straw pallet. Geoffrey then set about untangling the leather straps that had to bind his couters and poleyns. Both were simple in design, but they were solid, so he was confident that his elbows and knees would be protected, mostly. Geoffrey glanced at Jean. The Frenchman was deprived of even those basic bits of metal to protect himself, but he reckoned that the hoqueton and iron hat would be enough, considering that he, Geoffrey, would be facing the brunt of any likely attack on the militia. The chandler just needed to keep his end up and his head down.

Sergeant Alfonso was busy pushing the villeins into ranks when he met Geoffrey and Jean.

"Enjoy the banquet?" Alfonso asked.

"It was almost too much. I do not recall ever having eaten so well. I found the condottieri to be lively company, although that Florentine captain did not do much for his reputation, did he?"

"Well, you get yet another honor tonight. Congratulations, master pikeman, you are now the corporal of the second file." Sergeant Alfonso clapped Geoffrey on the shoulder and grinned.

"Corporal! I cannot even talk to these villeins. I don't need to be a corporal of anything. I decline the honor. Let one of *them* be a corporal." Geoffrey waved in the general direction of the militia. "They're likely to see the back of me soon anyway."

"Listen," Alfonso said as he tightened his grip in the squire's shoulder. "I'm stuck running this rabble because they can't do it themselves, so if I have to be captain, then you will be corporal. Or would you like to be a *pavesaro* again, boy?"

Geoffrey sighed and mumbled his agreement. "But how will I give orders, or pass on yours?" he asked.

"Use your second, the Frenchman. He's been turning a local tongue, and if it's not good enough, have him turn it again. Now, let's get your file on the road, corporal."

Sergeant Alfonso stepped back to address the full array of Spoletan militia, as well as the sergeants and senior bowmen of the Catalonian company, which was assembling nearby. "The column will march in tight ranks!" he yelled. "All pikes and crossbows will remain in the wagon. Everyone will carry a sword and heater. I know they'll be a burden, but the road is short and the area has not been fully scouted. Militia will flank the crossbowmen with their heaters showing outwards. At least we won't have horsemen in front of us. That place has been given to Attendolo."

"Then you haven't heard how the men of the Romagna fart like horses," one of the company's older veterans quipped.

The joke was well timed to break the tension. Everyone laughed, even Geoffrey, who somehow understood the Catalon words for 'fart' and 'horse'. Sergeant Alfonso ended his speech with the order that final deployment would be made at Narni.

The trumpet of Captain Prospero's gonfalonier sounded the call to form ranks. The blast set in motion nearly a thousand men with clanking iron and grinding leather. The moon was at its brightest when after the shouts and prods of their captains, the column began to shuffle westwards.

"So how much did you win?" Geoffrey asked Jean after about half an hour. The march was expected to take close to four hours, which should bring the army to the gates of Narni just before dawn.

"You can't win if you don't play," Jean answered, suppressing a yawn. "And you can't play if you haven't any money. Need I remind you that the gross sum of our meager *prestanza* went for your fancy harness? What little we hold between us must suffice for a good while. Now that we are taking this damned city by peace rather than by force, we shall get nothing for our trouble."

"So now you are anxious for battle, when only yesterday you were praying that we would be held back. Be mindful that we're not in the alehouses of Narni yet."

Geoffrey was alert and in good spirits despite his earlier reservations. The pace of the column was swift and orderly, which gave him satisfaction. The army was resolute; the enemy was proving to be weak. The moon was bright enough to illuminate both the road and the verge that might hide attackers, and the weather was ideal for marching. From their outward appearance, the signs favored success.

"Unless our captains put on another banquet, we'll be hard pressed to enjoy the comforts of any alehouse," Jean said. "What troubles me more, though, is that his papal legate lordship will quickly send us to take some other town, and then another, until we find ourselves thrust into some unpleasantness."

"I believe Captain Prospero leads this host," Geoffrey declared, "and if he requires us to carry on all the way to Jerusalem, then that is what we shall do. My only concern is that I will miss the *Cacho* game again if we're billeted too far away from the company. Then, just you watch how I can turn our silver pennies into gold."

Now he thinks he's a bloody alchemist, Jean thought, but he merely shrugged, then feeling a pinch on his right shoulder adjusted the heater that was weighing heavily on it. He could not see them staying in Narni for long – if they truly had been granted unopposed entry. If the rumors he had heard at the *Cacho* game were true, that other captains were reconsidering their fidelity too, the course of the war might suddenly shift, or grow to enflame all of Italy. These prospects put Jean in a mood of great uncertainty; he had done nothing to get his English squire to Florence or collect his debt.

The men grew quiet as the enlivening effects of alcohol gave way to deadening feelings of sobriety. Only the mounted captains remained boisterous, riding up and down the column, exhorting the *pedites* and conducting impromptu meetings with their peers. Geoffrey counted

OF FAITH AND FIDELITY

seven times that Captain Prospero visited Captain Vilardell for hushed exchanges. It was hard to make out the German in his black mantle, but the frequency of the talks suggested to Geoffrey that the captain-general was very concerned about the operation, despite the assurances given at the banquet. The captain-general went so far as to speak with the lances Tarlati had sent to guide the papal army himself, interrogating them at length to ensure that no ambush was imminent before allowing the column to advance further.

Narni appeared as a distant shadow, still and foreboding. Captain Prospero halted the column and ordered his entire compliment of horsemen to form into squadrons and scout the perimeter of the city, while the men-at-arms were told to ordain into squares in an open field about a mile from the city walls. The Catalonian crossbowmen were divided in half and placed on its flanks while the peasant militia ranged into ranks behind them.

Sergeant Alfonso ordered Geoffrey to take his file of militiamen – a dozen in all – to the end of the right flank immediately behind the crossbowmen. After some confusion between Geoffrey and Jean on how to manage this awkward command system, Jean got the message through, and with a little snickering, the villeins did as they were told.

With the companies set, Captain Prospero ordered the pages and servants to distribute the pikes and crossbows.

"Did you mark our pike?" Geoffrey asked Jean.

"Mark it for what? It doesn't belong to us."

"Whether it belongs to us or not makes not a jot of difference because we are responsible for it. I will be made to look the fool if I'm not properly armed. On my oath, you are as lacking as a lamp with no light. Now go and find it!"

"Calm down. Our pike is the shortest of the bunch, so I'm sure everyone in our company knows who is *responsible* for it. I do feel like a leper when holding it, though."

Jean was right. Shortly after his dismissive remark a page thrust their short English pike into his hand.

When dawn broke and the first rays of light struck the fields surrounding the captive city, Captain Prospero's square was surprised to be confronted by its reflection dead ahead, defending the main gate. The parallel host was smaller and free of flanking crossbowmen, but it looked solid just the same. However, they were less surprised to see the mess of broken siege engines, half-dug trenches, overturned wagons, uprooted trees, and other detritus of war Tarlati had cast aside when he abandoned the siege.

Prospero shook his head at the disorder and signaled to his captains to follow him, apparently heedless of the likely danger. The rival host sent out its own representatives, and the two parties met on an open stretch of ground midway between the armies. As the sun rose higher, Geoffrey was able to recognize the richly adorned Tomacelli brothers and Tarlati. The other men were unknown to him, but he assumed they were Tarlati's. The discussion looked serious, and after half an hour some of the younger soldiers began to comment worriedly, wondering why the transfer of authority was taking so long. The sergeants repeatedly demanded silence, but they only succeeded in reducing the volume of the loose talk.

Geoffrey kept quiet, his eyes fixed on Captain Prospero. He saw the German shake his head a few times and the Italians gesticulate, but otherwise he sat still and tall in his saddle, appearing to say just a few words. Then Andrea Tomacelli trotted up to him and touched him on the arm. The nodding of exalted heads unmistakably implied that an accord had been reached. A few moments later Prospero and his captains returned to the square and issued orders.

"Captain Tarlati's company will camp on the east side of the city," Alfonso explained to his corporals, "while we will take the west side.

OF FAITH AND FIDELITY

They are with us now, but until the *condotta* is drawn up they will remain separate. The gate is open, but Captain Prospero's men are still locked in the citadel, so no one is allowed into the city yet for fear of provocation. Well, I should say no one is allowed in except for the militia."

When asked why the good captain could not just ride in alone and free his men, the sergeant said that he needed some protection and that he would not detach his own men from the army, implying that he still did not trust Tarlati not to attack the papal host.

Captain Prospero scrutinized the peasant militia from astride his horse and warned them that he would not tolerate pillaging or anything that might oblige him to hang them and their dogs.

"Did you understand what I said?" the captain asked Geoffrey, who was standing at the head of his file.

"Yes, your lordship, and I will be the one to make the noose, should any part of this rabble disgrace you," Geoffrey answered.

Prospero smiled. "Call me captain. Now, come with me, squire. I have something better for you to do."

"But I cannot abandon the company, captain. These men need to be led."

"They will follow you because you will be carrying the crossed-keys flag of the throne of St. Peter into the city."

The streets of Narni were deathly quiet, even so early a morning. True to his word Tarlati had evacuated his men from the city, but it seemed as though he had also taken its citizens with him. Broken doors and the charred heaps of a few houses testified to some pillaging having taken place, but overall Narni appeared to have suffered little from the siege.

Captain Prospero's column advanced slowly and in tight ranks, still fearing betrayal. Geoffrey was concerned that some of the peasants in his file would bolt at the first sight of the spoliation. He threw fierce looks at his tiny company and even threatened one with the papal gonfalon when the man stepped out of rank.

At the walled-up gate to the citadel Prospero called out in German to his men. A few tense moments passed before someone inside responded in kind. After an exchange of serious words the scraping of heavy stone echoed down the street and within an hour the relieved soldiers filed out of the battered fortress. To Geoffrey, they looked tired but well fed. Perhaps Italian warfare was not such a dangerous thing after all, he thought.

Not wishing to linger, Captain Prospero ordered his relieved half-company to split into three columns and march down Narni's main streets to demonstrate before the citizens. Geoffrey marched alongside Prospero's horse down the high street, as he was still the provisional gonfalonier. They had almost reached the gatehouse when Geoffrey spied a couple of men scurrying out of a nearby tower. He thought about San Bernardino and the Bretons.

"Looters!" Geoffrey yelled. "Shall I dispatch them, captain?"

Prospero looked at the fleeing men and shook his head.

"We should not break up the column. And besides, it didn't look like they were carrying anything. Still, we had better inspect that tower to see if it's still intact. Tarlati might have made holes anywhere."

The tower looked to be sound from the inside, but the captain wanted to be sure that it had not been undermined, damage that was hard to detect from the outside. The door to the dungeon was jammed, but a couple of his men broke it down. When the torches were lit they saw over a dozen richly clad corpses heaped in a corner. Prospero pointed at the pools of blood oozing from beneath them.

"These men were recently killed," Prospero said.

One of his newly freed men identified them as members of the city commune.

"Damn them!" Prospero shouted. "This will not do! I will not have murders while I'm in command!"

OF FAITH AND FIDELITY

Florence

"You seemed to enjoy yourself with your countrymen last night, Godwin," Chancellor Salutati said, "especially the green-clad knight. Why, he was even fatter than you. I was surprised not to see you on their ship when they departed this morning."

Godwin shuffled on the dusty floor of the copper-beater's cellar. "I may still be a subject of my king," Godwin began, "but my king has not chosen to subject me to his will, and so any passage to my distant patria would have been the subject of his majesty's captain, who would have demanded more than the poor fare of an exposition on the subject of goodwill and promises. You still hold my purse strings, and they are as yet well fastened to your belt."

Salutati turned his head and coughed violently. "You are unusually patient for an Englishman, Godwin," Salutati said at last. "The long years in Italy must have worn you to a fine finish, for I insult you. In truth, though, you executed your commission far better than I had expected, or indeed desired. I received word today that Giovanni Tarlati di Pietramala has broken his *condotta* with Malatesta and joined the papal side."

"That is good," Godwin said warily. "So, why am I here?"

"That is good, yes. However, Tarlati has taken Brandolino Brandolini with him, which is not so good." Events were moving too fast in the field. If the balance of forces tilted too far in favor of Boniface, then the French might involve themselves, or worse – Tarlati might have the time to advance on Arezzo.

Godwin shrugged. "Rats leaving the sinking ship," he said. "You should be pleased because now the cause of his holiness the true pope Boniface is truly blessed. His hand has been strengthened to strike a serious blow against Clement and the Visconti. Who knows where this year's campaign will lead?"

The chancellor sighed. He sat down on a stool and bid Godwin to do likewise. "You express the situation correctly. Who knows where this will lead? Of course, the Republic is most desirous to see the Church recover its patrimony."

Godwin again stroked his greying beard. Despite the chancellor's misgivings, he was confident that anything he said had value; otherwise he would not give it voice.

"You have not seen Tarlati's company," Godwin said. "I have. You paid Tarlati far more florins than he's worth, and trust me when I say that I pocketed not a single penny."

"That is comforting. So, you found no indication of hidden companies waiting to cross into Tuscany? The French are preparing to seize Genoa on behalf of one of their flatulent princes with the support of the Visconti, and Genoa is uncomfortably close to us." Salutati also had England in mind, but he said nothing about it.

Godwin shook his head. "What do you want, chancellor?"

"Your compatriots were missing a young man from their party, a squire, they said."

"I heard. A tall beggar, apparently. I hardly made a suitable replacement."

Salutati ignored the joke. "He was a man of the Duke of Lancaster. Did you encounter such a man on your visit to Tarlati or heard rumors about him?"

"About unusually tall English squires? Well, I heard that a company of Catalonian crossbowmen that had recently crossed into Umbria was trailing a couple of foreigners with it, including an Englishman."

Salutati frowned. "Are you sure? Might there not be some English *routiers* still plying their trade here? After all, Umbria is attracting all sorts of condottieri."

"No, this man has no name or rank, apparently, and was alone."

Salutati fell silent. John of Gaunt was a powerful lord, in France as well as in England. If Florence would do him a favor, like returning a prized squire, then he might reciprocate with something like raiding the lands of the French knights who were investing Genoa and threatening the Patrimony. The green English knight had let slip that the duke had recently cancelled one such raid, but was planning another.

"Do you think you can find him?" Salutati asked.

Godwin fixed a hard stare at the chancellor. "Look, I've already done you one favor by being your bagman to Tarlati, and I am not about to do another. You owe me."

"You know more people than all my spies put together, so this task should be as easy as the first. You are the only person I have who might identify a man of Gaunt. You campaigned alongside his son Edward before you came to Italy, so you should not err in your judgment. I don't need any other English squire."

"I don't see why I should help you. What is this boy to me, or Gaunt, for that matter? Find another tracker." Godwin turned to go.

"This is not a request, sergeant."

Godwin sighed and turned back. "Then this will be my next to last departure from Florence. You will have my accounts and whatever else belongs to me released by the time I return?"

"They will be ready. You have my word, and I assure you that it is good. Now, go find your compatriot."

Narni

"*You* are coming with me," Captain Prospero ordered Geoffrey, who was in the throes of rolling up the captain-general's gonfalon while one of his sergeants was waiting patiently to receive it, and walked away.

Geoffrey was surprised to hear the captain-general speak with such emotion, though he was much relieved that the captain had finally changed his tune from the dry "This will not do," which he had continually muttered all the way back to camp. After hastily handing over the standard, Geoffrey ran after the captain-general.

"Captain," Geoffrey said, once he had caught up to Prospero, who was taking brisk steps, "should I call on the rest of my lance and Captain Vilardell to accompany us?" Geoffrey ambled awkwardly, since he had not been given time to remove his harness.

"There's no need," Prospero answered curtly. "Your lance second can take care of camp business alone and we should meet Vilardell very soon."

Geoffrey offered no rejoinder to this, but asked instead, "I should at least know where I am being led so that I can prepare myself."

"We are going to the war council. I need you there."

Geoffrey had to assume that Captain Prospero was not interested in his strategic advice or to promote him for a display of valor he had not made. "I am honored, naturally, but what sort of contribution do you think I can make, your lor ... er, captain?"

"You are my witness to the appalling acts committed in that city *after* our occupation of it, and I will not have my name associated with them!"

His thoughts ran towards Tarlati and the crimes his Bretons committed at San Bernardino. "Maybe we should take some of the peasants with us as more witnesses?"

"They are peasants and you are not. Lord knows what they might say, if they say anything at all. I can't trust them. I trust you. And before you ask, my men won't do either, since their fidelity to me might cast doubt on their honesty in this matter. No, my good squire, you are the most useful, as regrettable as that sounds."

When Geoffrey entered the great, red and white striped pavilion in which the war council had convened, he could see by the way the captains were arrayed that Andrea Tomacelli had assumed the most honored place.

Duke Gianello was standing to the right one pace behind his brother, staring at a map of eastern Umbria and looking rather content to do so. If he was aware of how his brother had usurped him, he did not show it. The petty captains, Bartolomeo Altoviti, Bosio Attendolo, Gherardo Aldighieri, and Braccio di Montone, were grouped together on the papal legate's left side, silently awaiting the formal convocation of the council. Giovanni Colonna stood apart, emphasizing his particular status no doubt, and was fingering the stiletto dagger gripped in his right hand. Only he rivaled Captain Prospero in looking grave. Berenguar Vilardell had taken a place between the duke and Colonna. The duke's quartermaster was also in attendance, as usual, but conspicuous by his absence was the erstwhile occupier of Narni, Giovanni Tarlati.

"You needn't have brought your valet with you, captain-general," Andrea Tomacelli said, nodding at Geoffrey, who was two lingering paces behind the captain. "I, for one, think that you are finely dressed." The papal legate looked as though he was about to smile, but did not.

"Everything after a fashion, everything after a fashion," Prospero answered as he approached the table. He directed Geoffrey to stand next to Captain Colonna. "I prefer to eschew coarser threads since they are unsuitable for winding a strong weave, lest they break apart at the softest blow."

The petty condottieri shifted uneasily. They could hear in the timbre of the German's voice that he was angry, and they all knew that something serious had to happen to make Corrado Prospero angry.

"I do not think that I would be putting you on the spot by saying that something solemn is troubling you, although I must advise you against allowing it to distract you from your duties," Andrea said.

Prospero composed himself, straightened his doublet and took inventory of what lay on the table: maps, silver, seals, a stack of documents, the duke's feathered hat, three bronze tankards emblazoned with the papal arms. "My main duty is to ensure the successful prosecution of this campaign towards ridding the land of the Avignonese heretics, and I am quite grateful for it. Thus, having been elected to lead the papal host in Umbria by the highest authority, I am responsible for all plans and deeds concerning that host, including excesses and unauthorized acts."

Andrea noted Prospero's oblique appeal to the condottieri, each of whom had a say in the selection of their campaign leader, and took it as a threat. As papal legate, Andrea had the right to overrule any order issued by the captain-general, regardless of the rights and privileges given in his *condotta*, and so this challenge to his authority could not go unanswered.

"The war council is collectively responsible for the welfare of the army," Andrea said with deliberate emphasis. "You forget that the papal host does not comprise your esteemed company alone. There are six other captains here, or rather seven now, in addition to my brother, the Duke of Spoleto, with whom you signed your *condotta*. You might be the first among equals, but you are an equal nonetheless."

"Be that as it may, an arbitrary action taken by any one of us undermines the authority of all and plays upon the dignity of each. The captain-general must be privy to all decisions, for that is what dictates his distinction as, like you say, first among equals. I will not permit any act, deed or venture that might threaten the moral integrity of this army. We face enough threats from our enemy and our Lord's wild nature without our making fresh ones."

Andrea believed he had given Prospero plenty of opportunity to extinguish the flame fuelling his impudence, so the time had come to confront him openly. Discord within the war council would be an unfortunate result, but the hierarchy had to be maintained, and with the easy victory over the Malatesta at Narni, the papal legate had a considerable amount of goodwill from his brothers on his side. "Not the Lord, his holiness the pope or I indulge in arbitrariness of any sort, my good captain. It is not even a consideration. But I should ask you so that it is clear to all of us here gathered: do you accord the same dignity to the one true pontiff's enemies as to his friends?"

Geoffrey sensed that the papal legate was baiting Captain Prospero, although he could not understand why for all that is sacred he would be looking to escalate the confrontation. Instead, the papal legate, as the supreme pontiff's ultimate representative on the war council, should be endeavoring to bring peaceful resolution to whatever was troubling the captain-general. Then it struck him: Captain Prospero was accusing the papal legate of having had a hand in making the corpses in the dungeon of that tower. At least, that was how he understood it. They were speaking in a mix of Italian and Latin, so Geoffrey strained to recognize tones, inflections and gestures in order to follow the debate properly. Until now he had been certain that the massacre was a random, desperate crime committed by the worst of Tarlati's men as they were abandoning the city, or an act of pillage gone too far. Not for a moment had it occurred to Geoffrey to suspect that the supreme pontiff's brother might have ordered the murder of unarmed men. A cold fear gripped Geoffrey, especially as he could see that Captain Prospero was not about to back down.

Prospero straightened his shoulders. "I *do* accord the same dignity to the pope's enemies as to his friends, should they be worthy. They may be deceived, but they carry the same soul as the rest of us, damned as it may be. However, that is not what is at issue here. I will not tolerate the arbitrary murder of citizens of any rank of any city, for their sakes, for my sake, for the sake of this campaign, and for the sake of the pope in Rome!"

"And you have evidence that someone from our noble host has committed an excess? If so, then bring him forward and he will be punished and his captain will be held accountable, but above all be certain of guilt." Andrea Tomacelli was giving Prospero one last opportunity to extricate himself from the confrontation. The execution of a common soldier would satisfy any indignant party, as well as reinforce discipline, not to mention permit Prospero to preserve his dignity without having to follow through with a direct accusation.

"I saw the handiwork of Tarlati's men in Narni today. The siege was well over yet the killings were recent; the blood of the victims was still flowing from their bodies. The city had been given over to our rule. We take prisoners. That was the arrangement and nothing more," Prospero curtly explained.

Andrea Tomacelli's patience ran out. He had given this German mercenary captain enough time to smooth out the wrinkle he had made in the fold, but now his accusation was all but in the open. He detected the interest of the other captains in this test of wills, especially that of Colonna, who was by far and away the most important of the lot. "Giovanni Tarlati was our enemy yesterday and he is our friend today," he began with a voice that was strong and stern, "but as accountable as he might be for the behavior of his men, we must consider making allowances in delicate situations, especially considering the natural hazards and confusion of war. Undertake an investigation if you must, but it would be foolish to restore an enemy. The campaign must press on."

"I saw the freshly hewn bodies of citizens and merchants. You explain to me and to the other captains here how such men could survive the occupation of Giovanni Tarlati and his Bretons yet have their throats slit the moment it's all over – by the same company."

"It might have been pillaging, captain," Gianello suggested.

"It was not," Prospero said without looking at the duke. "That much is certain."

"While I will agree that Tarlati's men are not the most disciplined soldiers, they will fight on our side," Andrea said. "Like I said, have an investigation if you wish, but we must not delay; further victories are at hand."

OF FAITH AND FIDELITY

Prospero would not be deterred. With an uncharacteristically abrupt move he lunged towards Geoffrey, grabbed him by the sleeve and dragged him to the center of the pavilion. "This Englishman is a witness. He knows what a murder looks like, and so he can testify that men of Narni were slaughtered not because they were armed or were holding a bag of gems, but because of who they were. This was *purposefully* done, *signore*, not random killing, and I want to know why."

Geoffrey was able to easily follow the captain's speech because he had switched to French, but since no one was actually asking him a question, he remained silent. He wanted to ask in plain language if any of the captains knew of this crime, but he understood that Captain Prospero's intention was not to openly accuse any of them. Geoffrey admired the captain-general's speaking in such a way that avoided humiliating a guilty captain in front of his peers. Geoffrey also sensed that something else was simmering beneath the words Prospero and Tomacelli were exchanging, as though each was referring to something other than the subject at hand. He was troubled by the papal legate's diversionary tactics, though, for Geoffrey believed that if anyone should be concerned about discreet murders and breakdowns in discipline it should be the pope's own representative. However, this was Italy, and he was fast learning that words were as often used to disguise meanings as to reveal them.

Captain Vilardell stepped towards the Tomacelli brothers. He recognized that one of his men, even if he was only a bondsman in the company, was about to be sacrificed as a pawn in a struggle between great men, and that gave him license to enter the fray, however reluctantly. He could not afford to let scandal touch his company so early in the campaign season.

"Please, gentlemen and princes of the Church," Berenguar began in a soft and solemn voice, "if we move on to the next subject for discussion then all our differences will be happily resolved. See these rolls? They are lists of prisoners and petitions from the townspeople formerly under siege. I believe that a return to order will cool our passions and put paid our harried suspicions." Berenguar looked meaningfully at Andrea and his brother. While the rolls were genuine, the subject was false.

Andrea made the briefest of nods and looked at Captain Prospero, who still had a handful of Geoffrey's tabard. Colonna coughed and mumbled support for the captain of crossbowmen. Prospero slowly released his grip then said, "The Englishman stays."

Geoffrey returned to his place without protest.

Vilardell was conscious of the threat of his upstaging both the papal legate and the captain-general, so without a word he gave the floor to the Duke of Spoleto, who, bearing the highest title, had the right to dispose of prisoners. With a sweeping gesture of his right arm Captain Vilardell invited him to the table.

Gianello Tomacelli was not sure what to do, but seeing that a path had been opened for him, he moved forward without any obvious intent. At the table he began to poke around, tracing a few roads on one of the maps and wondering how he could maintain his threatened dignity. Fortunately for everyone's sake, Captain Colonna came to his rescue.

"Forgive me, my lord," Colonna began with feigned contrition, "but in my haste I failed to inform you that the list of prisoners taken at Narni lies on the pile stamped with the mark of my family. It should be with the petitions from the citizens of the same city."

The duke leafed through the stack of parchment until he came across the sheet Colonna had indicated. He would have simply begun to read out the names and ranks of the prisoners taken, starting from the most esteemed lord down to the lowest bachelor knight, had he not known that the council had yet to agree on the manner of division of the human spoils. This left him confused, but again someone came to his rescue.

"Forgive my impertinence, Lord Gianello," Prospero began, "but I do not believe it necessary to say a single name on that list." His voice was strong and steady, held at a respectful tone so that neither Tomacelli would have an excuse to charge him with abuse.

The pavilion was silent.

"I would be content not to consider an investigation into the murders I discovered in the city," Prospero continued, "and would joyfully proceed with the war council in its normal work if the lords and captains present will agree to release all prisoners taken at Narni without ransom and with the promise to never again bolt their doors against the pope's captains."

The petty captains were stunned, but they would not speak unless one of the senior captains spoke first. Berenguar produced a barely perceptive smile. Colonna, Geoffrey and Gianello turned to look at the papal legate, and they did not like what they saw. Andrea's face was like stone, his eyes were on fire and his hands had shrunk into fists.

"Would you have our enemies laugh in our faces before they stab us in the back?!" Andrea said in an icy tone that sent shivers down Geoffrey's spine. "Things are difficult enough without leaving behind the seeds of insurrection. Why do you think your emperors failed to conquer Italy?"

Prospero would not be intimidated. He had campaigned against so many unstable, arrogant, petty lords over the years that almost no reaction surprised him. Moreover, seeing that the papal legate was losing control of his passions, he believed that it was now possible to draw a confession from him.

"We are not here to conquer Italy. We are here to defeat the enemies of the supreme pontiff. But if you antagonize those who would be our friends, it may come to a bloody conquest, and then we are lost, like those failed emperors."

"The enemies of the Church must be destroyed," Andrea declared. "With your talk you would let heretics run the Curia!"

Captain Prospero continued to speak with the certainty of balanced reason. "Our enemy came to our side yesterday. The city had surrendered. All prisoners, therefore, belong to the war council, not to your brother alone. Narni might be located within the *dominium* of the papacy, but it also has a freely elected commune. Should you choose to enforce one set of rights while ignoring others, you sow the seeds of rebellion. Murders water it. We all remember the thunderous repercussions of Captain Panicale's murder."

Everyone except for Geoffrey gasped.

"We should consider Captain Prospero's proposition," Gianello suggested. "While I will not presume to be his advocate, the focus of my campaign is to defeat Clement and reunite the Patrimony, not ransack towns. Should we decide to treat the prisoners as conquered foes to be ransomed, it might reflect poorly on me. We need to keep this campaign moving forward!" Gianello punched the air with his fist.

The captains liked the speech, since it cleared a path to quick resolution of the current discord.

"Yes, but examples must be made, my brother," Andrea declared. "Any act that might have been done to punish those who betrayed you would be right and proper. It is very likely that a band of greedy men, seduced by the wealth offered by city life and led astray by our enemies, combined to make common cause with Clement and his hired sword, Malatesta Malatesta. The cities must learn to show uncompromised fidelity as vassals. Should they fail or willfully ignore their duty, they must be treated accordingly, up to and including administering the ultimate penalty. Boniface entrusted me to enforce not only the rights but also the will of the Church. However, in matters of war, of course, the war council reigns supreme."

The petty captains breathed a collective sigh of relief when they heard this final, conciliatory statement by Tomacelli. All were anxious to return to the business of campaigning rather than discussing the nature of jurisdictional rights or customary law and were prepared to sacrifice any ransom they might receive if the disputing sides would only make peace.

"Our next move cannot be considered until the fate of the prisoners is decided," Prospero declared. "The manner by which we treat them will serve as a message to the citizens of the next cities we invest and, as such, will affect our manner of conducting the respective sieges."

"Let us put this matter to a vote," Vilardell suggested. He was not keen on drawing attention to himself, but he feared that the war council would collapse if an accord was not soon struck. "Time is running short and the number of prisoners is small anyway." The other captains agreed.

"Give me your hat," Andrea demanded from Vilardell. He too recognized the custom and was certain of victory. "I shall give each captain a gold bezant. He who wishes the prisoners to be set free will scratch the face of the eastern emperor before giving to the Catalonian's hat. He who wants the prisoners kept in the custody of the war council will leave the face unblemished. Are we agreed?" He looked at Prospero, who nodded. There were no dissenting voices. "Englishman," the papal legate called. "You are the only man without an interest in this dispute, so I grant you the honor of selecting the coins. Captain Vilardell can show you which the bezants are, since I doubt you have ever handled such wealth."

Geoffrey nodded and with his captain counted out nine bezants and then handed them each to the six captains, the duke, the papal legate and Prospero.

"Take this and stand in the middle of the tent until you feel the correct weight. You can also play treasurer," Andrea instructed as he thrust out Vilardell's hat.

After the votes were cast, Geoffrey thrice tallied the results: six unmarked emperors to three marked.

"It is settled," Andrea said solemnly. "I should also inform the war council that I will be asking his holiness to send a special commission to Narni to question those prisoners who were a part of the surrender of the city to the false pope. The rest will be divided amongst the captains to be ransomed, although I would advise the council to set a low ceiling as a gesture of goodwill to the citizens of Narni."

The papal legate was triumphant and the strength of his words made it known to all the captains. As far as he was concerned, this trivial matter of prisoner disposal was closed; even the captain-general should be able to see the sense in that, he thought.

Prospero said nothing. The supports had been kicked out from beneath him and he was reeling from the fall. Henceforth, the war council would treat him as the senior strategist, a military councilor, and nothing more. The leadership was now fully in the hands of the papal legate. It was, above all, an insult to his dignity, since for him to rise to such heights as captain-general of a papal host only to be cut down for no sound military reason was unjust, an affront, a sign of bad faith. Should the cities and *signori* of the Patrimony resent the treatment of Narni and rally to Malatesta, or should the army advance too quickly and find itself beset on all sides by hostile forces, then all of Captain Prospero's plans would come to naught.

"Your presence here is no longer required," the papal legate said to Geoffrey. "You may return to your company."

CHAPTER 11

GEOFFREY had much to think about on the march back to Spoleto. What bothered him was not the open discord amongst the captains, as he knew that great men often came to blows in the heat of a campaign, but the nagging feeling that Captain Prospero had been absolutely correct in his desire to have the prisoners released unharmed and un-ransomed. The people of Narni were not prisoners of war. No battle had been fought. No contest between peers had taken place. Only bandits ransom common folk, Geoffrey knew from his talks with the old knights in the squires hall. Ghosts of the bloody horror in that tower arose before him in the midday heat. It was Tarlati's doing, he was sure. The heinous acts his men had committed at San Bernardino were enough to condemn him.

However, Captain Prospero seemed to think that the papal legate, the pope's own brother, was somehow complicit and not just condoning the "excess", as he had put it. While those dead men in the tower were not nobility, they were not lowly villeins either. Their violent end seemed unjust, even if they had denied fidelity to their lord. Maybe the war council should have accepted the captain-general's proposal of amnesty, he thought.

Then Geoffrey mulled over the reaction of Captain Vilardell in all this, or rather the lack thereof. For a man who had saved his life, enrolled him in his own company without a name or recommendation, and risked his men to chase down and destroy a corsair vessel, his quiescence in the matter of the prisoners was surprising. Perhaps he poorly followed the debate, his being from Barcelona, Geoffrey thought, but he quickly cast aside this doubt when he recalled how fluent the captain's conversations with the Italians had been. Geoffrey was sure, at least, that Captain Vilardell was one of the three who had scratched the eastern emperor, with Prospero and Colonna being the others, but the issue was moot now. Yet Geoffrey remained troubled, and he could not help but sense that this was a bad omen.

"I was speaking with the lads," Jean said, as he caught up with the squire, "and they are expecting to set up *Cacho* tonight, although no one is sure who will host. Geoffrey? Oh, for all that is holy, can you not listen to me for once?"

"I always listen," Geoffrey said and he slapped Jean across the chest with the back of his hand. "You just have to say something useful."

"You insult me, but I'll let it go." Jean shook his head in disgust. After all he had done for the squire, the least he could do was acknowledge his efforts. He was no better than the Gamesmaster, including having to fight to get what is owed him. "And don't walk so fast. You are outpacing the company, and Sanchez ordered us to keep good order."

"Hang that sergeant!" Geoffrey said aloud. "Are you happy serving with those villeins? I should be campaigning alongside a knight by now." He kicked a stone up the road.

"Well, no one is happy. Those villeins got wind of the Tomacelli brothers taking hostages at Narni, including members of some local guilds and confraternities. To seize citizens in such a rough manner after it was made known that the town was to be surrendered without the sack, well, some of them are starting to worry about their own families."

Geoffrey waved his hand. "They would be put to better use doing the work for which they were intended, namely tilling the soil for their lords. After the honor Captain Prospero bestowed upon me at the war council yesterday, I should think I will be removed from this band of peasants."

"So, that is where you were! And here I thought you were delayed because you were busy polishing the armor of Prospero's newly freed men. You haven't been promoted again, have you?" Jean rolled his shoulders and then wiped the sweat from his brow. He was not used to marching.

Geoffrey recounted the events at the war council.

"So, Prospero believes that those men in Narni were murdered by Tarlati and the papal legate knew about it, am I right?" Jean asked.

Geoffrey nodded.

"And Prospero is sure that some of the prisoners will suffer a similar fate, which he believes is unjust, and so demanded that the lot be released without ransom, yes?"

"Precisely. Then the captains voted on whether they should be released without demanding ransoms. I believe that Captain Vilardell voted for releasing the prisoners, much to his credit."

"So, you are taking Prospero's side. Did you see the prisoners?"

"No, but I saw the slaughter. Captain Prospero is clearly trying to hold up the dignity of his station. He despises Tarlati, I am told, and then there are those Bretons of his. The captain-general is definitely in a quandary over this."

"As well he should be." Jean rubbed his chin. "But if the militia is disbanded, would Vilardell take us back? Would he make you a *pavesaro* again?"

Geoffrey shivered and spat away from Jean. "I cannot go back to that. Captain Vilardell was to help me get to Florence and I believe he has yet to lift a finger to do so. I am indebted to him for my life, and that cannot be changed, but he is treating me as a member of his company. Therefore, if he no longer requires my service, he can release us to enlist elsewhere."

"Like with Captain Prospero, for instance?"

"When Captain Vilardell's indenture expires ..."

"*Condotta*," Jean interrupted. "It's called a *condotta*."

"Whatever it is called, when the terms of the *condotta* are fulfilled, then I should be free to seek service elsewhere, perhaps with Captain Prospero."

Jean took a breath and eyed his companion to make sure he wasn't joking. "That is a risky plan, and the remainder of our pay wouldn't last us a month, let alone get us the additional stuff we'd need that the crossbowmen now supply. Listen, Geoff, I have an idea. If we offer to help protect some merchant convoy on its way to the coast or even to Florence, we could settle all and be on our way home in a week!"

"I understand your desire to return, but I still must consider my petition to the papal legate," Geoffrey countered. "And I have not lost his seal. He might even provide me with an escort all the way to Florence. And don't worry, Jean, I will ask for you to accompany me."

"You are too generous." Jean looked up. The day was warm, but he felt oppressed by the thick clouds that stretched far into the horizon. He had little idea of even the direction they were headed.

"Have you any idea where we are going, Geoff? My boots are not nearly as good as yours."

"We are to strike at Clement simultaneously across the Patrimony."

"Yes, but where specifically. Where are *we* going? North, I think."

"At the war council, the papal legate wanted to press our advantage by dividing the army and plunging deep into Umbria, but Captain Prospero suggested that the entire host should march up the Tiber River, taking fortified places along the way. The papal legate could then lead his companies from the Marche westwards and threaten Perugia. Prospero is against bypassing enemy-held castles for fear of exposing his rear and supply line."

"Sounds like Captain Prospero does not want to campaign alongside the papal legate."

"When the two strategies were put to the captains, they came down on the side of his grace. So, the duke is taking Tarlati, Brandolino Brandolini and Bosio Attendolo up the Tiber River to chase down Malatesta, while Captain Prospero has us, Braccio di Montone and Gherardo Aldighieri to march up the Vale of Spoleto."

"Wonderful. How far?"

"As far as it takes."

"And that would be…"

"Assisi. I told you I had to go there."

Umbertide, Patrimony of St. Peter

Godwin had decided to take the safest route possible into the Patrimony, visiting only those cities whose lords he knew well, which was why he was on the pilgrim route that passed through Sansepalcro and the forbidding Mountains of the Moon. He also had decided to play the role of a pilgrim, so he was traveling light – no harness, no sword, not even a crossbow. For a charm he had dusted off and brought along his blue embroidered riding cap, which was the only bit of color on him, since to complete his disguise he had chosen to wear an unbleached penitent's tunic and cheap woolen hose. If only Hawkwood could see him now, Godwin thought, how he would laugh.

Godwin tried to remember the last time he traveled this road, but it had been so long now that his memory failed him. He could identify the landmarks, though, and his linking them to long past campaigns rejuvenated his spirits. He had resented the idleness imposed on him by the retirement of his late master as well as having to remain in Florence as a purposeless advisor to the Signoria. He could simply ride north now, through the Romagna, into Lombardy and over the mountain passes into France. He was short of silver, of course, though he could still count on a few friends to help, but Salutati had such a long reach that he would never reach home. He was no one's man now.

Then there was the question of what exactly he would do in England, should he ever return. His boast about marrying a knight's daughter was high fancy. Even if he was able to collect that money he had long been saving in the tight banks of Siena and Arezzo, he could not be sure what it might buy him, or if he would be happy to return to a land he hardly remembered. Godwin had always been certain, while fighting beneath the gonfalon of his great captain, that he would never miss Italy, with its deceit, its treachery, its inconstancy, but now that he was back in the saddle, if not the harness, he was not so sure. In his newly minted solitude the veteran sergeant let watery recollections of beautiful women, extravagant feasts and cascades of money that could be heard leagues away sugar his mind. Perhaps he was fated to die here, just as he had been fated to ply his trade here.

Realizing that the heady mountain air was fuelling such womanly sentiments, Godwin reined in his attention to address the matter at hand, which was to write a report for the chancellor. A deal had been struck with that old fiend, and he would stick to it. If he could say nothing else to his confessor with his dying breath, he could at least state with a clear conscience that he had always shown faith and fidelity.

As it stood, however, he had heard nothing about an English squire. Things had been quiet for some time in these parts, so the news was mostly bland, but now people were nervous. The Tomacelli's capture of Narni and defections from Malatesta Malatesta were creating the fear that the war would move northwards. Then Godwin encountered news that Brandolini had met and driven off Malatesta at San Giovanni Bridge on the Tiber River north of Deruta, causing him to pull back the remainder of his forces westwards in order to avoid the advancing papal host.

Well, so be it then – it had nothing to do with him.

OF FAITH AND FIDELITY

Assisi, Patrimony of St. Peter
May

It took Prospero's division a full week to march from Narni back to Spoleto and northwards along the old Roman road through Trevi, Foligno, Spello, and finally Assisi, because he would regularly stop to ensure that garrisons were in good spirits and well supplied. While this did afford Geoffrey time to buy a new doublet similar to the one he had lost at sea, such caution troubled him. For a while he was disappointed that he was not with the duke's group, but the more he saw how the captain-general inspired fidelity amongst his men, the more he admired him. There was no spoliation during the march. His men kept good order and looked fitter to fight than any other company in the papal host. Geoffrey recognized a quiet dignity about the man that demanded respect. As they marched through the Porto Nuovo of Assisi, Geoffrey felt a wave of confidence surge in his breast.

"I heard the company *Cacho* game will be renewed this afternoon at an alehouse called the Grey Boar," Jean announced. "What say you, Geoff? It has been a while since you played."

"Sounds good, but I want to visit some holy sites first," Geoffrey said. He was anxious to play again, but the lure of one of the busiest pilgrimage centers in all of Christendom was greater.

"Suit yourself, but with all the silver Captain Vilardell gave out, the stakes should be high." Jean hid his disappointment with a smile and a clap on the squire's shoulder, but he figured that touring churches and basilicas would keep him away from trouble. "I need to see the master victualler, so you will have to tour alone. I will see you at the Grey Boar later."

The crossbowmen and militia were billeted in the southern quarter of the city, mostly around the hay market between Santa Chiara and

Porta Nuova, which meant that Geoffrey had to traverse the entire length of Assisi – uphill – to reach the Basilica of St. Francis. Out of respect, Geoffrey decided to borrow the blue tunic the villeins from Spoleto had lent him in Terni, which was close to a pilgrim's smock anyway. After giving his buskins a light polish and his hose a firm tug, Geoffrey carefully secured his *couteau* to his belt just above his left hip, for if nothing else, he hoped to find a priest to bless his sword and only worthwhile possession.

Geoffrey was unsure about *Cacho* now anyway. The pots tended to be small, which to add insult to injury the Catalonians endeavored to have evenly distributed by the end of the night's wagering. He was coming to the conclusion that the company's perpetual *Cacho* game would only end when Our Lord and Savior Jesus Christ finally returned to bring paradise back to the world. Assisi attracted pilgrims from all over Christendom, many of whom he was sure brought their games with them, like Hazard. Throwing dice was no slower than *Cacho*, but the wagers were larger and the potential winnings correspondingly greater. With any luck he might also find a respected knight playing the old game; he had yet to find anyone of a respectable rank playing *Cacho*.

Geoffrey was now more anxious about needing to consort more with his peers and betters not only for the sake of his dignity, but also to find an elevated place of service. He was a common pikeman in a peasant militia attached to a company of missile-throwers who played low-stake games of chance. It was all becoming hard to bear; he was a proper squire in a respectable hall, whether anyone in this damned far and distant land cared to acknowledge it or not. If he could not make himself known in a pass of arms, then perhaps he could in a pass at the gaming table.

The closer he got to the basilica, the greater the number of pilgrims' lodgings he passed, including one honoring John the Baptist. This reminded Geoffrey about his friend and erstwhile companion-in-arms Roger Swynford. He must be healthy by now, he thought. The bloodletter had been confident that a few more bleedings would rebalance Roger's humors nicely, he recalled, and the monks of the St. John's hospital seemed to be of the good sort. He thought about how great it would be to pay a chantry priest at the Basilica of St. Francis to pray for Roger, but the few coins that remained in his possession, since Jean had taken most of them for some necessities or other, he had already set aside for a blessing of his *couteau*. Nevertheless, Geoffrey promised to find time to pray for his friend himself.

Jean found the Gamesmaster's partner in a small room abutting the south side of the cloister next to an impressive chantry chapel that, while not in the cathedral proper, could lay claim to being a part of the Basilica of St. Francis. Jean's first impression was that the man had done very well for himself. Although furnished in a modest manner befitting the humble monks of St. Francis, its very location at the heart of one of the most prestigious shrines in Christendom spoke volumes about his likely power and influence. Jean had not been given a name, only a place. A nondescript monk had given him leave to enter the room after Jean had showed him the small lead seal the Gamesmaster had given him on the eve of his departure from Avignon.

Fortune was smiling on him at last. After being unable to contact directly either of the Gamesmaster's associates in Viterbo or Spoleto, Jean was relieved to finally find someone to whom he could pass on a report of his activities and a request for some assistance, like getting him and the obtuse squire to Florence. Jean had not lost count of the amount the English squire was owing to his employer, including interest, and to Sergeant Alfonso, as well as his own small pecuniary debt of gratitude to the company's master victualler. In sum, that made three people with a share in the unsuspecting squire's debt, including himself. If he was to collect any of it, he had better make a stronger effort to push Geoffrey in a more profitable direction, whether gaming, hiring himself out to a condottiere or rejoining the English royal commission.

The monk closed the door and shot the bolt behind him. The room was empty of candles, votive or otherwise, but the braziers were emitting enough of a glow for Jean to find a collapsible wooden chair. The long trudge up to the basilica coupled with the weeks of hard marching had wearied him. After slumping into the chair, Jean feared that he might fall asleep before the Gamesmaster's partner arrived, since the intoxicating incense together with the warm chamber were already lulling him into the arms of Morpheus. However, the sharp clang of a metal bolt put Jean's senses on alert. He felt a slight breeze and his eyes caught a shiver in the tapestry on the far wall. A shapeless shadow emerged and, hugging the wall, steadily approached. Jean did not move or speak, fearing that the fiend had sent a specter to frighten him. He blinked once and then again, but there was no mistaking the figure now – it was the astrologer Catherine.

Geoffrey knew little about the life of St. Francis of Assisi. He had encountered many Franciscans in and around Avignon to be sure and had even taken a few shillings from them in the gaming rooms now and again, but there was little he could say with any degree of precision about their customs or their rules. The order was dedicated to charity, Geoffrey knew, as they were rivals of the Cistercians. One of his teachers had been so tonsured, Brother Something-or-other, who had been if not particularly kind, then at least competent in his attempts to educate. All he needed was to find a chapel and a suitable priest who would bless his *couteau* and listen to his prayer for Roger. Assuming that the upper chapel would be superior in every way, Geoffrey began climbing the wide stairs to the main doors. At the top he was accosted by the usual wretched company of lame children, blind men and mad women, all begging for alms, food

OF FAITH AND FIDELITY

or anything that might sustain them until the next miserable day. Then a monk asked if he would like to deposit his sword for safekeeping. Geoffrey declined the offer; he would no more be again parted from his *couteau* as he would his leg.

The nave was remarkably spacious, which was convenient since the number of pilgrims to the tomb of St. Francis certainly exceeded the number of supplicants at the court of the pontiff in Avignon on any given day. The groined vaults looked as though they could only have been raised by angels, so lofty were their heights, so delicate was their filigree. Just enough light filtered in long strips through the stained glass to give the pilgrims below a sense of eternity. The distant altar seemed unattainable, but Geoffrey sought it out as the starting place for his chantry priest search.

When Geoffrey reached the altar, after cutting a long and circuitous path through the multitude, he was startled by the massive and vibrant paintings that enveloped the apse. This was one thing Avignon did not possess. Geoffrey stared at the panel farthest to the right. There, depicted in bold colors, was St. Francis preaching to a flock of birds. However, Geoffrey ignored the story and instead compared the rendering of those images he saw all but floating before him with the ones he knew. The tiniest leaves of the trees were vividly rendered; the sky was mottled in several shades of blue; the birds looked as though they would swoop out of the painting at any moment. Geoffrey tried to think of a word that could describe the contrast between the styles. After a quarter of an hour of staring at the wall it came to him: movement. This painting projected movement such as he would see it in the raw streets outside the cathedral; this movement brought the story of St. Francis down to him. Geoffrey likened it to the passion plays he sometimes attended when a troupe of actors would come to town, or when one of the guilds organized a show to benefit a charity. The painting was kindling a warm spirit in his breast and it made him glad.

"So, you like our Giotto then?" a familiar voice asked in English.

Geoffrey turned and was startled to see the astrologer Catherine. He noticed that she was dressed more modestly than when he had first met her in Viterbo.

"Lady Catherine," Geoffrey said in a respectful tone, "are you searching for inspiration for your next reading with Captain Vilardell?"

"I am here to read these wondrous works," Catherine answered.

Geoffrey would have willingly continued to exchange wits with this woman, but he took Catherine's unexpected appearance as a sign that he should not remain idle, that he still had important tasks to complete before entertainments could be considered. So, he decided to bid the lady farewell.

"But you did not answer my question?" Catherine asked, taking one step forward.

"And what question would that be?" Geoffrey could not be rude, least of all beneath the dome of such a famous shrine, so he allowed himself to indulge the astrologer.

"I asked if you liked the Giotto? It is well and truly awe-inspiring, or so people say."

Geoffrey frowned. He knew that English had many dialects spoken with many accents, but the word 'jyotow' was wholly unfamiliar to him. Of course, he had never set foot in England and those with whom he would speak English were always either wellborn folk or book-readers, meaning that the slurry of vulgar English phrases rarely filled his ears or crossed his tongue. However, the woman had pronounced the word with an Italian lilt, so Geoffrey decided to guess its meaning instead of asking it. "I have never seen one quite like that, but as far as my humble tastes will allow, it falls well upon my eyes. The color suits you."

It was Catherine's turn to frown. "The painting has nothing to do with me, good squire, but I thank you for the compliment all the same. I, for one, consider it a marvel. It has a life all its own. Never have I seen brushstrokes so accurately capture ecstasy as these. Have you?"

Geoffrey looked at Catherine's headdress, which was made from light blue satin and fastened on her head with an expensive piece of lace, at the image of St. Francis preaching to the birds, then back again. His cheeks burned with embarrassment when he understood his error. Nevertheless, he suppressed the anger and resentment building in his chest for the sake of St. Francis and his most holy shrine. "I like its ... movement," he answered in a quiet, unsure voice.

Catherine flashed a look of surprise, but Geoffrey did not notice. He was again staring at the imploring St. Francis, the scattering birds and the living colors. However, Geoffrey soon found that he could not stand still against such vitality, and so he began to fidget. When his fingers brushed his *couteau*, he was reminded of the tasks he had pledged to fulfill. Turning back towards Catherine he said, "It seems as though you know this cathedral well. If that is true, then perhaps you can recommend to me a priest who might assist me in a benediction for my ill friend and my sword."

"Are you sure you have enough money for both?"

Geoffrey refused to answer. The question was an insult, but he could expect nothing less from such a woman, so he refused to dignify her question with a show of offence. He returned his attention to the Giotto.

Catherine understood what the squire's abrupt silence denoted, and so she became more accommodating for the sake of harmony. "Yes, I am acquainted with one or two reliable priests here who would accept your requests. They are young, so they work in the side chapels."

"Any assistance would evoke my most heartfelt gratitude." Geoffrey was calm again and he offered Catherine his arm. She took it. As they were passing by the screen that divided the nave from the choir, Geoffrey was certain that he recognized a man hurrying towards the main doors. "That looks like Jean."

"Who? Your chandler friend?" Catherine responded. "It's a bit far and all sorts pass through here." She ushered the curious squire around a very thick pillar. Then, after pairing Geoffrey with a priest, she retreated to the cloister.

Were he able to fully understand what the chantry priest was saying to him, Geoffrey would have felt more confident, more devoted, when he committed his prayers to his sword and to his friend. His Latin education had been rudimentary and his lecturers dull-witted souls incapable of sparking bookish learning. Nevertheless, this priest was his guide, and so all he had to do was follow his voice and pay him, then all would be well. The more pertinent question of the moment, however, was whether he should ask this man of the cloth to bless his sword before or after reciting prayers for his wounded friend. Geoffrey dropped his eyes to his *couteau*, which the priest had taken and laid at the base of the stone altar. He could not decide. While his *couteau* was the instrument and symbol of his ambition, Roger was his peer, his friend, and someone in need of the healing power of prayer. Let the priest decide, he thought.

The chapel grew silent and Geoffrey turned to the priest with a questioning look, who responded by pronouncing two sums: one for each benediction. Geoffrey checked his purse. Judging by its weight, he would not have enough money to pay for both. As he was dumping the sad, few coins into his hand, Catherine reappeared, chalice in hand.

"I would like to contribute to the good health of your friend, good squire," Catherine said, holding out the cup to the priest.

Geoffrey stared at the gilded vessel as it passed over his head. He frowned before rocking backwards in surprise.

"Yes," said Catherine, "this is the same chalice that you left in Viterbo. I redeemed it for you."

OF FAITH AND FIDELITY

As he negotiated the winding streets and slippery steps that sprawled away from the basilica, Jean was preoccupied with the idea that Captain Vilardell's astrologer was in league with the devil. This was the only way he could explain how she could have gained the confidence of the Gamesmaster. And confidence it was, since the Gamesmaster had explicitly stated that his partner in Assisi was one of his best and most trusted. Of course, considering the distance between Avignon and Assisi, it was possible that he had never met her, but the Gamesmaster was a man in the know and not easily deceived. His master had dealings with wizards, Jean knew, but never witches. Of course, there was a lot that Jean did not know about the Gamesmaster. He might even be Jewish, considering the superiority of his money-handling skills. Jean resolved at that moment to learn more about his master, should he ever return to Avignon.

However, the strange partnership was not the worst revelation to come out of his meeting with Catherine: she had managed to coax from him the secret of Roger Swynford's death. No doubt she had put some wicked potion in those fragrant braziers to loosen his tongue, Jean reasoned. He could not for the salvation of his eternal soul remember when it had happened, but the witch had spared no time in using the information. Under a vague threat of betraying his secret to Geoffrey, she had demanded an interest in the squire's debt above what was owed to the Gamesmaster. She was not stupid, however, and neither was Jean. Knowing full well that Jean was closer to his master than she was, Catherine had judiciously offered to 'assist' him if he would bring the squire to a gaming hall of her choosing that night and they would split his winnings down the middle, minus a five-florin fee for each game she arranged. In truth, Jean thought, it was not a bad deal. The astrologer's demands were surprisingly modest and the offer would benefit Jean personally, allowing him the means to possibly collect the squire's debt and to return to Avignon in some comfort. Still, he hated being manipulated. May the Catalonians be damned about his being their bondsman and may Sergeant Alfonso be cursed for all his remaining days for his sin of greed! There was nothing Jean could do but agree and hope that Catherine would not betray him to Geoffrey, Vilardell, Prospero, the municipal authorities, or the Gamesmaster himself.

Jean inhaled deeply and set himself to the painful proposition of calculating the English squire's total debt to all who had an interest in it: there was the ten pounds plus the four sous per week interest owed the Gamesmaster, which now after eight weeks came to over eleven pounds and twelve sous; there was the one-third of the principal debt that the now damned Catalonian sergeant had extorted shortly after their liberation (liberation! Hah!) at Corneto; to the master victualler Jean had been obliged to promise one month's wages of a standard lance and a good word with the victualling guilds in Avignon, connections with which Jean had boasted; finally, there was the percentage that witch in the sacristy demanded. Life was becoming complicated.

Jean calculated and recalculated using first the accounts-reckoning method of the Gamesmaster, then that of the Catalonian company's treasurer and finally by the Italian money-changers he had observed in Viterbo and Spoleto, since each valued French and Italian silver differently. Regardless of the system he employed, the result was disquieting, ranging from sixteen pounds and half a dozen sous to nearly eighteen pounds in white money. The calculations came surprisingly easy to him, but irrespective of the sums, he still had to share the profits from the English squire's mounting debt and find a way to retain some for himself. In addition, he had to prevent the death of Roger Swynford from reaching the light of day, lead the squire to Florence and find a route back to Avignon, not to mention keep out of harm's way amidst the struggle between the two halves of the Church.

Jean sighed as he strolled into the hay market, but before he could

OF FAITH AND FIDELITY

reach the warehouse, a page belonging to the peasant militia approached him bearing the message that Captain Prospero wanted to see the English lance as soon as possible. Jean made a wry smile when he heard the phrase 'English lance'. His only certainty was that the best he and the squire could do behind the pike would be to lance a boil!

Geoffrey met up with Jean at their lodgings, where they saw Captain Prospero talking with Sergeant Alfonso and other men of rank.

"So, what are the orders, sergeant?" Geoffrey asked.

"For me, it's garrison duty. For you, I don't know." The sergeant took his leave.

"Hotspur! You're late." Prospero said.

Geoffrey started to explain his absence when the captain waved him off.

"Never mind, it no longer matters. Tell me something, though. What is the morale of the militia, your companions from Spoleto?"

Geoffrey bristled at the captain-general's suggestion of such close familiarity, but before he could find an answer, Jean took up the thread. "They grumble about having to march so much. Their crops will start to ripen soon and if they find themselves too far from home, well, I don't know what then."

"Anything else troubling them?" Prospero asked.

"Narni, captain. They're hearing many unsettling rumors about what went on at Narni," Jean said.

"I suspected as much. I shall make my words brief," Prospero stated dryly and without emotion. "Our victorious advance stops at Assisi. To consolidate our gains, I have been asked to strengthen key points in this region. I need you and the militia, but only if they are reliable."

"I cannot vouch for that, captain," Geoffrey said.

"That is too bad. Inform me if their mood improves. Good day."

Geoffrey was about to offer his own sword when the captain-general galloped off. He then thought about telling Jean that he intended to seek service with Captain Prospero, but he had not decided what to do about the Frenchman in this matter. Jean was part of his lance, after all, and Geoffrey would need a servant sooner or later.

"How did Captain Prospero's curious questions strike you?" Jean asked.

Geoffrey was quick to answer. "I believe he fears their idleness, that those peasants will get up to no good. They need action. He needs action. Captain Prospero should not be made to sit and watch while lesser captains earn fame by striking blows against the pope's enemies, especially that Tarlati. Could you not hear the frustration? It is unjust."

"I agree with you, Geoff, but if this is the decision of the war council, then it must be for the best. Nevertheless, this *idleness*, as you put it, does present you with the opportunity to get close to Prospero. You have been taken into his confidence evidently, so he might be willing to arrange a review of your petition. I haven't heard anything from Captain Vilardell about this, so perhaps it is our captain-general's turn to help you get to Florence. Andrea Tomacelli is still in Assisi, as far as I know."

"I shall ask Captain Vilardell one last time, out of courtesy," Geoffrey declared, "and he should be informed about the poor state of his peasant guard."

When the bailiff announced to Captain Vilardell that the pikemen Geoffrey Hotspur and Jean Lagoustine had come to see him, he ordered that they be made to wait for half an hour before being allowed an audience.

"There is wine on the sideboard next to that ridiculous tapestry," the captain glumly said when the pikemen entered. "It comprises the last of the company's stock of fine Catalonian red." He swung a silver goblet at a threadbare image of St. Francis rapt in prayer atop a mountain. The tapestry was so twisted by age that the monk's shoulders were riding above

OF FAITH AND FIDELITY

his ears.

Geoffrey and Jean walked in, but they stopped short when they saw that Captain Vilardell was alone. There were indeed wine bottles on the sideboard beneath the ragged St. Francis and several more on the table in front of the captain, as well as stacks of documents, numerous quills, empty leather coin pouches, and his hat.

"Don't stand on ceremony for my sake. Take a goblet. It's easy, since you don't have to bother winning one now," Berenguar said. His tone was abrupt, sarcastic and dismissive.

Accepting the invitation at face value, Jean approached the sideboard and poured himself a full measure of wine. He was sure, however, to choose a modest vessel, similar to the one from which the captain was drinking, but in pewter. Jean lifted his goblet to honor the captain, victory, the fine vintners of Barcelona, and finally Geoffrey before taking a deep draught.

Captain Vilardell did not drink with Jean. Instead, he slammed his goblet on the table, causing a wave of wine to slop over the rim and douse his hand. Geoffrey and Jean made eye contact and gave each other a knowing look: the captain was not in a pristine state of sobriety.

"As much as I appreciate the generous offer of your precious Catalonian wine, I will not deceive you by accepting an invitation to be your guest, my lord, and so I say that I have urgent business with you. It's about my petition."

For a moment it looked as though Captain Vilardell had stopped listening, as his eyes did not appear to focus on anything in particular and his body was as still as stone. Jean took a sip of wine, content to quietly await another act of generosity. At last, the captain raised his head. His brow was furrowed from some troubling thought, but he seemed to lose its thread when he again recognized his guests. "Show me that sword of yours, Englishman" Berenguar said with a thick tongue. "I don't think I've ever seen one like it. Wait, no, don't bother. I really have no need and

I would hate to be disappointed. I will no longer sponsor your petition. I believe that your vain is in purpose ... your *purpose* is in *vain*. Did that make sense? No matter. Have some more wine."

Captain Vilardell's outburst provoked Geoffrey to think that maybe he was planning to give him the commission his station merited, or recommend him to someone else, like Captain Prospero. The forced idleness at Assisi would have given the Catalonian condottiere time to rate his most excellent men and, as a result, now valued the English squire considerably above a common pikeman. Geoffrey poured some wine and all but toasted himself on his well-earned success.

Jean was more circumspect. He asked the good captain for an explanation.

"Has Sergeant Alfonso not told you what is happening with the company? No, I don't suppose word has reached you yet, although maybe he hasn't told anybody. The arrangements have not been finalized."

"What arrangements?" Geoffrey and Jean asked in unison.

"I fear that we are as likely as not to see each other again. Tomacelli, the smart one, has offered me a new *condotta* for when the old one expires. Very efficient, he is. The pecuniary terms are the same, which to be honest are quite generous, but it comes with a clause that I am not sure I can bear. I would have to give command of my company to that fool of a duke, his brother."

"Would the situation be any different from how it is now?" Geoffrey asked.

"I dare say it would, squire! There would be no more voting on prisoners, for one thing. And what is worse is that he, Tomacelli, the smart one, has ordered me to split my company, the best damn crossbowmen in Christendom, to strengthen the garrisons of three castles. The order came from Prospero, but I know he had no hand in this. It's intolerable, I tell you! Breaking up any company goes roughly – roughly I say – against good military sense. Also, he, Tomacelli, the smart one, wants the St. George's Company to train those garrisons. Now, I don't mind garrison duty – it's easy money and the work is usually not dangerous – but training fat *citizens* to load and shoot that most complicated of arms is an outrageous request. I have half a mind not to sign this *condotta* and join the other side."

Geoffrey was aghast. To be so close to victory and then to betray the victor was not something he could stomach, especially when the prospective victor was the head of Christendom. Also, Geoffrey was in favor of the papal legate's proposition – the more regimented the chain of command the better, he believed. Mercenaries needed to be under the hand of someone with supreme rank and honor. Geoffrey could not resist speaking his mind.

"I would sign the *condotta* if I were you, captain, if only because I can think of no good reason not to."

Berenguar focused on Geoffrey. "Oh you would, would you? My company fights as a whole, or not at all. To make pieces of it would ruin its effectiveness. This isn't the relic of a saint we're talking about here. And speaking about relics, with which piece of my company would rest the most sacred relic of St. George? It would break my beloved company." Berenguar slapped the table hard, but the puff of anger dissipated like steam on a hot day and he slumped in his chair. Then, after heaving an anguished sigh, he reached for a full bottle of wine and added, "Well, I had better make this outrage worth my while, all the same."

"What do you mean?" Jean asked, eager not to let Geoffrey risk being imprisoned for the crime of impudence.

The captain shrugged his shoulders and took a final, sloppy draught from his silver goblet. "Well, maybe my men need to line their purses a bit thicker in order to keep them warm and content in those cursed castles. With ransom and pillage now out of the question, I might have to economize on my *condotta*, for you see, master squire, I'm not sure how much use a peasant militia will be in garrison duty. In my experience, it just gets in the way."

Jean realized the implications of this statement before Geoffrey did. "To disband the militia now might send the wrong message to the papal legate and to the people of the Patrimony, not to mention Captain Prospero. But, of course, I am just a chandler."

"The militia is mine to do with as I wish. I am very well aware how those peasants reacted to the murders at Narni, so it might not be a bad idea to disband the lot anyway."

"And would that include us as well?" Geoffrey asked solemnly. The image of him serving as a proper liegeman rather than as a common soldier in a mob of pike-wielding peasants was fading fast.

"Well, why not? Be gone, all of you! Take your chances with the papal legate, or the duke, or Clement and his champion Malatesta, for I care. And besides, we're not budging from Assisi, now that the summer is nearly on us, so any chance of getting into battle is about the same as … as you winning the company *Cacho* game."

"The petition on my behalf to the papal legate and his brother the duke still goes unanswered, then?"

"The what? Oh, yes. I was supposed to ask them to send to Florence concerning some English party of fools, wasn't I? I do recall mentioning something about it in Terni, but nothing seems to have come of it. Well, I no longer believe that Florence will answer for you anyway, master squire."

Geoffrey was crestfallen by Captain Vilardell's admission that he was derelict in his duty, but his heart felt lighter because of it all the same. It was something akin to clarity of his non-status, and he no longer need rely on the charity of this Catalonian commoner. This broken vow reminded Geoffrey of his own pledge to ensure the restitution of the ruined chapel at San Bernardino.

OF FAITH AND FIDELITY

"Tell me, captain," Geoffrey said. "Did Tarlati ever pay for those crimes that we so solemnly and with heavy heart witnessed on our journey to Spoleto?"

"Eh? What are you talking about, Englishman? Crimes? Did he steal someone's *condotta*?" Berenguar frowned and made a sour face, as though via grotesque gestures he could reorder his thoughts.

"I am speaking of the chapel his Bretons destroyed. He was to make restitution, was he not, as part of his joining the papal host?"

Vilardell coughed out a rude laugh. "Now I remember. No, I don't think he did anything of the sort, and nor do I suspect anyone asked him to. It's all been forgotten, I'm sure."

"Not forgotten by those villeins who relied on that church for succor and salvation!" The Catalonian's flippancy angered Geoffrey.

"Well, you do it then, if it troubles you so much. I did my bit. You go and tell Tarlati to do whatever it is that will satisfy your insulted dignity, or conscience. I want to hear no more about it. I am a busy man and I have my own problems." Berenguar waved his hand as though batting a fly.

Jean was anxious to change the subject, lest this chapel business get the better of Geoffrey, so he asked, "And so you will not sign the new *condotta* then?"

"That is none of your business. My decision is made. I hope you enjoyed my wine. Now, I am a busy man, so if you please…" Vilardell sat back in his chair, lolled his head to the right and stared through Geoffrey and Jean at the door.

Geoffrey was close to uttering a curse on the house of Vilardell for his apparent treachery, but his gratitude held fast the impetuous words. Instead, he consigned himself to offering his former master a curt bow and a view of his back.

While Jean was relieved to be discharged from military service, his being struck from the company rolls meant that he lost access to the trickle of silver flowing from his enlistment. The best he could do, or rather the only option he saw left open to him, was to stick with the English squire and try again to profit from him. To this end he tugged at Geoffrey's sleeve.

"I have an idea," Jean began quietly and he pulled Geoffrey into the shade. "If the peasant militia is dismissed from the company, then it no longer has a captain. Sergeant Alfonso was always whining about that. Now, if *you* were to captain them, Master Hotspur, you might be able to catch the eye of the duke or Prospero and receive your own damn *condotta*. You are a free lance now, and those peasants are, or will soon be, free of any service obligation. It could eventually get us to Florence."

"And what role would you play in such a farce?" Geoffrey's voice was tinged with contempt, but he was mulling over the idea.

"How about master victualler, or quartermaster? I wouldn't really need to fight, would I, since I'm not a squire, knight or soldier."

Geoffrey snorted from the humor he saw in Jean's words.

"In the meantime," Jean continued, "we might do well to safe-keep our valuables away from the eyes of the company, and since your *couteau* comprises the bulk of the inventory, we need not immediately return to the hay market." He was thinking about Sergeant Alfonso and how he might want to seize the squire's fancy sword, since after all, they were now out of the famous Catalonian Company of Crossbowmen of the Guild of Vintners of Barcelona, which meant that his debt was due.

"I will not entrust it to a banker," Geoffrey warned, but before he could continue some shouting erupted from the direction of the basilica. Geoffrey and Jean turned to see two beggars fighting over a loose coin and a monk trying to restrain them. This gave Geoffrey an idea.

CHAPTER 12

Florence

May

Two recent events gave Chancellor Salutati cause for joy and comfort. At the University of Paris, where King Charles recently called upon the resident clergy and scholars to consider ways to end the war for the throne of St. Peter, embassies were reporting that the king had come to see the Way of Force as an unsuitable means for ending the sixteen-year division, particularly as it was steadily draining France of needed resources. Therefore, it was much to his pleasure that the priests and scholars almost to a man had come down on the side of the Way of Cession as the most favorable means of reuniting Christendom.

This was a clear sign that the pontiff in Avignon had finally lost the support of France, the chancellor reasoned, and with that essential prop knocked out, others were sure to follow. Salutati was certain that the momentous ruling of the learned Frenchmen had made possible the second joyous event. The Malatesta family in Rimini and Andrea Tomacelli were negotiating a treaty, thereby for all intents and purposes ending Pope Boniface's war of 'pacification' in the Marche. Although the document had yet to be signed, the chancellor's men in the respective camps there had informed him that the treaty was favorable to both sides, with the Malatesta family retaining the lordships and vicariates of all that they currently held in the Marche in exchange for enforcing the pope's will throughout the region.

How the treaty would affect the young Malatesta Malatesta was unclear. However, what was clear was that Andrea Tomacelli was unlikely to let his army linger in the Marche for long, with his brother still chasing after Clement's captain-general. Perhaps he had misjudged the situation, Salutati thought. Perhaps the war will indeed be over at the conclusion of this year's campaign season.

Thoughts of the war in Umbria flowed into consideration of the old English sergeant the chancellor had sent to fetch a wayward squire. He had received only occasional messages from him in the past several weeks, always with the same news – no squire. He would be disappointed not to be able to return the young man to the Duke of Lancaster. The French were still pressing hard on Genoa. If the city should fall, the chivalry of France might be sent to reinforce the young Malatesta's sagging fortunes. Furrowing his brow in annoyance, Salutati came to the frustrating conclusion that he would have to wait on the dyspeptic soldier.

Because he recognized himself as being stranded in Assisi, Geoffrey had no qualms about leaving his *couteau* with the good monks of the Basilica of St. Francis. It was an honor even, although how Jean had managed it at no cost Geoffrey could not say. Perhaps the Frenchman was recognizing his duty to assist his superior in any way possible, since Jean was still the anchorman in his lance, after all.

What saddened him, however, was the departure of Captain Prospero with his company to besiege Deruta, as it deprived Geoffrey of the opportunity to offer his sword to the captain-general. The good captain had accomplished his mission to occupy the Vale of Spoleto and secure key castles near Perugia, so it was rumored that the papal legate had ordered him to take Deruta while his brother received the glory of chasing down Malatesta.

Geoffrey was now faced with the prospect of following Captain

OF FAITH AND FIDELITY

Prospero across country, remaining in Assisi or accepting Jean's suggestion that he assume the captaincy of the Spoletan peasant militia. So, in the absence of reliable counsel, he began to calculate odds. Traveling alone in the shadow of Perugia would be dangerous, and there was no guarantee that Captain Prospero would accept him, despite their cordial relations. The stakes of such a wager would be high and the odds discouraging, dissuasive even. Assisi, meanwhile, offered the dual attractions of holy sites and games of chance. However, neither was likely to get him closer to Florence or to a knighthood, while taking the tonsure was now far removed from consideration; Catherine and Jean had made certain of that. Of course, Captain Prospero might soon return from Deruta, but sieges were notoriously lengthy affairs, so there was every chance that he would be in for a long wait. No matter how he looked at it, Geoffrey gave this option even odds with a protracted stay in the house.

The more he thought about it, the more the idea of creating his own company appealed to Geoffrey. To bring order to a rabble of villeins might serve as good practice for when he finally commanded his own powerful host of knights. Captain Vilardell did not want them, nor did the garrison of Assisi, since the last he heard the Spoletans were still quartered on their own and without duty. He would have to consult Jean about this. The petty details of organizing a free company were naturally compatible with his sorts of skills.

Of course, the larger question was what he would do with such a company. To fight alongside a respected lord in Italy he would need to procure that thing called a *condotta*, which sounded rather undignified, even if he knew how to go about it *and* had any intention of staying in Italy. Favorable odds, low stakes, little purpose. Another option was to enter service with some other lord, but a lord who could help propel him out of Italy. Andrea Tomacelli still owed Geoffrey an audience. He pulled out the papal legate's seal and rubbed it. This option better resembled a debt from the house, which was quite a slippery thing but at least held the promise of silver owed.

After going back and forth comparing the odds and potential return of the various paths, and putting plenty of wear on his buskins in the process, Geoffrey concluded that the last way offered the most favorable balance between risk and reward. Staring out towards the dimming western horizon, he recognized that his heart held the same determination as in Gaunt's hall, when he decided to join the royal commission, and with this familiar feeling Geoffrey reaffirmed his resolve to obtain an audience with Andrea Tomacelli, the consequences be damned.

Jean emerged from the basilica. "The long summer dusk, I feel, has begun its lethargic advance," he drawled. "It might be in our interest to find somewhere to dine and enjoy ourselves. I recommend a new place, as our humors might be thrown askew should we sup with the ungrateful Catalonians." He handed Geoffrey a small wooden tag notched with a Roman numeral.

Geoffrey tucked the tag into his belt without so much as a simple 'thank you' to Jean for securing his precious *couteau*. His eyes remained transfixed on the view the steep steps of the basilica afforded. It all looked as impressive as Avignon – a fortress of God, which made it all the more strange that Assisi was now a frontier town in the struggle between the two halves of the Church. Geoffrey scanned the horizon and caught sight of the Spoletan peasant militia drilling on a common pasture below the outer wall. At a distance they looked impressive, their ranks and files advancing and retreating with relative precision. Despite not having a sergeant or a captain to command them, Geoffrey decided that the peasants were making a good show of themselves. Of course, an empty commons was no field of battle.

"Yes, some sort of roast would suit me down to the ground right about now," Geoffrey said as last. "Trudging up and down these streets has worn me out. Find me a fine inn or an alehouse and I will show you my home for the evening."

Those were the words Jean had been waiting for. "Well, I have been keeping my ears and eyes open for such an important thing, and the word around the trading stalls is that the Pearl is the finest establishment for the *milites* of the Church." In truth, this was the word of Catherine.

"I am not in the mood to consort with tradesmen, regardless of how palatable their banquets might be. What else have you heard?"

"You misunderstand. The Pearl is not for either tradesmen or the common soldiery. I dare say we might find ourselves sharing a table with lords and high officials, should we be permitted ingress."

"Should we be permitted what?"

"Should they let us in."

Geoffrey soured his face. "Oh, for the love of … And afterwards? While I'm not against a few tankards of ale before matins, I will need a warm bed at the end of it all. No doubt the Catalonians have already seized our gear and locked that stable they call lodgings, although even if they haven't, I have no desire again to be indebted to Captain Vilardell."

"I assure you that will not be a problem."

"What do you mean?"

"You will see."

Geoffrey saw the location of the Pearl behind the English pilgrims' hospice as a good sign. He anticipated a successful evening.

"If we can find a tender side of beef and a healthy pint of ale, I might be here until our Lord's return," Geoffrey announced with such cheer that Jean was taken aback.

"I would settle for a chicken and a swig of something harder," Jean retorted. The squire's new mood caused him to recall that other squire, Roger Swynford, and Jean hoped that nothing in the Pearl would remind Geoffrey about his dead friend.

"Don't talk to me about wine," Geoffrey warned. "It reminds me of the Catalonians, and I definitely do not want to hear about those wretched people or their wine on this night."

"I suppose you expect me to pay." Jean pulled up the right side of his jupon and bunched the shoulder padding.

"Well, you have the silver, if I recall correctly." Had Jean a less prudent nature, he would have smiled broadly the moment the English squire verbally transferred all responsibility for his personal finances to him. Jean could almost hear the thirty-six solidi worth of Italian currencies, valued at the Assisi rate, coming alive in his purse. Admittedly, this was not a great sum – about two month's wages for an average lance – but the silver was connected by a golden thread to a promise of relinquishing debt should the squire seduce Fortuna at the tables.

Geoffrey beat a path to the kitchens, but to get there he had to wade through a sea of richly dressed men and women. Behind him he heard Jean comment on how their colorful raiment made the princely courts in Avignon look like poor pageants by comparison, and he had to agree. The fashions flowing around him were more elaborate and florid than anything he had seen, although it all reminded him of the slaughtered citizens he and Captain Prospero had found in Narni.

Geoffrey swiveled his head back, thinking he had caught sight of a couple of the captains, but the crowd quickly swallowed them. Then, at the main archway leading into the kitchens he spotted Andrea Tomacelli. Few courtiers graced his circle, as the bulk of the court from Spoleto had chosen to escort his brother, the duke, to the other side of the Patrimony.

"Find us a table, will you Jean, and learn the quality of the fare on offer," Geoffrey ordered. "I will course the hall."

"I hardly need another master," Jean mumbled, but he went all the same.

Geoffrey compared the luxury of the Italians to his own simple blue

OF FAITH AND FIDELITY

doublet, unadorned belt and grey, woolen hose and immediately felt self-conscious. He began to hope that the guests would respect him for the austerity of his style rather than pity him for his poverty. More important than good fashion sense, however, was courtesy, Geoffrey was convinced. If he attempted something so rude as to walk up to the papal legate, flash the papal legate's seal and declare his petition, he would likely be chastised for lack of propriety and summarily dismissed as an ignorant commoner. Geoffrey could approach him as a fellow officer in the papal army by holding his nose and calling himself captain of the Spoletan peasant militia, but considering that this would be about as impressive to such a grand knight of the Church as assuming the title of fool-king at a village fair, he was likely to be ignored. Then he had it. However, the moment's exaltation collapsed under the weight of that most usual of dilemmas – someone had to introduce him.

But Geoffrey could not despair, as the boisterous crowd buoyed his spirits. He looked over the bobbing heads around him in search of a familiar crown. The petty captains would not do, as they seemed too preoccupied with drink, women or wagering – or all three – to be of use. He was not acquainted with any member of the clergy, which was also well represented in the main hall. Captain Vilardell was out of the question. Then he spotted the astrologer Catherine in her familiar dark blue taffeta gown and a black domino encrusted with tiny diamonds. As loathe as he was to admit it, the woman was ideal for such a mission – she enjoyed a degree of familiarity in such exalted circles and she had no reason to hinder his chances with the papal legate. In truth, the astrologer should be gratified to learn of his modest success with the papal host, as it validated her prophesy about him.

Geoffrey resurrected Captain Prospero's once enigmatic command to him: "You are coming with me." He instinctively reached out to grab Catherine's arm but pulled it back at the last moment, fearing a breach of

Italian custom.

Catherine gave a little gasp of surprise upon seeing the English squire and ignored his order. "I was looking for you among the games of chance, but all I saw were well-dressed knights." She smiled and drew herself up to her full height so that her eyes were level with Geoffrey's chin.

Geoffrey ignored the slight. He was anxious not to lose his opportunity to meet the papal legate, since he was expected to leave for the Marche any day now. "You are known to His Grace Andrea Tomacelli, are you not?" Geoffrey asked impatiently. "I was told you read for all the captains, when they pay, of course. You must introduce me."

Catherine saw the intensity in the squire's eyes. There was no doubt that she would do as he asked, for she wanted to keep the squire as amiable as possible while he remained in the Pearl, wagering to be sure. Nevertheless, she would make him state his purpose with clarity of vision. "*Signore* Tomacelli is an exalted personage. Why should I risk compromising myself by doing him the dishonor of having to meet a common pikeman? He might not trust my readings thereafter, or pay less for them."

With time being of the essence, Geoffrey would not stoop to exchanging insults. He knew his purpose and would not be deflected from it. "I am a squire of the Duke of Lancaster tonight. I am no longer in Captain Vilardell's service, or rather in his company. I can represent my true station now."

"Well, that *does* put a different light on it. You are not planning to represent the English duke, are you? I was not aware that you carried his seal."

Geoffrey understood that he would have to lay out his *naipes*, so to speak, before this woman if she was to do his bidding. She had held his confidence and he did owe her a favor – two, in truth, considering the chalice and the chantry priest. His face softened as he briefly told her how he needed the papal legate to give him leave and safe conduct to

Florence in order to fulfill his commission with the King of England. He did not say that he was seeking a place at his court. Then, to Geoffrey's surprise, without so much as a condescending look or belittling comment, Catherine agreed.

The introduction was brief, though courteous, and once the usual pleasantries had been exchanged Catherine excused herself on the grounds that she was being called to read for Captain Vilardell.

The papal legate's attire was amongst the most modest in the hall. He wore a long white tunic and a yellow robe without trim, and he would have been mistaken for a minor courtier were he not so well known. "It must be difficult for a squire such as yourself to be cast so far adrift from your native shores and not know when the winds will blow you back. You are enrolled with the Catalonians, are you not? Your face looks familiar, or rather your height."

That the papal legate had initiated the conversation surprised and gratified Geoffrey. "Captain Vilardell is no longer my captain," Geoffrey answered. "At the moment, I serve no one but myself on this fair but foreign soil."

"Well, such is the fate of men oft times when they are torn from their roots." Tomacelli sipped his wine. A local dignitary bowed to him while passing and the papal legate nodded in return.

"My lord, the Duke of Lancaster, is of the same belief. I once carried his badge, but it was lost."

The papal legate produced a thin smile. "That is a rather large thing for you to lose. I should be more careful next time. The wrath of your duke is terrible to behold, I am told, but I am curious. Tell about the court he keeps."

At first, Geoffrey had trouble finding the rights words to describe the great hall in Avignon, but after a few halting attempts, he spoke of the squire hall, the old knights he met as a page and the huge hearth, until he found his rhythm and talked for a quarter of an hour, concluding with his low station in the Hawkwood commission.

"Perhaps this war will furnish me with the chance to show myself, but it seems I no longer have a place in it, much to my regret. You know that I am wanted in Florence."

Tomacelli returned the bow of another local notable. If he had heard Geoffrey's last words, he gave no indication of it. Rather he was looking over the multitude to see who was talking to whom. The dark mood of his captain-general was troubling him, and he was concerned that it might infect the other captains. He knew that Corrado Prospero was an honest man and would never break a *condotta* without just cause, but the sin of pride by nature runs in all *condottieri*, so he had to be watched. Also, the recently taken territory needed a strong hand, and while he would have preferred to leave the German captain in the field, it was more important to show that his brother the duke was leading the campaign against Clement.

After a long silence, Geoffrey grew nervous and considered taking his leave; however, the stark realization that another private audience with the papal legate was highly unlikely girded his confidence, so he continued to speak. "My problem is that I have nothing to vouchsafe me and my appeals have gone unheeded."

Tomacelli answered without taking his eyes off the crowd. "Captain Vilardell will not speak for you?"

Geoffrey thought that his relating in any detail Captain Vilardell's state of inebriation and despair would be indiscreet and, therefore, would reflect badly on his manners, so he declined to mention his most recent encounter with the captain. Instead, he told how he was accorded the dignity of bearing the captain-general's gonfalon at Narni, hoping that the papal legate would connect the petition Captain Prospero had made in the command pavilion to release prisoners with his own petition.

OF FAITH AND FIDELITY

A look of recognition brightened Tomacelli's face and he turned to Geoffrey. "You're that English squire Captain Prospero dragged into my tent. I am heartened by your desire to stay with us."

Judging by tone and by words, Geoffrey concluded that the papal legate was ambivalent towards him and not in the least troubled by his having been Prospero's witness in the affair at Narni. "I must admit that such a fortunate circumstance is not likely to last, as I am without rank or station in this country."

"I understand your meaning. It would not do for an English squire to be on his own here, as he would find few friends." Tomacelli looked thoughtful.

"It has been my good fortune to be well received at all stations along my long road to this place. It has been a trial, I must admit, though mainly a trial of waiting for my captain to fulfill his pledge. I now know that this will not happen, yet I am still bound to your host by virtue of this signet." Geoffrey pulled out the seal of the Papal Legate to the Marche and held it out in plain view.

Andrea raised his eyebrows. "It seems as though I am obliged to hear you, good squire."

Geoffrey saw his opportunity and he blurted: "I am your man, my lord." He bowed and held out his right hand.

Tomacelli was far from taken aback by the sudden declaration, since he was quite used to supplicants of all ranks and stations seeking his patronage. He merely acknowledged Geoffrey's pledge with a nod. "You are Gaunt's man; he should have you back."

"I am, yet I have been carried to Assisi without him." Geoffrey straightened his back, but kept his eyes lowered.

A page approached the papal legate and reported that several messages had arrived from his brothers, the Duke of Spoleto and His Holiness Pope Boniface. Andrea turned to go.

Geoffrey made another bow and asked, "Am I likely to see you at the gaming tables, my lord? I shall be there straight away."

But the papal legate was already leading the page out of the hall.

Geoffrey was pleased with the exchange, despite its meager promise, as the papal legate seemed to show an interest in him. However, his protesting stomach cut short such reflection, and so Geoffrey decided to search for the rest of his lance. He found Jean seated at a table near the back of the hall with a large plate of roast beef in front of him. Its sight and scent brought a smile to Geoffrey's face, as here was yet another sign that the evening would bring him advantage. After wading through the remaining crowd, he seated himself next to the Frenchman and without a word tucked into the beef while commandeering a mug of ale that had been left unattended.

"You're lucky you chose that cup," Jean said when he was sure Geoffrey was listening. "I saw one of the captains spit in the one next to it."

"Fortune is the byword for me tonight, I'll have you know. I just took leave of *Signore* Andrea Tomacelli and he was quite courteous. I might not need to seek command of that militia mob after all." Geoffrey tore a piece of flat bread from a pewter platter and began to vigorously mop up the beef drippings on his plate.

Jean passed Geoffrey a bowl of mixed shallots, peas and turnips, followed by another filled with dates to divert him from consuming all the meat. "You still mean to pledge yourself to a lord, then?" Jean asked.

"I do indeed. It's a pity that Captain Prospero is on the other side of these walls, but perhaps it is the Lord's will, as his absence has allowed me to buy several blessings, leave the crossbowmen and cultivate the goodwill of a great lord. Yes, I am certain that much advantage will come from this here."

"But what about Florence? Have you forgotten your commission to that other lord, King Richard, not to mention that you are still a man of

OF FAITH AND FIDELITY

Gaunt?"

"There is no need for you to be concerned on those accounts," Geoffrey replied brusquely. "Now that we are no longer enrolled with the Catalonians or even a part of the papal host, you are free to fulfill the purpose for which your guild sent you to Italy. Or, you can make your way to Florence alone and catch one of those wretched caravels back to Avignon. I will return to Gaunt when the papal legate no longer needs me. If it is money that concerns you, and I have seen just how expensive this land can be, then I shall give you half my winnings here tonight to facilitate your journey onwards. Wait. I shall be generous and offer you a full two-thirds. What say you?" With charity Geoffrey hoped to curry more divine favor.

Jean could only be pleased with the offer. Should the squire win big, he might be able to pay off the sergeant and the astrologer and still have enough to give to the Gamesmaster, that is, if he indeed wanted to hand over anything. He could very well take the money and leave the Catalonian and the woman high and dry, abandon the Englishman with his debts and return to France. However, the fly in the ointment was that he could not be certain of getting very far before someone tracked him down; Catherine was a partner of the Gamesmaster and evidently well connected in Italy, not to mention the Catalonians and even the master victualler, for that matter. Jean could not decide, so he resolved to let the final reckoning of the squire's winnings determine his course of action, even though relying on the fickle Lady Fortuna unnerved him.

"Since I am still the second in your lance, I have no reason not to defer to your judgment."

Geoffrey nodded. He would have shaken hands with Jean, but they were coated with grease. "I am certain I heard the sweet clatter of dice being rolled," Geoffrey said. "It is time to weave my fortune."

"Have you the silver?"

"No, but I know you do. Where is that great mass of coins I won in Spoleto the last time round at *Cacho*, anyway?"

"It was only a few sous and I spent it on provisions and such. However, the captain was kind enough to pay out next month's wages, which I suppose we'll have to return now, and the master victualler finally handed over the few florins he owed me." These were all lies, of course, but Jean had to find a way to explain the 36 solidi he suddenly had on his person.

"Well, perhaps the time has come for me to bear that heavy burden."

"Indeed? Just be sure not to let too much silver slip through your greasy fingers. And make yourself presentable, for all that his holy." Jean unlaced the purse attached to his belt, withdrew from his boot a stack of coins wrapped in felt, removed a gold florin from the cuff of his sleeve, and placed the lot in front of Geoffrey, who, after wiping his hands and mouth with the tablecloth, scraped the money into one hand and left. Jean was about to follow when he caught sight of a familiar pendant of a certain guild lodged into the headdress atop a familiar head. Jean excused himself from accompanying Geoffrey on the grounds of needing to pay for the meal.

"Should you really let him go unattended like that? He might fall in with the wrong company, meaning those who would fleece him of his last penny," Catherine chided.

"Of course he will. We are in Italy, are we not? The squire is a gamer, not a grumbler, and from now until the drawing of the dawn I myself will wager that he scarcely budges from the tables. He's like a Flagellant, you see; once he whips up his wagering fury he falls into ecstasy," Jean replied.

Catherine nodded, but her eyes were following Geoffrey through the crowd of revelers. "Who has he met?" she asked.

"You should know. You introduced him to Tomacelli."

"Anyone else?"

"No one that I'm aware of. Why, does it matter?"

"Of course if matters. In Italy all conversations are thick, like your accent, with meaning and significance. Can you at least tell me why he is so interested in the papal legate? I know about the petition, but that cannot be all."

"I'm not sure that I should. It is a personal matter, not a pecuniary one. Why did you so quickly abandon him if you are so desirous of knowing the Englishman's intentions?"

"The papal legate would never speak freely in my presence, so I was obliged to leave them in peace. And I should tell you that if anyone speaks with the pope's favorite brother, it is almost certainly about more than personal matters."

"If what you say is true, then I should be scrupulous with my answers."

"As you are scrupulous with your debts?"

"The good squire is my debt, madam, and we shall not be seeing him until the morrow."

"I was not speaking of your pledge to your lance. Can the squire play?"

"The squire can play. Dice is his game, and no doubt he is casting at this very moment. Jean hesitated before offering Catherine a version of the truth concerning Geoffrey's interest with Andrea Tomacelli. After all, he could not be sure that she did not already know it. "He is thinking of pledging himself to the papal legate. The Catalonians dismissed us today."

"You should have told me earlier."

"It only just happened, and it will not affect our arrangement. I'm just worried that the house will not accept his word to play on tick if he starts wagering like a bishop. Nothing has been pawned and I have not been able to speak to the local gamesmaster, or whatever this hall's cashier is called."

"That is all taken care of. The table masters have been informed about the squire."

Jean looked at Catherine with admiration and contempt. He feared that she might attempt to assume command of the squire's debt and leave him with no prospects. He was still an outsider here, and that weakness was a considerable disadvantage in the game he and the astrologer were playing.

"Nevertheless, I shall keep watch," Catherine informed. "I know of vantages that will make me invisible to him."

Geoffrey was surprised by the absence of a table for *naipes*. He had assumed that if a band of crossbowmen from across the sea had them, then Italian lords would certainly have imported the game as well. But Geoffrey was in no mood to fondle *naipes*. He was hearing the seductive song of dice and he had to follow it. He passed tables offering other games, children's games to his mind, like pebble-toss and number lotteries, all the while keeping one eye out for Andrea Tomacelli. He soon spotted him at an elaborately crafted dice table. Geoffrey peered into the shallow table and saw that the players had already wagered on a main point.

"I wager ten solidi on the chance point and another two on the nick," Geoffrey announced to the table master.

People turned their heads to gaze at the French-speaker with the unrefined accent, including Andrea Tomacelli.

"We do not accept stakes made on the nick or on the crab, sir, only on the main roll, unless the caster chooses to accept them," the table master explained in Italian.

Geoffrey understood enough to look at the caster, who in turn passed an imploring look on to Andrea.

"As I am the one staking him," Tomacelli explained, "then I should decide. What was the main roll?"

The table master stated that the main roll was 'six'.

Tomacelli was impassive, but had no intention of letting the English squire seize control of the game. The aggressive wager, made without decorum, was an act of bravado rather than good strategy. The money was of no consequence, since the pot was only up to forty solidi. He would much rather see how the squire reacted to the humiliation of rejection.

"I will abide by the house rules," Andrea announced. "All wagering ceases the moment the main roll is cast."

Geoffrey nodded solemnly and withdrew his hand from the table without protest; the papal legate's right to deference crushed any seed of anger that might have germinated in the squire's breast. While the caster was throwing his dice, Geoffrey worked himself into a player's place.

The chance point came to 'eleven'. Had the main point been 'seven', the caster would have won on the nick, so the chance point had to be thrown again.

'Ten'. Now, another 'ten' or a 'twelve' was needed. Geoffrey was sure that the next cast would be a 'seven', recalling seeing that combination the most often after three casts.

'Seven'. Had this been Avignon, he would have been allowed to wager on each cast after the chance point was set, but again he had to suffer the house rules.

Another 'seven'. Geoffrey kept his eyes on the dice as they spilled out of their leather casting drum and listened carefully to how they fell. Unlike the rough mat at the Blue Boar, the casting surface at the Pearl was a high table covered by a thin layer of green felt, which reduced the normal clatter of ivory dice to a series of low, muffled thumps. Nevertheless, after a few throws Geoffrey determined that they were not loaded, for even muffled thumps varied in pitch.

'Three'. The caster had crabbed out.

Andrea covered the wagers and the table master called for a new caster.

Geoffrey could not contain himself. "It is the custom in my land for the honor of first cast to go to newcomers in the hall," he announced loudly and with precise enunciation in order to grab the attention of the dozen-odd men and pair of courtesans who enveloped the dice table.

"Pray someone tell me that this noble custom holds true in the Patrimony of St. Peter. I would not want to suffer the pain of insulting the dignity of this noble company."

The courtesans were charmed by Geoffrey's simple speech as by his less than sumptuous attire. The table master looked at Tomacelli for a sign, who nodded to indicate that the house rules should prevail.

"Have you the money to cover the wagers, sir?" the table master asked.

Geoffrey threw his coins onto the table. The table master raked them towards himself with a long, curved stick and after counting the contents etched a number on a small slate to indicate the maximum total wager – thirty-six solidi. He then asked Geoffrey whether he would be willing to accept a house debt at the house rate should he require it. Geoffrey immediately nodded his ascent, so anxious was he to show his mettle at the gaming table. The thirty-six solidi were returned.

Geoffrey started out very well. On his first throw he won on a nick of 'eleven' after throwing a main point of 'seven'. He then won the next three throws by making his chance point before crabbing out on his fifth throw. And the money he won was not insubstantial. From the first cast with a stake of five solidi he won twenty-five. The same result favored the second cast, giving him eighty-six solidi in total. For the third cast Geoffrey doubled the stake, but with just three players knocking he was only able to collect a modest thirty solidi. For the fourth cast he dropped the stake to eight solidi, which attracted another player and led to a thirty-six-solidus win.

The burgeoning crowd around Geoffrey's table began to draw players from other games, but none could make their way through the growing throng. The same four players remained to wager against Geoffrey's ten-solidus stake for the fifth cast, which cost him forty but left him with 132 solidi as he passed the casting drum.

"You should be well pleased with your good fortune, dear squire. You should be able to buy a fine harness and surcoat with those winnings," Tomacelli said.

"I would rather use the money to marry or fund a chapel," Geoffrey answered with a mask of sincerity.

The crowd applauded and Geoffrey became the most popular man in the hall. The flock of courtesans tightened around him.

Andrea laughed. "Were you to bed your bride in those clothes, she would no doubt flee from your affections, regardless of how fat your purse was."

"Then perhaps a chapel is in order, or maybe I could fund a company of knights. His holiness would not object to more men to help defeat the enemies of the Church. I have already served him once, and it would be an honor to serve him again."

"I have to warn you, good squire, that with your handful of silver you would be hard pressed to recruit even the worst company in Italy, although you might be able to find a few Bretons to do your bidding. At least they might understand you."

"Then pray give me some useful advice. Your free companies do not interest me. And besides, I should win at least three handfuls of silver tonight. Today is indeed one of good fortune for me." Geoffrey grabbed a tankard of ale from a passing server and threw a grosso onto the tray.

"Be careful that no one parts you from your newly won wealth, since I know how much squires value their silver."

"Noble service can be a well-minted currency too, but I am sorely impoverished in that treasure at the moment. You are not playing tonight?" Geoffrey waved his tankard over the table.

"I am already wagering that my captains fulfill their duty, and that is quite enough to leave to chance."

"I am sure they will, and I should imagine their success will draw Italy's finest knights to serve his holiness. It will be wonderful to see the glittering ranks of Italian chivalry riding down the poor hirelings of the antipope in a grand pass of arms."

"Would that were so, my dear squire, would that were so. I am afraid that our chivalry has found virtue in the sin of sloth, excepting that of my native land of Naples. Were the French not stirring the cauldron of discontent for my cousins, they would ride north at the head of ten thousand knights to smother these rebellions."

"Remember that I am a man of the Duke of Lancaster, uncle of the English king, and without land or relations in France, my lord." Then a strange and exciting idea blossomed in Geoffrey's head. "I would venture to wager on a place at your court."

"I have no need of your silver, master squire, nor have I a place at my court to stake. I keep a small household, as everyone knows."

Geoffrey was crestfallen. He had already gone so far as to place coin values on the ranks of courtiers and hoped, with the aid of Fortuna, to make enough casts of the dice to win the post of groom, or even keeper of the seal.

"Blessed am I in silver, but it seems that silver can no longer buy a blessing, alas," Geoffrey said as he sighed.

Andrea raised his eyebrows to show that he was amused by the squire's clever turn of phrase and was about to answer with yet another friendly quip when he noticed a dark pall descend upon the squire's face. He followed the young man's eyes until he found them resting on a new arrival – Tarlati.

"God's bones!" Jean exclaimed to Catherine. "What is he doing here? Shouldn't he be with the Duke of Spoleto somewhere to the west? This does not bode well for our affairs." Jean began to awkwardly make his way to Geoffrey, for he was still on the other side of the gaming hall, but Catherine held him back with a fistful of sleeve.

"Do not rush in, you fool," she commanded. "We do not want to brighten the spectacle with a violent act. Let us quietly work ourselves around the hall to get closer to our friend. I cannot see a reason why our interest in the squire should be made known, and in such a coarse fashion yet."

"I will again defer to your judgment, but pray tell me why he is in Assisi? His hellish Bretons are not encamped nearby, are they?"

"I will make enquiries." Catherine looked around until she found a courtesan she knew and accosted her. After a brief exchange, she returned to Jean's side with an answer. "Captain Prospero sent him here from Deruta, although no one seems to know why. Fortunately, his Bretons are still ravaging their way up the Tiber in the wake of Malatesta's retreat. Now that your idle curiosity is satisfied, let us take care of our squire."

Geoffrey rose to full stature, which impressed the ladies even more. A few blinks broke the power of his gaze. Ignoring the calls of the table master to play on, he addressed the players who were clinging to the opposite end of the table. "Make way for a true knight of the Church," he bade them, "a man who leaves no stone atop another in his search for the enemies of the one true pope and who, thus, should be honored accordingly."

All faces turned towards Tarlati, who was now at the papal legate's side. He looked confused by the attention and did not recognize Geoffrey until Tomacelli whispered his identity. Then, seeing by the attention he was receiving that the peculiar greeting could not go unacknowledged lest he risk incurring ridicule, Tarlati stepped forward.

"I regret to inform you all that I shall not be gaming this evening," Tarlati announced, "so please find a more ardent player who might be worthy of an honor such as this." It was a simple deflection of address and a respectable retreat from the field. He made a slight bow and was about to speak to the papal legate when he again heard the English squire's voice rise above all others.

"You have decided to donate your stake to make good the unfortunate consequences of this war within the Church, have you then?" Geoffrey asked with a presumptuous tone. "It should go a long way towards clearing your conscience." If Geoffrey had expected this arrow to hit its mark, he was sorely disappointed.

"We are all so heavily laden with sin that it would take until the Last Judgement for each of us to give voice to them all, although a babe like you might be closer to innocence that the rest of us," Tarlati answered.

The crowd laughed, but Geoffrey would not be deterred by Tarlati's quick wit. For him, the affair of the ruined village chapel was no laughing matter and he refused to allow it be trivialized by some condottiere.

"So, you have made a good and honest restitution, like a true knight and servant of our Lord, by sending monies and apologies to the good people of San Bernardino for the ruin your men made there. I am pleased." Geoffrey's tone was challenging.

"What are you talking about, boy? San Bernardino? The only apology that need be made is you for your appalling taste," Tarlati answered, gesturing towards Geoffrey's doublet.

With the blood roaring in his ears, Geoffrey did not hear the laughter behind him. "As you well know, my words concern the chapel of a village near the castle of Orte, which your Breton company destroyed for no reason worthy of a true knight and Christian. It must be restored. Have you restored it?"

"I have no recollection of this village *chapel*. No report was made to me. Anyway, these are the hazards of war. I have no regrets if my Bretons don't. You above all, being English, should appreciate the sentiment." Tarlati smiled and bowed to Andrea as a gesture of deference and an invitation for him to end the discussion.

The truth is known, Geoffrey thought. Captain Vilardell was right. He now thought to sting the captain with a remark about his betrayal of the false pope in Avignon, but now, of course, he was on the right side, so such an epigram would almost certainly fall flat. Nevertheless, he needed to respond to the captain and he needed to do so in a hurry or risk being pelted with ridicule by the crowd. It was clear that an open condemnation of his company and an unadulterated demand for restitution of the ruined chapel would mean little in this crowd and even less to a man like Giovanni Tarlati. He had to defeat him in a pass of wits, not in a recitation of his crimes and an appeal to his conscience.

A glance at the papal legate reminded Geoffrey of Captain Prospero and how they nearly came to blows in the war council pavilion at Narni. The captain-general had held Tarlati in contempt, he remembered. Perhaps that was the way to get to him.

"I agree that only our ultimate Lord can judge us our sins," Geoffrey began haughtily, "but who will avenge the slaughter of innocents, I ask you? Just as the sins of this world will not go unpunished in the next without redemption, so too our earthly crimes should be redeemed as befit them, or we are guilty of reckless folly that makes us unworthy of salvation. I believe that our captain-general, the esteemed Corrado Prospero, would agree."

The guests oohed and aahed and the courtesans beamed admiration for the squire, while Tomacelli's silence implied neutrality in the verbal dual between the squire and the captain.

Tarlati knew that he must respond, and respond decisively. "I would be very wary about speaking for your betters, boy, when you are so ignorant about their affairs," Tarlati said evenly.

"Nevertheless, as he is the captain-general of this campaign to defeat the abomination that resides in Avignon, it would be an insult to Captain Prospero's dignity if reckless murders were made in his name or without his approval." Geoffrey still had the dice drum firmly gripped in his hand, despite the urgings of the discomfited table master.

Andrea looked annoyed, but he said nothing, while Tarlati remained defiant and continued to press. "So you are the good captain's gonfalonier then, are you?" Tarlati said. "Why are you so concerned about the state of the captain-general's dignity, pray? Are you his champion, or do you hold some other more vulgar office in his retinue?"

Geoffrey anticipated Tarlati's barb and this emboldened him. "We should all be his champions, as he is busy championing the just cause of his holiness the supreme pontiff in a noble pass of arms with his holiness's enemies, as you should be."

The crowd had begun to jeer, and Geoffrey could hear in the cruel captain's voice that he was becoming impatient.

"I see that you have won a knight's ransom. Now you can go home and buy a herd of swine with all that suspect silver and marry the blacksmith's daughter," Tarlati spat out in disgust.

"I am surprised to hear you talk of ransoms, my good captain, since I know how you dislike them so. But this is all empty talk because since you decline my challenge at the gaming table, I would expect you would retreat from my pass on the lists, and I never run someone through from the backside up."

The crowd howled and the courtesans tightened their grip on Geoffrey's arms and waist.

"Should you stay under Captain Prospero, such an opportunity would never present itself, as it is well known that our esteemed captain-general prefers to avoid battle rather than seek it. Perhaps his dignity is not in danger after all?" Tarlati addressed the question to the crowd.

Geoffrey shook himself free of his admirers and pushed his way around the table in order to get to Tarlati, but instead of emerging face to face with his challenger, he found himself confronted by the astrologer Catherine.

"Wine fires the passions of the young more quickly than those of the old, would you not agree *Signore* Tomacelli, your lordship?" Catherine said in a voice so nuanced as to hold the arguing parties at bay.

The papal legate smiled at this timely intervention and made a deferential nod in her direction. He then spoke a few ameliorating words to Tarlati before addressing Geoffrey. "Come see me in the morning, master squire," Tomacelli said. "I will be riding out to the Marche."

"I am your man," Geoffrey declared.

The papal legate and Tarlati soon left the hall, followed by the small condottieri. Catherine mixed with the remaining guests, though always with one eye trained on the English squire. Jean, meanwhile, his remaining strength having been drained by Geoffrey's encounter with Tarlati, returned to his lodgings. Geoffrey, however, was so invigorated by his excoriation of the despised butcher of San Bernardino that he remained at the dice table for the rest of the night, retiring only when the hall's gamesmaster closed the wagering.

CHAPTER 13

"So, these are your lodgings now, are they? Of all the shrines in the holy city of Assisi you choose to pay homage to Our Lady of the Rented Venus." Jean, who was on whole amused by the scene but piqued at not having been invited to this apparent debauchery, kicked Geoffrey's uncovered foot to get his attention. On his right lay the courtesan who had escorted him during the bulk of the previous evening, asleep and smelling sweetly of wine. It was mid-morning.

Geoffrey opened his eyes and stared at the ceiling. He was sure he should recognize the voice, but he could not quite place it. Oh right, he realized; the chandler. He opened his mouth to offer a rebuttal, but his parched throat stifled any sound. Then he coughed, which shook the bed, bringing the huddled figure beside him closer.

"Homage is about all I have to offer, Jean," Geoffrey managed to squeeze out after much effort. "Now make yourself useful and find me a glass of water, or wine, or something to cleanse my salty tongue."

Jean rummaged around the small but sumptuous room until he found a ewer partially hidden by a rumpled headscarf. The room was almost exactly as Catherine had described it last night as they together watched Geoffrey leave with one of her acquaintances, which gave grounds for Jean to suspect that she supplemented the income from her astrological readings with more than just usury. He poured each of them a goblet of cool clean water, passed one to Geoffrey and made a silent salute with his own. Looking out the window, Jean judged that Andrea Tomacelli should be well underway preparing to leave for his army in the east. What a shame it would be were the notable English squire to miss his appointment, Jean slyly reckoned.

Geoffrey gulped down the water in a single draught, sighed and then threw himself out of the courtesan's bed. To Jean's relief, he was wearing a long white shift that must have been borrowed from his still sleeping companion.

"In truth, I was not wholly honest with you just now," Geoffrey said. "I can pay homage to a lord or I can pay some of this." He dragged a small wooden chest off a sideboard and dumped its contents on the bed.

Jean peered into the newly dug depression and was astounded to see it filled with coins. And not just any old coins. Amidst the shiny silver pennies and grossi Jean spotted at least three florin d'oro.

"I'm not sure whether you look pleased or troubled, Jean, as my eyes are still weak and weary." Geoffrey picked up a coin stamped with the profile of the Roman pope and threw it at the courtesan. It landed in the luxuriant trusses of her hair, hardly causing her to stir.

"How much is she?" Jean asked, then immediately regretted it. He did not want to look as though he had any interest in the squire's business, personal or otherwise. He had to continue presenting himself as an accidental and indifferent companion, lost in the same wilderness of strange customs and languages as the Englishman.

Geoffrey blinked a few times then turned to look at the girl. Until now, the idea of paying for anything that had passed between them had never entered his mind. "Perhaps I should ask her," he suggested, "although it hardly matters now though, does it?" He grabbed a few more coins and threw them at the courtesan.

This time she awoke with a start. After a bit of eye-rubbing, she noticed Jean standing at the foot of the bed, cup in hand, but if she was surprised by his presence, she did not show it.

"What gifts should I bestow upon you this morning, fine mistress?"

Geoffrey asked in a loud affected voice. "You were my talisman last night, my charm and my guide. I will give you all that I have for a single kind word from your sweet lips." He poured a cascade of silver down the front of her chemise.

The girl was far too experienced to allow herself to be carried away by the flowery words of the squire. She merely asked for the amount her hand could collect in one scoop of coins and a goblet of wine from the squire's valet.

Geoffrey laughed and with a sweep of his arm bid her do as she wished. He wanted to say more, but he could not for the life of him remember her name.

Very adroitly, the courtesan gathered in her small white hand a pound's worth of metal, being careful to gather only two gold florins, and dropped them into another small chest built into the corner of the bed. Then, sensing that Jean had arrived to take the squire away, she kissed Geoffrey lightly on the lips and scurried into an adjoining room.

"Will she let you keep the box at least?" Jean asked, pointing at the empty chest that lay at Geoffrey's side.

"It is not hers to give. I won this box along with all that filth you see before you. I told you the signs foretold of impending good fortune." Geoffrey slid the remaining coins into his chest and closed the lid, handing it to Jean once he secured the brass clasp.

"Very well. I'll take this and wait for you outside." Jean took his leave. He was sorely tempted to throw open the tiny casket and count Geoffrey's magnificent winnings. He was certain that it contained enough silver and gold to pay off all the squire's debts *and* for him to live comfortably for little while. Jean's fingers tingled from these thoughts, but all that would have to come later. Right now he had to figure out how to secure the money and come up with a plausible and safe way to declare his true self so that he could claim redemption of the debts. When should he do it?

Perhaps he should consult Catherine.

Geoffrey emerged looking content. Jean suggested that they breakfast at a small market located close to the English pilgrims' hospice, but Geoffrey wanted to collect his *couteau* from the basilica as soon as possible and to double his offering for chantry prayers for Roger Swynford. As he looked at the clear blue sky, however, he stopped in his tracks and an icy streak of fear ran through his back.

"By all that is holy, what hour is it!" Geoffrey cried. "The papal legate will have gone by now! Oh, curse the dastardly fiend that tempted me with the twin delights of women and wagering. How could I have let slip from my heart the one mission that was so dear to me. I must go at once!"

Jean grabbed hold of Geoffrey's doublet and said in a stern voice, "Calm yourself, man. There is plenty of time to reach the papal legate. These departures have a habit of being long in the making and you still need to collect your gear, as you yourself have clearly stated. Now, what time is our appointment with his grace?"

"What?! What are you saying? Oh, yes, of course." Geoffrey combed back his hair with his hand to steady himself. "But *we* do not have an appointment with his grace. I did not commit you to anything. You are a free man. I sought personal service and now I am about to be received in fealty by this distinguished Italian lord."

"So, you're breaking up our lance. I should be hurt."

"You should be overjoyed, for there is nothing to hold you here now. My burdens are not your burdens. Listen, I will split my winnings with you, like I vowed, and we can part as friends."

While Jean was thinking about how to respond to Geoffrey's decision to join the papal legate and his offer of a load of silver (and perhaps gold), the bells of the Basilica of St. Francis began to peal with unusual intensity, a clamor that quickly found its echo with other bells across the city.

"Matins are not over already, are they?" Geoffrey asked.

"They are long over, but that is not a call for matins. I fear that alarm is being sounded."

Geoffrey and Jean looked around them, but all shutters were closed and doors bolted.

"We should make for the English pilgrim hospice," Jean suggested. "They are sure to let us in."

Geoffrey sharply turned to Jean. "What? No, no, I must collect my blade and meet his grace. Climb up a tower and see what the alarm is all about."

"I cannot run with this chest of yours tucked under my arm," Jean complained. "Look: let's visit the basilica first and get your sword. We can view the whole city from there." Jean was also thinking that Catherine must be on her way to the sacristy, if she was not already there, where she could mind her and the Gamesmaster's newly won wealth. That would at least relieve him of some of the responsibility for the squire's debt should the town be sacked and the treasure lost. If the woman succeeded in keeping the chest out of harm's way, he should be able to track her down, whether through the Catalonian captain, one of the Gamesmaster's associates, or even the Gamesmaster himself.

"Good thinking, master chandler. I'll wager that the basilica serves as a mustering point too." Geoffrey slapped Jean on the back and set off at a brisk pace.

The monks would not let Geoffrey into the tower of the basilica, but they did direct him to a part of the curtain wall that had been built into one of the basilica's outer cloisters. There Geoffrey found a cluster of people staring southwards into the Vale of Spoleto. He followed their sight until he too saw the rapid advance of a large body of horsemen towards the two southernmost gates of Assisi. He could not determine who they were, since they were too far away for their banners to be clear, but the glint of light reflecting off their polished helmets and the heavy thundering of their horses made it certain that they had all points armed.

Geoffrey left the wall and ran to where he had stored his *couteau* the day before. The door was locked and there was no one about. Geoffrey kicked the door, but he only succeeded in bending the toe of his right buskin. He kicked it again and this time a wooden tag fell from his belt. Geoffrey picked it up after a moment's confusion, tucked it back into its fold and looked around for someone to help him. Hearing voices above him, he followed them up some stairs and into a cloister, where he spotted a pair of dark-clad figures hurrying through the far arcade. Geoffrey chased after them, but as he was rounding a corner, he nearly ran over Jean.

"I cannot reach my sword!" Geoffrey cried in frustration. "Where are those wretched monks? I thought I saw a couple of them roaming this corridor just now. They should be praying for the welfare of the city instead of gawking at some distant riders!"

Jean put a hand on the squire's shoulder to calm him down. "Not to worry. Your money is safely stored, first of all, and your *couteau* I am sure is in even safer hands. Let us visit the sacristy in the northern transept. That is where most of the keys are kept, from what I've seen, and it should not be abandoned."

Jean could feel Catherine's eyes watching him from somewhere near her little sanctuary. She had fastened Geoffrey's chest with one of her own locks. This was reasonable enough security, although it meant that he and the squire were once again penniless, since in his haste Jean had neglected to collect any silver for himself.

The sacristy was indeed full of monks and sextons scurrying to bring order to the room. Jean grabbed hold of a brother who was smaller than him and, with one fist wrapped in his robe and the other perched beneath his chin, explained that Geoffrey was a young captain in the papal army, and so it was of divine importance that he retrieve his sword before rejoining his company. The fib worked. The monk snatched a handful of keys and tramped down to the armory. At the bottom of the steps, Geoffrey duly turned over the wooden tag and the monk wasted no time in searching for and returning with the treasured sword. Then, with great care and reverence, Geoffrey affixed his *couteau* to his belt.

As soon as they were back in the cloister, Geoffrey turned to Jean and asked, "And now, what about my harness? I cannot face the Papal Legate to the Marche looking as though I had just left a courtesan's chamber."

"I've told you where it is, but I suppose that makes no difference. Now, we must go back to our lodgings."

The streets were empty of common folk, but the farther south Geoffrey and Jean traveled, the more soldiers and militia they encountered. Jean thought about making himself lost in the crowd, returning to the basilica and taking the money for himself. However, the flow of men carried them quickly to the hay market, where they discovered that not only had the threat not passed, but the organization of the city's defence was in full swing. On the market square proper several ranks of men-at-arms and local militia were mustering, sergeants were yelling and soldiers were fumbling with their arming points. No one paid Geoffrey and Jean any mind, although for an instant they caught the eye of Sergeant Alfonso, who was trying to establish order while fending off questions from a clutch of citizens. The pair ignored the shouting Catalonian and pushed forward towards their former lodgings.

When they reached their room, they saw that all the crates and chests had been thrown open, but fortune was still smiling on Geoffrey's lance, as they found both harnesses, scattered, but complete. They made haste. Anything that could not be worn was stuffed into a sack and shoved into a pile of hay. This left them reasonably well armored but poorly armed, despite Geoffrey's *couteau*, as their English pike remained with the Catalonians.

On their way out, a glint of metal caught Jean's eye. He peered into the corner and saw Geoffrey's chalice. "I'll have that," he said as he picked it up. The lip was bent and half the gems were missing.

"Take it," Geoffrey said. "You can use it as a mace."

"Well, what now, squire?" Jean asked once they were back on the square. Seeing no way of escaping the moment, he deferred to the Englishman.

Geoffrey looked around and reviewed his options. The Catalonians were out. Prospero was out. Rejoining the Spoletan militia was possible, and they must need a captain, but he did not know their language. And besides, Geoffrey was sure they would be panicking by now. What Geoffrey wanted to do was find Andrea Tomacelli, pledge his sword and ask to join a knight. That was the best plan, he decided. But before Geoffrey could explain anything to Jean, the shrill voice of a crier announced that all men-at-arms must make for the main citadel with all possible speed. Immediately the great mass of mustered and unordained men began to pour into the streets leading eastwards.

"It seems as though our course has been set," Jean sighed, trying hard to hide his ambivalence. "Shall we go?"

Geoffrey gave his companion a sharp look. "I have an appointment to keep. No doubt his lordship is rallying the army at the main citadel. I shall go there. You are still free, although it might do you well to continue serving in my lance. As a stranger here, I doubt you will easily find refuge."

The open field at the base of the main citadel was strangely tranquil. The sergeants and criers were now silent, as though the battle was already over. Strangest of all, however, was the absence of captains or town officials. Both Geoffrey and Jean had expected the papal legate, the city's *podestá* and the guild captains to have convened on some high ground to direct the defence of the city, but even the bridge that led to the citadel's main gate was showing no earnest activity.

Jean asked one of the Catalonians if he knew anything.

"What did he say?" Geoffrey asked. He had his left hand wrapped around the pommel of his *couteau* and his right hand tucked into his belt.

"He says that the gates to the citadel are closed. The same goes for the minor citadel. Beyond that, nothing."

"So, we have to wait?"

"We have to wait. We should have brought some *naipes*."

Geoffrey frowned. He pushed passed the Catalonians and waded into the dense mass of local militia, but he did not get far. Not happy about being jostled by an excited squire yelling and cajoling in a foreign language, the more hot tempered citizen-soldiers began to push back until finally Geoffrey was thrust out of their company altogether.

"Fie on you!" Geoffrey cried at the militia as he retraced his steps to Jean. "I would no more be captain of your womanly rabble than I would a band of blind nuns! Jean! What else have you learned? And where is His Grace Andrea Tomacelli?"

Jean shrugged and pointed at the squadrons of heavily armored horsemen that were appearing at the heads of the streets and alleys that led away from the main citadel. They were deploying in such a way as to prevent anyone from entering or leaving the field. The disorderly host began to stir, particularly as the long spears of the strange horsemen were being leveled at it. The Catalonians emerged as the best organized of the lot, with their crossbows armed and set to knock down any knight who would dare to ride them down. The militia seemed to have no idea what to do while the peasant-soldiers of Spoleto formed three ragged ranks backed against a sheer rock face. The men of the companies of the petty condottieri, meanwhile, were still deciding whether or not it would be just wiser to lay down arms and surrender.

"Maybe I should lead the Spoletan militia and form them into proper ranks before they panic," Geoffrey suggested. His eyes darted around the field looking for a place to set arms. "We could defend the flanks of the crossbowmen, then. I know it's an odd way to ordain a battle, with crossbows in the center, but at least anyone will think twice about running us through."

Jean was about to agree to the plan, in the absence of a safe alternative, when his eye caught a pair of richly clad figures separating themselves from the mysterious horsemen near the citadel's main gate.

"Is that Captain Prospero?" Jean asked, tugging Geoffrey's sleeve and pointing.

Geoffrey squinted into the sun and recognized the colors and trappings of the captain-general's horse. "God's bones, so it is!" Geoffrey cried. "We must go to him. There is no danger for us now."

"If no danger remains, then why do the bells continue to peal so violently?" Jean said. He did not share Geoffrey's certainty.

"It must be a clarion for the men to arm all points. Captain Prospero has no doubt discovered the threat to the city and needs us with all speed," Geoffrey declared.

Geoffrey and Jean threaded their way through the nervous soldiery, calmly this time, and the squire's confidence grew further when he saw trailing the captain-general: Captain Vilardell, the abbot of the Basilica of St. Francis, the city's *podestá*, and other local notables. Next to Captain Prospero, however, was a man neither Geoffrey nor Jean recognized, but only one name was whispered around them: Malatesta.

Geoffrey and Jean had just reached the verge of the citadel road when a herald stepped out from between a couple of horsemen and announced with the full force of his voice, "By the peaceful agreement of the *podestá* of Assisi, the abbot of the Basilica of St. Francis, the chancellor of the commune of Assisi, and his lordship Malatesta Malatesta of Bologna, the city and commune of Assisi are hereby confiscated by his lordship Malatesta Malatesta of Bologna. All those bearing arms will lay them down and follow his lordship's men into the main citadel at their direction. All captains and sergeants are to likewise submit and to remain with their companies until further notice is given." The herald stepped back and the horsemen closed ranks.

The full impact of the proclamation hit Geoffrey only after his ears stopped ringing. The city had surrendered to Clement. Captain Prospero, far from being a prisoner, seemed to be leading the forces of his now erstwhile foe. Geoffrey could not believe it. Leaving Jean behind, he ran towards Captain Prospero to demand an explanation, but men with clubs and chains were already descending into the defeated host, preventing him from reaching the captain.

Captain Prospero noticed the struggling squire, but he merely nodded to him before riding onwards into the citadel.

"You say you're looking for a lost English squire?" Captain Prospero asked William Godwin.

"Don't tell me you found one, Conrad," Godwin answered. "It seems as though Assisi has a blessing for both of us."

"Yes, well I don't think anyone else is willing to pay his ransom, so if you are truly interested …"

"What! You want me to *pay* you to take him off your hands?"

"It wouldn't be much, say … five silver florins."

"I'll give you two and not a penny more, and be thankful to get that much."

"I thought you were in the pay of Florence? The *Signoria* there is almost as wealthy as the Church. It should be they who pay, not you."

"Regardless, my conscience allows me to redeem only at true value."

Prospero laughed. "You sound like a crusader!" he teased. "Conscience, indeed. Did Florence redeem *that* for you? I thought you'd pawned your principles ages ago. So be it. I'll take your two florins, in unclipped coins if you would do me that courtesy, and release him to you. And one more thing. He has formed a free lance since he was thrown upon these shores, so you will get the lot – the English squire and some French chandler who serves as his valet. Ask Sergeant Alfonso of the Catalonians if you are in need of more details. I only plan to spend a couple of hours here before returning to Deruta."

Godwin snorted to signify his agreement before walking away to the kitchens to find something to eat.

Geoffrey looked lost in the shadow of the main gate as he searched for the man who had paroled him. Only moments ago he had been marching with a mixed group of prisoners, glum and confused, towards an unknown fate when a man yanked him out of the queue and told him to report to Captain Prospero. Leaving his companion-in-arms behind, Geoffrey worked his way past the sad column and soon found himself alone and disoriented in the main citadel's courtyard.

Prospero had dismounted and was in the midst of sorting some documents. At the first call, he did not hear Geoffrey, but upon the second, louder address, he looked up and nodded at the squire, as he had outside the citadel.

"Does the papal legate request my presence?" Geoffrey asked, refusing to believe that Prospero had switched sides.

Prospero rose to his full height and assumed his most dour demeanor. "The papal legate has escaped," he said without emotion.

Geoffrey silently pronounced the word 'escaped'. "I don't understand," Geoffrey said.

"There is no need for you to understand. You are out of it. You belong to him now."

Captain Prospero pointed with his riding crop at a grey-bearded man ambling towards them with a leg of mutton in one hand and a cup of ale in the other.

Geoffrey gave Prospero a quizzical look. "You betrayed Boniface? You are under Clement now?"

Prospero jabbed the tip of his riding crop into Geoffrey's chin. "I am not under anyone! They betrayed me!" He pulled the riding crop back and exhaled. "Go home, boy."

"And Tarlati?" Geoffrey felt a surge of anger flow alongside his confusion. He clenched his fist and stared hard at the captain.

"He fled during the night, not surprisingly. Now go to the man who ransomed you. He is one of your countrymen."

"Ransomed?"

"Of course. You are a prisoner, are you not? Twice over, from what I understand of your situation. He's called William Godwin."

"William Goodswine?"

"Godwin, of the White Company. One of old John Hawkwood's companions-in-arms. Bow to him, if you wish to bow to anyone. You belong to him now." Prospero returned his attention to the documents, having no more to say.

"I wonder for how much *I* was ransomed?" Jean quipped. He could not suppress his smile over the squire's sudden change in circumstances. However, the smile concealed a more serious concern, which was how to retrieve Geoffrey's money from the astrologer, now that the Tomacelli meeting was likely postponed indefinitely.

Geoffrey was not listening. He felt adrift from all around him. The papal host, the Catalonian company, Andrea Tomacelli, all seemed like parts of someone else's life. The royal commission to collect the remains of Sir John Hawkwood, *his* commission, now made manifest in the form of this strange grey-beard, roused him to his original purpose. It was another sign, but it left him no further ahead than when he had sailed from France two months ago. Perhaps he had finally failed, he thought. He had missed his appointment in Florence; he had been stricken from the rolls of the company that had saved him; and he had not gained favor with a prominent lord. He had done nothing of valor in Italy, leaving him without a shining example of prowess or courage by which he might be able to secure service with even the most obscure lord in Avignon. And while his faith in his station as a squire had been sorely tested, he had done nothing to demonstrate his fidelity. He was leaving, being taken away, and that was that. His heart was now as heavy as during his final hours in Avignon and his situation was no less uncertain than when he had first landed in Italy. Geoffrey's head began to swim, and he grabbed Jean's hoqueton to steady himself.

As it was clear that Captain Prospero had no intention of introducing them, Jean took the initiative. "You are William Godwin?" he asked when the grey-bearded man came to within a dozen paces of them.

"I am," Godwin mumbled as he chewed.

"We are your charges, sir," Jean said, speaking for Geoffrey as well.

"Don't call me 'sir', or 'your lordship', if that's what's next on your tongue. You sound like a man from Languedoc, so you must be the Frenchman. You may come with us, if you like, but you owe me nothing. You're free to do as you please." Godwin turned to Geoffrey and addressed him in English. "So, you are the missing English squire. What is your name again? Hotspur? All very well. We ride at noon for Perugia. You are not to be let out of my sight!"

Geoffrey was sullen as they rode down the road into the Vale of Spoleto on palfreys Godwin had secured. Although he had been unwillingly brought into the war between the rival pontiffs, he found himself unexpectedly sorry to be taken from it. He sensed that the campaign was about to culminate in a great battle somewhere in the Patrimony and he would have pledged his *couteau* to be part of it. However, far more than his forced return to quieter pastures, Geoffrey was troubled by Captain Prospero's apparent treachery. As the party was crossing the Chiasco River, he kept muttering, "I don't understand it, I just don't understand it."

Godwin could not stand it any longer. "You don't understand *what*?"

Geoffrey looked up. "What?"

"I said 'you don't understand what?' You were babbling like a brook back there."

"Captain Prospero. I don't understand how he could betray Boniface, the papal legate and the duke. We are on the cusp of victory over Clement, yet he…I can't even say it anymore." Geoffrey slumped in his saddle and let the afternoon sun beat down on his neck.

"He was insulted." Godwin shrugged his shoulders.

"That's it?" Geoffrey asked. "He was insulted? For all that is holy, he went against the supreme pontiff! He will be excommunicated for sure, and then where will his soul be?"

Godwin chuckled and mopped his brow. "You most certainly do not understand, boy. Now listen. Don't worry about Conrad's soul. Popes excommunicate condottieri all the time and no one pays it any mind, and before you ask why, I will tell you. It is because the soul doesn't enter into it. When a pope hires a captain, he is acting like a lord, not *the* Lord, so if a captain takes his holiness's money but breaks his *condotta*, no amount of scripture can be used to deny him the sacrament. He is not a heretic; he's just an unreliable soldier."

Geoffrey thought about this for a while before saying, "Yes, but to risk the wrath of one of the most powerful men in Christendom over an insult?"

"Reputation," Godwin answered.

"What?"

"Without one, a man is nothing, and a condottiere – less than nothing. Conrad told me all about what happened at Narni and how the Tomacelli usurped his command. He left to protect his reputation."

Geoffrey nodded. He understood the value of a man's reputation, his dignity, and the need to ensure that it remains untarnished, but to risk anathema? That was a strange thing. Upon further reflection, Geoffrey decided that in good conscience he could never bring himself to raise his sword against the supreme pontiff in Rome.

"Is the White Company with Clement?" Geoffrey asked after a lengthy silence. Only now were Captain Prospero's parting words registering.

"The White Company!" Godwin snorted then spat something vile into the verge. "No, the White Company is long gone, I'm afraid. It departed this earth before the death of Captain Hawkwood. Even the St. George's Company has broken up."

"I was with the St. George's Company," Geoffrey stated plainly.

"What kind of St. George's Company? I am speaking about *the* St. George's Company, blast you, which was before your time, if I reckon correctly."

"Catalonian crossbowmen."

"What?! Who?! Don't tell me you were with that son-of-a-vintner Vilardell. No wonder you survived this long without getting a scratch on you."

"So, you are not in this war, then."

"No. Best thing, really. It's getting bigger all the time and without an end in sight. The sooner we are out of the Patrimony, the safer we'll be."

"Bigger? I thought that it already involved all of Christendom."

Godwin sighed. "I mean bigger on the field. More and more lords and condottieri are being drawn in. Silver is flowing like that river we just crossed. Best to stand clear, I say, because none'll win this one. It's not like the usual quarrel between lords or cities. I foresee no end to this struggle, especially if we start to see the northern kings taking up the sword themselves instead of sending their poor cousins to trumpet their interests for them. I pray that it won't come to that, for the soldiers' sakes, since it is well known that kings and pontiffs prefer to root out the weeds of their private affairs than tend to the flower of their armies. That was the one good thing about fighting for the cities here; they were timelier with their obligations to those who protected and defended them."

"What do you mean 'was'? Does your company no longer take the field? Having trouble getting a *condotta*?" Geoffrey asked. He was interested in hearing the old man's opinions because he seemed to be so forthright and honest with them.

Godwin coughed out a wheezy laugh. "So, you've been picking up some of the language, eh? Well, once I return you to Florence, I leave this land for good, and then I won't have to hear that miserable, fiendish word *condotta* again. England awaits."

It was after Perugia that the trio heard that Andrea Tomacelli had left the Duke of Spoleto in charge of the entire papal host in the western half of the Patrimony in the wake of the defection of Captain Prospero to campaign in the Marche. How he had managed to avoid capture at Assisi no one could say, although the papal legate was known to be an early riser. Also, it was rumored that Berenguar Vilardell's company of Catalonian crossbowmen might have had something to do with it, since he had declined an offer to join Clement and instead decided to leave the war altogether.

Jean was listening to the conversation between the young squire and the old sergeant, but he did not care enough to participate. His mind was on Catherine and the money he had lost, or rather the money she had taken from him and declared it for the Gamesmaster. When he had finally found her in the Pearl, she declared the squire's total debt with the various interests at over sixteen pounds, plus half of whatever Geoffrey had stuffed into the chest he had won. Such a sum would keep about three hardy knights for a year in France, Jean calculated. Because the winnings could not cover all of Geoffrey's debts, the witch had confiscated the lot. When he threatened to denounce her as a spy, sorceress, or usurer if she did not give the money back to him, she said that she would denounce him back as a man of Clement. He left with nothing but a promise that the Gamesmaster would receive his share.

From time to time Jean would sigh and consider turning his back on everyone and everything and try his fortune elsewhere. He even nearly convinced himself that Geoffrey was a curse, or worse, that the squire had been right about the evils of silver, but such morbid thoughts did not sit well with his humors, and regardless he could not betray his imposture as a simple but useful chandler with no particular interest in the squire. But the horror of his penurious state kept praying on his mind, so much so that in order to defeat that demon, he decided to interrogate Sergeant Godwin as they rode the road to Umbertide, in spite of the old man's obvious dislike of him.

"I understand from your words yesterday that you are anxious to leave this fair land," Jean said. They were already traveling upland into the hilly country of northern Umbria. The road was wide enough to ride three abreast.

"Aren't *you*? I have no reason to stay here." Godwin's answer was gruff, but the cool morning air combined with the surety that this was to be his final journey in the service of someone other than himself had softened his mood.

"You found no wife, no title, no place here? I find that hard to believe, master sergeant. The wine is so fine as well." Jean wanted to impress that he was a light-hearted rather than a light-minded fool.

"Then you should hold fast to your drink. You're a chandler, are you not? You can find a place here, I'm sure. You seem to be well tried in casting about."

"My calling is in France, I must admit. I have had no luck on my commission to this land. Fortuna thumbed her nose at me from the moment I stepped foot onto this rough shore, or rather dragged onto it.

Anyway, France is no less beautiful than Italy, particularly the southern lands of Languedoc, and silver stretches further there. Was the White Company ever in France? Although if it was, that's nothing to me."

"My hatred of the French has long since faded, like the hair on my head and the black in my beard. The memories of my service with King Edward the Victor are so clouded that even the names of my companions-in-arms from those days have been blotted out. No, I shall return to the village of my birth, like the great captain, John Hawkwood."

"So, you will not be taking the squire back to Avignon yourself?"

"I don't see why I should. I was hired by Florence, not by Gaunt or King Richard, or anyone else. Why? Are you looking for safe passage back home?"

"You have seen through me, master sergeant. I am indeed without means to return to *my* village. As my story goes, Italy is cursed for me. Fortuna will only again turn her radiant face towards me when my feet feel their native soil."

Godwin chortled. "As opposed to Fortuna soiling your native feet. I'll tell you right now that you will have to ask the chancellor in Florence, or perhaps the squire himself. Our crossed paths diverge in Florence."

"But the English commission must have already left and the squire has no means of his own." Jean was inching towards the heart of his interest in Geoffrey.

"The chancellor will take charge of all that. He always does. The squire will be his ward when I turn him over in Florence." Godwin scrutinized Jean from the corner of his eye. He was not accustomed to talking in such great draughts, except with the Florentine chancellor, and then only out of duress. Even as the intelligence gatherer for his late master, all talk with his spies and agents rarely lasted as long as this one with the Frenchman. Were he not exhilarated by the prospect completing his final mission in Italy, he would not have bothered to spit in his direction.

"Then neither King Richard nor the Duke of Lancaster has sent someone to collect him?"

"That I cannot say, nor does it interest me. All I know is that *my* duty ends in Florence." Godwin could not see how the squire's fate interested the chandler. They appeared to be friends and companions-in-arms by accident, but it was clear that they were not equals, shared common aims, or were in any other way related. The squire, Godwin noticed, was showing no indication that he was listening. The boy was quiet, sullen even, and evidently distracted. He was keeping his head up, which was a good sign, but he had not said a word since they left the gates of Perugia. He would have to keep a close watch on him, Godwin decided.

"Well, *my* duty will not end until I report to the chandlers guild of Avignon on my disastrous journey," Jean said. He was certain that he would get no more out of the old sergeant for the moment. He was also coming to believe that little or no money awaited the squire upon his arrival at Florence. That was unfortunate. However, if the mighty Chancellor of Florence has a keen interest in the English squire, then at least a sliver of hope of a reward remained. Of course, if he could get the old sergeant to stake the squire at *naipes* or at dice along their journey to Florence, then he still might be able to earn a little silver for himself.

"How well do you know these trails?" Jean asked Godwin. They were passing woods as thick as those near San Bernardino.

The interruption was unwelcome. Godwin coughed and spat into the dusty road. He was just starting to enjoy the tranquility of this area. It was late afternoon, they were between largish villages and the low growl of the nearby Tiber River was playing in his ears.

"I know them better than you, but if you don't trust me then ride ahead and tell us what you find – tomorrow."

"I will do that. And so that I don't fly off my horse while I race up and down that mountain over there, I'll use that bag of coins you keep in your saddle to weigh me down. So, hand it over, sergeant." Jean stuck out his hand, palm upwards.

"If you ride that nag too hard, you'll miss all the ambush sites, and then where will you be when the village waifs jump you and trample you in the dirt? You're good for nothing else, besides troubling my peace."

"And you know where they are," Jean said flatly, his voice tinged with doubt.

"Know them? I made some of them myself, and so well, mind you, that the local lords have probably built castles over them."

The sergeant's mention of ambush drew Geoffrey's interest. "You were a cutpurse? That doesn't sound likely," Geoffrey scoffed.

"Of course not. The White Company used to pass through here on its way between Tuscany and the Marche, and not a few times, if my memory serves me rightly." Godwin looked up at the sky and then glanced at the twin mountains that were still a few hours away.

"You knew John Hawkwood well?" Geoffrey asked. He realized that he knew nothing about the late condottiere, despite a lively reputation in Avignon, whose bones he had once been entrusted to find and return to their native soil. Out of respect, since the captain had evidently been knighted, and as a small way towards redeeming himself before his lord and king, Geoffrey resolved to make the man known to him.

"I was with him since Poitiers, more than thirty years ago, and accompanied him on his first journey to Italy. I was just a common archer then, though don't ask me to string a bow now. A better captain there never was, nor ever likely to be." Godwin had no intention of sounding wistful, but he was not used to looking at the past, whether of glorious adventures or strenuous trials, so his words contained a raw emotive power that surprised him.

"Who knighted him? Whose man was he?" Geoffrey asked.

"He was his own man, that's for sure," Godwin claimed with pride.

The rekindling of these ancient memories warmed him, making him more voluble. "I don't think he ever served a lord after he left France, at least not in the way you might think, boy. After our great victory at Poitiers, good King Edward no longer needed him, or the rest of us for that matter, so we all became our own men."

"Yes, but how did he become *Sir* John, if he had no lord to grant him arms?"

"Edward, son of Edward, the Prince of Wales."

"A prince of the realm knighted John Hawkwood?"

"Yes, of course. It was during the Reims Campaign, and it was well deserved. He received a mighty fine set of spurs, as I recall. Never wore them in battle though. He thought it would be tempting fate. Ha!"

Geoffrey was impressed by the old sergeant's words. "How did he go from serving the King of England to serving the city of Florence?"

"He served many masters as captain of the White Company. I do believe that we stepped foot into every city in Italy at one time or another, and not a few in France as well." Godwin looked at the sky and then inspected the mountains for signs of suspicious movement, as was his habit. The late afternoon sun was exceptionally hot, he thought, as he pulled his blue riding cap down over his eyes.

"Was your late master a man of virtue?" Geoffrey asked, emphasizing each word. He did not wish to cause offence, but he needed to know. It reminded Geoffrey of how Gaunt used to talk to him during his the early days in Avignon.

Godwin gave the question serious thought before answering. As the main protector of Hawkwood's memory he had to be discreet about his life and deeds, for he understood as well as the wisest scholar that the most valuable treasure a man can bequeath to the future is his good name. His only rival in this matter was the soulless *Signoria* of Florence, and he would be damned if he let that band of wool-sellers and moneychangers control it.

Squinting into the blazing sun and stroking his beard, Sergeant Godwin at last said, "He was indeed. He honored his debts, respected his men and made sure that the reputation of the company was always above all others. A good man all round."

"I mean did he conduct himself well with other knights? Was he a virtuous man?"

"He was not a courtier, if that's what you mean, and he had no court of his own, other than his captaincy. You're starting to sound like a priest, boy. Take off your hat. I want to see your tonsure or burn your scalp trying."

Jean laughed, but Geoffrey was too earnest in his inquiry to be bothered by the mild jape. "Could he be relied on to defend the Church, perhaps I should ask? He served the supreme pontiff, I am sure, but did he ever protect the Church? Was he a man of great chivalry, like a true knight?"

"Hawkwood was a condottiere, not a chevalier," Godwin said shortly. "He showed *virtu* rather than virtues. Knights of the kind you seem to have in mind do not survive in Italy for very long."

"I don't understand your words. What is *virtu*? Is it not the same as virtue, in the meaning of loyalty and humility before the Lord?"

Godwin's first instinct was to tell the squire to mind his mount and let him learn the hard way about the life of soldiering. He recalled the ear-numbing lecturing of Salutati with a shudder and resolved not to replay that dull spectacle. However, if he ignored the question, that bloody Frenchman was sure to pester him until he answered, so he might as well do it once and do it right. Keep it short and sweet, though, and let neither fool interrupt.

"*Virtu* is what keeps a great captain in the saddle amidst a large and unruly company. It is how he conducts himself as a leader of men. It consists of virtues, perhaps, for any great captain needs to know when to be loyal, when to be generous or when to show strength of purpose.

He cannot be forever bound to one man, excepting our Lord and Savior. I don't know any other way to explain it. Maybe ask a priest, since they spend most of their time idling in thought. If you want to wield the white baton properly, then you must act as though you deserve it. That no one else is worthy. That's how it's done here. There is no king."

After the old sergeant had whipped his palfrey and rode ahead a few lengths, Geoffrey thought long and hard about these last words. Geoffrey had always believed that the essential virtues of a knight were eternal and housed in the heart. Loyalty and devotion could not be broken except by mutual consent, or by betrayal, but he did not want to think about that. He understood that above all a knight owes *fidelitas* to his lord and to the Church, all the way up the natural order to the king. However, here in Italy chivalry was defined by other customs. These condottieri, who were men of no one unless paid, were knights of a different sort. Again, the corruption of silver, Geoffrey thought and he was sad.

The night and the next day passed quietly, with conversation as stilted and heavy as the air. More villages started to appear, which elevated the mood somewhat, until at last they saw Umbertide resting on a bend of the Tiber. The *signore* did welcome Godwin and his charges, feted them in accordance with their stations and let them wander the small, neatly appointed city at their will. Godwin had no fear of losing the English squire, but just to be certain of his whereabouts he had Geoffrey agree to meet him at the big alehouse on the main square before compline hour, where he promised to spin a few tales about the campaigns of the White Company. In the meantime, Godwin went in search of a notary so that he could send a coded message to his employer about his discovery of the English squire. He reckoned that Salutati had been kept in the dark long enough.

Jean was pleased not to know the name of Godwin's alehouse, although

OF FAITH AND FIDELITY

if the bloody place had anything to do with boars, he swore that he would piss himself and then take the tonsure. He felt worse, though, when he learned that the wretched place had no hall for dice, *naipes* and any other means of gaming. Even so, he did not think that he could muster the desire to support Geoffrey in another bout of manic wagering anyway. When no one was looking, Jean smashed an empty bottle against the wall near the kitchens. His nerves were fraying at the prospect of having to return to the Gamesmaster with nothing but debts on his shoulders. He was growing tired of spinning lies to no end. It was time to finally leave this miserable lot and find his own way: the miserly Gamesmaster, Geoffrey the English millstone, Catherine the thieving witch, Berenguar the Catalonian fool, Prospero, Tarlati, the Roman pontiff, the French pontiff, condottieri, may they all be captured by Saracens and made galley slaves, so long as they ended up as far away from him as possible. He had nothing left.

Jean chuckled bitterly at the irony of his feeling as the young squire had on that very first day in Spoleto when he suffered a crisis of conscience. Perhaps, with some luck, they would be set upon and murdered by *routiers*, but Fortuna would never be so kind.

Jean began to order ale by the quart. It was good, strong ale, and so it not only eroded his fears, it also scraped and smoothed the hide of his troubles. The faces around him started to dance like the flame of a candle.

"I found a solemn and respectable chapel today," Geoffrey announced after Godwin was seated and comfortable. It was near the hour of vespers, so he was getting hungry. "It was built by crusaders at the time of our king of blessed memory Richard Lionheart. Do you know it? I haven't seen many crusader chapels in Italy, at least not where I've been. I am taking it as a good sign."

"I cannot recall it offhand, but I'd wager my own weight in silver that I stepped foot inside at one time or another," Godwin answered. He stopped a passing serving maid and ordered a full plate of roast pork with as many vegetables as the plate could hold and another round of ale.

"I should like to pray there tonight. Will you join me? I have seen nothing else to distract me."

"You could pray for that astrologer woman to come to us," Jean suggested. He was starting to feel ill, since he too had not eaten since morning.

"I will pray for the ruin of Tarlati," Geoffrey said.

"Oh, enough about Tarlati!" Jean shouted. "Let him be already!"

Geoffrey was taken aback, but upon seeing how drunk the chandler was, he let the outburst pass.

"I was also thinking about praying for Roger's swift return to health, although that doubtless has been accomplished."

"That would be one, long prayer," Jean slurred. He groaned as he watched a plate of roast pork being delivered to their table.

Godwin hacked off a large piece of meat and began to chew on it with the ferocity of a lion. He was glad that the Frenchman's interruption had forestalled his having to answer the squire, so he said nothing.

"What do you mean, Master Chandler?" Geoffrey asked.

Jean waved him off, realizing how loose his tongue was. "I mean that it should be a long time before another trouble besets your Master Swynford," Jean said, "considering how well his bleedings went."

Godwin's ears pricked up. "This would not be the great Swynford family what attends the royal court, would it? Are you a member of the Swynford household? I might have been away from England for the better part of my life, but I still know who's who out there." Godwin thought about Salutati and all the secrets he held. He was certain that money lingered at the back of the chancellor's mind, like the fiend waiting to seduce the unwary.

"My friend and fellow squire Roger Swynford is related to that family, yes. He was wounded in a brawl just before I left Avignon and was faring poorly."

"Did he attend the court of the Duke of Lancaster as well?"

"How do you mean 'did'? I should hardly think that the duke would exile him just for fighting a few heated commoners. Our cause was just."

It was time for Jean's ears to prick up. Although money-drunk and despondent, he did not like the way the conversation was going. He could not let Geoffrey know that his good friend was dead. But, then again, why not? He had failed the Gamesmaster. He could not see how he could collect the debt from the squire – the English sergeant was making sure of that – and he saw only a remote possibility of any sort of legacy awaiting him in Florence. There was a greater chance of the squire being clamped in irons and thrown onto the first galley bound for Avignon, just to be sure that he did not stray again. A few days ago, he was fashioning an opportunity for the squire to fight for one side or the other in this war for St. Peter's throne. He had seen the amount of wealth that was regularly exchanging hands, even among the lowborn, in such a venture. Now, this Godwin fellow was taking away his squire. Well, blast him anyway! He was the one person in Italy to whom he was not indebted. Old and feeble best described him. Jean could run if he needed to, or run the blackguard through. He had been running for the whole of his time in Italy, after all.

"Roger is no more," Jean slurred. He strained to pull his right shoulder up, but he only succeeded in bashing his head against an oak beam.

"Roger is no more what? You look swine-drunk, Jean," Geoffrey said.

Jean rubbed his head and then downed the rest of his ale before making his grand declaration. The more he thought about it, the better the idea seemed. He was through playing games with the squire. The irony made him laugh. "Roger gave up his immortal soul before we left Avignon. A page told me as we were boarding the caravel."

"Fie on you for uttering such words!" Geoffrey looked at Jean with incredulity, but after scrutinizing his face he saw that the Frenchman was in earnest. All blood drained from his face and he slumped back against the wall.

"Yes, he's dead, dead, dead," Jean mumbled into his empty tankard, finding a deep echo with the final 'dead'. "He has no more humors to balance. He's just dead, empty of spirit, only dead, gone."

"Enough!" Geoffrey croaked. "You are too drunk to think straight."

"Well, that bloodletter the monks cleaved to him was serious and dedicated enough to have drained your squire friend through to his soul. He *must* be dead."

"What do you know about bloodletters? And what do you know about pages, for that matter. Who was this page anyway? How can you be sure that he wasn't some dock waif playing a prank on you?" Geoffrey's voice began to tremble and his hand was unsteady. He instinctively reached for the pommel of his *couteau*.

"He was from the hospital, and he pronounced our names and the dead squire's name with absolute precision. He declared on all that was holy that the wounded squire Swynford was dead. I might have even paid him for the information." Jean banged his tankard on the table several times to declare that it needed to be refilled.

"*He* should be here instead of you."

"If he was here he would be dead, and dead again." Jean laughed bitterly.

Jean's words were too much for Geoffrey to bear. He jerked himself off the wall and smacked Jean's tankard out of his hands. Godwin was about to interfere, but Geoffrey was too quick for the old man. He leapt over the table and tackled Jean to the ale-washed floor.

"Get off me! I'm drunk and you're penniless," Jean cried out while covering his face to shield himself from the hard blows Geoffrey was administering. "If it wasn't for me you'd be serving the Saracens by now, as a galley slave or in some other less dignified position."

"I'll show you what dignity is! Get up off that floor and face me!" Geoffrey pulled himself up with the help of the table, but before he could draw his sword Godwin had him by the collar.

"We're not playing these games here tonight, gentlemen. Don't force me to drag you to Florence in chains. Now, settle down and bury your noses in more ale." He gave Jean a sharp kick in the stomach and threw Geoffrey back down on the bench.

Geoffrey stared wild-eyed. Then, while Godwin was calming a discomfited serving maid, he bolted.

CHAPTER 14

Umbertide

Even if Jean had not been drunk, Sergeant Godwin still would have been able to beat him to within an inch of his life. They might have been roughly the same height and build, but the old sergeant's years of fighting experience far outweighed any benefit age might have afforded the Frenchman. After finding a blind alley, Godwin had proceeded to interrogate Jean with a mixture of fists and threats, so that by the time he finally pried the truth out of him, Jean was curled up on the ground with blood streaming from his nose and mouth.

"There is nothing else you want to tell me, you worm?" Godwin said, pulling Jean upright along the wall.

"I could tell you the name of the pig that knew your mother to produce your horrible self," Jean sputtered. The abundant ale coursing through his veins had dulled his nerves and sharpened his wit, so the fierce blows the English sergeant had applied to his body hurt considerably less than he expected.

"Tell me something I don't know. However, I do know that your name is indeed Jean Lagoustine, as if it really mattered, and you work for the Gamesmaster of Avignon as a debt collector. You have been following this young squire around Italy with the purpose of eventually collecting his debt on behalf of your master, but the squire believed that you were an ordinary chandler," Godwin recited.

"He believed that I was an *exceptional* chandler, in truth. He'd be languishing in the hold of a Saracen galley right now if it hadn't been for me. Or is this your way of thanking people? Remind me never to be kind to the English again."

Jean tried to remember what he had spilled. The sergeant now knew about his master and his commission, not to mention Geoffrey's debt to the Gamesmaster, but did he spit out any other names during the beating? He did not hear himself mention either the astrologer Catherine or the sergeant Alfonso. In between groans he might have said that he had been an assistant to the master victualler of the Catalonian crossbow company, but he was certain that the only debt Godwin had learned about from his tongue was the one of Geoffrey Hotspur to the Gamesmaster.

"How well do you know the Swynford family?" Godwin demanded, raising a bruised fist above his head. "Did this Roger Swynford have a debt with your master too? You can either tell me now or tell your confessor later, when I drag you to your deathbed."

Jean shifted his aching body until he was almost eye to eye with his attacker. "No, the Swynfords are strange to me. They don't have a hall in Avignon as far as I know. The squire, Roger, was alone at the court of Gaunt. On my oath, I met him but once, when he was wounded. Ask the St. John's Hospital if you don't believe me." Jean clutched his side after a jolt of pain announced that he was suffering from a cracked rib.

"Your oath is worth about as much as your life. Now, this is your last chance. Have you nothing else to say, besides common insults?"

Jean shook his head.

"So be it," Godwin said. He straightened Jean's jupon. "I don't have all night to make sure of this. We need to find that squire. What's his name again? Oh yes, Geoffrey Hotspur. A funny name, that is. *You* will now help me find him."

"Yes, well, I need him too." Jean rolled his right shoulder.

"I don't see how that will help matters, and it has nothing to do with me," Godwin declared. "He survived until now without knowing what breed of snake you are. Where might he have gone?"

"He could be anywhere. He could be in a chapel bruising his knees on its stone floor, or he might be in a gaming hall running up a debt. The English squire suffers from bouts of piety. One moment he's laughing about taking a huge trick at *Cacho* and the next moment he's pledging all his piddling wealth to the Lord."

"*Cacho*? How long were you two with the Catalonians anyway?" Godwin asked.

"Since a couple of days out of Avignon. Geoffrey told you how we served with the crossbowmen at Narni." Jean wiped a trickle of blood from the side of his mouth.

"That's a lot of ground to cover." Godwin stared at the starry sky.

"We should separate. You may have first choice of place," Jean suggested.

"You're not slipping out of my sight, you eel."

Godwin grabbed a fistful of Jean's jupon, taking a strip of his shoulder with it. Jean winced and he would have plunged a dagger into the old sergeant's belly if he had one. "Worm, snake, eel … can you really not decide what I am? I feel like a witch's familiar."

"Let's start with our lodgings." Godwin pushed Jean into the street.

Geoffrey walked the streets of Umbertide for hours without rest. His long strides carried him to the main gate, up to the citadel, around the curtain wall, through the cathedral square, and down narrow lanes that were empty but for mangy cats and offal. He could not stop as long as the passions roared inside him; anger, grief, sadness, frustration, confusion, and regret were tearing at his heart. He had failed his friend; he had failed his lord; he had failed to show virtue. Jean was false; Vilardell was unreliable; Andrea Tomacelli kept bad company; Prospero had betrayed his lord. No, that was not true. Captain Prospero had broken his *condotta*, that strange Italian thing that was not an indenture. He remembered what old Godwin had said about reputation and dignity. He was a man without a place, like himself, a foreigner. Memories flooded back about the war council at Narni, where he was asked to serve as a witness to murder, and the hall at Terni, where he learned of Captain Prospero's history with Giovanni Tarlati.

Geoffrey smashed his fist against a thick oaken door he was passing. The hollow sound he made reverberated in his ears and he looked up. The door belonged to a small, round chapel. Geoffrey tried the handle, but it remained fast. He turned away and was again pounding his soles on the cobblestones when he nearly ran into someone. He looked up and saw a helmed man in a long dark cloak.

"Out of my way!" Geoffrey said, and he reached out to shove the man aside. However, Geoffrey suddenly felt his right arm being twisted around his back and his face pressed up against the nearest wall.

The helmed man said something, which Geoffrey did not understand. He just mumbled an English oath, which brought the point of a dagger to his ribcage. The threat made Geoffrey even more inflamed, and he tore away from the man and unsheathed his sword. He tried to plant his feet, but the ale was in league with his heated passions to make him unsteady.

Someone yelled "*guardia*", and Geoffrey realized that the man must be from the night watch. Soon several other men, dressed in similar attire but more heavily armed, arrived and surrounded the squire. Geoffrey looked at the ranks set against him and decided that he would not break the peace. He sheathed his *couteau* and walked calmly and purposefully back down the way he came. Several guards moved to intercept him, but Geoffrey did not break stride. One man grabbed his shoulder, but he shook it off. Then another guard clamped his hand around Geoffrey's sword arm. Geoffrey tried pulled away, but soon another hand was on him, and then another.

OF FAITH AND FIDELITY

"Let me be, for the love of Saint Mary!" he cried. He began to struggle as one by one the guards took hold of him. He felt an arm snake around his neck and soon he was falling backwards. A fist crashed down on his jaw. He tasted blood. Then he felt the burn of rope around his wrists, but his fury continued unabated until the night watch bodily lifted Geoffrey from the ground.

"What do we do now?" Jean asked. He and Godwin were standing in the narrow doorway of a prison cell. Early that morning, a messenger from the *signore* of Umbertide had arrived at the lodgings of Sergeant Godwin to inform him that one of their party had been apprehended last night for breaking the peace.

"Go and talk to him," Godwin ordered in a whisper. "You're the one who caused this."

They peered into the cell. Geoffrey was crouched in a corner, head on chest and very still.

"He looks asleep. Let's come back later, after we have eaten."

"So, wake him up." Godwin slapped Jean on the back of the head.

"Listen. He's your ward now, isn't he? You ransomed the bastard, for the love of Christ. *You* take care of him. You don't even want me here."

"I want you here now. I won't spill blood in my friend's city, but I can drag you outside the walls just as I did from the White Boar tavern and lay into you. If you start pulling my shank, it's liable to kick you in your softest parts."

"Hey!" Jean said in a half-whisper. "Who knows him better, me or you? Who has kept him going, kept him out of harm's way, for the past three months? If I say that his humors are so imbalanced that any attempt to disturb him now would result in ... I don't know ... something bad, then that's how it is."

"I am taking him to Florence in whatever state," Godwin declared, raising his voice a little. "We have to get him out of here and on the road to Arezzo. Do I need to remind you about the Gamesmaster? I am certain that for you too the squire's progress into Tuscany is a matter of urgency."

Jean sighed and looked askance at Godwin. He had to talk to the squire sooner or later, so it might as well be now. He gingerly stepped inside the cell and sat on the wooden bench next to Geoffrey.

"Geoff. I don't know what to say. Roger is gone. He is … with our Lord and Savior now." Jean awaited a response, but after seeing no movement and hearing nothing but the impatient rustling of the sergeant behind him, he added, "He died with honor."

"Yes. Of that I am glad," Geoffrey said. His voice was almost ethereal, as though it was emanating from the walls. He did not move though, not even a twitch of a shoulder.

"The truth is that I am not a chandler." Jean looked back at Godwin. He had better make a clean breast of it. He had wondered when he would tell the squire all, and now he knew. "I am a debt collector for the Gamesmaster of Avignon, and I have been shadowing you since you made your debt with him. It is what I do."

"Chandler, debt collector, pikeman, it matters not. You did not kill Roger and you did serve me well…at times. My anger is gone. I shall leave today, assuming they let me out of here," Geoffrey said.

"God be praised," Godwin said flatly. It was Friday, July 3, St. Thomas's Day, Godwin realized, and although he was well-practised in ignoring signs, he prayed that the squire's doubt had finally fled him. "Everything is ready. We can leave as soon as you have eaten. The road to Arezzo is still open, according to my old friend, the *signore*. I already collected your *couteau*, so you needn't worry."

"I am not going to Arezzo."

"Well, the way to Florence by way of Sansepalcro is long and holds more dangers, so …"

"I am not going to Florence. There is no need. I need to prove my faith and fidelity through noble service, so I shall return south and pledge my sword to Captain Prospero."

"Faith and fidelity! What do you know of those words, boy? They are not to be spoken of lightly, no matter how easily they might slide off the tongue! Guard! Lock up this cell!" Godwin took a deep breath to cool his anger.

"I have been thinking and praying all night, and I came to realize that everyone I have encountered has failed to fulfill their pledges – the papal legate, Jean, Prospero…they all betrayed something, but at least Captain Prospero is striving for restitution now, like me. I will serve him."

"Listen boy, you can serve the just as well from Florence. You will be serving Gaunt, and I will even help you. Also, Captain Prospero, lest you have forgotten, is now fighting *against* the Church. You will be excommunicated and thus condemned, and what of your faith and fidelity then?"

"I am condemned otherwise and will never be able to earn my spurs. His Lordship the Duke of Lancaster will refuse me entry to his hall. Besides, you said yourself that his holiness should not find grounds for condemnation on such a matter. You don't understand. I must seek restitution for the destruction of that chapel. It has become my duty. Fidelity to my mission is an act of faith. Captain Prospero will understand, and so will everyone else."

Godwin didn't. He was confused and annoyed, so he turned to Jean for an explanation.

"Are you talking about that ruined chapel we saw on our way to Spoleto?" Jean asked, although he was sure that it was.

"That is the one. In truth, I should thank you for your unintended revelation about Roger's death, for it reminded me that I must fulfill my pledges. I pledged to avenge and seek restitution for the destruction of that house of God and I pledged to serve Captain Prospero. He valued my service once and I repaid that trust by considering service with another, who I see now was unworthy."

Godwin stormed into the cell. He grabbed Jean by his sore shoulder and gave him a fierce, questioning look. Jean responded by slipping out from under the sergeant's painful grasp and moving to the other side of Geoffrey. He then briefly described the encounter between the Catalonian crossbowmen and the Breton mercenaries of Giovanni Tarlati, the murders at Narni and Geoffrey's erstwhile intention to join Andrea Tomacelli.

Godwin understood, but he was unimpressed. He was well familiar with the reputations of both Prospero and Tomacelli, and while he considered both men to be worthy to serve in a soldiering capacity, he would hesitate recommending anyone pledge fidelity to either man. "You are my ward, so you will do as I say. I ransomed you, and that's a pledge."

"I will accompany you to Florence *after* my mission is complete. You may wait here if you like." Geoffrey stood up on unsteady feet.

It was Jean's turn to grab Godwin by the shoulder, and he dragged him aside. He was weary of the ex-sergeant's overbearing nature, so in a fit of spite he said, "Now you know what he's like. What we need to do now is accompany him to Prospero's camp and make sure he doesn't get into trouble. You know the German, so you should be able to convince him to help us. What say you?"

Godwin stroked his beard and squinted at the ceiling. He felt his heart contract. "Yes, I know Prospero, and that is something at least. I should put you in here instead, but you still might be of some use."

After dismissing the guard who was about to close the cell door, Godwin leaned over the squire and said, "We leave in one hour."

It took them more than a week to find Captain Prospero at Acquasparta. Godwin kept a slow pace in the hope that the squire would change his mind about Prospero, while the German seemed to be always on the move. After coordinating the storming of Assisi, the combined host of Malatesta and Prospero had made a triumphant march southwards on the Via Flaminia and along the Tiber River as far as Orte, overrunning Captains Attendolo and Altoviti at Fratta Todina and Castello di Vibio. This forced the Duke of Spoleto to fall back to his springtime position on the Nera River to form the Foligno-Spoleto-Terni-Narni line in order to avoid being cut off and risk losing Spoleto itself. He sent Broglia to retake Assisi and a messenger to the Marche to ask his brother for help. By the middle of July, Prospero and Malatesta were in Acquasparta, where Malatesta suspended their advance so that he could consult with his family in light of their making peace with Andrea Tomacelli. As a result, Corrado Prospero had the white baton of captain-general.

When the page announced that they would be received in the command pavilion, Geoffrey strode in ahead of Godwin, knelt and doffed his small arming cap before Prospero.

"I come to offer you my sword, my liege, and my loyalty as a humble servant of your lordship," Geoffrey declared and he held out his *couteau* flat on the palms of his hands.

Captain Prospero stared at Geoffrey and then at Godwin. He was bent over a table carpeted in maps. "You told me you were taking the English squire to Florence, Will. Did you get lost or did you simply want to return my horses before you hobbled them?" Prospero said.

Godwin shrugged, but added a run of facial gestures that suggested they would speak later about this business.

Prospero looked down at Geoffrey "I am not in need of servants, my good squire, nor courtiers to lay about in a court that does not exist, and you already know that I am not such a lord who can grant you a knight's fee, so why are you here?" Prospero reminded himself about why he was no longer interested in the English squire. Word of his good treatment of the boy received was supposed to reach the Duke of Lancaster and King Richard via Godwin. He was not pleased to see the old sergeant return him to his company.

"I would like to enroll in your company as a free lance."

After carefully weighing his options and obligations, Captain Prospero decided to hear the squire out before rendering a final decision. "Have you a destrier, squire? I need horsemen, not foot soldiers."

"I have neither, captain. If your company cannot accommodate me, then perhaps another under your command will, a knight, perhaps."

Prospero shook his head. "That is not possible, I'm afraid. The *condotti* for the next two months have already been signed and advances given out. Go to Florence. It will be safer and more profitable for you."

"My prayers have led me here," Geoffrey said solemnly. "I must make Tarlati account for his crimes. He must be made to pay."

Prospero leaned back and scratched his cheek. "Tarlati. I will make him pay when I defeat him, rest assured."

"Captain Vilardell made the same promise. With respect, I cannot chance it."

"I don't need some beardless youth hell bent on vengeance in my army," Prospero said angrily. "I cannot chance you causing disorder."

"This is not about vengeance; it is about fidelity. You must understand." Geoffrey's icy blue eyes stared with an intensity that startled the German.

"You know I fight for Clement now. You might be risking more than you think."

"I have thought about it, and with respect, captain, that need not be your concern. You are fighting for your reputation, and even though I have no name, so am I."

A severe look crossed the captain-general's face at the squire's implication that they were somehow equals.

"I might have room for a *pavesaro*," Prospero said, wanting to test the squire's resolve. "I know you possess experience with that rank."

Geoffrey winced. "I have a proper lance."

"Where is your lance?" Prospero asked.

"The rest of my lance is behind me."

The captain looked at Jean and then at Godwin, who again caught his eye. "You are not serious. An untried English squire, a gouty old man and – who are you again – Oh, some French lathe-spinner? This will not do."

Godwin stepped forward to offer a suggestion. His acute hunger was making him impatient. "Conrad, why don't you just enrol his lance as a company without any provisions for pay, advances or rations? I know there is such a thing. I wrote up a few such ghost *condotti* myself when I was still a player in this game. You're the captain-general, so I know you can do it."

"I cannot give out a *condotta* with just the snap of my fingers. I have Malatesta to answer to and I fear that the other captains would be gravely insulted were they to learn that a single barbuta lance had received a proper *condotta*."

"They don't have to know," Godwin said.

"They will know. Malatesta's treasurer and my company scribe maintain strict accounts of all documents issued within the host. It would get out."

Silence descended on the pavilion as each man considered a way out of the awkward situation. Captain Prospero needed to maintain the dignity of the captains, as well as ensure that all accounts were done right and proper, yet he did not want to dismiss the squire out of hand, as he should still get to Gaunt. He also saw that Godwin wanted everything resolved without ambiguity: either the squire was to be enrolled with the antipapal host or he was to be sent on his way. He would not agree to let the squire languish in the baggage train or wander about his camp.

Jean, who had thought it prudent to act invisible for as long as possible, had an idea. "Why don't you wager for it?"

All stared at Jean as though he had just arrived from the land of the

Turk.

"I don't see how that will resolve anything," Prospero said.

"Listen. Make it known that you had wagered for a *condotta*, a small one, in Assisi, and lost, and now you are bound by honor to issue it. The treasurer would understand, and if Captain Malatesta is as true to his reputation as I hear he is, then he'd understand as well. I would venture to say that he might even applaud the gesture." Jean really had little inkling about Malatesta Malatesta's thoughts on such things, but the ruse was worth a try.

"Yes, but the gesture would reflect badly on *my* reputation. All I need is to trail hordes of poor lances in my wake asking me to wager on a *condotta* for them."

"I would argue that such a gesture would enhance your reputation, captain," Jean said, although he was not sure how.

"It would reflect brightly on your honor," Geoffrey said. "It would illustrate your chivalry towards lesser knights."

"And I would ensure that everybody knew," Godwin added. "I as yet have some influence in condottiere circles. Hawkwood's name still carries weight in Italy."

Recalling that Godwin had something to say to him about this affair and being pressed for time, Captain Prospero demurred. However, he stated categorically that the *condotta* would be arranged wholly on his terms, for no money, victuals, privileges, shares in booty, rank, or the right to appeal to either the company priest or the field court, and he would draw up the list of articles. "So, what shall we call you, then? Godwin. You've never commanded a company in your life. This can be your final glory in Italy."

Godwin winced and shook his head. "Never have, never will. I don't want the responsibility or to look foolish. I've done too much of both in my time."

OF FAITH AND FIDELITY

"Of course not. The *condotta* has to be made under some name, though, so whose will it be? If not yours, Will, then the boy's here. The Frenchman is out of the question." Prospero tapped a leaf of parchment with his finger.

"I don't want the boy's name in print. It is a matter of discretion. Salutati is involved," Godwin said quietly.

Prospero's eyes widened and he smiled. "Fine. I will just enroll you sad lot as the English Free Company. That should raise a few eyebrows yet reveal nothing."

While Geoffrey dropped to one knee to recite a little prayer for his good fortune, Prospero pulled Godwin to one side.

"What are you playing at, Will? I thought you were out of this game? That squire should be raising dust on the road to Florence." His voice was suffused with concern and annoyance.

"Don't worry, Conrad. If you'll allow me, I will keep the squire out of harm's way. I have no choice but to let him get this restitution nonsense out of his system. This is the summer season, is it not? Well then, once he starts marching around under the hot Italian sun, the heat should burn the mood out of him." Godwin was thinking about what the Frenchman had said to him about Geoffrey and his delicate temper.

Prospero looked down at the table and scratched his cheek. "Very well," He said at last. "This is what I will do. The boy can remain with my army, but you will have to join my council. You still know people in the western Patrimony from your Hawkwood days, so you should do better than any of my agents gathering intelligence. Do you agree?"

Godwin thought about Salutati and snorted. "I agree."

Castelfidardo, the Marche
July

Despite his unprecedented success at having returned the last of the rebellious families to *fidelitas* with the Church via the Treaty of Castelfidardo, Andrea Tomacelli was glum. The message from his brother meant that his Grand Strategy of bringing all of the Patrimony to heel this season was in a very bad state, although he refused to believe that it could not be salvaged. He had done his bit in the Marche, to which the recent treaty was witness, but the loss of Assisi and defection of Prospero would make restoration difficult. He would have to return to his brother's side as soon as possible, and with as large a force as possible. At least Captain Broglia was already galloping westwards to buttress his brother's host. The only ray of light he could see shining through this dark cloud of misfortune was that Captain Vilardell and all his crossbowmen had resigned with his brother, although the terms of his *condotta* were disturbingly liberal with the cost high. Nevertheless, it was a start. After steadying himself with another read of the freshly signed treaty, the papal legate ordered his groom to saddle his best horse.

But what should he do about Corrado Prospero? This desire to restore his reputation, such as it was, was blinding him to good sense. If his skills were as good as he thought they were, then he would not have lost the winter campaign for his brother, so it was just as well that strategic planning had been taken away from him, Andrea reasoned. Well, if the German wanted to bear a grudge against his family, then he will answer for it. When his host is destroyed and the great captain himself taken, he should expect no ransom. If he wanted to hang his reputation on the point of a pike like a proud knight, as the popular captain Boldrino de Panicale once did, then he could expect to see it be knocked down to the very depths of Hell!

As he spurred his horse onto the road to Macerata, Andrea thought about what Boniface had said to him about prudence back in March. Well, the time for that had passed. He had done well for both his brothers, but Andrea believed that neither truly understood how to conduct war in the

OF FAITH AND FIDELITY

Patrimony. He would take the battle to his faithless captain-general and destroy him in a single pass of arms, and with him the hopes of Clement to win the Patrimony.

Acquasparta

"My intention is to make a fair pass of arms with Andrea Tomacelli," Prospero explained to Godwin as they inspected the city walls. "That is all. I will embarrass him as he did me in front of my peers."

"So, the decision to offer battle is on your head, not on Malatesta's. That sounds about right. You have a habit of taking too much on your own shoulders, Conrad." Godwin looked over the fields. He was thinking about San Donato and how the Chancellor of Florence had got him here. Godwin hoped he was tearing what was left of his hair out waiting for delivery of the lost English squire.

"Are you saying that I am wrong? Look: if Malatesta returns, there will be no battle. He is too weak and has little prospect of bringing either Broglia or Brandolini back," Prospero challenged. "And let me assure you that I take on precisely what is equal to the weight my shoulders can bear."

"Whoa, whoa, Conrad. Don't let your pride get the better of you. All I meant was that it was quite a risky maneuver taking Assisi like that right after you tore up your *condotta*. If you had failed, it would have been just you facing the wrath of the Tomacelli, without Malatesta's company."

"Yes, well, I will admit that this burden of mine is digging into my flesh, and it seems to have barbed my tongue to boot. What is done is done. I need to find a place to offer battle, and soon."

"Of course," Godwin acknowledged. "Have you any idea where yet?"

"No. The duke is the key. I need to draw him out of his nest at Spoleto and then his brother will follow in short order."

"And the war for the throne of St. Peter?" Godwin asked. "It has nothing to do with me, but if you defeat the Tomacelli, the Patrimony will be lost for Boniface. Are you prepared for that?"

"Then he deserves to lose it," Prospero said sharply. "It has nothing to do with me either, but if I am known as the man who won the Patrimony, it could hardly hurt my reputation."

"Your pride has turned to arrogance, and I would watch that if I were you. Now, if you want my advice, here it is: keep moving. That should also forestall Malatesta should he decide to change strategy, keep the Bretons on the road and out of trouble and prevent you getting stuck in a city, as what happened at Narni. A moving army is difficult to stop. This is none of my affair, mind you, and I would be just as content for you to pull your men back all the way to Florence."

"If I did that, I'd have to contend with that spider Salutati, and I am already too close to his web for comfort. But in all seriousness, your assessment and mine are in accord, and with the hot weather now upon us and our barrels full of victuals, a good march should hold back the plague of lethargy. I propose to threaten Narni to see what the duke's reaction will be. Yes, marching in this heat will be tough, but the city is not far, the roads are dry and we will course the river. I will engage all the companies for the purpose of making it look serious. I know the defences of Narni like the back of my hand, and its recapture by Malatesta's host will resonate throughout northern Italy. If the duke takes the bait and drives towards Narni, I shall pull the army gradually westwards until I find a place of my choosing to give battle"

Geoffrey was happy to be on the march again. His very bones trembled with the ever-approaching pass of arms that he knew would occur between Captain Prospero and Captain Tarlati. It was the sole purpose of this campaign to his mind, and he believed in it. The prospect possessed

OF FAITH AND FIDELITY

the certainty of a tournament joust. While one, both or neither knight might become crestfallen, passes would be made and made again until one knight would be forced to concede. In the strange fancy of his imagination, Geoffrey saw Corrado Prospero as Richard Lionheart, a knight in spirit with the prowess and wisdom of a king, although not the Richard Lionheart of Roger's dream. That was someone else, whose true meaning he would be made to understand one day. Giovanni Tarlati, meanwhile, was like Saladin, the enemy and infidel, although without the dignity of the greatest of the crusaders' enemies. Therefore, there was no question in the squire's mind as to who would hold the field.

Geoffrey was also excited by the *un*certainty of the campaign. Captain Prospero was wagering on so many odds, like casts of the dice, and with such high stakes that Geoffrey almost felt kinship with him; his army was outnumbered; he was marching deep into enemy territory; his captain-general was in faraway Bologna. However, the captain had the determination of a bull and the skills of a fox, Geoffrey thought, as well as just cause on his side.

Now that he, or rather his lance, was formally enlisted in the antipapal host, Geoffrey was obliged to march in formation with Malatesta's *pedites*, which consisted of the captain-general's company of 500 heavy lances he had left to Prospero's care, or 2,500 men in total, and a few hundred Bretons. With the addition of Captain Prospero's 400 mounted men-at-arms (the other 100 horsemen were galloping around southern Umbria looking for a battle) and the 80 lances of the captains Attendolo and Altoviti, a modest but well-fed army of 3,500 men went in search of the papal host.

Geoffrey was disappointed to lose Sergeant Godwin, however. The captain-general was always calling him away, perhaps to reminisce about Hawkwood. At every city they captured or threatened, he would suddenly disappear and return only when the army was on the march again. This act was repeated for two weeks until the word came down that the Duke of Spoleto had finally risen from his slumber and was setting out after them. He had had enough of losing bits of the Patrimony, apparently. Geoffrey then found himself marching southwards, along the same route by which had first journeyed to Spoleto. This was good, and Geoffrey thought about what feats of arms he might accomplish in full view of the masters of the field.

On the left bank of the Tiber, in the shadow of the small, under-provisioned town of Orte, Prospero ended the long march and took council with his captains, quartermaster and old Sergeant Godwin. After over an hour of deliberations and planning, Godwin returned to the main body of Malatesta's men-at-arms and found Geoffrey and Jean lounging by a rotting stump on the bank of the Tiber.

"Sergeant! What news? Will we have battle tomorrow?" Geoffrey leapt up to greet the old man, who was ambling down a path towards him.

"Captain!" Godwin said after he had caught his breath. "You have received an honor."

"You do not need to call me captain," Geoffrey said. "What honor? Am I to be made corporal again? Say it's not so."

"The duke's army is less than a day's march behind us. Captain Prospero has decided to offer battle on the morrow. We will camp on the slope of the citadel."

Geoffrey clapped his hands while Jean slumped against the stump.

"Why don't we just hole up in Orte for a while and pray for the rain to come and wash the duke's army into the Tiber?" Jean suggested.

"Orte is not big enough, for one thing, and for another even if the rain comes and washes away the duke and his men, his brother is fast on his heels. To invite a siege would be foolish anyway, since Malatesta is in no position to come in relief and the French have their own problems at Genoa."

"Captain Prospero wants to make a proper pass of arms here, then, not repel a siege?" Geoffrey asked.

"He does. He knows that the duke needs to take Orte in order to secure a way to Rome and Viterbo. He wants a decisive battle here and now."

"Here?" Jean repeated. "What's so good about *here*? *Here* does not look like a good place for anything other than to ford the river for us to get over *there*, away from any senseless battle."

Godwin and Geoffrey ignored Jean: Godwin because he knew down to the marrow of his bones that Prospero was set to fight somewhere on the left bank of the Tiber and Geoffrey because he was anxious to meet Giovanni Tarlati on the lists – anywhere.

"Are we well-armed to discomfit our opponent?" Geoffrey asked. "What does Captain Prospero say? Speak plainly, for I am prepared to challenge Tarlati face to face, if need be."

Godwin shook his head and winked at the sky. "Conserve your passion, squire. It is best not to speak of such things now, for we do not want to curse our luck. I only know that we shall be crossing swords with a couple of the best companies in central Italy. You may want to look for signs of our impending fortune."

Geoffrey obeyed the sergeant, so he decided to return to the original subject. "So, what is this honor you mentioned? Will I be set in the bottom rank," Geoffrey asked eagerly.

"Captain Prospero has agreed to let you captain the guard of the *carrioccio*."

"The what?" Geoffrey and Jean said in unison.

"The *carrioccio*. The war wagon. That big trough with four wheels and pennons sticking out of it."

Geoffrey and Jean looked at one another in confusion and then stared blankly at Godwin.

"The *carioccio* is the main rallying point for the entire army," Godwin continued. "In France, I still believe that the royal standard-bearer serves that function. This is the same, but with a cart. If the *carrioccio* falls, then the battle is lost. It *is* an honor. Not the losing-the-battle bit but guarding the wagon. All company and family banners, pennons and gonfalons will be set there for protection and inspiration. You should be thrilled."

Geoffrey was not thrilled. He did not have to ask to know that this *carrioccio* would be located as far back from the action as possible. "I will ask the captain for a different honor," Geoffrey declared. However, as he stepped on the path, his chest caught Godwin's stony hand.

"This is the honor the captain-general has seen fit to give you, so this is the honor you will accept," Godwin stated. His voice had never sounded more threatening. He had indulged the English squire beyond what his patience would normally allow, so now the time had come to enforce his authority. Prospero had made good on his word to protect him and his ward by keeping them behind the ranks. If he knew Conrad Prospero, the *carrioccio* was as safe a place as any, since he would never let a battle get out of hand and risk a rout of his company. As to the squire's desire to avenge this chapel of his on Tarlati, Godwin would have to work that bit out later; the fast approaching clash of arms was quite enough for the moment. "I have had enough of your haughty behavior, boy. I will not allow you to insult my old fighting companion or me by letting you throw that honor back in his face. It would be disgraceful."

The hard words rooted Geoffrey to the spot. The old sergeant was right. Who was he to reject an honor bestowed by the captain-general of the army when he was fortunate to be allowed a part in it at all? His chest heaved and his fists clenched in frustration, but he would not overthrow the man who had ransomed him. The black mood seeped away and he stepped back from the hand blocking him. From what he had learned in the halls of Gaunt, he knew that battles were seldom as predictable as they might seem at the outset. They were occasions of great opportunity.

"You are right, sergeant. Forgive me. I am impetuous. I will not embarrass the company."

Godwin nodded his head in approval. "The sun is setting. You should use these final hours to polish your armor, mend your harnesses, and hone your weapons."

"How about some sleep?" Jean asked. "Can we do that too?"

"If you can sleep, sleep, but I know you won't," Godwin said. He looked over to where most of the army was encamped and then turned to Geoffrey. "You are a captain, boy, now go act like one and prepare your English Free Company."

Geoffrey smiled. "A captain, yes, a knight, no. You are a part of my company. We should prepare arms together."

"I've done this a thousand times. We will share wine later, but I have to speak with the captain-general."

Sergeant Godwin found it strange to see so little activity around Captain Prospero's command pavilion. Normally on the eve of battle he should see the comings and goings of great number of captains, victuallers, embassies, communal delegates, harlots, assorted officers, and a host of other ranks trying to remove as much uncertainty from the upcoming engagement as possible. Of course, the hour was late and no doubt many had taken refuge in Orte instead of braving the elements in camp. To his credit, Captain Prospero had decided to show the strength of his position by remaining with his men outside the city. Godwin entered the pavilion and found the captain-general engrossed in an array of objects curiously positioned on his desk.

"Come in, Will," Prospero said quietly. "As you can see, I am in need of some company." He smiled and returned his attention to the desk.

"And here I thought I was interrupting the final gathering of the war council, or are we so well counseled already that you have spare time to play with sticks and stones?"

"What? Oh, yes, well this is the battle I have arrayed for tomorrow. It looks impressive enough with such dumb objects, don't you think?" Prospero pushed a black stone across his pretend field until it collided with a brass buckle.

"And soldiers are not dumb objects? You have been hiding in this tent for too long, my friend, for your ideals are getting the better of you." Godwin lifted the captain-general's white baton and weighed it in his hand.

"Kindly return the gently sloping heights to where it belongs." Prospero took the baton from Godwin and placed it behind the buckle and next to a tallying stick.

"Those are your heights, are they? Well, where are your depths, or do you not account for such things."

Prospero smiled. "You know that I intend to make a pass of arms tomorrow, do you not? I plan no second course of action."

"Of course. Otherwise you'd be locked away in the keep of that town yonder. All the men know and they seem content. Have you decided how to ordain your companies? I recall an empty field on the other side of the Tiber for just such a purpose."

"You are looking at it now, that and how I intend to discomfit Tomacelli. I have had it well scouted." Prospero rearranged the stones and sticks and buckle and proceeded to show Godwin how he intended to win the morrow's battle. "You sound like a green captain. I would have thought that you of all people would understand my aim, but your mind is as rusty as your skills, no doubt, so I will have you know my reasoning. I intend to keep the companies off that empty field of yours for two reasons. The first is that its slope, as represented by my white baton, cannot give me advantage, since its angle will favor the duke; the second is that the field is too close to the bridge, which might tempt some of our less sturdy men to beat an early retreat, should we find ourselves discomfited. A longer run to the safety of Orte offers the risk of being cut down by pursuing horsemen – mine, most likely. Rather, my plan is thus: I intend occupy the heights above the field and let the duke and his captains come to me. Retreat is not an option on this day."

"Are you really that put upon by circumstance, Conrad, or is your pride just acting up again? I am surprised to hear that you wish to fight defensively against mounted knights heavy with arms and steel. You do know that Brandolini is sure to be with the duke, don't you?"

"I agree that we are comparatively deficient in good horsemen, but we should be able to even up the sides with our superior vantage. I am sure the duke will think that *he* is superior with his many good horsemen, and this should embolden his haughty captains to seek glory on their own. The duke's council will be divided, since his lordship is weak and unworthy of command, and Tarlati cannot be trusted regardless. So, I intend to frustrate them with a sturdy wall of well-fitted men-at-arms until they are forced to dismount to engage my men on foot – or fall back to Narni. However, I believe the latter result very unlikely, despite the duke's mobility, because the youngest Tomacelli has yet to prove himself in a pass of arms. Another retreat after what he has suffered this year would be a devastating humiliation, and what is worse: it would give greater resolve to those cities that were thinking of switching *fidelitas* to Clement."

"That sounds reasonable, although it seems a bit risky for your tastes. Tell me, though, will you ask Giovanni Tarlati to come out in a knightly duel with you? Now that would make a fine tale to tell the lads and lasses on a dark and dreary eve in England." Godwin squinted and smiled slyly at Prospero. To his surprise, he was not at all nervous about the battle. He had seen and fought so many in his day – much bigger ones than this one promised to be – that it hardly crossed his mind. Most of his attention had to be devoted to the young squire since, considering what happened in Umbertide, he could not even hazard a guess as to how he will react when the trumpets blare, horses charge and arms clash.

"I do not foresee such a happy circumstance arising, especially since it would not settle matters between me and the Tomacelli. This battle must be fought and it can only be fought now."

"And my squire will be right here for the whole day, right?" Godwin put his finger on a red stone that was serving as the *carrioccio*. "I just want to confirm it. I appreciate you letting him trail along as though he had a real *condotta*, yet letting him get at least a whiff of battle. That should satisfy him."

"He will be the closest to the bridge, likely with whatever militia I can get out of the city. Under almost any circumstance, you will be able to haul him off to Orte and from there take him north to Florence. Besides, it will be good having you at the war wagon keeping an eye on the rear, since I don't have any men to spare for such duty. I think the sums of favors between us are equal now, don't you?"

Godwin tore his eyes away from the mock battle on the table and searched the pavilion for a suitably comfortable chair. When he found one, he plunked himself down on it, leaned back, folded his arms, and let out a long sigh that the guards at the pavilion's entrance mistook for a sickly wheeze. "And from here where will *you* go, Conrad? Service with the Visconti, maybe, or a well-provisioned town to hold at your pleasure until winter sets in, perhaps? I promise not to tell anyone."

"I have no shortage of lucrative options, let me tell you. I might even return to Germany. You're sure you have no desire to get back in the game, Will? There is always room on my *condotta* for an experienced sergeant."

Godwin harrumphed and said that he no longer burned with the desire to follow the white baton.

OF FAITH AND FIDELITY

Geoffrey was honing his *couteau* with such vigor, that Jean could not concentrate on mending his jupon.

"It's sharp enough to slice stone already!" Jean shouted. He then pricked his thumb with a needle. He threw his jupon to the ground and balled his fist. "Fie on both popes!" He cried. "May they both rot in the steaming bowels of the fiend!"

Geoffrey put down his tools and turned to Jean. "Forget about them for now. Did I ever tell you about my sword? What I once thought its pommel contained?" His voice was calm.

Jean stared at the squire. He inhaled deeply and then sighed aloud. "I remember you telling me something about it on the caravel, before we were attacked."

"I see. Well, did I ever tell you how I was given the name Hotspur?"

"I've always been curious about that," Jean said, leaning over to pick up his jupon. "You were found by the Duke of Lancaster, right? So, why are you not called Calais, or Foundling, or Beanpole? Any of those names would suit you better."

"The name was given to me by his lordship himself, when I tried to follow his retinue as they were leaving for a campaign. I was maybe five years old at the time. I tore away from the ladies who were taking care of me – many were the wives of the very knights who were riding out – and ran after the knights. Other boys ran too, but I was the fastest. Apparently, and his lordship told me this himself, I grabbed the spur of his best knight and held on even as he dragged me. My hand was wrapped around the rowel with such force that it bit deeply into my childish flesh, yet I would not let go. I screamed until the ladies fetched me, and then I screamed some more in the hall until I fell asleep. My hands were well bloodied. Look, I still have the scars." Geoffrey showed the palms of his hands.

"It is dark, but I trust it is as you say," Jean said quietly. "Geoff. Let's go for some ale. You should be with the other captains anyway and the odds of my not sleeping tonight are incalculable."

"You are right." Geoffrey stood up and straightened his doublet. He looked out at the camp fires blazing beneath the moonlight and thought about Roger. Perhaps he was with Lady Fortuna, looking down on him, trying to convince her to smile upon him. "A walk will calm your nerves. Then we should train for tomorrow."

"What, for standing around a war wagon? I think we should be all right."

"And if a rogue lance breaks through?"

"Hit them with the war chest, because that's what I'll be sitting on until this thing is over."

The camp grew livelier the closer they got to where the captains were gathered. The men-at-arms were keeping their spirits raised by playing games, telling jokes and otherwise distracting themselves. Girlish giggling could be heard from time to time, though only Geoffrey and Jean seemed to notice. Sone were attending their arms, like Godwin had suggested, and none were looking ready to sleep.

When they finally found where the captains were gathered, Attendolo quickly got up and greeted Geoffrey as though he were a long lost brother, slapping him on the back and offering him a tankard of ale.

"That's what I am here for, but I have my own vessel." Geoffrey reached back and pulled from his belt the chalice he had won from Captain Vilardell so many months ago. "For luck," he said and pulled himself a pint.

"I can't believe you're a captain," Altoviti said. "What did you do? Wager Prospero for a *condotta*?"

"Nah, our esteemed captain-general is too sober for such nonsense," Attendolo declared and he passed the tankard to the Breton captain. "I'm sure he would keep ale and women away from his host if he could. Thank God I signed with Malatesta instead of him."

OF FAITH AND FIDELITY

The two young captains clinked tankards and took long swigs.

"Don't I get a drink?" Jean asked.

"You're French, so no, you don't," Attendolo said. "I jest. Take from the keg yourself. The citizens of Orte are paying for it."

"What about women? Am I entitled to them too?"

Attendolo sized Jean up before saying, "I don't think we have any blind harlots here. Where *did* you get that lump of a nose of yours?"

The captains laughed while Jean just shrugged and went to find the ale.

Geoffrey sat on another keg next to Attendolo and whispered in earnest, "You know, Jean, my sergeant, is not for Clement. If anything, he is for himself, but he will fight tomorrow, rest assured."

"If you trust him, so much the better," Attendolo said.

"Are you not concerned about your reputation?" Geoffrey asked. "I mean, should Captain Prospero prevail, you might be known for siding with Clement."

"I'm more worried about my company," Altoviti said. "I have few men, and should they be lost, I would have a hard time finding more. Had I not signed with Malatesta after he took Fratta Todina I would be languishing in a dungeon somewhere, or paroled without a company to lead. Now *that* is condemnation."

"So, you both are for Boniface?" Jean asked. He had already downed two tankards of ale.

"We are," Altoviti said slowly, "but popes come and go, don't they? How many times was Hawkwood denied the sacrament, yet his final confession was taken? Anyway, both Boniface and Clement are Christians."

Attendolo stood up and dusted off his doublet. "This talk is too serious. How about some *Cacho*?" he suggested. "I know the Catalonians are the best at it, or the most devious, but I know Malatesta's men like to play the game."

Geoffrey smiled. "Lead me to it."

CHAPTER 15

Orte

August

Dawn broke just beyond the even row of hills where Captain Prospero was planning to array his army. A fine mist was hanging low over the Tiber and a local astrologer forecast that the day would be hot and muggy, though rain was unlikely. The camp began to stir, but the morning's rituals were soon disrupted by Captain Malatesta's small Breton company. The 200-odd men had left the safe confines of Orte and were dragging and cajoling an equal number of dispirited local militiamen behind them on the Narni road. Then the sergeants, as though goaded into action themselves by this messy cavalcade, began shouting for reports, waking soldiers and ordering ranks to put on arms and muster within the hour.

Geoffrey opened his eyes and saw blurry light. He blinked until he could see clearly the pieces of his harness lying neatly on the tent floor beside him. Looking down he noticed that he was still wearing his blue doublet and buskins. Geoffrey chuckled and looked over to see if Jean was awake yet.

"Hey! The hour draws near," Geoffrey said excitedly. "Look alive!"

Jean had his eyes open, but his body was still and his face was ashen.

"What if you don't see Tarlati on the field today?" Jean asked as he stared at the tent ceiling. It was a question that had been plaguing him for several days. Geoffrey had promised to go to Florence and then home if Fortuna succeeded in rolling his chance point. However, what if Fortuna crabbed out? What if he or Prospero did not cross swords with Tarlati? Would Geoffrey follow him to the ends of the Earth? Jean shivered at the thought of accompanying a deranged English squire across the length and breadth of Italy, anxious to ensure restitution for a village and a chapel whose spoliation everyone else had long forgotten.

"I pledged to follow Captain Prospero. He will meet Tarlati. He would not have offered battle here were he not certain of it. All will be resolved today."

"You had better be right, but not at the expense of my life," Jean mumbled.

"The priest is offering a benediction this morning," Geoffrey said. "Will you go?"

"Take your sword instead. It will do both us some good."

After splashing his face with cold water and combing his hair flat, Geoffrey asked, "Why do I never see you at prayer? You avoid taking the sacrament as though it carried a plague."

"You pray enough for both of us. And besides, my good works speak louder for the salvation of my soul than any prayer I might mumble. Remember who saved your hide in Avignon? Remember who got us out of the slave pen in Corneto? That should be quite enough to keep my soul bathed in holy light and away from evil shade, I should say."

Geoffrey threw Jean's jupon at him, hitting him in the face.

"But not Roger's," Geoffrey said solemnly. "I cannot blame you for that, but you have demonstrated some virtue, despite all your falsehoods. Show fidelity to me one last time, and we will be even."

"Do I get a hauberk, like you?" Jean looked at his harness. Malatesta's men had been about as generous with armor as had the Catalonians. He had a coat-of-plates and an old Norman helmet.

"You won't need one where we will be." Geoffrey shook his hauberk, laid out his pourpoint and aligned his arm harnesses. He had nothing to protect his legs.

"So, how will you get to Tarlati if we are kept in the war wagon?"

"He will be brought to me," Geoffrey said with conviction. "Captain Prospero will make him yield, if not here, then at the next pass of arms."

Jean rolled his eyes in horror and fell back on his cot.

"There might be some silver in this," Jean said quietly to himself. The other side is bound to be armed better than me." He stood up and turned to Geoffrey. "And remember when we talked about ransoms? Even if we are on that war wagon, we should get a share of the booty." Jean's spirits suddenly rose. He had to look forward to something. "How much is Tarlati worth?"

"A chapel," Geoffrey answered without hesitation. "I am looking for restitution, not ransom this time, but you are right. We should get our just share, and then you can go back to Avignon and perform for the Gamesmaster. You can even have my portion, if yours is not enough."

Jean shook his head and walked to the entrance of the tent. "I'm going to get us something to eat."

"Why aren't you two armed yet?" Godwin asked as he strode into the tent. He bumped Jean backwards with his chest. The sergeant had all points armed with a thick leather jack, studded leather cuisses and steel gauntlets. He was also carrying an English-style barbuta helm and an old sword stained with a line of rust along its fuller.

"I just need a little more time," Geoffrey said as he struggled with his buttons. "My fellow pikeman is of no help."

"Oh, for the love of ... Let me do it. I've done it a thousand times and under more trying circumstances that this." Godwin dropped his helm and went to set and then reset the squire's harness.

"Sergeant," Geoffrey began. "I never thanked you for escorting me here. I would have never found Captain Prospero without you as my guide."

"What else had I to do? You can thank me when we embrace after the battle." Godwin lashed Geoffrey's spaulders.

"After we have won?" Geoffrey's sudden movement nearly toppled Godwin.

"Well, what are we here for? There, done." Godwin stepped back. "Let's go!"

Godwin led the one-lance company to the bridge, where they found the *carrioccio*. Geoffrey was astounded by its immense size and luxury. Pulled by four oxen, the wagon was blazoned with the arms of the many captains who had served with the Malatesta family over the years. A small tower was mounted in its center and well decorated with colorful standards and pennons, which were set at various heights to reflect the seniority and dignity of the captains, lords and officials represented in the army. Completing the pageant was a dedicated band of drummers, pipers and trumpeters, who at the moment were annoying the quartermaster by making rude and other inharmonious noises with their instruments. After bustling his way through the coalescing field army, Godwin located the Gonfalonier of the Army, who by custom commanded the *carrioccio*.

"Is this all there is?" Godwin asked, looking around at the musicians.

"Captain Malatesta took most of his retinue with him and Captain Prospero will not spare men. Are you the new English captain?" the gonfalonier asked. He was an Italian and affable, but his rapid speech revealed that he was nervous about the day.

Godwin corrected the gonfalonier by introducing Geoffrey Hotspur, who was immediately given instruction about how he should conduct himself during the battle, which gonfalon belonged to which lord or captain, and other essential knowledge. However, few around them believed that the gonfalonier was more than superficially relinquishing command. In short order, Geoffrey found himself on his borrowed palfrey riding alongside the drive team as it passed over the bridge. The gonfalonier rode in the wagon itself, and while he invited Geoffrey to share his vantage,

OF FAITH AND FIDELITY

Geoffrey said that he preferred the horse. He too understood that his position in the *carrioccio* was as much honorary as it was an honor, so he did not wish to impose himself and risk offending his superiors.

After the wagon crossed to the left bank of the Tiber, the gonfalonier ordered the driver to pull it off the road and make for the white pennon that a scout had planted the night before to designate the rallying point – a level spot on the crest that divided the riverbank and the field proper.

The moment the *carrioccio* and its retinue reached their station, Captain Prospero appeared with his full retinue and the other captains. He was richly clad in a crimson brocade and black velvet surcoat that well hid his harness. He could have been mistaken for a somber provincial courtier were it not for the white baton, the symbol of his supreme command, gripped in his right hand. He held it aloft and ordered the gonfalonier to sound the trumpets.

The host stirred. Captain Prospero spurred his horse and led the way. Their goal was the heights situated a mile east of the Orte bridge on the north side of the Narni road.

"A fine morning to you, Will, and to you, Captain Hotspur," Captain Prospero greeted them after he had ordered a band of horsemen to scout the road ahead. "You found yourself a harness, I see, sergeant."

"Yes, it's not much, but it should do, since I do not anticipate seeing the point of a pike today. Isn't that right, Conrad?" Godwin wiggled his shoulders to loosen the jack.

"I cannot foresee what the next hour will bring." Prospero gathered his war council on the verge to await the report of the scouts and began to discuss deployment.

Geoffrey smiled as he listened to the urgent words of the captains and their sergeants, for although he might not get his *couteau* bloodied today, at least he would be part of a genuine pass of arms. Perhaps he will be called upon to defend the *carrioccio*. He knew nothing about the ebb and flow of battle, but it was ever possible that the ranks would be pushed back, or that the rallying point would become the heart of the storm, or … something would happen to oblige him to draw his sword.

The report from the scouts was not good. When they had reached the heights they observed a large body of enemy horsemen testing the ground below them, the very ground that was to serve as the lists for their tilt.

Prospero ordered a general halt and sent two of his own squadrons to drive off the unexpected company, but after an hour, instead of his men the captain saw another force appear on the horizon: the duke's main body was approaching, and without the drag of foot men-at-arms to slow it down, even the most generous estimate gave only two hours before they arrived on the heights. That was not enough time for Captain Prospero's men to finish driving off the enemy and deploy his ranks in the strong defensive stand he wanted.

A war council was hastily arranged near the *carrioccio*, involving Prospero, Godwin, Attendolo, Altoviti, the senior sergeant from Malatesta's company, and the Breton captain.

"We should fall back on Orte," Sergeant Godwin suggested. "Cut the bridge and hold the town until Malatesta returns. We should have a clear run up the Tiber for supplies."

"Is that a Hawkwood stratagem, Will?" Prospero asked sarcastically. "And the answer to that question is a resounding 'no'. We give battle today."

"With the slope against us? Are you mad, Conrad?" Godwin said. He pointed at the heights and made a downward motion with his hand. "*That* would definitely not be a Hawkwood stratagem."

"What you do not realize, is that Andrea Tomacelli is coming. This is my chance. The battle has to be now."

"Could you not send your company to meet whoever's out there while the foot companies occupy the heights?" Attendolo suggested. "A

OF FAITH AND FIDELITY

diversion."

"And if my men get crushed, or ambushed, or you are too slow up that slope?" Prospero queried, shaking his gloves as he spoke. "I will not divide my companies. Now, look." He rode passed the *carrioccio* to a place where he would have an unobstructed view. "The field is narrow between the Tiber and Nera rivers. We can concentrate the foot companies there. Malatesta's company wear such thick armor that even the best crossbowmen could not pierce. Yes, we shall ordain here."

"And what if Fortuna sets her odds against you?" Godwin said. "If their numbers are great, they will run you through like butter!"

"If we abandon the field, it will be much the same. The die is cast!"

Prospero gave the order for his horsemen to harry the enemy without making contact to slow their advance. He set a guard near the bridge so that no one would be tempted to cross back.

The trumpets around the *carrioccio* blared and the entire army shifted direction. The gonfalonier frowned and began to scream at the drive team. The oxen pulled and bellowed at having to turn around, but they were eventually made to go the right way, which was back towards the bridge.

"Maybe the safest place for this *carrioccio* is behind the battlements of the city," Jean joked. "Let us ask the bullocks what they think."

"Or maybe we should ask the fiendish Bretons what they think. Why don't you approach them for advice? I'm sure they wouldn't slit your throat behind a tree and throw your body in the river, or anything like that," Geoffrey answered.

If Jean had responded to his jibe, Geoffrey did not hear, for an agitated bullock suddenly jerked and nearly gored his palfrey, forcing him to rein his horse out of harm's way. Finding himself off the road and facing the field, Geoffrey became distracted by the deployment of the Captain Prospero's main brigade to the middle of the field. As the captains and sergeants bellowed, men-at-arms fanned out across the field that gently sloped down towards the Tiber. Their movements were orderly. Captain Malatesta's men were disciplined and marched in dense squares with pikes pointed at the sky. Captain Prospero's horsemen screened them on the heights, which they finally took only to abandon it once the *pedites* were deployed to Prospero's liking, returning by the Narni road. The field had already been cut for hay, leaving a flat, stubbly surface that led almost to the water's edge. The field's northern fringe sank into a shallow marsh that gradually grew into some woods, which caressed the edge of the heights. Thus, a square field nearly one mile by one mile was created.

Surveying how the field affected the array of his army, Captain Prospero considered the various stratagems he had learned over the years to compensate for his tactical disadvantage. There were few to be sure, but he patched together a plan that, while risky, might succeed in at least saving his own company should the battle not go his way. Although he had openly boasted about closing all paths to retreat, in truth he would not risk the capture or ruin of his company should either result seem likely – he could probably make Todi, if he was careful. As for old Godwin, well he was just an old sergeant who had not retired when he should have.

Prospero began by ordaining the foot companies into a harrow formation, with the tapering flanks drawn ahead of the main body by several ranks. On the Narni road, which bordered his right flank, he deployed Malatesta's Breton company. Doing away with the customary vanguard for lack of men, Prospero placed all of Malatesta's and the other captains' men in the main – 580 lances in all – stretched across the breadth of the field. Their heavy pikes bristled from the six dense squares arranged as a row. Prospero concentrated his own company behind the main – 400 heavy mounted men-at-arms in a dozen squadrons. Behind Prospero's company at a healthy distance sat the lonely *carrioccio*. That just left the Orte militia to set, but where? They had to be kept away from the Bretons and the bridge, but Prospero could not reasonably give them a place in the main. Besides, they needed a strong hand to enforce discipline, especially now that his army was forced into a weaker position. They might not be well-trained, but they were not stupid. He could not think of anyone to spare. Prospero looked around and found that resolution was close at hand. He spurred his horse and promptly rode up to the *carrioccio*.

"Captain Hotspur!" Prospero shouted, frightening the gonfalonier.

Geoffrey hesitated for a moment, looked around in surprise and then bowed his head to his captain when he realized that it was indeed he who was being addressed.

"You commanded a company of local militia when you served me in the host of the Duke of Spoleto, did you not?" He gave Geoffrey a look that said he should carefully weigh his answer.

Geoffrey straightened his posture and scrutinized the captain-general's features. He smiled and responded in a deep, loud, English voice: "Indeed, I did, sir."

"Then you are relieved of this duty. Collect your lance and follow me immediately!"

Godwin heard all this and maneuvered his horse so that Captain Prospero could not avoid him. "Where are you taking him?" he demanded.

The captain-general flashed Godwin an annoyed look and brought his horse alongside the sergeant's. "Don't try me, Will. We are striking steel today. According to the squire's *condotta*, the terms of his service are defined at my discretion, so I have decided that he will now do service as captain of the Orte militia on the far left flank," Prospero explained. "As part of his lance, you will accompany him there."

"Throwing him on the field at the end of the line does not constitute keeping him safe. That is what we agreed, Conrad." Godwin was so vexed that he nearly fell off his horse.

"This will not do. Had we been able to hold the heights, it would have been different, but now I need all the men I can muster to show as big a force as possible. I need to stretch the field. Do you think I want to deploy that mob of a militia the Bretons dragged down here? Not on your life, I say, but there it is; they're with us now. Besides, *you* will be there to keep him safe. Now, out of my way! I have a battle to lead!" Prospero spurred his horse, forcing Godwin's palfrey to jump back.

Geoffrey was stunned. While this was not quite the opportunity he had anticipated, at least it would bring him closer to the battle. He had hoped that Captain Prospero would remove him from the *carrioccio* and make him a squire to one of the knights he expected the captain-general to make just before the battle, or at least promise to make. It was the place he had wanted Sir John to grant him on the eve of the *chevauchée*. Nevertheless, he could not refuse the honor. As Sergeant Godwin was bringing his horse back under control, Geoffrey and Jean trotted passed in the captain's retinue.

No one saw the riders course behind the rear ranks, as every man-at-arms had his eyes on the crest of the eastern heights. Prospero made well-rehearsed boasts to his veterans as he passed the aligned squadrons, as was customary, promising them all the riches of the duke and his jumped-up brothers. They were in good spirits, though anxious about their disadvantage, and gave triumphant shouts when Prospero's retinue rode by them.

"Form your ranks, captain," Prospero ordered Geoffrey when they reached the disorderly group of militiamen squatting in the reeds near the riverbank, hoping they had been forgotten. The quacking of ducks in the marsh on their left nearly drowned out Prospero's voice. Geoffrey took this to be a good sign. "I give you this militia to captain until dusk. Do whatever it takes to make them battle-worthy." Prospero slapped his hand on Geoffrey's shoulder. "You are our reserve, but do not be downhearted, for I am sure to ask you to arm and draw to the field in due course."

Geoffrey fixed his icy blue eyes on the heights. He knew this was an opportunity to show his prowess, prove his mettle, display his courage, even reveal a bit of that *virtu* Sergeant Godwin had told him about, but for the life of him he did not precisely know his purpose. He clenched his left hand around the pommel of his *couteau* as he looked over the sad collection of men and boys clustered before him. Watching them shuffle nervously, he thought: at the least those peasants from Spoleto had some enthusiasm for their venture.

"Did you not hear me, captain? You do understand my orders, do you not?" Captain Prospero spoke in English.

"Yes, my lord, I mean captain. I shall get these men into ranks," Geoffrey said mechanically, for he was already searching for the commands he would need to issue. He frantically tried to remember the words and phrases Sergeant Alfonso had spoken on the day they occupied Narni, but it was a mix of Catalan and the Spoletan dialect, both of which he was far from mastering. Geoffrey turned towards the captain, but Prospero was already on his way back to the *carrioccio*.

"If you're looking for the baggage train, it is on the other side of the river, corporal," Attendolo mocked when Prospero was beyond earshot. He captained the square that comprised his and Altoviti's company, which was ordained in front of the cowering militia.

Geoffrey recognized the voice from the banquet in Terni and turned to confront it. "The rank is captain, and you confuse me since, seeing the poor dress of your company, I thought that I *had* found the baggage train."

Attendolo grunted and uttered a Romagnian oath. "Captain?! You dare jest on such a serious occasion as this? So be it. Just don't trip over yourself and your band of citizens while you watch our backs."

"I am more likely to trip over your head on my way to the papal legate's baggage train." Geoffrey yanked the reins and began to move aggressively towards Attendolo. However, Godwin turned his palfrey to stop him.

"You!" Godwin shouted at Attendolo. "Mind your men before another captain takes them away from you. We are fighting together here."

Attendolo nodded and turned his attention elsewhere, as he recognized by the fury in his face that Sergeant Godwin was not to be trifled with.

"Sergeant! How do I speak to this mob? I need to array them as simply as possible so that I can get a good look at them." Geoffrey tried to sound gruff, like a veteran frustrated by the ineptitude of his charges.

Godwin rubbed his beard and squinted into the sun. "It's been so long since I fought in the ranks. Give me a moment to find those days inside my head."

"I remember," Jean declared, riding up to the other two members of the English Free Company. He was disconsolate about Geoffrey's promotion, since it took him away from the safety of the war wagon, but he could not let the squire fail again. Then, who knew what he would do.

"Excellent. Now, order them to form ranks of twenty, a *vingtaine*, as it is called," Geoffrey said with authority.

Jean turned to the militia. He barked a few words and received some in return. What was worse, from Geoffrey's point of view, was that none of the citizens had moved.

"What's the problem? Did you not make the right phrases with the proper tone?" Geoffrey asked. He recalled the ridicule he had suffered from the wealthy squires on account of his peculiar accent when he arrived in the Duke of Lancaster's halls. "I know you're not used to giving orders, but you can't be shy now."

Jean squinted in annoyance at the squire. "They say that they are missing their gonfaloniers, and so they cannot fight."

"The what? No, I don't care. I heard the clarion very clearly this morning, so they can't be still sleeping."

"I don't know," Jean answered.

"Of course you don't, but one of them must, so ask!" Geoffrey turned to see if he had an audience for his poor captaining, particularly Captain

OF FAITH AND FIDELITY

Prospero, but so far the men-at-arms were ignoring them.

Jean picked out the militiaman who looked the least likely to bolt from the field and risk his neck in the Tiber. They had a quiet exchange, at the end of which Jean shook the man's hand.

"It's Malatesta's Bretons, Geoff," Jean explained. "When those blackguards came storming into their town the other week all the guild captains, the gonfaloniers, grabbed what valuables they could carry and escaped to Viterbo. Well, most of them did; the Bretons caught the others and hanged them. In truth, no one answered the call this morning; the Bretons just went around prodding men at knife-point to come out."

Jean half expected Geoffrey to fly into a rage, but instead he heaved a sigh, dismounted and stepped forward to address the militia directly. "Translate for me, will you, Jean?"

Jean nodded and took his place to the right of the English squire.

"Men of Orte, I sympathize with your losses." Geoffrey's voice was loud, but flat, and he at once knew that it would not do. This field was not a gaming hall, where cajoling and joking could win friends and allies, and these men were not fellow squires. He gritted his teeth and held fast to the pommel of his *couteau*. Then he heard Jean whisper from behind him, "Confidence." Geoffrey raised himself to his full stature and released the pommel. "I too have suffered at the hands of the Breton bands of thieves and murderers," he continued, "and I am here today seeking restitution for their outrages. My name is Geoffrey Hotspur and I am your captain by the grace of the esteemed captain-general of this great host, Corrado Prospero. I may not be a native of your land and I may not owe fealty to any of your lords, but I have sworn *fidelitas* to the cause of making right what has been wronged, and to that end your duty to restore that what was lost to you has become my own. I was at San Bernardino when the Bretons came. Even though none of us can claim to be a knight, we will prevail in this passing of arms by virtue of our own stubborn prowess, hewn from a single purpose. Have faith in this, and we will be rewarded!"

After Jean had finished translating, silence descended on the militia. Geoffrey was not sure what to make of this, so to emphasize at once his authority and devotion he unsheathed his sword and by the blade held it aloft. The ruby-colored pommel glowed in the sunlight.

An older man-at-arms with greying hair gingerly stepped forward and in a low voice spoke to Jean. Another followed, and then another, until Jean and Geoffrey were surrounded.

With his *couteau* still raised, Geoffrey turned to Jean and asked, "You didn't tell them that I'm English, did you?"

"I told them that you were the *pavesaro* who had pledged to rebuild the chapel that Tarlati's Bretons had destroyed in San Bernardino. Some of them have heard about you, from the widows, and so they will follow you. However, one of them did ask about your strange accent, to which I replied that you are Hungarian and honed your craft fighting the Turks. That seems to have calmed them a little. They do have one request, though. They say that they will only form ranks by quarter."

"They will only form ranks by quarter, will they? What does that mean?" Geoffrey lowered his sword.

Godwin answered for Jean. He had used the occasion of Geoffrey's speech to carefully scrutinize the militia, and so had already come to some conclusions about their fighting ability. "It means that each man enrolled by way of the quarter in Orte where his family lives. All cities in Italy are like that."

"May the Lord curse all common folk!" Geoffrey said aloud in English. "Very well. Let them form ranks the way they want to, just so long as they form them!"

Geoffrey marked with his sword the place where the bottom rank should array, which was parallel with Attendolo and Altoviti's square.

Jean made a conciliatory statement to the militia, which did the trick, and the men of Orte began to move into place. The Bretons had managed to seize no more than 180 men in all, but they were fairly well armed, since Prospero had seen fit to issue the company with sixty long Italian pikes – one for every three men. Armor was a problem though. None possessed a hauberk and only a few had arm or leg harnesses, leaving the militiamen to hope that the gambeson or leather jack and simple metal helm each wore would secure them.

"Two brigades, I should think," Godwin said.

"Why?" Geoffrey asked. "They should be made thick in one square. They will have more confidence then and be less inclined to flee."

Godwin shook his head. "There's too many. If you try and move them, they'll be tripping over one another. And we don't have the space back here."

Geoffrey looked around and grimaced as he thought about when he and Jean had attempted *hastiludia* in Spoleto. "You did this with Hawkwood?"

"We made men-at-arms out of the worst rabble. I'll take the left brigade and the Frenchman can take the right one."

"So be it! I will stand at the bottom rank between you."

Geoffrey told Jean to get the Italians to learn which quarters were on the friendliest terms and for them to assemble accordingly.

"I think I had better stay at your side, boy," Godwin said. Jean had already taken a few steps towards his assignment, but stopped and turned back upon hearing the old sergeant's voice.

"There's no need, sergeant. I have led such Italian militia ranks before. It's not that difficult, aside from the language," Geoffrey answered.

"Don't be arrogant! This isn't some tournament or a routine taking of an open town. Those condottieri coming to meet us have tilted more times than you've had shits, and I am not about to let you be run through, or me." Godwin wheezed a great sigh and squinted at the crest of the heights nearly a mile distant.

"All right, young whelp, let's do it," Godwin said. "You, Frenchman, come here. We need to get the calls straightened out; otherwise you'll find yourself marching your brigade into a pass with those noisy ducks!"

Geoffrey, Jean and Godwin held a brief council where Godwin had the other two memorize a list of Prospero's commands and made farting noises to roughly, if rudely, imitate the trumpet signals they were likely to hear during the course of battle. Then he and Jean compared Italian field commands and settled on a simple lexicon that even Geoffrey could understand. After a round of handshakes, the trio broke to take their places.

Andrea Tomacelli reached Narni with a sweaty brow and a lame horse. His squadrons were still a day behind him, but in light of the recent news about the impending confrontation at Orte, he could not afford to wait for them. Besides, if he were to exhaust his men, they would be of no use in battle. Regardless, it was clear that his brother was more in need of a strong hand to control his proud captains than additional lances. The Tiber River could yet be reclaimed, Andrea believed, since he still had a sizable host at his disposal, but only if this obstacle before Orte could be cleared. Then, with Malatesta's and Prospero's companies gone, *all* the cities should surrender, now with no one to defend them. His dear brother just had to keep vigilant, which would be no small task for him. He hoped Gianello would heed the advice he had sent, which was to pursue the antipapal army, protect his rear, await reinforcements, and keep his captains close. He recalled his elder brother's words: Umbria is the keystone in the arch; as it goes, so goes the Patrimony and any hope of ending the war for St. Peter's throne this year.

The rumble of trotting horses rolled down the slope and beneath the feet of the deployed men-at-arms as the Duke of Spoleto began to gather

OF FAITH AND FIDELITY

his forces on the heights. The first banner to appear was that of the duke himself, and was quickly followed by the pennons and gonfalons of the companies of Ceccolo Broglia, Brandolino Brandolini and finally Giovanni Tarlati. The enemy was arriving by the squadron and for a while they looked disorderly as they gazed down on the assembled host ready to meet them, but in less than an hour the squadrons had formed into companies, and the companies into a grand host that stretched over the crest. The number passing through the ranks of Malatesta's men was around a thousand horsemen, not counting what reserves were gathering on the other side of the heights. This meant that Prospero's company, the only mounted force with the antipapal army now, was outnumbered by a ratio of almost three to one. The duke's extreme flanks were bare, though, leaving the road to Narni and a large gap by the woods unoccupied, but no one was fooled into believing that they would remain unordained for long. The hour was past tierce.

"So, Ceccolo Broglia is here too," Prospero whispered and he scratched his cheek. "That was unexpected. Godwin is losing his touch. Well, this will have to do."

A lone horseman brandishing a white flag rode out from behind the duke's army and made his way to the middle of the field. Captain Prospero, understanding that the duke wished to parley before the lists were drawn, sent one of his pages to meet him, who soon returned with a note. Prospero called his captains to the *carrioccio*, including Geoffrey.

"Gianello Tomacelli, Duke of Spoleto and captain-general of the papal host in Umbria and brother of the false pontiff who against all reason and nature occupies the most holy throne of St. Peter," Captain Prospero announced with derisive humor, "is demanding that I surrender the citadel of Orte and betray my lord, Captain Malatesta Malatesta, by retiring my company from the field so that Captain Malatesta's company can be discomfited and taken at the duke's leisure. What say you esteemed captains and sergeants to this most generous offer?"

The captains responded with laughter and ridicule, except for Geoffrey, who was unsure how to react, since he assumed that the note was in earnest. However, it soon became clear that Prospero was being so rude because he had no intention of surrendering to the duke or negotiating any peaceful settlement, and he wanted to make sure that Malatesta's men did not either. Geoffrey reasoned that their ransoms would be high and that some of them would be subject to excommunication, or worse.

"Should I take your mirth to signify that I must reject this offer?" Prospero asked rhetorically. "Very well then, I shall draft a suitable reply." He called over the page who had received the duke's message and dictated the following: "To the captain-general of the host of Pietro Tomacelli in Umbria: I shall only consider divesting myself of the citadel which you most urgently desire if you agree to arrest Andrea Tomacelli, *signore* of Naples, disarm his company and turn him over to me to answer for his insults to my dignity and slanders upon my reputation, after which I shall give him in custody to Clement of Avignon."

"And Tarlati for his spoliation of consecrated property," Geoffrey added.

Captain Prospero looked at Geoffrey with surprise and amusement. He recalled the English squire's resentment of Tarlati on this particular account and thought that now was as good a time as any to remedy it. After all, why should he not twist the dagger of animosity at this irrevocably confrontational stage? "Add that bit to the note as well," the captain-general told the page.

The captains and sergeants were sent back to their respective companies with the order to maintain their defensive formations.

Geoffrey duly reported all that had transpired to Godwin and Jean. Infused with the pride of responsibility, he assumed a very serious demeanor and was careful to explain the most trivial details of the exchange, the mood of the other captains as well as their opinions, facetious and otherwise.

In response, the other two members of his lance took turns relating the fear and uncertainty rippling through the ranks. The growing mass of heavily armed men-at-arms and their horses snorting less than a mile away from a superior vantage was having its intended effect on the militia of Orte. Godwin had already overheard a few men discussing flight, but the old sergeant berated them for cowardice and threatened them with violence, and then just to make his point clear, warned them all of the consequences defeat would have for their families before moving some of the agitators to the bottom ranks, where he could keep an eye on them. Overall, the two brigades were holding together, particularly with the safety of the marsh on their left, the dense ranks of Malatesta's men-at-arms in front of them and Captain Prospero's reserve to their right.

"Perhaps we shall not see any fighting today," Jean said hopefully. "It seems to me that the weave of politics is too tight for any of the captains to unravel it. Maybe this Malatesta and Andrea Tomacelli have cooked up something together to settle this war finally. Where are they, after all? They might be negotiating as we speak."

"Captain Prospero will fight. I am certain of it," Geoffrey answered.

The others detected strong resolve in the squire's voice. Godwin above all appreciated it, since such fortitude would go a long way towards instilling discipline and obedience in what was, quite frankly, a poor and undermanned company.

"Prospero said nothing about retreat, did he?" Godwin asked. "I don't want to be left here to feel the hot blade of a sword on my neck. Now, think carefully." He had seen the gonfalons of his old companions-in-arms, Broglia and Brandolini, rise above the heights. He was certain that they still held him in high regard, so while he could expect no quarter on the lists, they might be able to save him if Prospero's host becomes routed.

Geoffrey assumed the same concerned look as his old sergeant and responded in a forthright manner, as when the astrologer Catherine read for him in Spoleto. "Captain Prospero knows that the duke is playing for time with his parley while he waits for his brother. He told us, though, that he has a plan that involves all the companies, but he will only reveal it to us when he is certain of the enemy's full strength."

"And that is all?" Godwin asked.

"Yes. I remember well."

"Perhaps he's waiting for a better offer," Godwin mumbled to himself and he kicked hard at the flanks of his palfrey.

"What's all this about waiting for the brother?!" Godwin yelled as he approached the captain-general. "The time to strike is now. Take the younger Tomacelli and the older one will follow."

"Back to your ranks, sergeant!"

"Oh no, Conrad. You made me a part of your council, and even though you have failed on your end of the deal, I won't fail on mine." Godwin shifted his horse to block Prospero's mount.

"Out of my way, fool! You are senile. You never should have left your soft bed in Florence." Prospero brandished the white baton.

"Pride has made you blind. You want to restore your reputation as a great condottiere? Then act like one! One Tomacelli brother, the other… it's all the same. That is *their* army ordaining on those hills yonder, and if you want to push them off it, you had better do it now!" Godwin reined his palfrey to give Prospero full view of the heights. They again stared at the foreign host blanketing the distant rise. The horsemen there still had not formed into tight ranks, although more banners and pennons had appeared. All anxiously looked for the gonfalon of the Papal Legate to the Marche, but it was not among them. An hour had elapsed since the duke sent his messenger to Prospero and some of the men were becoming restless.

OF FAITH AND FIDELITY

"Damn you, sergeant, you are right. Return to your company. We set on shortly."

Godwin said nothing to either to the squire or the debt collect. Instead, he distracted the militia by inspecting harnesses, resetting buckles, tugging laces and various arming points, and ensuring that each lance was fully complimented with a fearless head man, a stable second and a heavy-set anchor man. Geoffrey followed suit, as did Jean, albeit reluctantly and with little skill.

A storm of chilling war cries rolled across the field from the Narni road, startling Geoffrey's men. Because the militia was standing several dozen yards behind the harrow of men-at-arms, they enjoyed an unobstructed view of Malatesta's Breton company moving forward, led by a thin screen of Prospero's horsemen.

The fog of confusion was soon dispelled when a page galloped up to Geoffrey's position and explained that Captain Prospero, not having received the duke's response within what he considered to be a reasonable amount of time, decided to make his impatience felt by letting the Bretons loose to stir the duke's ranks, if not his bowels.

After the messenger left, everyone watched as the screen of horsemen rode to within two hundred yards of Brandolini's company, wheeled around and raced across the field, opening the way for the Bretons to abruptly stop, form several ranks and in quick succession let loose a rain of spears. The main of the antipapal army cheered with each contact of point on armor. A few men-at-arms were knocked off their horses by the blows, but Brandolini's company was too experienced to be frightened off by a few missiles. The assault caused little damage in the end, but it did have the intended effect of provoking activity on the heights. The Bretons, meanwhile, returned to their position in good order and excellent mood.

A second emissary waving a white flag emerged from the duke's ranks. His message was no less definitive but considerably more abusive that the first one, and there was no question that Giovanni Tarlati had a hand in composing it. This time, Captain Prospero did not even bother calling his captains and sergeants to the *carrioccio*. Instead, he merely ordered his pages to memorize its general contents and to go from rank to rank and recite them.

"What did he say?" Geoffrey asked Jean, who was standing nearby. The page's heavily accented Italian had prevented Geoffrey from understanding even the most Latin-like words.

"He said that the Duke of Spoleto now demands that Captain Prospero order the entire host to lay down its arms and surrender en masse to him; otherwise he will make it known in princely courts and condottiere circles alike that Corrado Prospero is a false soldier and agent of Clement," Jean explained. "That sounds pretty nasty to me, Geoff. I think we're in for a real fight now."

"Excellent! The duke and Tarlati have revealed their true unworthy selves. Captain Prospero did not dishonor himself at Assisi and this battle will prove it. He cannot go back now. I take this as a very good sign." Geoffrey turned to locate the captain-general and his retinue.

"But would the astrologer Catherine?" Jean asked. A discussion about victual prices in Orte with some of the militiamen of his brigade had stimulated Jean to think about that woman who had taken his and Geoffrey's treasure. Was she in the camp of the duke? She was the Catalonian Vilardell's astrologer, so if the crossbowmen had indeed refused a summer *condotta* with the papal army, it would be unlikely that she was anywhere near Orte. She might even still be in Assisi.

"It is too late to consider that now," Geoffrey answered. "Her magic is made before battle, not during, and this game is well underway. What say we wager on the outcome? We've not done that, you and I." Geoffrey could not resist smiling.

"What? Should we wager on whether we win or lose or on how much blood each of us spills here today? I am not a soldier, but I *am* certain that such a challenge to Fortuna would cause her to rain bad luck upon us, not unlike those Breton spears. Beg a wager of Sergeant Godwin, if you must, but leave me out of it."

"You wail like a woman, Jean. I would never wager on blood. To do so is profane, although how would you know that? We can wager on how many prisoners we capture or who gets to Tarlati first, me or Captain Prospero."

"Those would be fine wagers, Geoff, but need I remind you that neither of us has even the lowest of black money with which to lay any sort of bet?"

Geoffrey broadened his smile and patted his *couteau*. "We could wager with the booty that we seize. I am good for a debt anyway."

Sergeant Godwin approached the young captain and his new sergeant. "You had better return to the ranks, boys. Look!" Godwin pointed at the heights, where they saw considerable movement involving Captain Broglia's and Captain Brandolini's horsemen. Their squadrons were being ordained into brigades.

At the same time as the activity on the heights was gathering momentum, a column of foot soldiers appeared on the duke's side of the Narni road. Word quickly flowed through the harrow of ranks that Tarlati's company of Bretons was taking up position directly across from their compatriots.

"This should neutralize our right flank and the duke's left flank," Godwin explained. "Bretons almost never fight one other if faced with even odds."

Geoffrey scrutinized the one thousand-strong mass of mounted men-at-arms. "This field will not hold such a crush of knights unless it be stretched a mile in both directions," he said loud enough for Godwin to hear. "Otherwise the weight of their charge would carry them right into the Tiber."

"Expect to see them more than once today, boy, for as sure as fire burns the duke will issue charges upon us at least thrice. He is no fool, with his council of able captains, since a single pass made by his host would be too risky a venture to ensure success against us. He is not French, after all, who like to send the flower of their chivalry against a foe in a single go."

"You have much experience with the French way of war?" Geoffrey asked, keenly interested. "You have been in Italy for so long. Can you be sure?"

"You have forgotten that I was at Poitiers. Regardless, the time for parleying is over."

"It looks as though Captain Malatesta will not arrive with all the condottieri of his family after all," Attendolo called out to his men. "He must already be in Spoleto."

Geoffrey thought the captain's jovial mood out of place, considering that his men were likely about to feel the *furioso* of a thousand charging horse. He was about to call out to Attendolo when Jean shouted over him. "Are we expecting him? How close is he to us?"

"The devil knows where he is right now," Attendolo answered.

"What do you mean? Are we about to fight this battle for nothing?"

"We haven't heard from the captain-general for over a week now, and doubtless our German field captain hasn't either." He spat on the ground and surveyed the heights.

"What do we know about what's going on up north?" Geoffrey asked.

"The last we heard was that the other Malatesta were doing fine work keeping Andrea Tomacelli's men of the Marche from making ground in the Patrimony," Attendolo described, "but for all we know now the papal legate could be marshaling his forces on the blind side of the heights as we speak."

The noon bells began to peal in Orte. When they finished, tremendous

OF FAITH AND FIDELITY

shouting went up on Geoffrey's right side, but this time it was not the Breton marauders screaming bloody murder but rather the sharp repetition of distinct orders being relayed through the six squares of Malatesta's and the small captains' companies. Something was happening and Geoffrey was in the dark about it. He looked around for a page of his own to send for an explanation, but his bare-bones militia company did not have any, and he certainly could not afford to peel even one pikeman from the ranks. Instead, Geoffrey mounted his palfrey to review the ranks, though as he did so he glanced at the *carrioccio*, where he saw several officers riding away from Captain Prospero and his field retinue. He looked for the good captain's company and was surprised to see half of his horsemen pacing towards the Narni road. For a horrifying moment Geoffrey thought that Captain Prospero was leaving the field, but when he saw the Bretons forming ranks again with their long pikes stretching out towards the enemy, he understood that the captain-general was finally taking the initiative. Surveying the bustling ranks of men-at-arms arrayed in front of him, Geoffrey saw that they too were about to be drawn deeper onto the field. The long, heavy pikes that once pointed at the sky were steadily craning downwards at various angles, depending on depth of rank, readying for an advance. Geoffrey's heart thumped wildly at the prospect of imminent battle.

A trumpet blared. Then a tug on Geoffrey's surcoat brought his eyes downward.

"You'd better get off that horse, boy, or you'll be shot off it. We have work to do," Sergeant Godwin said and he pointed towards the far right flank of the enemy.

Geoffrey had to squint to see what was happening in the shade of the distant woods. At first he thought another company of Bretons had just arrived, judging by the light harnesses they seemed to be wearing. They were foot soldiers to be sure, though they were not carrying the long pikes typical of Italian men-at-arms. The mystery was solved when the red and yellow flag of the St. George's Company of Crossbowmen of the Vintners Guild of Barcelona rose from behind them. Geoffrey dismounted and gave the reins to Godwin.

"What do you want *me* to do with this beast? I'm not a groom." Not waiting for an answer, Godwin turned the palfrey towards the *carroccio* and slapped it hard on its rump. "You can claim her after the battle," he said.

Geoffrey ignored Godwin's disposal of his mount, since it was no longer needed and the Catalonians were excellent marksmen. "Tell me what this means, sergeant."

"It means Captain Malatesta's company has been ordered to issue forth. Yours hasn't. So, be patient and keep your ears open and mind your station. I shall have my eye on you," Godwin said, and he left Geoffrey to assume a place between the squire and the right brigade.

The men-at-arms started to advance, pikes forward at the ready. Sergeants yelled and armor jangled, while the crunch of fallow stalks being trampled by 3,000 feet muffled the din. The squares shortened the battlefield by 200 yards before stopping, as though on cue. The Bretons advanced by the same distance as well, while Prospero's horsemen were still busy redeploying their squadrons behind the main.

The tactic seemed to work. Broglia's and Brandolini's horsemen appeared to be surprised by the advance as they continued to ordain brigades, but they still showed no sign of assembling for a charge. Then part of Brandolini's company broke away to cover Tarlati's Bretons, who had reacted nervously to the advance of their compatriots, and Tarlati's company of 200 heavy mounted men-at-arms took its place.

Another series of trumpet blasts from Malatesta's *carroccio* echoed across the field, prompting more movement. This time the six squares of men-at-arms that had just advanced subdivided, reforming into twelve squares and stretching the field by another hundred yards, so that it created an unbroken line from the very edge of the woods to the Narni road. Thus, the harrow was refashioned into a scythe, but it now blocked the Orte militia's view.

"I don't understand what the captain-general is doing," Geoffrey said to Godwin. There was no panic in his voice - just frustration and consternation. Geoffrey glanced at the ranks of citizens to gauge their likely effectiveness against a mounted charge. No matter how he ordained them, Geoffrey had to admit that he was none too hopeful.

Godwin squinted at the heights and stroked his beard. "It's obvious, boy. Prospero is shortening the field to reduce the force of a charge. We're on the wrong end of the slope, you see, and also by making a quek board out of Malatesta's company he is challenging the duke to so issue forth."

Geoffrey nodded. The move bolstered his confidence in his captain-general, but it still did not alleviate his concern about being kept away from the bottom rank. "Do you think he'll send his own men out, sergeant? I see horses going into position across from Tarlati's Bretons."

"That I do not know. We shall have to wait and see. It's good we have this marsh beside us. I can't see any of the duke's horsemen getting through there." Godwin smiled at his flippant remark. It was safe, since he had spoken it in English, but Geoffrey did not hear. He had been distracted by Vilardell's crossbowmen unexpectedly retreating back behind the heights.

After some thought and cheek-scratching, Prospero inferred that the disappearance of the Catalonians without having shot a single bolt and the prolonged inactivity of the mounted men-at-arms meant that the opposing captains had fallen out with each other. While Prospero's feint by Malatesta's Bretons and his horsemen might explain the quiescence of the duke's main, it could not answer for the simultaneous departure of the crossbowmen.

The moment his horsemen returned to their rear positions Prospero ordered the main to advance another 200 yards in tight formation, closing the gap between the opposing armies to almost half of what it had been at tierce hour. They were now in the middle of the field. Although the grade of the slope was a little steeper, the real difference in elevation between them and the crest was considerably lessened. His men-at-arms found purchase in the soft ground and held their pikes at the ready.

Once the maneuver was completed, Prospero again divided his own company, sending one half to array fifty yards behind the top-most rank on the left flank and the other half to do likewise in the center. The Bretons he ordered to stay put and tighten their formation. He wanted to give the impression that he was committing his reserves to a stout defence while provoking the duke to attack.

The duke reacted unexpectedly. Instead of drawing up ranks to charge or even abandoning the field for fear of disorder, the antipapal host witnessed some of Broglia's and Brandolini's companies, as well as a few knights from the duke's retinue, dismounting and forming thin lines on the left and right flanks of perhaps 100 men in total. The explanation for this action came with the reappearance of Vilardell's crossbowmen, again on the duke's right flank. Within moments of reforming behind the wall of the newly dismounted men-at-arms, the crossbowmen let loose a shower of quarrels into the center ranks of Malatesta's company.

The pikemen tried to raise shields, but many were struck hard by the screaming missiles. Men fell or were thrown back by the force of the bolts. The shortened field gave the crossbowmen an advantage in accuracy and velocity, but the men-at-arms understood there was no going back; even an orderly retreat of a few hundred yards could be deadly, as the opposing horsemen could take advantage of the backward movement to quickly close ranks and charge. Sergeants called for the men to hold steady. More shields went up and the bottom ranks tightened.

"They will be soon setting on," Godwin said. "Vilardell would not waste a bolt if they weren't."

Geoffrey did not hear. The blood pounding in his ears had deafened him and he was still, but for the hand trembling around the ruby pommel.

The day was nearing mid-afternoon and the sun was growing hot.

CHAPTER 16

D UKE Gianello watched the final volley of quarrels crash into the middle squares of the enemy below and was shocked by the violence of the blows. The Catalonians were good, he mused, and he hoped that Captain Broglia was just as good so that he could drive the reeling men-at-arms from the field before his brother arrived. The captain had already ordained his men in front of him, since he had accorded himself the privilege of first setter-on against the main of the cursed antipope's army. No one had opposed Broglia at the final war council meeting, which was testimony the esteem held by his peers, not least Tarlati, who had argued in favor of himself striking last in order to finish off those who still would stand against the might of Broglia and Brandolini. It was fortunate that all the captains were anxious for battle, though the duke was troubled by their respective motives: Broglia ultimately wanted to take Assisi; Brandolini wanted to besiege Todi; Tarlati wanted to drive towards his home town Arezzo; all wanted to finish the affair with Prospero before Andrea could arrive to share in the glory. He would have rather had at the forefront of their aims the desire to rid Italy of the supporters of Clement. Only the Catalonian captain had expressed any reservations about attacking at this time, suggesting that they await the arrival of the papal legate before making any pass of arms. He would not delay. If the day grows any older, Prospero might just return to the safety of Orte, force a siege and await the return of Malatesta. Well, never mind who is not here, Gianello thought to bolster his confidence. He was the captain-general on this field at this hour and he was holding the advantage.

The duke then caught the eye of his first setter-on. Broglia's men numbered over 400, grouped into ten squadrons of 40-45 horsemen stretched across 200 yards of front. All were wearing the full complement of the latest Italian harness, which included a long hauberk and a steel breastplate, and each man carried a thick lance that was over four yards long. Captain Broglia positioned himself at the head of the center brigade, as it was his custom to ride with his men. He had a reputation for strength and prowess and it was said that the captain himself had put up a bounty of twenty florins for the first man who could knock him off his charger in any pass. Captain Brandolini, meanwhile, had his men just behind his friend Broglia's, and with the Catalonians occupying the far right plus his own retinue, the heights were crowded. As for the *carrioccio*, he had been obliged to park it by the Narni road. Tarlati had suggested this place, although it meant that the war wagon would not be visible from the field, thereby cancelling its use as a rallying point. He had had the foresight, however, to double the guard with men from his own retinue, lest the Bretons lose interest in the engagement and decide to loot whatever was at hand. He had also taken the precaution of entrusting the companies' war chests to the Catalonians. They were a reliable lot, by all accounts, and since they were on foot they could not to wander too far, should they too take it into their heads to run off with the treasure.

What was nagging at Gianello, from a tactical point of view, was that he lacked a solid cohort of *pedites* to cover the crossbowmen, protect the crest and form an adequate reserve. None of the three captains were willing to dismount their men, particularly Tarlati, who argued that his Bretons disqualified him from the request anyway. It had required a despairing amount of effort to convince the captains Broglia and Brandolini to dismount a handful of their lances for duty to protect the Catalonians, which he supplemented with several of his own men. Curse their pride, the duke thought – none of them would have dared to argue with his brother

OF FAITH AND FIDELITY

on such a key aspect of deployment. Well, at least Captain Prospero was about to pay for his pride. He had rejected his offers, which were made in earnest, to save his skin as well as his soul, so the time had come for a more violent reckoning. "Their tempers will change once I have done this noble feat of arms for the sake of the Church and my brother, the one true pontiff in Rome," he whispered to himself. Then, seeing Captain Broglia staring hard back at him, Gianello signaled his trumpeter to sound the attack.

As soon as the final notes of the trumpet had died away, Ceccolo Broglia shook his lance and called for his men to answer. A cry of "Boniface!" went up from the dense pack of horsemen. They lowered their lances and with their captain in the lead they spurred their mounts forward. At first the horses were slow and unsure of their footing on the declining slope, but as they grew accustomed to the gradient, as they made sure of their traction, as their riders tightened their ranks, their confidence grew. The mass of horse and rider gathered momentum. The boom of hooves sent tremors all the way to the Tiber. The spray of dirt and grass being thrown up by the charging ranks blinded Malatesta's company to everything but the bottom rank of destriers and their determined riders.

The first touch of lance did not pierce the forward squares of Malatesta's company so much as bowl them over into their supporting compatriots, like so many nine-pins. Men were impaled on both sides and shields fell, but the center of Malatesta's company held. Unable to achieve full gallop, Broglia had succeeded only in denting the ranks of men-at-arms instead of scattering them to the wind as they had hoped. Now, caught amidst a dense mass of wounded and frantically regrouping men, horses began to rear and whinny, causing Broglia's squadrons to break up. Their lances now ineffective, the horsemen cast them aside and drew swords to hew at the bristling pikes trying to overthrow them.

Seeing how the flanking squares were quickly regrouping and closing to remake the harrow, Gianello told his trumpeter to sound the retreat.

Immediately, Broglia's disciplined company broke out of the potential encirclement and returned to the heights. To cover their retreat and to soften up the twisting squares for the next pass, the Catalonians let loose several hundred more quarrels.

Brandolini's company, which was just under 400 strong, moved into the place vacated by Broglia. However, instead of concentrating his ranks along a narrow front, as Broglia had done, Brandolini stretched his squadrons to cover a width of 400 yards.

"What is he doing?" Gianello asked aloud. "I do not understand Captain Brandolini's purpose. He should concentrate his ranks, not disperse them. I fear his men will be discomfited without the strong center."

"Calm yourself," Tarlati said. "The enemy has been weakened, but he does not want to risk envelopment like Broglia, so he is expecting to bend that harrow out of shape and maybe even send a few squares to flight. You can reckon for yourself that Prospero's horse cannot be enough to effectively counter."

"It is a wise decision," someone said behind them, "but it has been rashly made. What have you done, my brother?"

Captain Prospero dismounted half his company and sent them to reinforce the center of his line while the men-at-arms who had taken the brunt of Broglia's charge reformed their squares in the face of the newly ordained ranks of horsemen. Prospero understood Brandolini's purpose; now that his center was weak, even if he would issue his reserve to strengthen it, he could expect the next setting on to fragment more squares and open up his line. He was not confident that Malatesta's men would survive a third charge, whether by horse or by foot, if they were not broken by Brandolini's imminent attack, of course, and his reserves were few. Therefore, he was pleased to see that Captain Brandolini was taking his time ordaining his company and not to see either Tarlati's men or the duke's retinue

OF FAITH AND FIDELITY

forming ranks to quickly follow it. The standard order of battle right across Christendom was for a host to ordain three brigades: the van, the main and the rear. To be sure, Prospero had encountered numerous variations to this rule, but even so he had been surprised to see Broglia form up as the van, since that was a role better suited to the Bretons, or the duke's band of knights. He would have had Broglia's company serve as the core of the main. Perhaps the duke had hoped that his ranks would be wholly ruined after a single pass, Prospero speculated, or maybe Broglia had been impatient and demanded the first run at Malatesta's men. Also, Tarlati's Bretons were not moving. He sensed conflict confounding the duke's war council and he was about to smile at the prospect of piecemeal destruction of the duke's host when he saw Andrea Tomacelli.

"All the better," Prospero whispered. "Now I can strike." He sent a page to order his remaining squadrons to return to their reserve position near the *carrioccio* and he spurred his horse and galloped towards the marsh.

"Captain Hotspur!" Prospero called out when he reached the top rank of the militia. He spotted Sergeant Godwin, but he would not talk to him.

Geoffrey attended his captain-general alone. "Yes, captain. My company is ready."

Prospero lifted his white baton and pointed beyond the left flank. "Take your entire company through that marsh. There are numerous paths there that enter the woods, with which some of your men should be familiar anyway. I am tasking you to get your company through those woods to a place just below the heights. When I send up a flaming arrow, you and your men will smash that crossbow company and everyone protecting it. And for God's sakes don't let anyone see you!"

Godwin raced to Geoffrey's side as fast as his constricting harness would allow, but he did manage to catch most of the order. "We are the only reserve company now, Conrad, and I'd advise you to keep it that way." He gave the captain-general a meaningful look that asked whether he was being betrayed.

"A few squadrons of my company are reserve enough," Prospero answered severely. "The English Free Company is under my command, and you are under Captain Hotspur, sergeant. I do not need you to question my orders. The time for that has passed. Now, ready your men. Exchange those pikes for falchions and other more appropriate arms. You still have eyes enough to see our situation."

But Godwin would not be deterred. He grabbed the bridle of Prospero's horse and said, "The duke will see us and send men – veteran men – to cut us to pieces in the woods. This is woolly-headed thinking – even the blind could see that."

"You yourself said I should not delay. If you march your ranks just behind the harrow you should be well shielded. I am confident that no one has been ordained to protect the Catalonians' right side. Now, let go of my horse."

Godwin obeyed and took a couple of steps back. There was nothing he could do. Flight was out of the question and he would not risk the wrath of Prospero, not at this moment. The only way out was forward, he reckoned.

Geoffrey's heart thumped harder than ever and he tasted blood in his throat. "Why should we wait? Perhaps we should fall on the crossbowmen as soon as possible to stop them from shooting again into our ranks."

"You should learn to take orders, Hotspur, if only to explain them properly to your sergeants." Then he gave Godwin a sharp look. "You will only attack after the duke has committed his main. Should you show yourself too early, he will just turn his horsemen and ride you down. And instead of wasting time thinking that he won't, pray that our center holds long enough for me to send up the flaming arrow."

"And if an arrow never comes?" Geoffrey asked.

"Then hope for a better ransom than the one I gave for you." With that final quip, Prospero galloped away.

Jean had arrived and was standing beside the troubled Godwin when Geoffrey said, "How should we issue forth?"

"We shall issue forth together," Godwin stated with resignation. "I've already told you that I plan to keep my eye on you, and that includes every minute of this day."

"Andrea!" Gianello cried and embraced his brother. "It is by the grace of the Lord Himself that you have arrived at the most propitious moment to help me lead our host to victory. We hold the advantage and the men acquit themselves well."

Andrea returned the greeting but quickly broke away to inspect the situation. He was impressed with the damage Broglia had done and he could see Prospero's men-at-arms dismounting to support what was left of his center. The youngest Tomacelli had not done badly, in truth, although Andrea found it surprising that some of his horsemen had been assigned to watch the crossbowmen. "Why are those men not mounted and preparing for a pass?" he asked Gianello, nodding towards the Catalonians' guard.

"Captain Vilardell demanded it," Gianello answered with some embarrassment. "He refused to array unless we gave him cover, and I could spare no others."

"Call him here and get those men back on their mounts!" Andrea shouted.

"We should make another pass now, your lordship." This was Tarlati's suggestion. A page from Captain Brandolini had come up to him asking why the duke had not given the signal to charge.

The papal legate looked hard at the condottiere. "We will do nothing of the kind until I bring order to this command. Where is Broglia? Call him to me as well."

No one moved, particularly since the papal legate had not issued his last order to anyone specific. Gianello was hesitant to repeat Andrea's commands. He would naturally defer to his brother's superior judgment, but the battle was well underway and it seemed to him that the condottiere captains knew what they were doing. He wondered if he should not just have Captain Brandolini make his pass.

"Broglia is rallying his men near my Bretons," Tarlati answered, "and Brandolini is ordaining his men to crush Prospero."

"He will have to wait. I want a full account before we proceed. Captain Tarlati: why have your Bretons done nothing? Are they the reserve? If so, then why are they on the Narni road? If not, they should have engaged the enemy already. I see that we are short on *pedites*, so we should be using our horsemen to better advantage."

"I believe that his lordship the duke is doing just that," Tarlati responded tersely. "We have three bodies of mounted men-at-arms ranked for successive passes, a load of crossbowmen and my Bretons to cover the left flank, not to mention that Captain Broglia is already regrouping for another pass, if need be. What more can you add?"

As the papal legate and Tarlati began to argue over how the companies should be formed and deployed, Captain Vilardell arrived and took his place beside the duke. "Who took away my guard?" he demanded. "Why have we opened the right flank? Oh, S*ignore* Tomacelli, you are here." He bowed to the papal legate.

Andrea broke with Tarlati and addressed the Catalonian captain. "I see no reason for you to weaken our horse by making an idle garrison of them. Our right flank is of no consequence since, as you can see, the enemy is in no condition to attack, and even if they were, your crossbowmen could easily retreat in good order without undue haste under the cover of your *pavesari*."

"I disagree. My *condotta* stipulates that my men must have a properly armed foot guard of at least two dozen lances. This is no time to dispute it."

"I think not!" Andrea bellowed. "You should be thankful for half of what you received."

The duke stepped in to mediate. "I shall send some of my men from the *carrioccio* to replace the others to alleviate the Catalonians' fear of being discomfited. What say you?"

Vilardell nodded and Andrea made an affirmative dismissal with a wave of his hand. "So be it, Gianello," Andrea said. "Ah! Captain Broglia has returned."

"And Captain Brandolini has yet to set on the enemy," Tarlati added. "The day is flying. We could retire to Narni and regroup."

"No," Gianello said. "We have already entered the lists. Just one more push and they will be in the Tiber!" He spurred his horse forward to survey the field.

"Why did you not have the Bretons attack Malatesta's company first?" Andrea asked. "Tarlati's horsemen could have covered our left flank."

"Captain Broglia wanted to be the first setter-on and the others agreed," Gianello answered. "I had the Catalonians thin their ranks before his charge, though."

"We are losing time, Andrea," Tarlati said. "My Bretons are restless and the day is hot. Either send Brandolini to finish them off or we retire."

"Who is captain-general here?" Andrea asked. "Mind your ranks, Giovanni."

"*I* am the captain-general," Gianello said, "and the battle goes well."

"The battle does not go well. You are too slow as usual, my brother. Look how well formed those squares are now."

"Fine." Gianello threw the white baton at Andrea. "You have taken command, so you can ordain the brigades. Prospero's argument is with you anyway. You may have the glory on this day, or the blame." He wheeled his horse around and galloped towards the *carrioccio*.

Andrea fumed. Gianello should have waited for him, regardless of how

Prospero might have deployed his men. He looked down and understood why Malatesta's company was so far up the slope. Broglia's pass had been only partially effective, so Brandolini would have to follow. There was no time to dismount and ordain anew the companies for an advance on foot, or to get the Bretons up on the heights. Andrea spat as he realized that he would have to see his brother's original plan through.

"Captain Brandolini!" Andrea shouted. "Prepare to charge. Tarlati! Form ranks behind him. Should Prospero's squares not be wholly discomfited by the second pass and break, to will follow shortly. Captain Broglia! Rally your company with the Bretons on the left. They will seize the bridge, so that Prospero cannot escape. Vilardell! Have your men train their crossbows on the bridge."

Brandolini's horsemen thundered down the slope with another cry of "Boniface!" Again, the front ranks of Malatesta's men-at-arms buckled from the force of the powerful strike, but the push was not as great with the squadrons stretched over twice the distance. Prospero's assumptions were correct – the forward squares collapsed and melted into the rear ones, but enough men held fast their pikes to unseat even more of Brandolini's riders. With his line still holding its ground – just – the captain-general ordered the last of his reserve to dismount and rush to support those threads of the line that looked to be in danger of breaking.

Prospero was now in the dangerous position of having no men held back, while it was too late to recall the Orte militia. He would have to press ahead and hope that the distraction Hotspur and his company were about to make would be enough to disorganize the duke's rear, thereby giving him time to exhaust Brandolini's horsemen and delay another charge by the other captains.

The square consisting of the captains Attendolo and Altoviti's men broke, leaving a gap on the left. Some of Malatesta's men shifted to fill the space, but their action opened another gap, one closer to the marsh. Seeing

OF FAITH AND FIDELITY

this success, Brandolini pressed with the attack instead of pulling back to regroup, as his fellow captain had done. If another square collapsed, Prospero's harrow would become short enough for Brandolini's men to outflank it.

Andrea and the *signore* of Arezzo witnessed this success and smiled. Brandolini had made the correct decision, they reckoned, and each could foresee Malatesta's men-at-arms collapsing into small groups for self-preservation. If Prospero's line fragmented thus, all would be lost for him, as the remaining horsemen, including Broglia's and Tarlati's, could take their time to encircle and force the isolated clusters to lay down their arms.

"Prospero has no reserve," Andrea announced. I think the time has come to end this fine pass of arms. "Captain Tarlati. Ready your men."

Geoffrey smiled when he saw the flaming arrow rise up above the treetops, spark noisily for a brilliant moment then explode with a hollow pop. He had led the men of Orte through the marsh and up into the woods, or rather they had led him, and found hiding places in the nooks and crevices only they knew. No one had seen them, for in their hurry to reach the heights and then just as quickly to leave them, the Catalonians had failed to scout the woods that lay to their right. From his vantage behind a fallen tree, Geoffrey could only catch glimpses of the ongoing battle. He had a better view of the heights and watched in awe as the mounted men-at-arms of Broglia and Brandolini assembled for their passes. The sound of violence when the galloping horsemen crashed into the dense squares of men-at-arms thrilled him, and he regretted Captain Prospero not permitting him to join the ranks of Malatesta's men. His role as leader of an ambush seemed undignified, but he had to accept his station in this host. He was not even a squire in good standing in the eyes of the Italians, he had with embarrassment discovered, let alone a knight. Was he a condottiere now, what with this *condotta* he had signed? At least he was not idle, watching the clash of arms from afar while minding a bloated war wagon. Setting his pride aside, Geoffrey focused on his aim to seek restitution for the chapel lying ruined just a few miles on the other side of Orte and to help Captain Prospero avenge his insulted dignity. Perhaps he should visit the mourning village once the battle was won? Well, let's not get ahead of ourselves, he thought. The day is far from won. There was still much to do, and so Geoffrey reviewed the plans that he, Jean and Godwin made before Brandolini's charge.

"I see Sergeant Alfonso," Jean had whispered when all the men were settled into their hiding places.

Geoffrey did not notice the Frenchman crawl up to him through the bramble. He had been staring at the crossbowmen, who themselves were observing the clash of men, horse and steel below them, and had spotted the Catalonian sergeant Alfonso Sanchez in a polished helm. He was speaking with Captain Vilardell, who was the only captain on the duke's side not on horseback.

"I think the best way to accomplish this feat of arms is to drive the 'bowmen off with a charge of fury, wheel right before full contact is made, and fall on the men-at-arms," Geoffrey suggested to Jean. "We should keep better order that way and have the advantage in numbers once the Catalonians are in flight; I count forty of the blackguards in all."

"Just like the Outer City ruffians had," Jean added morosely. He could not see their having any advantage against a company of disciplined crossbowmen and a band of veteran men-at-arms, however few and disgruntled they might be.

"We will set on in two waves," Godwin decided, ignoring Jean's dismissive comment. He had taken his brigade to the north almost behind the crossbowmen, where a large cairn added to their cover, and had returned to ensure that all was right with the squire. "Your plan is almost well considered boy, but you are putting too many eggs in one basket. If you get tangled up with Vilardell's men, then what? You will be crushed between the hammer of the men-at-arms and the anvil of the 'bowmen, that's what. Don't assume they'll run just because your war cries are loud. Now, listen: you and the Frenchman will rush in with swords drawn and make directly for the crossbowmen. I shall count to ten before taking my men in. The men-at-arms should be distracted by your attack, and my men, as much as they *are* men, will fall on them. *If* the Catalonians scatter, turn your brigade, as you said, to outflank the men-at-arms and we will meet. If the *pavesari* hold fast, return to the woods with all speed. To be honest, I don't think the men-at-arms will stand; from my years in the field I can tell that they aren't enjoying serving as common guards for foreign crossbowmen."

Geoffrey grimaced as he felt the point of the sergeant's final words. Of course, the old soldier was right and deference had to be given. Geoffrey had already put away his pride, so he listened and nodded. He now understood the captain-general's purpose: once they scared off the Catalonians and their weak defenders, Captain Prospero would issue his counter-attack with either his own company or the Bretons, or both. He did not think about what might then happen to him or to the Orte militia.

But Jean did. "And how will you fare alone, W*ill*, once we find shelter in the woods? You haven't accounted for yourself should our scheme be overturned."

For once Godwin looked uncomfortable, and he waited a minute or so before answering. "We take cover below the crest list-side and make for the marsh. The 'bowmen won't be able to array before we reach it."

After Geoffrey watched the flaming arrow float down to earth, a hand clapped his shoulder. He turned and saw Jean. For a moment he doubted that the chandler would follow him; entering a drunken fray from the shadows was one thing, but setting on into the teeth of battle was quite another.

But then again, how would he know? The siege of Narni really counted for very little in that regard and he had acquitted himself poorly against the corsairs. The Frenchman only owed him any *fidelitas* on account of his deception, as a debt of honor, and such a bond could not be all that strong for him. Yet it was a bond, and their creation of a free lance must make it fast. Yes, Geoffrey felt in his heart, Jean would fulfill the commission entrusted to him; otherwise he will be hunted down and made to pay for his treachery. The time had come for Geoffrey to demonstrate his prowess. After giving Jean a reassuring nod, he unsheathed his *couteau* and kissed it thrice where the crossguard was mounted against the hilt. Then, as he rubbed the strange pommel for luck, thoughts of Captain Prospero, Giovanni Tarlati, Gaunt, Roger Swynford, and St. John the Baptist flashed through his mind.

"Shall we go forth?" Jean asked.

Geoffrey raised his *couteau* high above his head and cried, "San Bernardino!"

As though rising from the dead, the Orte militia emerged from their hiding places. A few looked around with uncertainty, unsure whether to join the battle or simply remain safe and concealed amid the protective trees, but upon seeing the old Hawkwood sergeant and some of their fellow citizens poking and prodding them to advance, the men of Orte followed Geoffrey and Jean into the midday sun. Led by their short swords, spears and falchions, they ran through the small strip of woods that separated them from the heights. They gave no war cry or shouts of bloodlust; they just followed the squire forward.

Geoffrey held his sword high as he led his men along the narrow crest of the heights at the massed ranks of crossbowmen. He saw a few surprised faces, but he averted his eyes lest he recognize some of his erstwhile *Cacho* playing companions. Instead, Geoffrey focused his attention on the vintners guild charges blazoned on their chests. For an instant he wondered if he had the moral strength to bring his sword down and hew in two any of these men, but the red almost bleeding stripes reminded him of how the Catalonians lacked mercy in their assault on the Portuguese caravel, when they cut down corsair and sailor alike. Geoffrey furrowed his brow and quickened his pace.

Then the *pavesi* went up. Crossbows rattled as the Catalonians turned to see what was coming at them. A few got off a quarrel before Geoffrey brought down his *couteau* onto the front rank of *pavesari*, slicing one shield cleanly down the middle and kicking aside another. The Catalonians tried to fill the gap made by the squire, but the townsmen were already on them, pushing forward with their long weapons. A bolt whizzed passed Geoffrey's ear. He looked up and saw Sergeant Alfonso bent over his crossbow with one foot in the stirrup, but just as quickly his view was blocked as several *pavesari* set up their shields further back. Then he heard Captain Vilardell's voice and at once the crossbowmen started moving backwards.

Godwin had been right; Geoffrey went through the list of commands he had learned earlier and found the one for 'halt'. He repeated the order again and looked back at the crest for the now separated guard. The surprised men-at-arms were tentatively girding themselves for a counter-attack. He was about to give the order to his rallying militia to form ranks when Sergeant Godwin blazed passed him, his brigade pressing hard on his heels.

The dismounted men-at-arms suddenly had a change of heart. Seeing that the Catalonians were abandoning them and alarmed by the second band of skirmishers streaming out of the woods, they retreated in good order into the squadrons of Tarlati's readying horsemen. Godwin halted his men and the two sides stared at each other from a distance of about fifty yards.

Prospero saw Broglia's dismounted men advance on his right flank in support of Brandolini's men-at-arms. His men still held the line, but it was under heavy pressure and steadily falling back. Then he saw that Brandolini was working to outflank the left end of his line, so Prospero pulled back his center for the sake of his harrow formation. He could not rely on the Bretons to advance with their compatriots still opposing them, although he was confident that they would hold their ground. But if Broglia's men succeeded in breaking his right flank, the battle would be lost.

Then Prospero saw the success the Orte militia was having across the field and the confusion it was causing among the duke's remaining forces. Not only had the Catalonians retreated from view again, but Tarlati was having a hard time ordaining his squadrons in the face of unset groups of men-at-arms mixing with them. Prospero smiled as he recognized that fickle Fortuna had decided to give him a final chance for victory. This delay, coupled with Brandolini's earlier late charge, should be enough to save his men from being crushed, encircled or otherwise overwhelmed. The Catalonians, meanwhile, might return, but they would have to shoot down the militia first, and that would cause another delay for the papal legate to attack his main. So be it; the militia was expendable.

Captain Prospero decided that he could wait no longer to engage the final part of his plan: he ordered the Bretons to advance up the road to engage Broglia's men on his right flank and the last free squadron of his company to pressure the leftmost square of the line to pinch inwards. He still held numerical superiority on the field and could see that this should be enough to allow him to fold in the points of his harrow. With Broglia outflanked, Brandolini disorganized and Tarlati holding back his company, the captain-general was confident that he could create at least a partial encirclement of the duke's main body in quick order and force at least two of his captains to surrender.

OF FAITH AND FIDELITY

"We must keep these townsmen together," Godwin yelled at Geoffrey. "They don't understand that the battle is not over yet."

Geoffrey surveyed the bit of the heights that he had just captured and saw how many of his militiamen were bent over the few dead and wounded of the enemy stripping them of anything of value, while others were heading back into the woods, content that their work was done. A wave of panic swept over Geoffrey. He turned towards the Catalonian crossbowmen and saw that they were no longer fleeing. Instead of making for the *carrioccio* as they had shown, the Catalonians were regrouping on the field Captain Prospero had initially hoped to give battle. He then looked ahead and saw that the retiring men-at-arms were causing such disorder in Tarlati's ranks that they were having difficulty forming brigades. Then he saw the hated figure of Giovanni Tarlati. He looked to be arguing with Andrea Tomacelli in the midst of the confusion. The Duke of Spoleto, meanwhile, appeared to be taking what was left of his retinue to his *carrioccio*, to array again the crossbow company, Geoffrey assumed.

"We have no choice," Geoffrey declared. "We must press the attack. I cannot let Tarlati escape before Captain Prospero arrives to claim victory. Sergeant Godwin! Sergeant Lagoustine! Rally your men!"

Godwin wanted to restrain the squire's enthusiasm, for if there was anything a man had to keep cool on the field of battle it was his head, lest someone take it from him. However, first he had to return order to this band of citizens. Godwin looked around and quickly realized that shouting would not bring the men of Orte back together.

"Hotspur! Listen! Take command of my brigade and form what's left of them into a square, like what we had below, and face the horsemen. Put those with falchions in the bottom ranks and tell them that for the sake of their own lives they need to pack close together, no matter how small the square might look. With some luck Tarlati might think twice about running down a bunch of militia for sport before leaving the field. They do not look at all content. I'll get to the Frenchman and help him drag his brigade out of the woods. What say you?"

Geoffrey nodded. He again felt obliged to defer to the old man's judgement. He had fought with Sir John Hawkwood and the White Company, after all. So, as Godwin dashed towards the woods, he grabbed and yelled and cajoled the men of Orte to reform ranks, knocking loot out of their hands.

"Hey! Frenchman! Get your men together! You better not even be thinking about fleeing into the woods?" Godwin yelled as he ambled up to Jean, who was standing on the crest of the heights looking unsure.

"Not before I get my share," Jean answered, mocking Godwin's aggressive tone. "But those shield-bearers are a poor lot. If you have any ideas, I'm all ears." Jean shrugged and fingered the laces of his harness.

Godwin glowered at Jean, and showing that he had no tolerance for such insolence, grabbed the neck of a militiaman, who was busy crouched over one of the few corpses trying to pry off a piece of armor, and sliced off his ear.

"Here. *Now* you're all ears." Godwin flung the newly ripped piece of flesh at Jean's feet as the stricken man screamed and fled into the woods. "Now ordain these men, and don't be afraid to use your sword to do it!" Godwin turned around and marched back towards his own brigade, berating, threatening and ordering everyone in his path.

"God's bones!" Jean cried. "Not even I would lay into the most delinquent debtor so." But the old sergeant's brutal act was enough to jolt him to action. Jean grabbed the surcoats of two militiamen and together they proceeded to collect whoever was left to collect. They were able to form one band of 70 men, although one that was now better armed and in higher spirits in the wake of the easy victory. Jean ordained them hopefully out of range of the Catalonians. As he peered down at his old company to gauge their distance, he saw a solitary figure emerge from the defensive square the 'bowmen had formed. When the man stopped at the base of the heights, Jean recognized Sergeant Alfonso.

"I have been sent to negotiate terms with Captain Prospero," Alfonso called out.

Jean was taken aback. He looked around: Godwin was already with Geoffrey and they appeared to be marching away from him along the heights; the Bretons on the far side of the field were advancing along the Narni road; Prospero's and Malatesta's men were still engaged on the battlefield, gradually encircling Broglia's and Brandolini's companies. Then he thought: why shouldn't he play peace emissary? He had a bone to pick with Sergeant Alfonso anyway.

"I can speak for Captain Prospero," Jean answered and stepped away from his band to show himself.

Alfonso also took a step forward and squinted. "I know you. You're that French chandler who was following the English squire. I thought you'd be dead by now. And you still owe me; the astrologer gave me little out of that coffer of yours."

"I am alive and well, thank you, and it looks as though my side has won the day. You may surrender to me."

"Our position is not as weak as you might think. Be careful that our gracious captain does not decide simply to shoot you off that hill."

"If you do that, you will only open the way for Captain Prospero's knights to ride you down. If your position is so strong, then where is your guard? We scattered that first lot like sand in the wind, although you probably missed their flight, unless you have eyes on your backsides."

"I suggest you mind your own backside. I see what sort of men comprises your company. In any event, there is no longer cause to fight. We must negotiate, or we will simply leave with the duke's *carrioccio*."

"Let me come down to you." Jean did not want either Geoffrey or Godwin to either see or hear what he was doing. He descended the steep slope and met Alfonso midway. "I will send a man to Prospero just as soon as you tell me one thing: where is your astrologer, Catherine? Is she with you? She has something of mine and I want it back."

Sergeant Alfonso looked askance at Jean and smiled. "She is in Spoleto, or Assisi maybe. I don't know. When the captain first refused a new *condotta* from the duke, she left us. When the captain decided to accept the *condotta* after all, she was sought but could not be found before we had to march."

So that's why the Catalonians were so hesitant today, Jean thought. "Vilardell misses his magic mistress. Well, all for the better for him."

Alfonso tilted his head back before saying, "We have something better: the companies' war chests."

Now that at least a portion of his company was in order, if not enthusiastic about continuing the fight, Geoffrey resolved not to let the infamous captain flee unscathed. He was accountable for spoiling consecrated ground, for murdering unarmed citizens at Narni after the city had submitted and for besmirching Captain Prospero's dignity and reputation. It was time to ransom. "Brigade!" Geoffrey cried in his heavily accented Italian. "Prepare to set on! Arms at the ready! Slow pace! After me!" Geoffrey waved his *couteau* once around his head and found his place at the bottom of his small company. Satisfied that the militiamen were well ordained and happy to see that none were trying to flee, he motioned with his *couteau* to advance.

"What in Satan's fiery balls are you doing!" Sergeant Godwin cried when he caught up to his ward. "The battle is over. We should hold position until Prospero can get some horsemen up here. Do not tempt fate or you will live to regret it, or die, should Fate have that in store for you." The old sergeant was huffing from his constant running, but he managed to fall in step with Geoffrey.

"Fate has given me the chance to fulfill my pledge to *the* Lord and *my* lord and I must not ignore the sign. Tarlati must be made to yield."

"I have my pledges to honor as well, and the principal one is to ensure that you do not perish on the way to Florence. Does this look like Florence to you?"

Geoffrey ignored Godwin's words and ordered the militiamen to halt. They were within twenty yards of the nearest horseman. "Captain Giovanni Tarlati, *signore* of Arezzo!" Geoffrey yelled as loud as he could.

Tarlati suspended his heated conversation with the papal legate when the peculiar accent caught his ear. He looked up and saw the determined face of Geoffrey Hotspur staring out from beneath the old bascinet helmet that he was still wearing. He made a wry smile and said with amusement, "May the devil take me, if it's not the lonely squire. Go home to your mother, boy, or I will cleave you in two."

"You will do no such thing," Andrea Tomacelli commanded. "You will have your men arm all points and prepare to support captains Broglia and Brandolini on the right flank, where Prospero is weakest." He pointed towards the distant marsh with the white baton he had taken from his brother.

"And I've said that it would be better for us to pull back. My Bretons won't budge now that they have seen how that damnable Catalonian has decided to leave the field. You waited too long with Brandolini's pass."

Geoffrey took several steps forward and positioned himself en garde. "Captain Tarlati!" he called again with the strength of conviction. "I ask that you yield so that I might hold you to ransom, as is custom. What say you? *Signore* Tomacelli, for the generosity you have showed me, you may cede the field and leave with your brother in peace." Geoffrey pulled out the papal legate's seal from his belt and tossed it onto the ground before him. "My men are prepared to repeat the feat of arms that won them your flank."

Tarlati showed a look of incredulity, which quickly transformed to anger when he realized that Geoffrey was in earnest. "You yield, or I *will* run you and your peasants through. My charger is well rested and anxious to commit violence."

"It is time for you to pay. Dismount and kneel before me," Geoffrey commanded. His tone was solemn rather than threatening.

"Geoffrey, don't be daft, for the love of Christ," Godwin begged, for the first time letting the emotion of the battle seep into his speech. "Look about you, boy. Your Catalonian friends are not showing themselves to be finished for the day. See how they march back up the slope?"

Geoffrey did not want to tear his gaze away from Tarlati, but the familiar rattle of crossbows was too distracting to ignore. When he turned his head, however, the first thing Geoffrey noticed was that leading the Catalonian company alongside Captain Vilardell and Sergeant Alfonso was Jean Lagoustine. His brigade, meanwhile, was marching in escort along either side, like a guard company, as Geoffrey himself had once done on his way to the siege of Narni.

Andrea Tomacelli pulled his horse ahead of Tarlati's and said, "Leave now and take your rabble back to the swamp, or I will order these fine crossbowmen to blast you off this hill. The battle is not over and you play but a small role in it."

"Don't be so sure of your allies," Vilardell warned. He ordered his company to halt just as the slope was beginning to steepen; he did not want his men too close to the horsemen. "We have come to negotiate with Captain Prospero. You have lost my trust, as I see no unity in council here or respect for my men, and with the craven flight of those men-at-arms leaving me exposed, I have no choice but to withdraw from the field. Captain Hotspur, take your man." He really did not want to see the

OF FAITH AND FIDELITY

captain fall into the hands of an English squire, if only for the sake of decorum, but he needed to pressure the *signore* from Arezzo and discomfit the papal legate all the same. Despite the strength and experience of his men, his position was not as strong as he was making out.

"You would break your *condotta* with my brother and risk your reputation, Berenguar? The battle is nearly won!" Andrea said.

"I am not risking my reputation and my *condotta* clearly states that I have the right to retire from the field at my discretion if I feel that my company is in danger. Your brother did not provide me with suitable protection and, as sorry as I am to admit this, my company was driven from the field by Captain Hotspur," Berenguar explained. "And the lists as yet belong to neither side."

"But what about your soul? You may not owe *fidelitas* to my brother the duke, as you are neither his vassal nor his man, but as a Christian you owe *fidelitas* to the Church, and on this field I represent His Holiness the Vicar of Christ! Would you like me to issue for you and your company of madmen a bull of excommunication? Believe me when I say that I would not have trouble convincing my brother, the supreme pontiff in Rome, to put his seal on such a document."

"I would appeal it and I would be in the right. You feign confidence, *signore* - you would make a poor *naipes* player. The supreme pontiff has no grounds to withdraw the right to sacrament from any of us here. We have not defied the Church nor defiled Church property, and we are not heretics. Now, do you wish to be captured or not? I am a busy man."

"I am confident that I can convince my brothers to deal with you, and the squire here, harshly."

"That would be difficult from Clement's prison, especially being twice so unlucky in such close succession. Remember Macerata."

The mention of last year's humiliation cut the papal legate to the quick. His blood froze and his mind began to cloud. "You will not receive your silver, Catalonian," he blurted out, unable to think of anything else to say.

"Oh, I think I will." Vilardell smiled. "And you can ask your brother why."

"I will not surrender to any captain who is in the pay of the cursed Clement. Be warned that I may decide to withdraw my companies from the field and turn them on you!" Andrea seethed. "You will not cause us to lose St. Peter's throne!"

"You have no companies here to command, *signore*," Vilardell answered. "I do not wish to see you killed or captured on this day, for I believe in your cause. However, if you do not let the young squire here press his claim and us to negotiate with Captain Prospero, you might force my hand. My men have not shot their last bolts. Let the German have the day."

Andrea regained his composure and rose high in the saddle. He looked down at the battlefield and saw that the companies of Broglia and Brandolini were slowly but surely being encircled and that Tarlati's Bretons were doing nothing. The battle was lost, and if he did not sound the retreat, so too would be the Patrimony of St. Peter. His grand scheme to repeat the feat of the great Albornoz was collapsing before his eyes. He was failing his brother and his family. But he would fight another day, and at the head of his own companies, not those of his fool of a brother. Besides, how much would a naïve English squire without a name want for an Italian captain of arms anyway?

Geoffrey decided the time had come for him to interject. "I repeat that I have no interest in the papal legate. He honored me well in Assisi. He has suffered an indignity today, which will gladden Captain Prospero, but I see no reason for it to be compounded. I may wish to serve under him again."

Andrea knew that his own company was close, so he should regain the initiative in quick order, but it also meant that he had much less need for Tarlati now. Furrowing his brow and gritting his teeth, the Papal Legate to

OF FAITH AND FIDELITY

the Marche said, "Captain Hotspur, take your man." He then wheeled his horse around and galloped down the slope towards his brother's *carrioccio*.

"What?! He will do no such thing!" Tarlati yelled in disgust and brandished his sword. "One call from my trumpeter and my company will turn its arms against you, and then you shall see a fine slaughter, guildsman," he screamed at Vilardell.

The insult made Vilardell frown and spit. He whispered to Sergeant Alfonso, who then finished the climb up the slope in order to address Tarlati face to face.

Jean, meanwhile, had taken a circuitous path away from the arguing parties to get to Geoffrey's brigade. Just before he reached the bottom rank, however, he was confronted by Sergeant Godwin.

"What in blazes is going on now, Frenchman? You've not cooked up one of your foul schemes again, have you? Remember, your life is not worth a groat in my accounts." Godwin grabbed the sleeve of Jean's surcoat.

"Get out of my way for once! I am about to save your ward's life. Tarlati would hack him to pieces if the Catalonians weren't preventing him. If you want to see another tomorrow, you will unhand me and let me negotiate a finish to this … this pass of arms."

Jean's severe tone and sober countenance prompted Godwin to release him; he was in no position to do anything but watch. Any appeal to Captain Prospero would demand that he leave the heights and crawl through the marsh for anywhere up to an hour, time which he could ill afford to lose at this juncture, so he had to suffer the indignity of watching a duplicitous French commoner, a nameless English squire and a wily Catalonian sergeant of crossbowmen deal their way out of the remainder of the battle without spilling more blood.

When he reached Geoffrey's side, Jean gave a brief account of his most recent discussion with the Catalonians and suggested that it would be better for all involved to let his former captain serve as the negotiator for both sides, as it was clear that neither party was willing to give way.

"I will take him by force, if necessary," Geoffrey stated, injecting bile in his voice. "He must be made to pay. His ransom is not for me. I did not come here seeking personal glory. I came to fulfill the pledges I have made. It cannot be any other way."

"Has Captain Prospero's dignity been restored?"

"It should be, but my opinion carries no weight here."

"And if restitution for that village chapel is made, and thereby your vows are fulfilled, then your quest, as it were, will be at an end. Am I not right?" Jean asked.

"You are right."

"Then let the Catalonians solicit justice for your cause if it will mean avoiding bloodshed. They have experience in such matters."

"I am not afraid of bloodshed," Geoffrey boasted. "If I should spill blood for a just cause, then there is no sin in it."

Jean shuddered at the thought. During the surprise assail by his brigade, he had not so much as scratched a foe. "But what of the blood of others, Geoff? Consider the men of Orte. This is not their fight. They have done their duty by their lords, you and Captain Prospero. Let not their wives become widows and children made orphans because you want to bloody your sword one more time. That is vanity, Geoff."

Jean's words found purchase in the young squire. Geoffrey's grip on his *couteau* slackened, but the blade did not waver. After a moment's thought, he answered. "Let it be so. Let Captain Vilardell's man come and negotiate a bloodless settlement between me and Captain Tarlati. Are you amenable to these terms, captain?" Geoffrey called out to Tarlati.

Seeing over a hundred crossbows trained on him and what was left of the papal host on the heights and none on the English squire or his militia, Tarlati nodded his head and pushed his horse to the crest in order to meet an approaching Sergeant Alfonso.

OF FAITH AND FIDELITY

"Stay with the men, sergeant," Geoffrey ordered Godwin, and he and Jean walked to within ten yards of Tarlati and the small group of retainers he had selected to protect him. There they met Sergeant Alfonso, who nodded to show that they were in accord.

Godwin wanted to go too, but he knew that without his authority the citizen militia just might wander off and he would be exposed.

"Well, what are your terms?" Tarlati demanded haughtily. His eyes were on the diminishing spectacle of the duke's *carrioccio* rolling away into the distance.

Sergeant Alfonso was the first to speak. He and Jean had agreed that the Catalonians would be more effective in negotiating with an Italian condottiere than a French debt collector, an English squire, or an old sergeant.

"First, I shall inform you that we are in possession of your war chest, by the command of His Lordship Duke Gianello, I should add, so this cannot be charged as theft. My company will return the chest to you less the amount Captain Hotspur decides is suitable as just reparations for your spoliation of the chapel at San Bernardino, which is known to you, plus whatever ransom he decides is fair for only you – not for any of your officers or sergeants. Should you agree to these terms, you will not be committed to Captain Prospero's charge, but rather immediately released for you to rejoin your company. You will thenceforth harm neither the St. John's Company of Crossbowmen of the Vintners Guild of Barcelona nor the company of militia of the citizens of the city of Orte. Have we an accord, *signore?*"

Captain Tarlati chewed his lip as he ruminated over these terms. He looked around to see whether Broglia or Brandolini was coming to his aid, but the moment he spotted them he understood that their consolidating movements indicated that they had decided to end the battle before their losses ran too high. In quick succession two trumpets bleated the call for disengagement with the enemy. Their encirclement was nearly complete and Captain Prospero himself was riding forth to accept the surrender of the two captains. His Bretons were nowhere to be seen. Thus, Tarlati saw that he had precious little time with which to decide, as it was clear from the dying din of battle than Captain Prospero was about to enjoy a full triumph.

"And what do you, or your company, get out of this? I see no advantage in it for you. This seems to me a rather strange thing," Tarlati said.

"We would receive a letter from the Duke of Spoleto, which you will arrange, giving us safe passage through to Corneto, where the company intends to embark for Barcelona, during which time we will turn over your reparations to the said village."

"I should assume that you will be levying a fee for your services," Tarlati said.

"I suppose that would be just. Oh, and tell the good duke not to worry about paying out Captain Vilardell's *condotta*. Just tell him to reimburse *you* for the full amount. What say you, Captain Hotspur?"

"I will take no ransom for myself, or rather that to which I am entitled by right of capture I will use to pay my company for their fine deeds done today. But is this the custom by which ransoms are made in Italy?" Geoffrey asked. "You are Catalonian, sergeant. Perhaps we are in error. Should these arrangements offend Captain Prospero, they might be overturned. We might find that the prisoner belongs to him. I do not know."

Tarlati made an exasperated snort and tugged at his reins. He was about to issue a riposte when Captain Vilardell stepped forward to clarify matters.

"Captain Tarlati is not a prisoner of anyone," Vilardell stated. "We are negotiating the terms of his withdrawal, but he will be duty bound by his honor and have the status of a ransomed knight until he fulfills the terms of our immanent accord. Therefore, as it is us who are challenging him, we bear the responsibility."

"To this I agree," Tarlati said quickly.

"Nevertheless, Captain Prospero cannot be ignored in this matter. What about making amends for the indignity he has suffered?" Geoffrey asked. "It was for this reason that he brought you here to battle. What will be his reparation?"

Sergeant Alfonso looked to Captain Tarlati for an answer. He had done his part on behalf of his company and the Frenchman. Jean stepped forward in his stead.

"Perhaps a letter begging the pardon of the injured party would suffice," Jean suggested, "endorsed, of course, by the notaries of the papal legate." Jean looked at Geoffrey.

"I will agree to these terms and I am prepared to swear to abide by them," Geoffrey declared.

Tarlati made a sour face, but time had run out for him. He glanced nervously at the battlefield and saw Captain Prospero holding up his white baton in victory.

"Agreed!" Tarlati shouted. "Leave my war chest in a place where my men can retrieve it unmolested. I shall deliver your words. Now, let me pass."

"Do you swear on your honor?" Geoffrey demanded.

"Honor might not be good enough, Geoff," Jean said. "Have his sergeants swear as witnesses to this pact."

"There is no need, Jean. The Catalonians have his war chest and his fame rests on our goodwill. I am satisfied with that."

Jean nodded and turned towards Sergeant Alfonso for a few conciliatory words. "Remember," Jean whispered, "the debt slate is clean." Although the original deal was for Jean to pay Sergeant Alfonso twelve and a half percent of the principal of the English squire's debt to the

Gamesmaster of Avignon, which should have come to twenty-five sous, the sergeant had creatively calculated that Jean in truth owed him forty sous, or less than half of what Catherine had given him in Assisi. Jean had conceded, since it was not Jean's money that the sergeant would be taking what he wanted anyway.

"It is indeed. Fare thee well, sergeant." Alfonso smiled and returned to his waiting captain.

"Nevertheless, Captain Tarlati must swear on his honor, on his sword, or on his father's grave – it matters not which – as long as he gives his word to me that he will fulfill the terms of the ransom," Geoffrey said.

"Let it go, boy," Godwin said. When he saw that the negotiations were over and would result in the warring parties leaving the heights in peace, he ordered the ablest militiaman he could find to lead his brigade back down the slope and report to Captain Prospero, while he returned to Geoffrey's side. "This is not France and you got what … I mean your pledge is fulfilled. These Catalonians will give the money to the villagers and Andrea Tomacelli would not dare risk not affixing his seal to a letter vindicating Prospero's actions, not with the number of witnesses present. All is satisfied."

But Geoffrey was adamant. "I need to hear it," he said and strode towards the retiring men-at-arms. "Captain Tarlati! You must give me your word as a knight that you will abide by the terms of the ransom."

Tarlati turned his horse around and made a rude gesture. "Be gone with you! You have got more than your station or your ability warrant. I will concede no more!"

"You are in no position to offer terms, captain," Geoffrey answered.

"Hotspur! Get back!" Godwin warned and he grabbed the squire's sword hand.

"I have had just about all that I can take from you, damnable Englishman." Tarlati reined his horse to the left to bring himself parallel with the Catalonians. Then he reached down and snatched a loaded crossbow out of the hands of a distracted Catalonian and aimed it at the chest of the captain of the Orte militia.

Godwin pushed Geoffrey down the moment he saw Tarlati's murderous intent, but the quarrel caught the old sergeant in the neck. He fell without a sound.

Tarlati cursed his luck, threw away the crossbow and galloped off towards the Narni road. The Catalonians made no move to either seize Tarlati or shoot him down.

Geoffrey scrambled to his feet and poised himself to race after Tarlati, but the blood spurting from Godwin's neck made Geoffrey's hands too slick for them to handle the *couteau*, and so it slipped from his grasp. Fearing that the treacherous captain would get away while he retrieved his sword, Geoffrey shouted at the Catalonian crossbowmen, "Shoot the blackguard!"

But the crossbowmen ignored him. Some turned towards Captain Vilardell and Sergeant Alfonso, but the company's leaders shook their heads.

Jean ran after Geoffrey and caught him just as he was about to run down the slope after Tarlati unarmed. "It's no use, Geoff. The accord has been struck and all parties will hold to it. Let's see to the old man and await Prospero. He will want to hear an account of all this from you."

Geoffrey's fury was such that he hardly heard Jean, but seeing that neither the Catalonians nor his own men were about to do anything to recapture his prisoner, he held himself still and watched the vile figure of Giovanni Tarlati gallop after the Tomacelli brothers.

"Godwin!" Geoffrey cried, and he ran back up the slope.

He knelt at the side of the veteran sergeant, staining his buskins and hose red. Geoffrey looked down and saw Roger lying there, half dyed in a rich crimson, but he shook from his head the trick the fiend was playing on him, refocused his eyes and saw true. "Tarlati has fled, but I will catch him," Geoffrey pledged with all the conviction his voice could muster. "You will have your vengeance, by all that is holy! I got him once, and I'll get him again!"

Godwin was writhing hopelessly, like a baby, with one hand pressing against his bleeding wound and the other tearing at the grass.

"Don't waste your strength, boy," Godwin wheezed. "It will be a vicious circle and you will lose."

"Justice must be done! It's why I came here." Geoffrey looked at the gash between the sergeant's fingers and nearly retched. There was no stopping the blood. Not even Roger's wounds had been that bad.

"Do justice to yourself, squire. You've already proven that you're your own man. I'm not worth fussing over anyway."

"But-"

"Listen for once!" Godwin coughed and started to tremble. "Forget Tarlati. He's already forgotten you. Move on."

Geoffrey frowned and looked at the place where he had confronted Tarlati. He dropped his head onto his chest and began to sob. "Shall I take you back to England, sergeant?" Geoffrey asked. "I was entrusted once to collect an Englishman from this land for burial in his native soil. Perhaps I should finally fulfill that vow."

Godwin raised his hand slightly to show that he had heard the squire. He squinted at the sky, but his sight was already gone and he was starting to feel cold. "I have nothing there," Godwin croaked, "Just make me a soldier's grave where you can …"

"I should go to Florence then," Geoffrey said.

Godwin squinted again then let his hand drop to his side. "Florence? Be wary of Florence, boy." Sergeant Godwin's body shook one more time and went still.

The sound of a score of horses drew closer and stopped within a dozen

OF FAITH AND FIDELITY

yards of Geoffrey, Jean and the remains of William Godwin.

"This makes me sad," Captain Prospero said when he saw the dead sergeant.

Jean lifted himself off the ground and decided to address the captain-general on behalf of the conqueror of the heights. "As you can see, Tarlati shot him. Captain Vilardell awaits your pleasure. An accord has been struck."

"Yes, I know. Your men made an excellent report. They had the fear of the Bretons put into them, no doubt. I shall be meeting with Captain Vilardell forthwith."

Geoffrey looked up and, still kneeling, said, "I await your judgment on my deed of arms." He bowed his head and clasped his hands in front of him.

Prospero furrowed his brow and stared at the squire until he realized what he was asking.

"I cannot knight you, Hotspur," the captain said. "I am not a lord of the kind you might wish to believe. I have told you this, but it seems to bear repeating. The most I can offer you is a place in my company as a pikeman."

Geoffrey felt his heart contract. He looked up at Prospero and asked, "Will you be pursuing the papal legate?"

"Do I look like a fool? I have no need to hunt him now. I have defeated him in a well contested pass of arms and he is much the worse for it. Also, I have no desire to meet the Tomacelli again. I know that unfriendly men-at-arms from the Marche are very close. This campaign is over for me. I congratulate you on your success here, Captain Hotspur."

Geoffrey sighed and rose. His knees were sticky from the blood-soaked grass and the hem of his surcoat was black. "I still wish to serve, my lord."

"You no longer wish to travel to Florence?"

"No."

"A wise decision. The Florentines would fleece you something rotten. Your *condotta* is now expired and I relieve you of your command. However, should you desire another – a *condotta*, not another militia company – I am shortly to be off to the Romagna to assist in resolving a family dispute over the inheritance of a great city. Accomplished captains and respected free lances can always find lucrative opportunities in such a circumstance. Well, as Captain Vilardell likes to say, I am a busy man, and I must finish this bloody affair. Fare thee well, master squire."

Prospero smiled and then spurred his horse. There was no longer any need to get the squire to Florence now, as the fame of his victory was sure to reach the Duke of Lancaster's ears on its own. Prospero's retinue rode down the slope to meet the Catalonian company of crossbowmen, leaving Geoffrey and Jean alone on the heights.

"Should we make for Florence, Geoff, or follow the Catalonians to Corneto and board the first ship sailing to Avignon?" Jean asked.

Geoffrey craned his head back and squinted at the sky as Sergeant Godwin had once done. "To hell with Florence. It's time to go home, but first, we shall celebrate. I have won my first battle!" He smiled and held out his arms, but weariness was rapidly taking over his body as his bloodlust drained away. He wanted to sleep.

"So, you haven't forgotten Avignon," Jean said gruffly. "Shall we bury the old sergeant now? I see some of the militia still scratching the ground for loot."

"Do you think Boniface will win now? He still has a large host and Prospero did not take either Andrea or Gianello Tomacelli." Geoffrey looked eastwards, but all he could see was the final few ranks of the papal host's rearguard.

Jean shrugged. "The Gamesmaster once said that the throne of St. Peter will always be contested, but faith must remain constant. I don't know what that means, in truth, but it sounds like something you'd want to hear."

OF FAITH AND FIDELITY

Geoffrey turned to look at the debt collector-chandler-lance anchor-sergeant. At least he did not deceive me on this day, he thought. Geoffrey Hotspur was silent for a moment, but he then smiled at his friend and said, "Tell me, Jean. How much silver did you take from Tarlati's war chest?"

HISTORICAL NOTE

While the Battle of Orte that took place in August 1394 between armies in the pay of the rival popes in Rome and Avignon was not a well recorded encounter, it was a pivotal moment in the Western Schism of the Church. The battle represented the last opportunity for the supreme pontiff in Rome, Boniface IX, to consolidate his rule in central Italy and thereby give himself considerable leverage over his opponent in Avignon, Clement VII. Had the host of Boniface won at Orte, this triumph, in combination with earlier and subsequent events, would have put him in an excellent position to return the fidelity of the Papal States to St. Peter's throne and undermine what little authority his rival in Avignon had left in Christendom.

The Treaty of Castelfidardo signed on June 24 by representatives of Boniface and the Malatesta clan for all intents and purposes ended the war in the eastern papal provinces, and a victory in the western theater might have brought other clans to heel. Moreover, victory at Orte would have secured the Tiber River and given the Roman papal host strategic advantage in the field and ruined the morale of the forces loyal to Clement before the autumn campaign season. Indeed, the death of Clement on September 16, 1394 and the decision of King Charles of France and the influential University of Paris to withdraw their support from the Avignon papacy the following year, despite the election of another antipope, considerably undermined Avignon's power.

Although such a string of impressive military and political successes might have been enough to oblige the remaining supporters of Avignon to come to terms with Rome, especially considering that Boniface was widely respected for his moderation and diplomatic skills, it was not to be. As it was, the defeat at Orte helped save the cause of the antipope, prevented the return of papal power to central Italy until well into the fifteenth century, and allowed the Western Schism to drag on until 1417.

Some readers might find it peculiar that in a work that puts the papacy at its center they did not come across any theological references. The reason for this is that the Western Schism of the fourteenth and fifteenth centuries, unlike the Great Schism of the eleventh century, had nothing to do with doctrinal disputes. The election of two popes in Rome in 1378 was all about politics and personalities that had its roots in the removal of the papacy to Avignon at the beginning of that century.

In short, what happened was that the leading cardinals wanted to elect a pope who would not only keep the papacy in Rome near St. Peter's throne, but also would be pliant to the will of the Sacred College. However, things did not go as planned, and the new pope, Urban VI, quickly showed himself to be arrogant and reform-minded, alienating those who had elected him. In response, a group of offended cardinals elected one of their own to be pope, claiming that the first election had been illegitimate because the conclave had voted under duress caused by a Roman mob, which was demanding the election of an Italian pope. This was unlikely, but it was not without precedent, since the papacy had migrated to Avignon in the first place in 1309 because of the endemic violence and instability in Rome.

Unfortunately for the rebelling cardinals, they elected a Frenchman to be the antipope Clement VII, which inflamed the nativist sentiment of the Roman people and forced Clement and his supporters to flee – to Avignon. The Western Schism acquired an even more political character when the rulers of Europe chose sides based on naked strategic interests, ignoring the legalistic aspects of the respective elections. For the next twenty years, the rival popes would excommunicate each other, make war on each other, and create separate papal administrations until finally the leading lights of Christendom, as well as its rulers, got fed up and steadily drove the competing popes towards reconciliation. A series of councils starting from 1409 finally brought an effective end to the Western Schism in 1417.

HARALD HARDRADA

THE LAST VIKING

Michael Burr

KNOX ROBINSON
PUBLISHING
London • New York

PROLOGUE

*I*T is Yuletide in Nidaros, Norway in the year of our Lord 1066 and that needs to change soon. This pagan holiday must become Christ's Mass or the Feast of Our Lord at least. Indeed, since its last professed Christian monarch, this land has lain under the hand of a known pagan and before him a king much too busy for Christ. Yes, much must change. If God will allow me to do so, I will work for that change. I, the cripple, once the lowest of the low; once a captive and a trembling second away from the bite of the knife across my throat; once an object of derision and pity.

How did it begin, this story of mine? Much as any man's life begins – in the blood and suffering of women. It began thirty-five years ago when ruin and death burst from the sea to wash over a place where women practiced love in the service of God, reminding those who shut themselves away from the world that no refuge short of the Kingdom of Heaven is safe from Lucifer and his devils.

My story continued through blood, shed both in battle and out, through greed, envy and ambition. It saw me become wealthy. It saw me in the company of the great ones of an empire and in the bed of a queen. It made me the confidant of kings.

On the other side of things, it led me into the sin of easing my conscience by telling it that many small evils are excusable if they lead to the ending of a great evil.

Truly, the Book does not lie when it asks, "How are the mighty fallen?"

From henceforth I will make what amends I can and perform such penance as will mitigate my debt to God. I will build where once I helped tear down; I will heal where once I wounded; I will lead and guide where once I schemed *and deceived, and I will pass my life in love where once life only nursed and fed my hatred. And I will do these things for the good of my adopted country and for my own hope of eternal life.*

But if I am truly to atone for my past I must begin by confronting it; by living it once more, for the last time. So in these pages I lay it before you, as truthfully as it is already laid forth in God's great book.

By that same care for truth I say that mine is not a pretty story, and it does me no credit when I tell of how I passed my life in serving a man I hated and feared. Aye, I served him in battle, in council, in murder and intrigue, always to one end — to have my revenge. For what he was mocked God who had given him physical stature, shrewdness, charm and a skill at arms that made him the foremost soldier of my time. But the Devil gave him his soul, and in the end it outweighed the other gifts.

The man I knew as leder was born in 1015 in Ringerike, a district of Norway known as the Uplandende. He was of royal blood, on his mother's side at least, for Aasta Gudbrandsdatter was first queen to Harald Grenske of Norway and then wife to my leder's father, Sigurd Syr. It was always his boast that his father was the bastard grandson of Harald Fairhair, king of Norway; but the skald Askell's lips would twitch when this was mentioned. He would say as much or as little as would suggest to the speaker that tales told usually stretch with the telling and that being half-royal was surely better than being not royal in any degree.

Whatever the truth, the sons of Sigurd were half-brothers to the child of Aasta and Grenske, Olaf II, called St Olaf after his death, who unwisely made an enemy of the Dane called Cnut the Great, and died at the battle of Stiklestad. Olaf's youngest half-brother, the man who would become my master, Harald Sigurdsson, nearly died with him. Indeed, the then fifteen-year-old had fought a man's fight all that day and left the field senseless from the loss of blood that had followed the sword cut he took in killing a Danish berserker who had broken through the shield wall to Olaf's standard.

HARALD HARDRADA

Only the devotion of some of Olaf's carls had got Harald from the field to the safety of a peasant cottage where he spent long weeks of healing hidden from Cnut's hunters, while a drakkar, a Viking longship, was found and crewed to take Aasta's youngest into exile.

What was there for a princeling marked for death in his own land? Only exile and the chance to sell his sword to one in need of it - but in that, the strapping youth had one or two advantages. He was of royal descent to begin with, but was also a born leader of men who had known his own mind since the childhood during which he had boasted to his royal half-brother that he would rather harvest enemies than corn.

He remembered the sagas sung by the wandering skalds who sought the meal and bed they could always find at the hall of Sigurd Syr, and the sagas, in turn, made him a youth who would go out of his way to confront danger that he might stare it down in the manner of one worthy of Valhalla. And this he did with a ruthlessness and a strength of purpose that caused those who came to know of it to shake their heads and murmur prayers to their god.

I am The Scraeling and I served Harald Hardrada.

HARALD HARDRADA

BOOK ONE
OF THE RAIDER
1031–1034

> "At Haug the fire-sparks from his shield
>   Flew around the king's head on the field,
>   As blow for blow, for Olaf's sake,
>   His sword and shield would give and take.
>   Bulgaria's conqueror, I ween,
>   Had scarcely fifteen winters seen,
>   When from his murdered brother's side
>   His unhelmed head he had to hide."

The skald, Thiodolf, in 'The Heimskringla'

HARALD HARDRADA

The coast of Brittany
August 1031

There was menace in the air as the field mouse moved uncertainly through the moonlight that slid in and out of the clouds, dappling the land below with light and shade. The shifting light held danger in the mystery of its shadows, and the tiny creature in the long grass at the edge of the clearing suspected it enough to flare pink nostrils to the sky in search of the threat that lurked in the dark.

But nothing moved at ground level save the faintest of breezes and on it there was nothing but the faint tang of the sea a mile distant; nothing to alarm the rodent by sound, smell or vibration. So, hesitantly at first and then more boldly, it made towards the raspberries that clustered where the parent plant hung low in the deep shadow of a tree and there, its forebodings gone, the little creature began to gorge. Completely taken with its meal, it never saw the glint of moonlight on a silver streak of fur, and if it felt the air displaced by the armored claw that smashed it to extinction it had no time to react.

The badger dragged mouse, earth and berries towards its mouth and, in its turn, began to gorge. It was an old badger, ever alert for the scent and sound of man, so as the faintest of vibrations rolled through the ground and registered in its belly, it reared back and up to sniff the air just as the mouse had done. It caught a scent that caused it to move slowly back until a rear claw touched the lip of its sett and the thickset animal oozed slowly back over the edge of the burrow.

The vibration grew greater and the creature pressed backwards into its burrow as a shadow fell across the edge of the clearing. For a long moment nothing moved. A low hiss whispered through the air. The source of the shadow moved swiftly across the moonlit glade, followed by other shapes, grotesque and huge in the shifting light.

The men from the sea sank to cover in the trees on the far side of the clearing, waiting for the scout to return. Across the glade they grouped together and although no word was spoken by any, a longer shaft of light from the moon lit up bearded faces tense with expectation and alight with the anticipation of what was to come. Here and there a tongue moistened dry lips while broken-nailed fingers flexed on the shafts of swords, axes and spears.

At length, the scout returned and spoke in a low murmur to one of the crouching men, one whose face in the moonlight was incongruous in its youthfulness, his only flaw an arm hideously scarred by a crudely-done cauterization.

"Nothing moves, *leder*. No lights, no sound. What now?"

Harald looked about him, gestured to another shadowy form and pointed wide and to the right.

"Skallagrim - your party to cut the road."

"Aye, Harald."

Ten men rose and moved off at a trot in the direction given while the main body moved carefully and slowly through the trees until they thinned, revealing the outlines of several buildings clustered about a small, whitewashed church with a bell tower at its seaward end. Harald whistled softly and two men turned to him.

"Thorkill and Sweyn— to the church," he said. "That bell must not ring. Go."

And the two men slid forward to the door beneath the bell tower, losing themselves in the shadows of its deep recess.

"Bakehouse. Alehouse. Stables. There – " Harald said as he lifted his scarred arm in the moonlight, "there's where they sleep, and where we'll find them. Take your pleasure, but take it swiftly. What you can take will be all you will eat in these next days, so if you would fill your bellies then, be quick about filling theirs now!"

The group parted for Harald to move through and to the right, in the direction of the sleeping quarters. But they had hardly begun to skirt through the trees at the edge of the clearing when a dog's high bark of alarm sounded in the stillness and was immediately answered by several more.

"Odin's balls!" Harald snarled. "Skallagrim's clumsy bastards've roused the dogs. On! On!"

At his command, twenty men broke cover to sprint for the largest building, brandishing weapons and baying like hounds. A door at the far end of the building flew open and a woman in a white shift burst from it, racing toward the stables. She threw herself through the wicket door and slammed it shut behind her. Her pursuers arrived just in time to hear the thud of a heavy bar dropping into the sockets, locking the door from inside.

"Is there a door at the end?" Harald shouted. "Make for the door at the end!"

The raiders at the locked door swung axes and hammers against it. A few moments later and well ahead of the nearest raiders who were racing down the length of the building, a door at the other end of the stables crashed open and a horse erupted through it with a young man sprawled along its bare back. With its rider digging in heels, the horse bounded forward on to the road that led inland past the buildings that surrounded the convent.

"Leave it!" Harald snarled to those who bellowed their disappointment in the dust of the horse's passing.

"Leave him to Skallagrim! The church! The larders! The alehouse! Move, you droppings of the raven, move – look, there! See!"

The soft moonlight reached into the stable and a white shift gleamed in its radiance as two men sprang through the door left open by the horse and its rider to grab the woman who had barred the other door in their faces but a moment before. She was of middle age, her pock-marked face twisting as she screamed in terror and struggled against the rough hands that mauled her as the Vikings yanked her forward into the open yard.

"For you, Harald? First right?" one of the Vikings who held the struggling woman asked as he tightened his grip on her arm.

"No, let those nigh as old and ugly as she is have her – you and Ulf. The younger women are still abed! Come on!"

And Harald raced across the yard for the door through which the woman had come from the main building, and from which came a babel of cries as those within awoke to the tumult of Vikings rampaging through the buildings of the convent of Les Trois Étoiles, smashing doors and shutters. Then, the men were upstairs at the door of the nuns' dormitory and those who had given their lives to heaven found only hell.

The nuns fell silent and for a moment no one moved as the women looked wildly about them for deliverance from the nightmare of bearded faces and iron helmets as the rank odours of the male bodies pressed in upon them. Just as Harald arrived, one young nun screamed, and the spell was broken.

A young Viking, excited and clumsy on his first raid, reached for her and as she tried to jerk away from him she stumbled, sending them both backwards over a cot and on to the floor. His weight drove the breath from her and pinned her helpless while he tore at the tarred rope that held up his breeches until the cloth came free. As his breeches slid down his hips, he seized the front of the nun's nightshift in one huge hand and tore it from her. The woman screamed again as her shift fell away to reveal her nakedness. Grinning, the Viking fumbled between his legs a moment, grunted and then savagely thrust his hips forward with a yell of triumph as he penetrated the body of the young nun, bringing forth another agonized scream from her as she squirmed beneath him.

His fellows cheered him on and began to chant a count in time to the movement of his hips as they rose and plunged and rose again while he crushed the sobbing girl beneath his bulk and his hands mauled her breasts. At the count of twelve, the young Viking's eyes bulged as if they would start from the bearded face and he rammed his hips forward once more, clutching her tightly as the seed burst forth from him.

And that began the frenzy. A chorus of screams echoed throughout the room as women were seized between two and three men and the clothing torn from their bodies before they were cast upon a cot or upon the floor to be held by one while the other drove into her without regard or pity for age or condition. Harald watched the rape with his arms folded and his back against the door until he grew bored and turned to descend the stairs and walk out into the moonlight across the courtyard to the church.

On the threshold he stepped over the body of an elderly priest, dead from a head wound that still leaked blood and brains, and entered the small church where one of his men was fashioning an altar cloth into a sack for the collection of all that was valuable. Another lit candles to bring light to the darkness.

"He'll be the confessor. Only one?" Harald asked, nodding at the body.

"Aye, just the one. Went straight for the bell rope. Never even saw us, I reckon. I tripped him and Thorkill tapped him on the way down. How far away's the castle then?"

"Two leagues. Bit more maybe, but not much. Close enough if that bell had sounded – well done."

"Who was on the horse? Not one of the sisters, surely?" Thorkill asked.

"A groom, I reckon," Sweyn suggested, over his shoulder. "No nun would ride like that. He was like a demon."

"Anyone get him?" Thorkill asked.

Harald shrugged. "If Skallagrim had the road blocked by then. No one else got out, and if he's got him, he'll be back with his boys wanting some loot and some fucking."

"Wouldn't mind a bit of that myself," Thorkill said.

Harald smiled and slapped Thorkill on the back. "Plenty of it over there. You finished, Sweyn?" he called to the other man.

Sweyn nodded and hefted the altar-cloth filled with loot over a shoulder. The three stepped out of the church to cross back to the two-storeyed building. The screams had ceased to echo throughout the dormitory, but in their place came the despairing sobs of the women who huddled together, clutching what remained of their clothing in an attempt to cover their nakedness. One or two lay still while their violators sat or sprawled around the room exhausted from slaking their lust.

Harald glanced about him. "Half of you," he said, "empty the larders. Make a pile of all you find by the stables. The others, cut poles. Make stretchers. We carry or drag all we can back to the longship. The more we carry, the better we eat. Move! And you, Griss, get off her. If you haven't had enough by now, get more later. There's work to do."

Griss rolled off the woman and rose sullenly to his feet. Making no attempt to cover himself, he pointed an angry finger at Harald.

"I do my share, son of Sigurd, and no man tells me when to take my reward. No man!"

"I'll tell you what I wish, when I wish, Griss," Harald said, the softness of his voice failing to hide the steel within it as the room went quiet. Even the sobs of the women went quiet. "I command here and not by your leave. Don't point your cock at me lest I cut it from you and if you point your hand at me again, put a sword in it. Now, get to work and leave some for the others."

Griss turned away with a growl, fumbling for his breeches just as the door to the dormitory crashed opened with a force that threatened to tear it from its hinges.

"*Høvding*. Skallagrim's coming in!" one of the Vikings called.

Harald stepped through the doorway, rushed down the stairs and out into the night. From the direction of the inland road, they could soon make out the party of ten which had earlier circled the convent to block the road. Between them, they were dragging the slight figure of a captive.

"The rider?" Harald asked, and the burly, one-eyed Viking who walked in the lead nodded. "Aye. Got him with a rope across the road. Just a kid – a real skinny little weakling, but he can really manage a horse."

"And when the horse turns up at the castle …?"

"It won't. Broke its leg in the fall. Snorri shut it up. How's it here?"

"All we thought it would be. Loot, women, food. We've got the loot, we're getting the food, and the boys have had the women. In there, if you want some."

"Right enough, *høvding*. What'll we do with this?" and he indicated the captive who slumped, half-conscious, between two warriors. He was, Harald judged, at least two years younger than his own sixteen summers, short and slightly-built with dark, curling hair through which blood from a split scalp oozed to trickle slowly down his face.

"Give you some trouble?"

Skallagrim snorted. "What, this little boy? Nah, came off the horse a good one; landed on his head. Rides better than he walks though," and the man twisted the boy around.

For the first time, Harald noticed that the captive's left leg was short, hugely twisted and that the knee pointed more towards the other than it did forwards. He put a hand under the boy's chin and lifted his head, looking into eyes that even in a sudden shaft of moonlight were clouded and dazed.

"Only brought him back so he could tell us how often folk come here from the castle," Skallagrim said. "As we're not staying, we might as well cut his throat. You or me, *leder*?"

Harald smiled. " Neither. Let him live. He may be useful. Good effort, Skallagrim. Now, go!"

MICHAEL BURR

As he dismissed the Vikings, Harald casually lifted one brawny arm and smashed it backhand across the captive's head. The boy flew backwards, hit the wall and slid down it to lie unconscious at its foot.

Skallagrim hastened to the dormitory, while Harald turned to direct the gathering of the stores that came in a steady stream from the buildings and quickly grew into a pile by the stables. On his fourth trip, Griss lowered a half-carcass to the stack of goods and as he turned away to make his fifth trip, his eyes caught sight of something in the stable doorway that made him move closer for a better look.

"Freya's tits!" he chortled, "forgot about her! Hey, Ulf, you had this one eh? Well watch this, and ask her afterwards who she enjoyed most!" He reached into the shadows of the stable where the woman had shrunk back in a failed attempt to hide. By the hair, he dragged out the woman who had been used by Ulf and his companion after the rider had broken clear. She shrieked from a mouth that still bled, and raised an arm to ward him off, but he seized it and pushed hard backwards so that she staggered and fell upon her back.

Griss laughed. "Stay there," he commanded, "and open wide for my little friend here." He loosed his breeches to reveal a member hugely erect and throbbing with purpose. Laughing, he grasped himself and stood over the woman. "Look, bitch. You're ugly, but I'll do you a favour, right? And you can have it rough or you can have it …"

Before Griss could finish, there was a rush of wind and a loud, fleshy smack. The burly Viking staggered, screamed and clutched his groin before doubling over and collapsing. His companions spun around to see the captive boy swaying upon his feet with a sling in his right hand and fumbling within his waist-pouch for another stone. The nearest Viking leapt at him and clubbed him to the ground, ripping the sling from his grasp and kneeling upon the unresisting body.

Harald went to the writhing, screaming Griss and stooped to peer at the sharp stone that protruded from his groin, already spraying blood. "I told you that cock of yours would get you into trouble, Griss. Ulf, Asgeirr, get this free and see what you can do about stopping the bleeding. And if you can't, cut his throat or let him bleed to death here because we can't carry him."

Ulf and Asgeirr stooped over Griss while Harald moved to where the boy lay beneath the Viking.

"Dangerous little bastard, aren't you, *scraeling*?" he remarked, but there was no malice in it. "Sling around your middle, holding up your breeches. Dagger in your boot, aye?"

Stooping, he turned back the cuff of the right boot and withdrew a bone-hilted dagger. He looked at it thoughtfully, then balanced the dagger across a finger and commented to the Viking who pinned the boy. "A *krøpling*, Askell," Harald said, eyeing the boy's deformed leg. "A cripple. Since he can't fight man-to-man, he carries a sling and a dagger made for throwing. Bet me a gold piece he's handy with a bow too?" He nudged the boy with his foot. "Aye, *krøpling*? I wonder what else you can do. We'll find out. Askell, bind his hands behind him. He comes with us."

"Aye, Harald. And the woman here?"

"Up to you, but bring the *scraeling*."

Visit our website to download free historical fiction, historical romance and fantasy short stories by your favourite authors. While there, purchase our titles direct and earn loyalty points. Sign up for our newsletter and our free titles giveaway. Join our community to discuss history, romance and fantasy with fans of each genre. We also encourage you to submit your stories anonymously and let your peers review your writing.

www.knoxrobinsonpublishing.com